THE BOOK OF
REUBEN

Also by Tabitha King:

Small World
Caretakers
The Trap
Pearl
One on One

TABITHA KING

THE BOOK OF
REUBEN

A DUTTON BOOK

DUTTON
Published by the Penguin Group
Penguin Books USA Inc., 375 Hudson Street, New York, New York 10014, U.S.A.
Penguin Books Ltd, 27 Wrights Lane, London W8 5TZ, England
Penguin Books Australia Ltd, Ringwood, Victoria, Australia
Penguin Books Canada Ltd, 10 Alcorn Avenue, Toronto, Ontario, Canada M4V 3B2
Penguin Books (N.Z.) Ltd, 182–190 Wairau Road, Auckland 10, New Zealand

Penguin Books Ltd, Registered Offices: Harmondsworth, Middlesex, England

First published by Dutton, an imprint of Dutton Signet, a division of Penguin Books USA, Inc.
Distributed in Canada by McClelland & Stewart Inc.

First Printing, September, 1994
10 9 8 7 6 5 4 3 2 1

REGISTERED TRADEMARK—MARCA REGISTRADA

LIBRARY OF CONGRESS CATALOGING IN PUBLICATION DATA:
King, Tabitha.
  The book of Reuben / Tabitha King.
    p. cm.
  ISBN 0-525-93766-8
  1. Men—Maine—Fiction. 2. Marriage—Maine—Fiction. 3. Father and child—Maine—Fiction.
4. Man-woman relationships—Maine—Fiction. I. Title.
PS3561.I4835B66   1994
813'.54—dc20

                                                          94-7045
                                                          CIP

Printed in the United States of America
Set in Sabon
Designed by Leonard Telesca

PUBLISHER'S NOTE

To Chuck Verrill

This is to thank my agent, Chuck Verrill; my editor, Audrey LaFehr; and my publisher, Elaine Koster, for their counsel and work in bringing this manuscript to publication. My lawyer, Jay Kramer, and my assistant, Nancy Gilbert, were the movers and shakers who obtained a wealth of permissions for me. My first readers, Stephen, Naomi, Joe Hill, Leonora, Owen, and Shane provided me with additional editorial advice and support.

"What we have here is a failure to communicate."

—STROTHER MARTIN,
Cool Hand Luke

"Tell me tell me tell me
who wrote the book of love?"

—The Monotones,
"The Book of Love"

I

Twice a Day Even a Broken Clock tells the right time. So said Tiny Lunt.

Of all the sayings Tiny repeated, this one captured the boy's attention. Drawn to the mechanical, he had by age nine autopsied several kinds of timepieces—old clocks and watches—and studied the mechanisms by which time is counted. The word itself—timepiece—was admirable in its workmanlike simplicity. It worked, he would say if he were asked. And that which worked was a harmonious thing and beautiful in its way.

Twice a day—as the sun set, as the sun rose also—the lake was given to a particular calm. This observation inevitably brought to mind the broken clock and its twice daily instants of truth. The boy's inability to precisely connect the phenomena intensified in turn the mysterious nature of both. Thus the simple occasion of going fishing with his friend Sonny and Sonny's father, Hallie, placing him at the center of the dawn stillness of the lake, gave him the spooks.

Drop by drop without color, the ninety feet of water filling the lake's bed was a sheen of low-angled light. A drowning weightlessness. The boy breathed in the smell of the water, mingled with the oily odor of Hallie's chugging little motor that hung in the air like a fart or a spoiled fish. Slowly, slowly and noisily, they progressed into the North Bay and Hallie shut down the motor. As they baited the hooks they conversed in low tones—not out of consideration for sleeping summer folk in their lakeshore habitations but because the serenity of the lake invoked a degree of reverence.

"See the new place?" Hallie asked, the point of his finger sighting the expensive folly. "Never seen the like of it. Million dollars' worth of house, I hear, and all it's gonna do most of the year is keep snow offen the ground."

Sonny sniggered at his dad's wit.

But the boy only stared at the structure on the shore. It was not like any house he had ever seen. His eye struggled to reconcile the contradictions of its absurd planes and angles. The unweathered, unpainted wood framing expanses of glass looked naked. On the lake side, a glass wall threw back the flat, metallic eastern light. For an instant it was as if someone had cut a great hole in the world. The boy experienced a moment of vertigo, teetering on the edge of falling into it.

He closed his eyes, feeling the gentle rock of the boat on the water, smelling again Hallie's cigarette and the sick, dead sweetness of the motor's exhaust. Something tickled the back of his neck. Before he could raise his hand to slap it, the mosquito bit. He got it, though, and stared at the dead bug and his own blood on his fingers, then plunged his hand into the lake water to wash it.

When he looked up again, the current had shifted the boat and the new summer house on the shore stood in a different light. It was still strange, but all at once he could see the way in which it worked. Not his place to say so to a grown-up—Hallie—but it did work, at least on the outside. And he could not help a twinge of excitement. A house, a mere house, a place to live—and someone had had a vision to make it work at something else as well. He had not the language to explain what he saw at work—one day he would find the word esthetics, with another instant of recognition. He knew already that a thing that worked was somehow beautiful. The strange new house told him, with the mysteriousness of the momentarily accurate stopped clock, that beauty was itself a working thing. At least twice a day, he thought with a grin at his own joke.

* * *

Time and weather had somehow compressed the garage so even its shabbiness, its missing shingles and peeling paint and the astonishing clutter of auto parts and supplies in it, all fit together into a singular, indivisible organism. Disturb a jot or tittle of it and the whole thing might very well come tumbling down. Or collapse with a solid whump into a pile of dust.

Sixtus Rideout, the proprietor of the Texaco, was in a similarly dilapidated condition, resorting these days to a walker. Most of his customers didn't wait for him to lurch to the pumps but jumped out to set the nozzle themselves. As to the maintenance and repairs business he once had done—only the sort of people who didn't intend to pay the bill anyway would trust their vehicle to one of the procession of bums and boozers passing through Sixtus Rideout's employ.

One man's trouble is another man's opportunity—

* * *

Joe Nevers' truck stood at the pump. Next to it Joe Nevers himself listened to Sixtus Rideout jaw. Blazoned on the door of his truck was his name and the legend CARETAKER. The two men paused to watch an ancient bastardized farm truck jouncing up and then the driver's exit from its cab. They glanced at each other in rueful amusement; the driver was a barefaced youth who wore his body like a too-large suit of clothes. No need to speak aloud of how the looseness of his limbs, the coiled energy in his motion, emphasized by contrast the sensation of time dragging upon their own strength like the man hanging upon the hand of a great clock.

"Mr. Rideout, sir." The boy colored violently—in over his head at once, a man in a drowning panic.

Sixtus thumped the feet of his walker. "Whatcha want, buck? I ain't got all day"—a blatant untruth, for all day was exactly what he had—"sonuvabitch quit on me, lef' that Christless Ford on the lift"—he gestured sourly toward the garage bay "Spit it out, buck."

The boy rushed it out in one breath. "I come to ask about the job."

Sixtus Rideout's mouth fell open, permitting an exhalation like an irritated bull. Joe Nevers allowed himself a discreet smile.

"That right?" Sixtus asked, his wet lower lip pooching out as he looked the boy over critically.

A rack of bone and muscle with hands on him big as baseball mitts he was. A brute of a kid. Face blank as a slate and see-through as a pane of glass. Bigger than most men already and only half-growed—must eat a moose for breakfast every day. The boy had worked on his old man's machines since he could grip a wrench—bought secondhand parts and never asked how to use them neither. Might have thought of him sooner but for his age and him still being in school. Of course, there was only two things to keep him at the Academy past the first day he could legally quit—playing ball and the draft. Which meant he was looking to work part-time.

The more Sixtus considered it, the more he liked the idea of a broad-shouldered boy in love with motors but otherwise as numb as a lump of tar. And the kid wouldn't expect much pay. Might get two years out of him, maybe three, given the kid was no Einstein, before he turned draftbait. And there was always the chance the draft would pass on the kid on account of stupidity or too much of an interest in farm animals. Must be getting soft he didn't think of this solution sooner.

"Taking shop at the Academy, are you?" Joe Nevers asked in an idle way. Nudging the thing along and all the time studying a cigarillo like he just came down from the trees and might eat it.

The boy nodded.

The caretaker flicked a glance toward the lift. "Why not let him have a look at the Ford, Sixtus?" To the boy. "Clutch is slipping."

Sixtus grinned. "G'wan, buck. Have at it."

The ten-year-old Ford Customliner belonged to the post mistress. Having been behind her on occasion, the boy knew Miss Porter drove on her brakes. The clutch linkage was dry—binding for lack of lubrication. Joe Nevers and Sixtus Rideout grunted their agreement with the boy's diagnosis.

"G'wan," Sixtus urged.

The two men watched as the boy lubricated the linkage.

"Brakes are worn too," he advised. "She'd do better to drive an automatic."

"What the hell," Sixtus said. "The old cat drives with both feet on the brakes, keeps racking the clutch, it's money in the register when she needs'm fixed." He coughed and spat. "Jeez, if enjines burnt snot, I could pump it by the gallon. It's the goddamn lilacs flowering. Have a beer, Joe."

"Too early in the day for me."

"You, buck, fetch me one out of the icebox, will ya? Git one for yourself, you earned it."

The boy picked his way through a stunning clutter to a dirty little icebox.

"I said you too," Sixtus said irritably.

"Thank you, sir," the boy demurred, "but Pop would smell it on my breath."

"What's your pop got to say about you working for me?"

The boy's face set stubbornly. "I'll work it out."

Joe Nevers sucked thoughtfully at his cigarillo.

Sixtus sipped his beer. He came to an abrupt decision. Punching open the till he extracted a dollar, smoothed it between fat fingers, snapped it smartly and thrust it at the boy. "Stop in here after school, do the brakes. I oughta be able keep you busy, say twenny hours a week. Summertime, you work out, mebbe forty, mebbe sixty we have a good season. All I can afford is the minimum, but you'll get the world in experience."

"There's one thing, Mr. Rideout—"

Sixtus Rideout's long, wiry old-man eyebrow hairs fluttered.

"I'm playing ball," the boy said.

"And what the jeezly hell does that mean to me?"

"Got practice most days 'til six and games three days a week and sometimes on Saturday."

" 'N' I'm s'posed to 'commodate you," Sixtus growled.

"I'll work early and late and Sundays," the boy said in desperation.

Narrowing his eyes so his eyebrows looked ready to slide off down his face, Sixtus leaned forward on his walker. His upper plate dropped and he sucked it back into place. "Shoot me for a g.d. fool," he groaned. He fixed the boy with a livid eye. "Listen up now, buck. I'm telling you the rules. All you got to do is foller'm. See that till? You ever leave it open and unattended, it'll be the last time. All transactions is cash on the barrel head. I'm the only one around here's authorized to give credit. Some buddy a yours wants a buck's worth of gas or a can of motor oil on the arm, he can get it some'eres else. Same for butts or those propherlastics in the w.c. I ain't rich enough to pay for some other fella's pleasures, and them as needs to rent'm from me can't afford'm neither. I don't want none of your buddies hanging around during workin' hours and no twitches neither. Don't be leaving no dirty magazines in the w.c."—he winked heavily— "leave'm in the bottom drawer. And you get to work on time and work until the work's done. You got any problem with any of that, you don't work for me."

"No sir, no problem with any of it, Mr. Rideout."

"Alrighty, buck," Sixtus sighed. "I'll be lookin' for ya."

* * *

Bleak and isolate, the Styles farm saddled the height of land upon the Ridge. Its builder, the first Samuel Styles, had blasted a cellar hole out of the granite and bound the shattered stone into the foundation of his house. Though partially protected from the prevailing winds by the horsebarn, it was fiercely exposed and no one had ever tried to heat every room of it to anything like comfort. The fine Styles complexion and the family habit of early to rise and quick to work was owed to the chill of its bedrooms, where shivering was the main form of combustion and the icy floorboards underfoot cleared a sleepy head quickly.

There were other farms along the same road. The Witchers had a couple of chicken houses. The Sewalls were dairy farmers like Sam Styles. The Schotts kept sheep but, like Schotts the county wide, were more successful at getting children and breeding lice. The closest neighbors weren't farmers; Frank Haggerty was a state trooper. His wife, Maureen, and their four kids kept a small herd of goats and raised a truck garden that substantially fed them.

Sam Styles at half past seventy was yet unstooped by age—indeed, possessed the kind of strength that comes of a lifetime of unrelenting labor. He grew beans for a cannery in South Portland and feed for his horses and milkcows, the milk going to a dairy in Greenspark. The last farmer in the county to till his land with horse-drawn machinery, he presented a striking, anachronistic picture: an iron old giant guiding a plow behind a team of draft horses that would dwarf a man of ordinary size.

It was common knowledge the boy Reuben was a surprise and not a welcome one, his mother in fact through the Change or thought she was. Old Sam had not been amused either by nature's prank or his neighbors' snickers. And as the boy grew, the old man had become harder with him—though the consensus at the post office and in the general store and wherever the men loitered, running their gums, was Reuben was no more trouble than any boy and less than most. It was a puzzle—a boy with an arm like that one's on him and old Sam actually tried to stop him playing ball. In the end the boy *was* playing ball. Some town fathers—Joe Nevers among them—had had to spell it out to Sam how the town had been looking forward to a Nodd's Ridge surname engraved on some of the trophies in that fancy glass case in that fancy new high school their taxes had gone to build in Greenspark. So Sam gave way—but with an unexpected cost to the boy. The word was Reuben was living in the horsebarn. Ah well, he was mostly grown. In a couple of years he would be out on his own, and in the meantime—the size of him—he could fend for himself.

* * *

A daddy long-legs balanced its unlikely architecture on a dry chunk of maple—the very one over which Reuben's hand hovered, his own long fingers shadowing it. He remembered the old thunderstruck maple in the north pasture, the smell of newly cut hay in the air, the midges swarming, the pull of his muscles as he laid the ax to it, the crack and the crash of its falling. He remembered splitting it, stacking it, picking splinters of it from the calluses of his palms. One-handed he nudged the daddy long-legs off the chunk, stacked it on top of the ones already filling his embrace and delivered the armful to the woodbox in the kitchen. The maple thunked into the woodbox—by tomorrow it would be ashes, the combustion begun by the stroke of lightning three years ago at last complete.

The old man remained at table while Reuben's mother cleared the supper dishes. He read the newspaper, one ear tuned to the farm reports on the radio. When Reuben dropped the lid on the woodbox, the old man folded the paper and his reading glasses and rose slowly to take his jacket from the hook and followed the boy out to do the evening chores.

At the bottom of the steps Reuben braced him. "Mr. Rideout offered me a job. Twenty hours a week 'til summer, forty and overtime when school's out. Minimum wage."

The old man faltered and then frowned. "Out of the question. I'd have to hire someone to replace you."

"Then do it."

Astonishment briefly contorted the old man's face and then he laughed rudely. "And how do we pay him? Assuming I could find someone who wasn't a drunk or a layabout. Out of your wages from Rideout?" He hauled out a handkerchief and blew his nose, one nostril at a time. "What about school—and playing ball?"

"Pop." Reuben shifted from foot to foot, looking physically for the solid ground of argument he needed to take his stand. "You'll have to hire someone sooner or later. I'm not going to be a farmer. I want to own my own garage someday, and this is my chance to get started. I can finish school and play ball and work this job at Rideout's, I just can't work here too—"

Disbelieving rage crackled in the old man's eyes. But he restrained himself and indeed seemed to shrink almost visibly with the realization he could no longer make Reuben do his bidding out of fear of the strop or his hand. He was too old, the boy too big and strong. Reuben could leave tomorrow and there'd be no stopping him.

"You'll be quitting school next," the old man railed. "The draft'll be on you like the wolf on the fold. You want to come home in a box like the Farnsworth boy from Greenspark? Break your mother's heart? You won't be worth spit at soldiering. You won't be safe in a motorpool, boy, the Army don't work that way." The old man ran on with sudden querulousness. "They'll put a rifle in your hand and stick you out on the frontline. And you won't duck, you're full of John Wayne and all that talkie and TV horseshit. You won't live long enough to figure out the first job in a war is surviving it."

Reuben heard what he had come to recognize in the last year or so in his father's ranting—an impotent lashing out at a world moving on and leaving the old man behind. Fixing on the chimera of the draft was the same sort of thing as his sudden outbursts about the softheaded talkies and the mindless TV and the diddling-obsessed nigger noise on the radio and how it must all make the Reds grin to see fat, self-indulgent America digging its own grave.

"I'm not quitting school," Reuben said, exasperated. "By the time I graduate this war may be over. If it isn't there's naught I can do about it. The hell with it. I'm taking this job. I'll give you a third of my wages. It'll help some with hiring a man."

The mention of money helped the old man get a grip on it again. Cash was serious argument, one he could accept without loss of face. And savor as a kind of victory as he counted it. He could let Reuben have his way so long as Reuben paid for it.

"I'll think about it." As they finished the milking, he said, "Just don't get thinking you know shit from soda crackers just because you got some money in your pocket."

II

The Stone Walls Did Not Tumble nor the fields revert to forest though Reuben gave only an hour here and there to chores on the farm. Old Sam seemed to have as much time as ever to loiter in the post office parking lot, gossiping and maligning the government with other farmers. Reuben kept these observations to himself for the sake of the truce he had with the old man, seemingly placated by his cut of his pay.

Every week Reuben folded a few bucks into his mother's apron pocket. Next morning there would be an envelope addressed to his sister waiting to be mailed. His mother cobbled surreptitious lunches for him without his asking. Tucking them into his jacket pocket, she sometimes let slip a faint smile.

They were not allies against the old man. She had never stopped his father's hand or strop nor made any attempt that he knew to reverse his exile to the horsebarn. But she still fed him, washed and mended his clothes. Like his father she was old, older than the parents of his friends, and he suspected she had forgotten what it was like to be young. Her life had been as hard as any farmer's wife and she was only a woman, after all. He supposed the old man had taken it out of her long ago. She had long since become his father's creature.

As they all were. Himself. Every living being on his father's property. Cat, rat, dog, flea, chicken, cow. His roommates, the horses.

They were enormous, stolid draft animals, not hobby horses for riding. The old man had no affection for them—animals were tools and meat to him—but he was decent to them so long as they served his purposes. He named them by their colors: Blackie, Grey, Brownie, Whitey, Red, Red Junior, Pie. Perhaps they were names the beasts would have taken for themselves—the obvious, the simple, the minimum. They lifted their huge heads at the sound of the old man's voice. They ate enormous quantities of hay and feed, labored mightily and shat tons. The manure and feed drew rats. Consequently, the horsebarn as well as the cow barn supported an interbred clan of nameless cats. Occasionally a huge hoof caught an especially stupid and slow cat, and Reuben shoveled a limp feline corpse onto the muck pile, where doubtless the rats took their revenge.

Living in the horsebarn was like living in a zoo—a limited, unexotic one, to be sure, but unquestionably a zoo. It was the land of beasts in which Reuben was just another of slightly more complicated habit. He had tapped the socket of one of the bare bulbs that lit the cavernous dark, providing himself with a lamp by which to study and power for his radio and his suitcase record player. In booting him out of the house the old man had troubled to smash Reuben's handful of records—"Yakety-Yak," "Lucille," "Rocket '88' " among them—then kicked the shit out of the cheap little record player that had once been Ilene's. Reuben had put the record player back together in shop. It would take a little longer to replace the records, but once done he would play them as loudly as he liked, as loudly as he played his radio, without objection from the horses.

A mongrel kitten shared his exile with him. Until the weepy-eyed, runny-nosed little orphan took to claiming the warm spot on his cot as soon as he left it, Reuben had never had a pet. His father's dogs were a crew of nameless curs, kept chained and kenneled—whether to keep out intruders or in case he might need to track him or his mother if they ever tried to escape? Reuben sometimes wondered. Though in the interests of sneaking out at night undetected he had befriended the dogs, they were still a very long way from being pets. Close examination revealed the kitten to be a male. With no more imagination than his father in naming the horses, he called the kitten Barney.

He had made himself an oil-drum stove and insulated the walls of the tack room, and with the heat the horses threw off, it was as warm as his bedroom in the house ever had been. Warmer. In trade for some work on a teacher's clunker over the winter he had also acquired a beat-up Gibson guitar. He admitted to his friends that he could not play for shit. His hands seemed to be too big for the fretboard. The horses didn't mind his noodling with the Gibson any more than they objected to his radio.

He smelled of horses. The town girls had a tendency to giggle and back away. That was all right. He was in love with Laura Haggerty, who lived down the road. She was used to the smell of horseshit. Maybe even liked it.

Often he saw her in the distance of a misty dawn, herself as fragile as the colors of the early morning. She handled her quarter horse gelding as easily as she carried her books from class to class. Once at an eighth grade social he had kissed her clumsily in the cloakroom and since had been too embarrassed to more than mumble in her presence.

Most of the time she hardly seemed to know he existed, which was a relief. She hadn't yet found him wanting and rejected him out of hand. He had no time for dating or money to do it with, for that matter. He didn't expect her to be interested in him. She was delicate and beautiful as blue flag in a marsh, and he was just an overgrown farmboy. Her folks wouldn't care for her dating a Protestant either, especially a recalcitrant semi-pagan one. Let alone one who lived in a horsebarn. But sometimes she gave him a shy smile before she bent her head to the circle of her friends and the inevitable burst of giggles that followed. They were laughing at him, those girls—he knew—and he guessed he was a funny-looking geek.

He tried not to think about her, especially when he was horny—an exhausting amount of time—because it only made it worse and then he felt guilty for thinking things like that about a girl like Laura. He wondered sometimes what girls thought—of it—if they had the same feelings as he did or different ones or none at all. Some of his friends had had experiences or claimed to have, and they talked about the girls who would come across. Those girls, his friends said, they liked it plenty. But those were fast girls—and guys boasting too. Nice girls were different in some way, or else, he deduced, they would be fast girls too. Laura was a nice girl. A very nice girl. She went to Mass every Sunday with her prayer book in one gloved hand.

He sneaked out sometimes to meet his friends at the quarry. To the music from someone's transistor radio they played cards and smoked cigarettes—he didn't smoke himself, but Sonny Lunt always offered him one just to hear him say it was bad for your wind—which he always did because it was. Cost money too unless you cadged or kited'm, like Sonny did. They used to talk baseball and trade cards, but last summer there was less of sports and more talk of drinking they'd done, of vehicles and girls, women—by summer's end, pussy was the word they were using. They drank beer Sonny kited from his old man a bottle at a time when Hallie was too soaked to keep track of what was left in the case.

And they swam in the quarry.

It was dangerous, of course, diving into the water, which was hard-looking and black as anthracite. Kids had drowned in the quarry. You'd think the way their folks carried on about swimming there, it was the only way kids ever died. They could all recite gruesome legendary deaths of kids—the one hit in the mouth by the baseball that poisoned his heart with the stuff at its center, the one who tried to fly off the barn roof, the one who got turned to hamburg by the train, the one who was murdered by the crazy old homo. All proof midnight diving at the quarry was at the most a minor risk in a dangerous world.

He loved the sensation of the summer night on his bare skin—the immediate thickening of his cock it provoked. For an instant—between mossy ledge and the cold baptism of black water—he was untethered from all that bound him. Whether he tumbled through the violins of "Will You Still Love Me Tomorrow," and Shirley Owens warbling, "tonight the light of love is in your eyes" or through the pump of "Runaway," to Del Shannon asking, "why, why, why" or the tomcatting growl and strut of Wilson Pickett's "In the Midnight Hour," it was always an epiphany, an instant of conviction that if there was a good way to die it was just this one. He never told the others how he felt about it. He just did it.

And after, with his skin cold and goose-bumpy, hair on end, he reflected it was the next best thing to jacking off. He wondered what it would be like to touch someone else's cool and shivery skin. But like the others he fumbled hastily into his clothes to huddle by the fire a little while longer, listening to the shit being shot, prodigiously.

Working at Rideout's would make it much easier to slip off to the quarry or the public beach or the parties in the woods and at camps—the later he worked, the better. A minor thing compared to cash in his pocket or doing work he wanted to do instead of shoveling shit. Or freeing himself of the convulsive dead man's grip of the old man. Getting the job had some of the thrill of midnight quarry diving. He breathed a little more expansively, walked with a spring in his step. Grinned at the batter, threw lightning bolts, and strolled from the high school mound with the professional nervelessness of a major leaguer who regularly struck out the side.

* * *

The boneyard bloomed over the Memorial Day weekend, with plastic flowers and miniature flags, jars of narcissi, heavy-headed tulips and even an expensive arrangement or two from florists. Elderly folks in straw hats unpotted plants and shrubs upon the settled graves of their grandparents and parents and siblings. And the summer people came to open their camps and cottages for the season. With every ting of the bell line by the pumps, Sixtus Rideout thumped his walker in satisfaction.

It wasn't the first Cadillac of the day, only the dustiest—a sway-backed sedan of five years' vintage, with a loose fan belt and balding tires. Reuben deduced an elderly owner with failing vision and reflexes, given to fender benders and forgetfulness about maintenance—some leather-headed, cardiganed retiree in golfing pants. As he emerged from the cool, greasy dark of the garage bay into the blind brilliance of the day, he saw the driver was a woman in a big-brimmed hat. The noonday was thick with the smell of sun-warmed grease and oil and gasoline.

In the passenger seat a little towheaded girl, feet tucked under her, worked at a coloring book with busy fingers. The tip of her tongue stuck out to help her concentrate. The woman peered up at him from under the hat, her eyes hidden behind sunglasses that emphasized the shape of her face. She looked to be somewhere between twenty-five and thirty-five to him, but without a look at her eyes he couldn't cut it any closer. Her black halter top not only displayed a lot of freckled cleavage, her nipples were discernible beneath the fabric.

Her voice—instructing him to gas it—startled him out of his daze. Reminded now of what he was supposed to be doing—asking if he could help her and being smart about it, according to Sixtus—he fumbled through his rest of his lines.

"Yes, ma'am. Check the oil?"

"Oh sure."

"Pardon me, ma'am. Sounds like you've got a loose fan belt. Like it checked?"

"Fan belt?"

"Thwip-thwip." An impatient young voice mimicked the rhythm of the belt from the backseat.

Only there was no one visible on the back bench. The voice must have come from the floor in the back.

"Is that what that noise was, David?" asked the woman.

"Yes."

"Why didn't you say something?"

"I like it."

The little girl snickered. The woman almost smiled.

As he lifted the hood she got out. She wore shorts—not short shorts or tennis shorts but the kind lion hunters wear. She was small, an inch or three over five feet, and neatly engineered. Maybe a little top-heavy. She moved with a slight hesitation, as if she had a short somewhere in her wiring.

The little girl climbed out behind her, and taking each other by the hand they set off down the road toward Partridge's Store on the other side.

The rear door chunked open and a tall, bony boy in the neighborhood of ten or eleven materialized at Reuben's side. Catching him gawking after that little drift in the woman's walk.

A boy, Reuben assumed—the woman addressed him by a male name. But he needed a haircut so badly he certainly would be accused in the local school yard of being a sissy if not an outright queer. A shrunken, rusty black T-shirt showed three inches of his midriff. His too-short dungarees had holes in the knees, and his bare ankles stood out from the laceless, dirty sneakers. Hands in his pockets, he squinted at Reuben through round, gold-rimmed glasses with dirty lenses. If not for the frames, which appeared to have been handed down from some wealthy granddad, and the fact he had just stepped out of a Cadillac, the boy could have passed for the most neglected kid in Grant, just over the town line—a place synonymous with inbreeding, poverty and holy rollers. Past the ratty clothes and shaggy hair he was a handsome kid—worse, a confusingly beautiful one. As if embarrassed by his own looks, the boy avoided direct eye contact.

Ducking into the shadow of the hood, Reuben examined the fan belt. He could not forbear a hasty survey of the machine. The whole mill was filthy and encrusted. Everywhere were signs of neglect. He turned his attention back to the fan belt. The boy watched. Reuben had never felt so thoroughly watched in his life.

"You'll get another hundred miles out of this belt," he told the boy, since he had given sign of some automotive knowledge, "but it should be replaced soon."

"It looks like shit."

"It'll hold all the same. Thing doesn't have to look good to do the job. This machine needs a good bit of work, though."

The boy picked idly at a scab on his elbow as he studied Reuben at work but said nothing. He was still squinting, as if the brightness of the day bothered his eyes.

When Reuben finished tightening the belt he looked up to the boy again and got a nod of approval.

"Thwip," Reuben said with a grin.

The surprise in the laugh that escaped the boy gave Reuben a measure of satisfaction.

As he closed the hood the woman and the little girl were returning. Holding out a Popsicle for her brother, the little girl suddenly spurted across the road. The boy lunged a step toward her, saw there was no traffic—she was perfectly safe. He recovered himself, pretending he was never concerned. But Reuben marked the wild pulse in the boy's throat, a tremor in his hands and sudden perspiration on his upper lip.

The woman carried the bag of groceries awkwardly in one arm while keeping her hat from being lifted away by the breeze with the other. Conscious of the boy's ironic gaze, Reuben hastened to relieve her of the bag. Holding the car door for her, he was rewarded by the hitch of her shorts as she climbed in. Thigh muscles stretched above the knee and inside too, the skin there pale as ice on the lake thinning to melt. When she reached past the wheel to turn the key, the creamy tops of her breasts shivered. He managed to tell her what the damage was. While she rummaged around on the floor for a handbag, the changing vista had him spellbound.

The boy reached suddenly forward over her shoulder to drop a chunk of orange Popsicle neatly into her cleavage. The bills squirted from her hand and change tumbled over her thighs as she gave a little shriek of outrage and plucked out the piece of orange ice.

"You little shit!" she gasped, but she was also laughing.

She popped the chunk of Popsicle into her mouth.

And the little girl scrambled around for the money as if it were a game.

Temporarily incapable of counting it, Reuben clutched it numbly when she handed it through the window.

The boy ran down the rear window nearest him and smiled at him. He held out the rest of the Popsicle.

"Suck on this," he said.

"David!" the woman exclaimed.

As she twisted around to throw an inaccurate whack in the kid's general vicinity, one tit nearly popped out of her halter, right to wild rose nipple.

"What am I going to do with you?"

"Nothing," the little girl answered the woman's question. "He's incorrigible."

The boy threw himself down on the rear bench and hung his sneakers out the window as they drove off.

While Reuben rang up the sale, Sixtus wheezed at his elbows. "I heard what the little shite said. Needs his mouth warshed out with soap. He was my yowen, I'd cut his goddamn hair and put some decent duds on him and paddle his ass for good measure. Boy's father's dead and she lost her other boy, and now she's soft as rotten ice with that one. Brat's been booted out of every school she ever put him into—not that she cares, she drags both of'm from pillar to post like they was so much dirty laundry. Don't you leave nothin' lyin' around loose when he's skulkin' about—he's one of them rich kids steals for the hellavit." Sixtus hawked and spat. "Mebbe next time she comes in here, you could tear your peepers away from Missus Christopher's jugs and watch the little bastid don't empty the till. You do your job and pay attention to what's going on. You ain't being paid to review the Annual Parade of Titties."

Reuben held his tongue against the impulse to say he would happily do that job for free. Sixtus would retail it all over town in no time flat.

It was mid-June before he saw the neglected Caddie—still sorry-looking as a wet cat—again. The woman began to stop regularly for gasoline, but she didn't ask him to work on it. He didn't understand it. He couldn't conceive owning such a machine and yet not taking care of it. All he could think was that in widowhood she was overwhelmed with having to assume all the tasks of ordinary living that had once been her husband's, and this one, the maintenance of her vehicle, might be of distinctly lower priority than raising her children or managing the family finances.

Like most of the summer people—they tended to be a well-mannered lot—she said please and thank you, but her eyes remained hidden behind dark glasses and her smile was often glassy. He was always too tongue-tied in her presence to be able to articulate his concern for her automobile, and when he expressed it to Sixtus, the old fart snorted dismissively.

"Women don't know nothing about auto-mobiles, rich ones 'specially. You might's well let her run inta the ground and hope she burns that mill out on your shift. Make more money that way."

The children were never with her. He glimpsed the little girl being driven by a white-haired woman in a late-model Chevy woodie. They stopped at Partridge's for groceries, the post office for the mail and were parked at the public library for Story Hour. Presumably the boy had gone to camp.

It was common practice among the summer people to ship their get off for most of the season to enjoy a taste of communal living. Whatever it did for their heirs, it freed the rich folks for their own summer diversions—golf, sailing, boozing, diddling each other's wives—idle hands doing the Bad Man's work, according to Sixtus, whose views were in accord with the rest of the locals.

In time Reuben became aware the propertied people who spent their summers at the lake held a not dissimilar view of the locals— that colorfully spoken lot, given to getting sloshed playing ball at the town field behind the meeting house or beered up to hoot and holler at the demo derbies at Castle Rock Speedway or boozed up at the local roadhouses to brawl in the parking lot over each other's wives, in the long, precious light of summer's evenings.

III

His Head Felt Woozy. Somewhere inside he settled back to observe himself getting soused. Sonny had gotten hold of some hard stuff, and they were chasing beer with rum and Coca-Cola mixed in the empty long-necks. They were all well ahead of him—Reuben had gotten to the party late after work.

The sudden looseness in his joints, the slur in his speech, felt good and made him laugh. Reality slipped and slid between the intensely real and the misty—it was like trying to clear a spot in the windshield when it was snowing hard and the defogger was, as usual, on the fritz. The night was up his nose—the crystal sharp air making him breathe more deeply. And in his blood, alcohol and oxygen made an internal-combustion engine, spinning disconnected wheels.

They were at the public beach at the Narrows and it was nearly Christmas. Steady freezing since the beginning of December had made a rink of the lake. It was a perfect night for skating—clear and crisp but not so cold it hurt. Between the beach and the road the grove of widely spaced old pines was easily negotiated right to the water's edge. With just enough snow on the ground to pack hard, they drove into where they wanted, pulling their junkers up between the trees close to the beach and cranking the volume on their radios. The fall of the land from the road to the beach allowed a driftwood fire on the sand that was not visible to what little traffic there was.

They were all between fifteen and nineteen—not one yet of legal age and nearly all of them drinking. Kids from the Ridge, from Greenspark and the other little towns that sent students to Greenspark Academy. More boys than girls as always—fewer girls had wheels and their parents kept them on a tighter rein. It took some daring for a girl to be there, and unless they were with a steady they tended to travel in packs.

Around the fire and on the edge of the frozen beach the boys passed the booze and smoked their cigarettes and watched the girls skate to the music from the radios. Most of the girls had regular figure skates; the boys tended to be more raggedly equipped, with hand-me-down and homemade blades. Occasionally a boy worked up his courage and went out on the ice to cut a girl out to skate with him. And the other boys jeered at the Romeo and he would throw them all a finger and the girls would laugh too.

Among the girls on the ice were Laura and her friends—Heidi Robichaud and Janice Shumway and Joyce Sharrard and Bobbie Lovejoy. They were something to see—shrieking and clutching each other dramatically as if they really thought they were going to fall down.

Laura's hair floated around her shoulders as she spun and glided. Her face glowed with exertion and a few long strands of cornsilk blond stuck to her damp skin. She was a slim girl, hardly anything for breasts, but her bottom in her wool slacks had a woman's shape. Sometimes she glanced his way. He could hardly take his eyes off her. He thought she looked like the angel off the top of the Christmas tree they used to have at the church when he was a kid and his folks still went. Taking another swallow of his sticky rum and Coke, he savored the heat passing from mouth to throat to belly. He was almost tight enough to go out on the ice. Of course, he'd have to borrow blades, and he doubted anyone had any big enough for him.

Joyce broke away from the group and whooshed up to him as he teetered at the margin of snowy beach and ice. She reached out, shouting with laughter, and grabbed his hands. Startled, he let her tug him forward onto the ice. His boots slid on it and he nearly fell on his ass. Sonny and the other guys hooted at them. Suddenly Joyce was hanging on his neck and swaying to the "Dancing in the Street." She sang it to him mockingly. Her sweatered breasts brushed against him, and he could feel her body heat and smell her shampoo and perfume and her perspiration all mixed up together in a heady tingle in his nose. It was very very pleasant, very warming—well worth the laughter of his friends and hers. Her color was high with exertion and drink.

He stumbled and she made a face. Then his hands were empty and she was gone, racing back to the other girls.

Sonny promptly slung an arm around his shoulder and sprayed spit into his face. "You get a feel?"

It hardly required an answer. It was one of Sonny's favorite conversational gambits, right after "Wanna butt?" and "Wanna beer?" Sonny had the hots for Joyce. Sonny had the hots for whatever female was currently in his field of vision—so bad he could get off on the report of a feel.

All at once there was shrieking and screaming among the girls. At first Reuben couldn't make out what was happening, but then it was clear two girls were fighting. The circle of onlookers broke open and he could see the two girls down on the ice. Joyce and Laura. Laura tearing Joyce's hair out, Joyce clawing furiously.

"Bitcccch!" Laura wailed.

Sonny plunged in to seize Joyce by the waist and haul her off Laura, earning himself cheers from some and catcalls from others who wanted to see the fight continue.

As quickly as it ignited the fight was over. The party curdled into separate elements—boys drinking and smoking and joking nervously in the face of the outbreak of female hostilities, girls clustered around each combatant, and from those quarters there were sobs and tears and muffled plaints, punctuated with a stern tone of lecture from some authoritative confidante.

After a while the party picked up again. Joyce skated again and this time Sonny laced on his blades and joined her.

Reuben looked for Laura but didn't see her. Vanished. Without a car or even a license she must have come with Joyce, who was supposed to be her best friend, or else Heidi or Bobbie or Janice in someone's mom's car—that was how the girls got around. But she might have bummed a ride home with nearly anyone. Just his bad luck—missing the opportunity to take her home.

Then he spotted her slight figure huddled near the fire. Hugging her knees, she concentrated blindly on the flames. She had taken off her skates and put on her boots.

"You okay?" he asked her.

She glanced up at him and then back at the fire. Her hair was all messed up. Eyes puffy with weeping. She nodded quickly.

"I'm kind of—" He stopped and waggled the bottle he clutched by its long neck.

"I noticed."

He sat down abruptly. "I like your hair."

His face was hot with more than the fire so close and he felt like a fool, but she looked at him again. He reached out impulsively and touched the tangles that veiled one side of her face. It was astonishingly silky. As he drew it aside he saw the scratch furrowing her cheek.

"It's nothing," she said quickly.

She stared at him from under the flutter of her half-shut eyelids, and he bent quickly to kiss her. Her mouth yielded. Her lips were hot and moist, and he kissed her more eagerly and she pushed him suddenly away from her. And jumped up and walked away, arms wrapped around her midsection as if she hurt.

He started up after her, made it to his feet and then sat back down abruptly. Rolling over with a sigh, he stared up at the sky. The pines reached blackly toward the run of clouds that blotted out the stars and soaked up the moonlight. He closed his eyes a moment. It was dizzy inside with the shades drawn. He sat up, sucked at the bottle and then concentrated on regaining his feet.

The party was running down. People leaving. Laura was gone, her buddies too. *Joyceheidijanicebobbielaura.* A single creature, spiderish, eight times as female as one of them on her own. Hair and tits and fannies and legs. Big eyes and wet red lips. Funny how the bunch of them were always together. From overhearing them jabbering with each other he knew the first thing they all did when they got home was call each other. No wonder they fought with each other. Must be hell all stuck together like that.

He amused himself getting a couple of shitboxes going without managing to cross the jumper cables and blow up the batteries. Then he squatted by the fire with the last holdouts, Ridge boys all—Sonny and Ansel Partridge and Junior Witcher and Louie Foster and Dana Fullencamp—getting drunker. The degree of their inebriation became the primary source of hilarity, his own most of all since it was the first time he had ever been this fargone.

At some point he groped his keys from his pocket and piled into the high-nosed '49 Ford he'd bought with his summer's earnings at Ridcout's. The body looked like the dry brown molt of some enormous beetling insect. It was ugly. He loved it.

> *does he love me? I wanna know*
> *how can I tell if he loves me so?*
> *is it in his eyes?*
> *oh no you'll be deceived*
> *is it in his eyes?*
> *oh no he'll make believe*

if you wanna know
if he loves you so
it's in his kiss

poured from the radio, and he knew he was really very fargone, very shitfaced because he liked it he loved it he howled it along with Betty Everett.

Aside from that particular litmus test his reflexes were sloppy, and he knew almost immediately he was too drunk to drive. He slowed to a creep and with great effort wove his way along the road. Losing his fix on the center line, he drifted across it and back again, overcorrecting onto the shoulder, skidding on the icy shoulder and back onto pavement. And then without any memory of how he got there he was in the snow-filled ditch at the bottom of the road up to the farm.

He felt fine. Clear-headed. The truck was fine. He would roll out early and get it out of the ditch before anyone even knew it was there. Taking a shortcut uphill through the woods and across the fields, he plunged into brush that flailed at him with denuded branches. He knew these woods, this terrain as well as he did the ceiling of the tack room. He had negotiated them at night on many occasions. But not in this state of inebriation. He became confused. The drifted snow seemed to grab at him and drag him down. He fell among the frozen brambles and was flagellated by thorns. He heard in his struggle the distant baying of the old man's dogs rending the night.

* * *

A crack like the ice breaking on the lake reached him, but he was a long way down and it was a long, gasping, heavy-limbed swim back to consciousness. Yet the sound seemed still to reverberate as he became aware of his face against the snow, melted to hard shell by his body heat. He had dreamed the sound, he supposed. His body, his head, wanted to sink again beneath the surface and perhaps it did, perhaps more than once, but finally he really was conscious and cold, miserably frigging cold, and could not stop shivering.

He groped his way to his knees and then got hold of a tree trunk and used it to get to his feet. It was wonderfully solid and he leaned against it awhile until he was less dizzy and then he leaned against it some more while he pissed.

It was just light out. The sky lowered over him, heavy with more snow that he could smell and taste. The temperature had risen a little in the night, which was probably why he hadn't frozen to death. With his head a painful throb on his shoulders he slogged onward up the rise toward the barn. Every step made him feel seasick.

The old man would be up by now and milking. After the cows he tended the horses, and there was no way he would not notice the state he was in. Might as well face the music. But the cows lowed needily at the crunch of Reuben's step on the snow pack of the barnyard, and the horses nickered from their stalls.

The dogs were loose. They formed a pack around something on the ground and sat there barking and snarling and growling. Despite their obvious disturbance they were wary and oddly uncertain. One of them sprang to its feet and barked sharply at him in recognition or remonstrance. There was a wet darkness on its muzzle.

Even the feeble light hurt his eyes. There was a sudden sharp spurt of pain behind his left eye as he realized the thing the dogs encircled was the old man. Most of his head was gone, the bits blown about by a shotgun load, a red puddle formed under him. The smell of blood hung in the air like a storm coming. The old man's hand had released the shotgun to fall next to him. One of the dogs snapped at Reuben and growled and its teeth were washed red to the root. Reuben hunkered down to look closely and saw the dogs had fed where they hadn't ought to and then the smell got to him. He scrambled away down the fence line to cough up the contents of his stomach onto the glittering snow.

Wiping his mouth with the back of his hand, he blinked his eyes back into focus. There were things that had to be done. He made himself go back to the circle of dogs. Making a slow approach, he sank to his knees on the snow to show them his hands. Creeping on their bellies, whining, they sniffed cautiously, licking his fingers and his face and sticking their noses into his crotch. Their muzzles smeared blood and matter and slobber on his hands, his chin and throat and ear, his pants at the crotch. He scratched under the lead dog's chin and it relaxed, rolled over and showed its belly. As he coaxed it gently into the kennel, the others followed and then allowed himself a moment to lean against the wire.

He felt every step to the house in the roots of his teeth and realized his jaw was rigid—he was grinding his molars fiercely. He let himself in at the back door. His mother was at the stove in the kitchen, fussing and frowning, her braids still hanging over her shoulders. She usually pinned them up before she came down.

"Sam didn't kindle it," she said.

"I'll take care of it," Reuben told her.

She looked at him then—perhaps it was the tone of his voice and spoke more sharply. "What's the matter with you?"

"It's not me," he said. "It's Pop."

Confusion blurred her features. He moved immediately to her side and took her by the elbow and guided her into the rocking chair by the stove. She fixed on his face, trying to discern whatever he might know.

"I don't understand . . ."

"Did you hear anything?" he asked her.

Her eyes widened and a little gasp escaped her.

Sinking to his knees before her, he took her hands and she looked at him. He squeezed her hands.

"He put the four-ten in his mouth," he said.

Her body jerked in the chair and she glazed over on him.

He chewed his lip. She rocked slightly in her daze. He let go her hands and got up and went to the phone and called Frank Haggerty.

It was a short wait but he used it to kindle the fire in the range and put on the kettle, and then he went upstairs and came down with a couple of blankets. One he tucked around his mother. At his touch she came out of it a bit, raising her face to look at him with suddenly watering eyes.

"I'm going to go cover Pop," he explained to her.

Her gaze fell to the folded blanket in his hands and the shock reared up again and she shook in its grasp.

Haggerty came in his cruiser, but he didn't use the siren. He met Reuben coming back from covering the old man's body.

"I'm going back inside to my mother," Reuben told him, and Haggerty nodded and went on to look at the body.

He made tea and put a mug in her hands, and it seemed to revive her a little.

Haggerty came in and spoke his condolences to her in a reassuringly calm manner and said he had made a radio call and there would be help on hand shortly.

"Do you have any idea what happened?" he asked.

She frowned as she considered the question. "I don't know. I woke up to a gunshot, but it sounded far away, in the woods, and I thought it was a poacher—one of the Lunts maybe. I didn't even wake up all the way. Then I realized it was nearly time to get up anyway. I was so surprised. Sam always kindles the stove for me and it was nearly cold."

Reuben turned one of her hands over in his and patted it. "Maybe he had a reason, Ma. Maybe he was sick."

Her hands in his relaxed a little.

"He must have been sick," she agreed.

Reuben glanced up at Haggerty, who gave a quick nod of encouragement.

"Maybe there's a note," Reuben said.

She nodded.

But there was no neatly sealed and addressed envelope on the mantel in the parlor or in the Bible, no note to be found in the bedroom or anywhere in the farmhouse. The old man's desk was full of paperwork. It would take hours to sift through it all.

Frank Haggerty drew him out of his mother's range of hearing. "You got any idea?"

Reuben shook his head. "Hear those cows? He must not have seen to 'em before he did it. They should be tended."

"Somebody else'll do it."

Now there were sirens, more cops coming and along with them neighbors and townsfolk alerted by a nearly telepathic grapevine. Reuben went outside with Haggerty again. In short order a ragged circle of men surrounded the old man's body just as the dogs had.

Hallie Lunt's truck bumped into the yard. Sonny, Hallie and Tiny piled out as Reuben went down to meet them. Tiny snuffled on Reuben's shoulder for half a moment and then, with her infallible sense of ceremonial timing, let him go. She waddled purposively for the kitchen.

"Hallie," Haggerty prodded, "the animals need tending."

Hallie and Sonny, eyes downcast, paused long enough to shake Reuben's hand and then made for the barn.

Reuben and Haggerty trudged back to the body. What little talk there was among the waiting neighbors and the increasing contingent of cops fell off to coughing and rubbing of hands against the cold.

"I noticed dog tracks around the body," Haggerty said, "before everybody tracked over'm. There's still some tight in. I see some other sign, they were out awhile—"

"They were out when I found him. I kenneled them," Reuben told him.

"Would have had to be done anyway. It means you altered the scene, you see, but I don't imagine it matters. Was that usual? For your father to let out the dogs?"

"No."

Haggerty nodded and set about a quick examination of the body and found nothing by way of a note. There was more shuffling around, much throat clearing, avoidance of direct eye contact, men dealing with a situation by calling on procedure, men being men, doing their jobs, doing the proper thing. Acknowledging the enormity of death, and a self-inflicted one at that, by a ritual that in large part pretended the wreckage of a human body at their feet was hardly more distressing than someone inappropriately naked instead of inappropriately dead.

As he had assisted at road fatalities, Reuben helped the cops bag the body and put it in the meat wagon. Then it was gone and there was only the mess on the snow. He shoveled clean snow over it. But the snow was beaten down all around it where the men had loitered—the place as clearly marked as the frantic erasure of a child on a sheet of lined yellow school paper.

The women had taken the kitchen. His mother sat in the parlor with the minister Tiny Lunt had summoned.

He and Haggerty began to shuffle the papers in the old man's desk more thoroughly. Looking again for a note or some other explanation. Bankruptcy. Be a joke on them if the old man had secretly bet the farm on a commodities scheme or some such folly and lost it. A teakettle came to a screaming pitch in the kitchen. Reuben's ears hurt suddenly and he raised a shaking hand to his forehead.

"You're hungover," Haggerty said with a little sour surprise in his voice.

Reuben could hardly nod.

Haggerty grimaced and shook his head.

✳ ✳ ✳

Tiny wrapped his hands around a bottle in a brown paper bag as the Lunts took their departure. "I knowed there wouldn't be nothing in the house, so I brung this with me. Charge a this'll get her to sleep."

Cherry heering. Tiny had a taste for it at holiday time. His mother accepted the small glass he offered without hesitation and tossed it back as if it were a teaspoon of patent cough medicine. With a polite little cough she tapped her chest, breathed deeply and relaxed against her pillows. When he checked a quarter of an hour later she was asleep.

Reuben drank a glass of the liqueur while he cleaned his old twenty-two rifle he'd left in the back of the closet when the old man exiled him to the barn. It didn't need it—it had been cleaned recently—but he did it anyway. Why'd you clean this rifle, Pop? Just in the mood? Trying to make up your mind which one to use? Then again, the old man had always been fastidious with any tool. Probably every shooting iron in the house was in firing condition.

James Brown was on the radio. "Papa's Got a Brand New Bag." *Ain't no drag, Papa's got a brand new bag. Uptight. Outasight.* All wrong, James. Papa was a drag and now he's *in* a bag, the kind thoughtfully provided by the medical examiner. Last dance was the horizontal flop. Papa's got a brand new penthouse in hell, that's what Papa's got. *Outasight.*

Reuben was sober when he went out to the kennel. The dogs sat up at his approach. The twenty-two made a polite little crack like ice snapping underfoot. Just as politely the first dog flopped over. The others barked briefly and then cringed, their eyes bright and puzzled. He came in close and put a bullet into the base of each of their brains, though it was harder to do each time and before the last he had to stop and wipe his eyes. When they were all dead he unrolled an old tarp, piled their bodies on it, tied it up and threw it into the back of his truck. Work for the morrow: he would have to dig a pit in the woods, pitchfork the corpses into it, douse them in kerosene and burn them.

It wasn't their fault. The dogs had just done what came natural to them, but that didn't change the fact they'd tasted a man's blood and eaten of his body. It was a fatal breach of the bond between men and dogs, and there was no redemption for them. The old man must have known when he let them out they were likely to do it. He must have wanted company on his way to hell, or maybe he just wanted to make a bigger, nastier mess. Leave his son another shitty job and make him share in the violence.

Sitting on the back steps, looking at the emptied kennel and the beaten-down snow where there had been so much foot traffic around his father's body, he knocked back the rest of Tiny's liqueur. It didn't seem to make him drunk or sleepy either, just dizzy for a while. *Outasight*. He went upstairs at last and stretched out on his old bed, under the roof of his family home again, over the old man's dead body.

His mother rose around four and so did he. She had breakfast ready for him when he came in from the chores. Though she could see the empty kennel and the tarp in the back of the truck from the kitchen window, she said nothing to him about the dogs.

They sat in silence in the kitchen, watching the hands of the clock click inexorably on toward the moment his father had pulled the trigger twenty-four hours earlier.

IV

He Hardly Knew His Own Sister when Ilene
descended from the bus. It had been more than ten years; she had
been a teenager and now she was in her early thirties and the
mother of five, and somehow the snapshots and Christmas family
portraits had not prepared him adequately. He saw an answering
shock in her face as she realized he too was not the little boy she
had known anymore but an eerily young version of the father she
had returned to bury. Despite the years of letters and snapshots
they had become strangers physically and had first to grow accus-
tomed to each other's looks.

Until the children—the youngest, Ilene's only girl, cross and
sleepy and bewildered—had climbed down from the bus the previous day, they had been no more than cute kids in the packets of
snapshots wrapped in Ilene's letters. In the flesh, quite literally, the
family resemblance was overwhelming. Ilene's boys could have
been his younger brothers or even his own get if not for their ages;
her oldest was only seven years his junior. Still, they were strangers
to him by the space of a continent. It added to the sense of
dislocation—this family that was so substantial in the flesh, so ten-
uous otherwise.

The house became a boil of kids to rival that of the Lunts. As
Reuben went about the chores he found himself being spied upon
and gawked at and followed about by disembodied sniggering and
high-pitched giggles. He found himself grinning to himself. He
thought he would miss them all when they were gone.

During the visiting hours at the funeral parlor in Greenspark,
Sonny took him outside and they leaned against the side of the
Mercury and divided a six of Miller between them. Sonny gave
him another six to take home with him, and he woke up the
morning of the funeral with a slight headache. When Sonny turned
up at the funeral parlor to join the other bearers, he had a pint of

Ron Rico inside his suit jacket. He and Reuben wet their throats down behind a rack of floral remembrances. They had another quick jolt outside the church before the service.

Inside the farmhouse after the funeral there was no booze, but Hallie tapped a couple of kegs and left them on the back of his truck. There was a steady traffic to it and a crowd of men loitering in easy reach. The women held the kitchen and the parlor, where there was coffee and tea and enough food to feed most of Africa. The kids whipped around, with Ilene's kids surreptitiously showing the local ones the place where Granddad done it, to the intense envy of the local youngsters.

Reuben moved distractedly among his friends and neighbors, listening to their condolences, thanking them for being there. That was how it was done. He avoided Laura; his crush on her seemed somehow ludicrous, part and parcel of the childhood that he had now to put away. He was now head of a household, his status altered to a man by his father's demise. He visited the kegs frequently. He felt himself losing coherence. His body grew heavier and difficult to coordinate. His emotions clotted inside him like a sick stomach but he didn't care. He refused to care. He refused to give a shit. He listened to the other men tell stories about his father, turning him into an amusingly irascible old Yankee.

In the twilight Laura left the house, headed for the barn. Reuben watched her, hugging herself against the cold in a short thin jacket and a short tight skirt. He guessed she had volunteered to see the horses were fed and watered for the night. Emptying his cup, he threw it into the flatbed of Hallie's truck.

She looked up at him when he drifted in, saying nothing as he crossed the barn. The cold light of the bare bulbs glowed in her hair and on her skin. He took the mash bucket from her and put it carefully on the floor. He cupped her jaw and tipped her face to his mouth. Her mouth was very soft and she didn't resist his tongue. His right hand groped at her jacket, trying unsuccessfully, drunkenly, to find its way inside.

There was a step behind him and Frank Haggerty shoved Reuben away from Laura. She seemed dazed.

"Get out of here," Haggerty told her.

With her head down, she scurried away.

It was cold in the barn, a cold Reuben remembered too well. A sobering cold. His head ached, his ears throbbed. He wiped his nose with his hand and then picked up the bucket of mash and turned to the horses.

Haggerty hesitated and then he shook his head and went out as silently as he had entered.

The tack room was so close and his old bed was still there. The mattress was bare, but it was a place to sit down and once he'd done that, he wanted to lie down. He closed his eyes.

The inside of his head wheeled around like a sky full of stars. Laura's hair had glowed in the naked light of the barn and her mouth had been so soft and welcoming and his tongue had touched hers. And now he was hard and he wanted to be on the mattress in the tack room with Laura, her soft mouth open to his tongue and he didn't care, he didn't give a shit. He didn't care. Laura's mouth was so soft.

* * *

Along with several other little towns too small to support its own high school the Ridge paid tuition to Greenspark. In turn Greenspark got the extra bodies to fill its brand-new facility that had replaced the four-story Gothic building downtown, the one Reuben's sister, Ilene, had attended.

Greenspark smelled of the mills and the tannery, and there was a palpable grimness in the air. In summer, enormous old elms and maples and chestnuts alleviated the gracelessness of its small redbrick and granite downtown, but it was in every season alien to Reuben. It seemed to him a sickly, claustrophobic place, petty walls and corners everywhere one turned and the sky diminished, like a great open hand closed into a fist. With the stink of the mills in the air it was impossible to smell the weather in its fluxes. Some days his eyes actually watered at the foul atmosphere. Though he was himself enamored of the complicated odors of petrochemicals and metals and motors, he reckoned he would rather live even with the smell of horseshit than the tannery, the paper mills or the munitions factory.

Returning to school after his father's death, Reuben took with him the silence that was like the deafness following a loud explosion. It went on inside him and outside of him; nobody, least of all himself, knew what to say after the initial formulae of condolence. He kept to himself and his friends took the hint. Passing Laura in the hall between classes, he averted his eyes to save her averting hers.

Among the papers in his father's desk there were bills from a doctor in Greenspark. When Reuben called, the doctor said he had only been waiting to hear from some member of the family. His father, the doctor informed them, had come to him with symptoms of a serious illness; tests had been performed, a tentative diagnosis made. A course of treatment prescribed. Then his father had elected an alternative and self-administered treatment. The doctor was professionally saddened, not least because while the condition was terminal, in a man as old as his father cancer often took a longer, milder course. His father might well have had several quite bearable years left. But whether out of fear of pain and dependency or of despair the old man had taken his own way out. Reuben inquired as to bills. His father, the doctor assured him, had paid cash. Soon the medical examiner confirmed a postmortem diagnosis of bone cancer.

His mother accepted it. They didn't talk about it, so he didn't know if she blamed him at all. He told himself that most likely the old man had been too wrapped up in the issue of his own mortality to give much weight to however much of a vexation his son might be. But there was no way of knowing, no way of assessing his own culpability—only the cut-and-dried fact that in extremity his father had shut out son and wife both.

Dying intestate and uninsured, the old man had left five local bank accounts and a shoeboxful of cash in the back of the closet. Auctioning the livestock and renting the fields to George Partridge provided both immediate cash and a small income. The land could be mortgaged as well as rented out. After clearing taxes and bills, his mother and he agreed to set aside a third for Ilene.

"We can see you through high school," his mother said with some relief. "But what happens then?"

He knew she meant, what was going to happen to her? Would he take her on as his responsibility or leave her to eke out her remaining years on what the old man had left and what the Social Security and Veteran's Administration would grant her?

"I want to buy Rideout's," he told his mother, "soon as I'm out of school."

He saw the relief in her face. A small business. A young man's stamina. It was at least as secure a life as a farm being worked by antique methods by an old man. Her knitting needles never missed a click. "Everything your father left will be yours anyway when I go. Call it half yours now. We'll go in half and half. How's that sound? It all comes back to you in the end."

"If I get drafted"—her needles did pause at that but he went on—"there's enough for you to keep going 'til I'm back. I should get a notice soon as I graduate. If I'm passed over we'll go through with buying the garage."

The proposition crumpled Sixtus Rideout's face into a disbelieving grin. "So you want to buy this place soon as you get out of school if you don't get drafted. What the hell, I ain't gonna do no better and I know I'm a useless old stick. I ain't ready to retire altogether is all. You'll need some help, boy. I can't do much but I can make change and answer the phone."

It took Reuben awhile to get used to sleeping in the house again. And nightmares troubled him so often he began to avoid going to bed. He found ways to stay at the garage so his mother would not know. There was an old mattress in the back room at the garage where he could toss and sweat. He told her he had to work late. She never questioned him. After all the years of being dominated by his father she accepted Reuben as the adult male in her life who would protect and support her. In all decisions she deferred to him. It was strange and more than a little frightening to have his mother in his charge.

Yet the old man's dead hand still ruled, though the iron was rusted to irony. Without any discussion with his mother Reuben stopped playing basketball for Greenspark Academy. He wouldn't be playing baseball in the spring either. The more hours he worked, the more he brought home in his pay packet, the less they need invade the cash the old man had left and the more that remained to stake the garage.

✳ ✳ ✳

My baby does the hanky-panky, Tommy James informed Reuben with understandable glee. Reuben dialed up the volume and tried to get back into *Moby Dick*. Queequeg and his involuntary roommate, the erstwhile Ishmael, were up to some kind of hanky-panky with Queequeg's wooden god. He was beginning to suspect that idolatry was only a metaphor for some other kind of hanky-panky. It struck him suddenly that hanky-panky even sounded like a word from Queequeg's odd—or as Melville would have it, queer—lingo.

At getting on for ten he had the radio tuned to a Lewiston station. It had been quiet for a Friday night, not even Sonny dropping in to shoot the shit. Sonny was put out with him anyway for working all the time.

The whole weekend was supposed to be cold and rainy, adding to the water rising from the snow melt. Normal for April— sogging up the baseball fields, though. Not that it was of any import to him anymore. The one behind the meeting house would be dry by Memorial Day, and he could play pick up ball there all summer.

With that thought lifting his spirits he sang along with Fontella Bass:

> *You got me doin' what you want me*
> *baby why you wanna let go.*

A woman emerged from the darkness into the overlapping spills of light from the office windows and the floods over the pumps. The pencil he tapped to the beat froze between his fingers.

Missus Christopher—so Sixtus called her—of the dusty, underserviced Caddie. Joe Nevers always referred to her as just Missus. Her straight dress bared her shoulders. A pigeon's egg of amber in a gold cage nestled intimately in her cleavage. Her hair was pinned up somehow with a wave at the front. There was a cut on her forehead. Squinting into the light, she stepped from the two-lane blacktop to the gravel edging the cement apron around the pumps, and in spike heels she wobbled dangerously. She nearly fell but managed to recover herself in an awkward little sway that gave movement to her breasts.

The ironic subtleties of *Moby Dick* forgotten, he hurried outside.

On her forehead the shallow cut was swollen with bruise. Close up, the illusion of glamour was tarnished by the unflattering mix of lights. She was a grown woman, middle-aged in fact but not in the worn way of local women. There wasn't a local woman he could imagine in that dress.

His hands dangled from his wrists like mittens attached to his sleeves with safety pins. His thick fingers were callused and scabbed, the nails broken and deeply fouled. His prints were all over the paperback *Moby Dick*.

"I've ditched my car at the turn," she announced. And then she laughed. The laugh had a sloppy turn in it from the booze he could smell on her breath. With a loose, wide gesture she indicated the wrecker on the apron. "Tow it for me?"

"Yes, ma'am. You okay?"

She frowned in puzzlement at his question.

He brushed the cut on her forehead lightly, with the top of a finger. He was amazed it didn't sink right into the wound. Her fingers followed his in sudden curiosity.

"That's nothing," she said.

He ducked inside to look down on the register and propped the Be-Right-Back sign in the window. The glass framed her shivering, stamping her feet. He grabbed the wrecker keys and snagged his letter jacket from the back of the chair. When he draped his jacket over her shoulders, she drew it right around herself and looked suddenly like a schoolgirl.

Seeing the height of the cab from the ground and that there were no running boards, she burst out laughing as if it were a deliberate joke on her size. Of course it was the booze; she was at the point where nearly anything was hilarious.

Tentatively he put his hands on her waist and picked her up, a circus strongman hoisting a petite trick rider to the back of her pony. Her laugh turned breathless with surprise. She was wearing perfume, something they didn't sell at any five-and-dime. She twisted and their bodies made inadvertent contact in several places—a curve of her haunch against his hipbone as he lifted her, her ankle against his calf, the side of her breasts against his upper arms. She wriggled onto the seat and he let go of her waist.

Getting in on the other side, he found the cab's normal atmosphere of grease and oil and his own sweat had suddenly acquired heavy overtones of perfumed, boozy woman. She huddled inside the jacket. On ignition the radio blared. He turned it down hastily but hesitated at turning it off entirely.

"Do you mind?"

She shrugged. "It's your truck."

The curve was hardly a quarter mile from the garage, where the Portland Road and the Sabbatos Road briefly fused before joining the Main Road through the village. The wrecker could almost find its own way to the point where vehicles going at excessive speed with a sloppy driver at the helm sought the ditch. From the moment they turned off the Main Road they could see the headlights of the Cadillac. It sagged on a blown rear tire. The windshield on the driver's side was starred.

Running flashers, he positioned the wrecker to yank the sedan from the rear and then go out to take a look. The left rear was flat and the fender skirt, which on the '63 covered half the wheel, was crumpled into it where it had impacted on a boulder outcropping in the ditch. No other major damage, just scratches and dings to match the old ones on it.

She was still tucked up in the corner of the wrecker's cab.

"See where the fender's jammed against the wheel? Have to straighten that out so I can change the tire. The windshield has to be replaced. That's a problem. I'll have to fetch one from Greenspark tomorrow. Have it in by afternoon, though."

"Fuck a duck," she said.

Blood rushed to his face. "I'll change the tire and tow it to the garage. Give you a lift home."

"All right," she sighed.

She slid out of the cab behind him. He turned to catch her as she jumped down. Her breasts brushed his chest, and for a glorious fraction of a second she was hip to hip with him. Then she tripped away to the sedan and threw herself across the front bench to retrieve something in a brown paper bag from the floor.

"Goddamn," she said, sitting up, "I've ruined these stockings now."

With a practiced flick of her fingers she spun the cap of the bottle inside the brown paper bag and took a swallow. As it went down she closed her eyes.

It was none of his nevermind. She was off the road now: she could drink 'til she passed out and it wouldn't harm anybody but herself.

She came swaying up to him while he was changing the tire and thrust the bottle at him. " 'S cold out here and I'm wearing your jacket. Put a little fire in your belly."

She must have thought he was old enough. It embarrassed him how much he wanted her to go on thinking it. The intimacy of putting his mouth on the mouth of the bottle that was still warm from her lips thrilled him. The booze was warm all the way down and then warmer in the pit of his stomach. He peeled back the brown paper a little: Wild Turkey. Bourbon.

He helped her back into the cab and before he closed the door she passed the bottle back to him. He took another swallow, said thank you ma'am, and shut her up inside the wrecker.

No joke, it was cold. He was shivering by the time the tow was rigged, and he was grateful to climb into the heated cab. She offered the bottle again. The warmth going down was just what he needed.

As the big automobile came smoothly out of the ditch, she breathed an audible sigh of relief.

"Really the damage isn't bad," he told her. "Unless there's some damage to the axle I couldn't see in the dark. Needs a little body work and a new windshield and a new tire. And spare. That one's sorry."

"I don't care about the car," she said. "I was worried a cop would come along before you got it out and bust me for OUI. This time I could lose my license."

So boozing and cruising was one of her hobbies.

At the garage he tucked the sedan into the bay. While he was unchaining it from the wrecker she sat on the edge of the seat with the door open and took off her heels, then let herself down to the floor from the cab. And there in the middle of the garage she pulled up her skirt and unhooked her stockings from her garters. His jacket came down to about mid-thigh on her, but he still saw a lot of leg and garter. She peeled off the stockings and tossed them in the trash can before she tugged her skirt down. She shot him a brilliant ironic smile.

Hastily lowering his eyes, he passed a silent word with himself as he cleared the chain: *She's tight and feeling silly. Teasing. Better cool down, buck.*

She disappeared into the lavatory.

He parked the wrecker on the apron. When he came in to close the bay she was back inside the back of the Caddie, rooting around for something. He took a closer look; she was feeling around under the front seat.

"My evening bag's under here somewhere. It slid off the seat under it when I ditched the car. Maybe you could reach it."

She sat up on the backseat, evidently intending to watch him go fishing for it. The width of his shoulders nearly filled the rear foot well, which was like a tunnel between the front and back seats. Intensely aware of her body on the couch of the back bench so close to him, he began to sweat. His fingers turned unnaturally clumsy, but at last he got a grip on what felt like a suede pouch. It had shapes inside it—some tubes and flat disks he guessed to be makeup, a soft bundle that was likely a handkerchief. And something else, like a flat bottle, too big to be perfume—about pint-sized. He tugged it out and handed it to her.

She looked at it without reaction and then stuck it on the back deck. Then she waggled the bottle in her hand at him invitingly. Recumbent on the floor of the Cadillac, he held up his hand. This might be a mistake. But so far the stuff hadn't done anything but make him feel warmer and more relaxed. She was teasing him, reclining on the backseat with her dress hiked up carelessly. He didn't want her to stop. He had a hard-on, but he could assure her there was nothing alarming about it. If hard-ons were five-dollar bills he'd own the garage by now.

"I like to drink," she confided as he handed the bottle back. "I need to do some work, so I wasn't going to this weekend. I thought if I came out to the house it would be quiet and I'd get a lot done. But first I had to go to this cocktail party and it was so-o-o-o boring—"

She burst out laughing again, and the sound was so free and easy it made him smile. He watched her swallow and took another one himself, and the heat of the booze seemed to burst inside him like her laughing. He was beginning to feel a buzz—lightheadedness, a tremor in his thigh muscles. He had to drive her home, though, and it would be major embarrassment to ditch the wrecker.

Sitting up, he handed her the bourbon. Then he pushed off the seat to roll toward the door. Her fingers closed around his wrist. Her eyes locked with his and he froze a second, then his knees folded against the bench. Her hand groped up his thigh and she touched him, touched his hard-on through the heavy cotton of his coveralls. His breath stopped under his breastbone. *Hanky-panky.*

"You want to screw me, don't you?" she asked in a whisper.

V

She Wanted It, she wanted him to screw her. Trembling, he sank toward her, between her legs. He was so much bigger he was afraid he might crush her. She drew his hand to the neckline of her dress and inside it, along the swell of the breast to a nipple, rising to his touch. She guided his other hand to the hem of her skirt and under it, past the loose nubbins of a garter to the prow of her pubis. He could feel her sexual hair through a layer of something silky. His dirty fingers—those panties would be ruined. The tip of her tongue flicked over his lips and inside. Her mouth tasted of the bourbon and her tongue writhed like a slow snake. Her hands were all over him in a way that gave him an idea she was excited by the difference in their sizes. He pushed down the top of her dress and her breasts, lustrous and pillowy, were free to him.

"My hands are dirty," he blurted when he saw the smears he was leaving on her.

"Good," she murmured.

Her skin when he tasted it was slightly bitter—but the texture was as soft as flowing water. The bauble she wore swayed between them and bumped against his mouth; it was cool and hard to the touch as the sex under his fingers was warm and yielding. Her hair had loosened and partially come down, and he buried his face in its perfumed veil. His fingers found their own way under the edge of her panties, into silky fringe. His index finger slipped between the fleshy wings, unfolding them, and between it was hot and wet like the inside of her mouth to his tongue. She made a little choking noise in her throat at the intrusion. He straightened a second finger into the fever of her cunt, and she closed her eyes and writhed on them. The spice of her perfume had grown heavier with exertion and mingled with the low tide musk of her melt greasing his fingers.

She pulled his hand away and began to shimmy from her dress and underwear. He had never seen a grown woman unclothed outside of stroke book pictures. The reality—the soft, exposed defenselessness of the naked body—moved him intensely. The sag of breast and softness of belly spoke to her age, and yet the greater surprise was how young her body still was. Full and luxurious and taut. The creaminess of her flesh marked with smears like bruises. The purplish tinge of her sex peeping through made her pubic hair look carroty.

He had gotten only as far as his shoes. He excused himself to lock up and she reached for the bourbon.

Grateful for the respite, he flipped the sign to CLOSED, locked the door and shut down the pumps and nearly every light in the place. All that he left burning was a workbench light in the bay. The Cadillac's dome light still glowed. He ducked into the lavatory. Returning to the sedan, he placed the little packet on the roof. Amazingly, she was still there, naked as a pin-up on the back bench. Waiting for him.

He pushed down his shorts and reached for the rubber, but before he could rip it open she stopped him.

"You don't need that."

He supposed she meant she was on the Pill. It was a relief not to have to try to put the thing on and risk the embarrassment of mishandling it. As he knelt between her legs again she grasped his cock and stroked it. He wanted her to keep on doing it but he also wanted more, he wanted to fuck her. When she released him he took it for an invitation and moved forward. He cupped the muscles of her ass and she arched upward and took him inside her, into the stretch of her cunt around his cock, into the blissful hot crush. He heard her gasp near his ear as he ejaculated in an exquisite rush that seemed to go on, in slow motion, for about an hour. He dissolved, formless as a slick of rainbowed grease on the floor.

As his breath evened out he became aware of his weight on her and started to withdraw.

"Whoa," she said, "you haven't even gotten started yet, friend."

He blushed deeply, out of embarrassment at having been too quick. And then smiled to himself at the perfect irony of being sentenced to remain between her legs. The broken clock gave the right time twice a day.

Her hips rose and fell beneath him, her cunt milking his cock and making him fully hard again as she bore him like a wave. He lifted her higher until he was nearly kneeling between her thighs. And fucked her slowly and deeply for a long time, until her eyelids were heavy and her face was white and pearled with sweat. She rowed his back with her fingernails. He was drowning, his lungs straining in an alien medium. In the struggle he lost any sense of the boundaries of his own skin. He tucked his head to rest it against the side of hers and looking down, saw a few hairs from his chest curled on her breasts in their mutual sweat. He closed his eyes and let the tree fall take him again.

"All right," she murmured, "not bad."

* * *

"Take me home," she said when she emerged from the lavatory.

It was strange to be back in the armor of clothing. They were different people, themselves again, their public selves. Wearing their fig leaves. But it was then he blushed uncontrollably.

From the backseat of the Cadillac she retrieved her bottle and her evening bag. She had an overnight bag and a briefcase in the trunk of the sedan, and these he placed in the wrecker for her.

As he helped her into the wrecker, she put her arms around his neck. They stood there necking for three or four minutes. Then she bit his lower lip. Instinctively he flinched and heaved her unceremoniously into the cab. The back of his hand across his mouth came away bloody. She snatched his hand and licked the blood. And laughing at the shock he could not hide, she uncapped her bottle and chased the taste of his blood with a slug of bourbon.

"Home," she said.

Being bitten left him confused. He didn't know if he had done something wrong, if he should apologize or not. It was a mute four-mile run on empty Route 5 before they reached the graveled camp road to the summer house. He could think of nothing to say. She seemed considerably more interested in the bottle than in him.

It was from the lake he had seen her house as a boy. From this side, fetching home its owner, he saw only a great dark looming in the trees. As they descended the steep driveway, it seemed to breach the black sea of forest until at the bottom it hung above them like a breaking wave. Something—perhaps only the isolation of the place, the absence of people except for them—made him think the house was like a monument, one of those mysteries in the village boneyard on which crude and silent carvings bespoke grief as expired as the dead they marked.

He helped her from the wrecker. "When do you want the car?"

"When will it be fixed?"

"Mid-afternoon."

"I won't need it until Sunday afternoon."

Barefoot she walked over the cold ground to the black loom of the house while he brought her bag and briefcase. When she opened the door it was like standing at the entrance of a depthless cave—he sensed enormous empty spaces waiting to engulf him. In the cold overlapping of shadows—night, forest, house—he could smell her, the luxurious perfume mingled with more than cunt, his own sweat on her, his semen with her exudations. She flicked on the light in the hall, dazzling his eyes briefly. Taking her bag and briefcase in one hand, she closed the door in his face.

"Good night," he said to the panels of the door. "And thank you too."

It struck him as funny. He was laughing to himself as he took the wheel of the wrecker again. He sniffed the fingers of one hand as he turned the key. The feeling of wildness, blind and irresistible, surged through him.

His foot nudged something on the floor. Her bag, dropped and forgotten again. There was an inviting slosh inside it. His first impulse was to take it to her right then—and once the door opened, sweep her off her feet, throw her on the floor in front of the fireplace he had never seen but knew was there by the massive chimney outside and fuck her again into sweating exhaustion.

He picked it up, feeling the liquid shift inside the pint. He peeked. Still a few mouthfuls in it. She must have nearly drained it on the drive from the city. Uncapping the pint, he sniffed it. Spicy, stinging—it smelled the way her mouth tasted. His cock began again to stiffen. His stomach was uneasy too but maybe everybody felt vaguely nauseated after sexual intercourse. Capping the pint, he closed the bag.

His little buzz had worn off. Driving back to the garage, he was merely intensely aware of everything—the vacuous cold and the smell of woods in fall and the rain that was coming soon. He felt like someone who had survived a close call. A woman, one he had lusted after—with the same indiscriminate horniness that perturbed him a dozen times a day over countless girls and women in the flesh in images in memory or fantasy but without expectations—that woman had taken him into the back of her Cadillac as casually as if she were buying a pack of cigarettes. And fucked his socks off.

She hadn't spoken his name once—he wondered if she even knew it. Suregod he didn't know hers. Outside the stroke books and locker room bull sessions, stuff like this never happened. Except this time it had and to him.

At least she wasn't anybody's wife. She was somebody's widow—some doctor who'd worked himself into a coronary. She was the one who had started it. Did she do it often? Not around here, he thought; there'd have been talk or at least remarks made. Sometimes you could read a woman's reputation in the pause in the conversation when she passed by. Straining his brains to recall a significant silence, a raised eyebrow, smothered rude laughter—at the diner the post office the garage where men idled with Sixtus on occasion while he worked—but he could summon nothing. If not for the cool silver shape of the flask in the little evening bag and the smell on his fingers, he would have a hard time believing it hadn't all been a jack-off fantasy.

The garage seemed especially empty. After cashing up and locking down the register—reflecting all the while how many of Sixtus' rules he had broken—he killed the lights and took the dregs of the flask from her bag into the back room. While Billy Joe Royal sang "Down in the Boondocks," on the radio he flopped on the mattress in his shorts and knocked back the last mouthful of bourbon. He savored the warmth that started in his stomach and seeped into his muscles, making everything seem to let go. He floated.

What they had done was to masturbation as the automobile was to the horse. A horse would get you where you wanted to go, but it wasn't sprung half so well, the ride wasn't half so smooth. It was, he concluded, the difference in the female suspension.

* * *

"*Baby, Baby, Baby, don't leave me,*" crooned Diana Ross and he realized it was Saturday morning. Light diffuse and gray as if he had a sheet over his head—he could hear the patter of rain on the roof. I got laid last night, he thought. Grinning, he stretched and yawned and rolled out.

He went home to fill the woodbox and have breakfast with his mother. Shower, shave and change to clean clothes and he was back to start work on the Cadillac. He checked the frame and axles, finding no damage, then looked under the hood. Someone was still giving the machine a lick and a promise by way of maintenance. The oil was so low she would burn out on the trip back to Portland. The battery was weaker than Sixtus' back. Once the tire was turning freely past the fender skirt and the wheels were realigned, he changed the oil, replaced the battery and gave the Cadillac the tune-up it so desperately needed. The machine purred in gratitude.

After stopping to open the garage for business, he started cleaning up the sedan. The interior was littered with kid stuff: coloring books and crayons, some loose sheets of light-sensitive paper figured with the silhouettes of leaves and coins and ice cream paddles. There was a beautifully articulated doll, a ballerina he guessed from the pointy feet, one of which had a socket in it as if to fix it on a stand. The ballerina was without a shred of clothing, had lost one eye and been shorn to bald scrub. Worked into the backseat was a dog-eared baseball card: a rookie pitcher for the Dodgers named Sammy Koberg who'd won one game and lost three. Back in the minors already. It was hard to know what was trash or treasure. He dumped it all into a paper bag and set it aside.

With nothing more mechanical to occupy his mind than the cleaning, washing and waxing of the machine, it was impossible to avoid the drift of his thoughts back to the previous night. He slipped into remembrance of the act itself, which necessitated in short order a trip to the lavatory. Where he discovered masturbation was itself intensified by his new experience. Apparently there was no end to the benefits.

When Sixtus thumped in around ten-thirty the sedan was gleaming. "Ain't that a beaut. Missus C's boat, ain't it?"

"She put her into a ditch last night. Blew a tire, drove the fender skirt into it. Gotta take a run to Greenspark right away and pick up the new windshield."

Sixtus bent a little, grunting, to examine the work. "Good enough. Shitfaced, I s'pose. When's she want it?"

"Sunday afternoon."

"All righty."

Sixtus turned himself around, spread his rear end over the stool and opened the register to check the previous night's receipts. He lifted a ham slightly to blow off a fart, then sighed in satisfaction. It wasn't, Reuben reflected, any worse than the horses.

* * *

Hard rain and Sunday produced a particularly soothing quietude, indoors and out. Smoke feathered from the chimney of the summer house and mingled in the mist in the treetops. The Cadillac slipped down the steep driveway, and when he killed the engine he could hear the steady rattle of rain on dry leaves. Thick on the ground and wetted by the rain the desiccated leaf was slick under foot. The air was heavy with the smell of decay, humus, wet wood. At the back door the rain rushed off the roof and down the back of his neck.

She opened the door to his brisk knock and he stood there like a fool, struck dumb at the sight of her. Not only did he not know her first name, he thought, she was different, she was not the same woman. Older—lines and shadows around her eyes. And she was sober and had clothes on. Slacks and a sweater and the amber pendant. Hair up but much more simply, just getting it out of the way. She squinted at him as if she didn't recognize him. Mutely he offered her the keys. She stared down at them. He remembered the other thing—the paper bag of children's culch, her evening bag on top—and fumbled them from under his slicker.

She peered into it. Smiled crookedly and took out her bag, then stirred through the contents. And suddenly her smile was stricken and she pulled out the baseball card.

"Where did this come from?" Her question was blurted in shock and she didn't seem to hear his answer.

"Stuck behind the seat."

There was a transparency in her skin as if it were thinner than usual. It made her look fragile. She was fixed on the thing as if mesmerized.

"Are you all right?"

"What?"

"Are you all right?"

For a second she stared at him. "Come in out of the weather."

She disappeared down the hallway like a flitting ghost. Following her, he emerged in the central room, the other side of the blind lens he had seen from the lake as a small boy. The room was so large and open it took inside whatever the weather was. The sullen rain seemed touchable despite the wall of glass. Goose bumps roughened his skin only partly from the chill.

The furniture huddled in small islands in the watery gloom:

oval dining table circled by chairs on one Oriental rug, sofa, rocking chair and coffee table on another. The sofa was leather, the coffee table glass and chrome, under a strew of papers weighted down by a bottle of Wild Turkey. The evening bag, keys, paper bag, baseball card tumbled from her hands in a heap on the glass of the table.

"I haven't had a drink today." A glance at him and she straightened up. "What am I telling you for? Hang your slicker on the back of a chair and make yourself comfortable. Like a cup of tea?"

He nodded. She took the booze and went into the kitchen, which was a kind of galley opening onto the big room.

Sammy Koberg's water-blistered face stared up at him from the table.

"It was Tommy's," she told him from the kitchen.

Tommy. Her oldest boy. The one who died.

"Wasn't even his favorite. David took to dragging it around after he died. It'll disappear for a while, then he'll have it again. I thought he'd lost it somewhere for good." Seated opposite him in the rocker next to the fire, she brushed back her hair with her hands. "Joe Nevers stopped by yesterday to tell me what a good job you were doing on the car. He thinks highly of you, you know. He told me you're sixteen. I didn't know. I took you for eighteen or nineteen—the size of you."

He cleared his throat. "Goin' on seventeen."

She laughed carefully. "From what I read, most kids your age are screwing each other every Saturday night at the drive-in anyway. Was it the first time? Did you like it?"

The twitch of her mouth made him think she was enjoying his discomfort. He nodded.

"So did I. I even remember it. Sometimes I just come to and can't find my pants." Her eyes glittered with amusement at herself. "You want to do it again?"

"Yes—no—I'm sorry, I have to get back to work."

She washed her face with her hands so the smile and the crinkles at the corners of her mouth seemed to vanish, leaving behind a smooth, sedate expression. "Oh, have your tea. You're wet and cold, you need to warm up your insides."

The kettle shrieked, summoning her to the kitchen, giving him a moment to recover himself.

And the tea did warm up his insides. He hadn't realized what a chill the wet afternoon had laid on his bones.

Her tea went untouched. She looked into the fire, into some distance beyond the flames. She rubbed her hands together briefly and put them between her knees.

"Sixteen," she murmured. Then she raised her head, her eyes sparkling with glee. "Guess what? It doesn't matter. We're all dead meat, sooner or later." She rocked the chair forward, hopped up and grabbed his hands to tug him to his feet. "This is definitely against the rules, but I'm definitely against rules, so come on."

* * *

The rain from the drainspout thrummed on the deck planking outside like a horse pissing. She pushed his hand off her left breast, where it had come to rest. "That jar in the kitchen. Bring it to me, would you? Pour yourself one too."

The bathroom door clicked shut behind her and within, water began to gush. He would have liked to take a shower and even more to take one with her but he wasn't invited.

Jar. She meant the bourbon. He put his pants on, fetched it and a glass for her and knocked at the bathroom door. She opened it a crack to reach out with a damp hand. He caught a glimpse of moist pink nakedness before she shut the door again.

Once dressed and ready to go and with nothing else to do, he looked at the books stacked on the night table. They were all about archaeology. All small print on thin paper bound together in fat volumes. Footnotes and references at the ends of chapters and Latin abbreviations and set-off paragraphs in foreign languages. Made his eyes ache to look at them. The newest one had a familiar face pictured on the back cover. It was her, the widow, Missus, smiling, sitting in a Jeep in some hot country and wearing lion-hunting shorts. Now it was in his hands, he thought he had known vaguely she was or did something to do with archaeology or anthropology or whatever, but he hadn't had any idea she wrote books. But her name was on it.

He put the book back hastily at the sound of the bathroom door opening. She stalked out and dressed as if he weren't there. Right off he was as embarrassed as if he had marched into somebody's bathroom at a private moment and they were too polite to tell him he didn't belong there. He got up and went out and found his slicker and stood by the back door until she came out.

She drove. Overdrove. Like the Caddie was a Jeep and she was muscling it over bad roads. It was painful.

"Just drop me off at the Main Road, okay?" he asked.

She glanced at him and smiled and he blushed.

"See ya," she said when he got out.

He smiled at her and she smiled back, and then the window came up between them and she was just a blur.

VI

Laura among Her Familiars janicejoycebob-
bieheidi staked out a favorite corner by a certain stairwell every
morning. Barefaced, Laura looked all of twelve from the neck up.
With makeup, like a little girl wearing her mother's cosmetics. But
her sweater draped her tiny, perfect breasts and her short skirt
showed off her lithe legs. She smiled shyly at Reuben.

"Missed you at Joyce's Saturday night," she told him, saving
him finding the first words.

"Had to work." He cursed himself silently for sounding so
short.

For a moment they hung there in horrid awkwardness and then
he asked her if she needed a lift back to the Ridge after school.

Loitering within earshot *bobbieheidijanicejoyce* burst out in
dirty-sounding giggles.

Laura glowed, the color in her cheekbones a faint reflection of
the furious red in his. "Thanks—but I've got cheerleading practice."

"Oh." He backpedaled, feeling extraordinarily stupid at having
forgotten such a thing. "Well, if you need a ride sometime—"

"Sure," she said.

That evening Sonny turned up at the garage with a six-pack.
"Way you're goin' at it, you'll be getting a date with Laura around
the time you start collectin' Social Security."

Reuben brooded over the beer Sonny handed him. "I'll think of
something."

"Shoulda come to the party Sad'day night."

No one to stop him. Only he'd been skittish, half wild with the
remote possibility the widow might come looking for it again. She
had once. He'd had his hand in the cookie jar, and any fool could
see he had a marginally better chance of getting into her cookie jar
again than into Laura's. So he'd begged off the party on the truth-

ful grounds he had to be up early to oil the floor at Partridge's store—one of the odd jobs Joe Nevers was always turning up for him, as if a moment's idleness was sure to lead him into devilment.

"Next time I will."

"Sure. Myself, I think you must be suicidal, trying to make a state cop's daughter—"

"Who said anything about making her? I like her—"

"—ass. Seen you look at it. Besides, I got more tit than she does, so it's not her knockers you go all glassy-eyed over. Hey, the old man wants me to change the oil in the truck. Wanna watch?"

"My favo ite thing."

"I ever get a chance to screw Diana Rigg in one of them leather get-ups she wears," Sonny said, "I'll let you watch, okay?"

"Thanks. I thought you were hot for Joyce."

"That reminds me—I got it worked out—a double date. You and Laura, Joyce and me. You gotta get Friday night off—"

"No way."

Sonny rolled his eyes. "Jesus. All right. Sunday afternoon."

"All right. What are we doing?"

"Only thing you can on a Sunday afternoon—movies in Lewiston. I already asked Joyce for Friday night. Mentioned maybe you and Laura. No big deal to change it to Sunday. 'Less Laura's in church or something—Cat'licks don't do nothin' Sunday afternoon, do they?"

"How would I know? The pope didn't send me a schedule this week."

"Now you gotta let go of your dick long enough to ask Laura."

"What if she says no?"

"She won't. Joyce says so."

Laura didn't say no but her father did.

She called the garage and whispered the news of her father's veto. Reuben could only say it was all right, he understood. His fingertips and hers had touched fleetingly as he passed his note to her in the hall at school. And she'd slipped away, her slight figure lost in the traffic.

A few days later, Frank Haggerty drew up to the pumps in the family wagon, a year-old Falcon, the right rear tire worn unevenly. Haggerty or his wife occasionally bought gas or a can of oil but otherwise did little trade at the Texaco. Reuben suspected immediately he was in for a hard time.

"Put three bucks in it," Haggerty started.

While he did Haggerty watched him with a cop's appraising eyes.

"Look, Reuben," he said on handing over the three bucks. "I'm just looking out for Laura. It's my job."

"Yes sir." Reuben, blank-faced, took the man's money.

"She's going to college, you understand," Haggerty continued.

Reuben just looked at him. "Your right rear tire. It's worn."

Haggerty glanced at the tire, nodded, got back in and drove away.

Reuben couldn't see a way past him. From what he'd seen of Laura and her father together, she was a daddy's girl. She wouldn't run around behind her daddy's back.

And Reuben didn't need anybody to tell him just how bad an enemy a state cop could be. Not only was his own operator's license at risk, but there was no end to the permits and licenses and paper he would need to operate the garage once he owned it. As a cop Haggerty was connected all over. He could quite literally make Reuben's life impossible.

* * *

The shudder and pant of the Cadillac's striving engine, the rattle of gravel on the verge and the whisper of tires on the apron—he heard it from under the hood of George Partridge's Olds as he scraped the battery terminals. Noontime of the Saturday of Memorial Day weekend, a year to the day that he'd first lifted the Caddie's hood. His stomach jumped as if he were taking a dip in the road too fast.

Conscious of how filthy he was, he approached the sedan. The widow rolled down the window. Sunglasses masked her eyes as they had a year ago. Her hair was pinned up in the back the way Grace Kelly sometimes wore hers so it showed that vulnerable place at the nape of the neck.

"How does it sound this year?" she asked.

"Neglected."

The little girl—leggier than a year ago and bouncing on the seat—chortled. There was a snicker from the backseat.

"Goddamn it," the widow said.

She popped the release; he lifted the hood.

Folding her sunglasses onto the dash, she took the little girl to the lavatory. It was a cooler day than it had been the previous year, and the widow wore slacks and a sweater. Nothing showed the shape of a breast like a sweater, Reuben thought. If she never spared him another look he could jack off over the line of her ass in those tailored slacks and the curve of her cashmere tits for the rest of his life.

When the boy didn't get out to look under the hood with him, Reuben tapped on the rear window. It rolled halfway down. The boy was sprawled over the backseat with a book in his hand. His glasses were in the end of his nose. He squinted over the top of the book, over the glasses.

"How you doing?" Reuben asked.

"Six a one, half a dozen of the other."

The sarcasm was as thick as the mocking broad accent. He didn't sound very willing to be jollied.

"Well?" the widow asked when she returned.

Reuben opened the door for her. The smell of her perfume hit him and he bit his lip against the rush of desire it provoked.

"Hope you haven't been paying for maintenance. It hasn't been done."

Her jaw tensed as she looked up at him. "Those jerks. So what do I do now?"

"How long will you be here?"

"All summer."

"Leave it with me this afternoon, pick it up tonight. Or tomorrow, whatever suits. Or I'll deliver it."

He let the mask slip. *Tonight,* he told her with his fevered eyes—what he couldn't say aloud, not with her children in hearing range.

She gave him nothing back. Plucking her sunglasses from the dash, she covered her eyes.

David lurched suddenly forward over the backseat and pulled a couple of pins from her hair. It cascaded down as she jerked her head away.

She leaned back wearily. "Jesus. You know, we're almost home, David. Do you think you could act your age for a few minutes?"

"Piss up a rope," David said.

Reuben had gotten beatings for less mouth. He wanted to yank the kid through the open window and give him a good shaking.

The widow smiled thinly at him. "He's in a good mood, isn't he? I hope it doesn't last all summer."

They drove away and Reuben punched a Coke out of the machine with excessive force. He was clenched up like a fist in his

chest. In the lavatory he splashed cold water over his face and
head.

An hour later, she left the Cadillac. He was busy, both pumps
running, people waiting, and she tossed him the keys and jumped
into the housekeeper's idling wagon and was gone again. From the
back window of the wagon the little girl waved at him.

Between customers he worked on the Caddie, noting creases
and dents and scrapes acquired since last year and as yet unre-
paired. The rust was already at them. Maybe she would let him fix
them over the summer. It would be an excuse to have the Cadillac
in the bay.

Damn fool. Goddamned if he would spend the summer with his
tongue on the ground. Now the season was under way he would
have a little more bread in his pocket. The cure for this ludicrous
fever for the widow was some backseat loving with some other female. One of Joyce's round-heeled buddies. Blow his chance with
Laura but so what? He had exactly nothing with her. She was dating some good Baptist from Greenspark—he could only hope
Frank Haggerty was sweating that one. If he was honest about it,
his most urgent need was not true love or even a regular
girlfriend—it was simply a piece of ass.

At eleven he cashed up and closed. Saturday night: he could
look forward to his sleep being interrupted by road service calls.
But it was early yet. He took the wrecker to the public beach at
the Narrows.

The pine wood skirting it sheltered numerous parked vehicles.
He knew them all—there was Hallie Lunt's pickup, for one. Sonny
tooted his horn and flashed his headlights as did some of the others. They probably thought he was there on business, called out to
revive some battery dead from a couple of hours running the radio
at the submarine races. He threaded the wrecker through the pines
to the far edge of the beach, where he was least likely to stumble
over courting couples. It was a cool night and people had their
windows closed, but he could hear muted music from the radios.
There was an occasional carrying laugh, the nerve-jumping explosion of a glass bottle as some drunk pitched an empty and then
one, two, three engines—one of them Hallie's truck—came to life.
Calling it a night or going to parties where there might be a keg
with something still in it.

The beach was shaped like a shallow S, with the north scallop
smaller and tighter. At the northernmost end the sand petered out

to a blunted point, an outcropping of boulders scabbed with brambles. Sudden depth off the point made it the favorite diving spot. There the night black water glistened silkily, reflecting and multiplying diverse and minute sources of light—a quarter moon, faint stairs, the single outdoor light the town maintained near the picnic area under the pines.

Reuben hid his clothes carefully—it was worth some scratches from the brambles to make sure no joker took off with them. He had imagined this skinny dip most of the day—how the water would wash away weariness as well as sweat. It might even lift some grease and dirt.

Someone rolled down a window and a scrap of "Tobacco Road" thumped in the night air. From a running step he arrowed toward the lovely dark of the water. And with an uneven startlement of horns a blinding fusillade of headlights caught him at the key of his arc. He dropped through the light in a fraction of a second, hearing Sonny's bellow of laughter as he entered the water headfirst. Rolling onto his back, he saw the wash of dilute light above him. Deliberately he thrust his fist above the water, the middle digit extended first. Even underwater he heard the horns playing their Bronx cheers in response.

He swam underwater at an angle, away from the point, before he surfaced. Filling his lungs, he glimpsed Hallie's truck and a couple of other vehicles backing away. He assumed they weren't sticking around to see if he found the prank as funny as they had.

But when he emerged from the water Hallie's truck was parked next to the wrecker. Joyce lounged on the wrecker's hood with Sonny leaning against it next to her, one hand comfortable just above her knee. At first sight of Reuben scrambling bare-ass for his clothes Joyce sat up and applauded. Several horns blatted briefly and some lights flashed. There were a few cheers too.

Joyce exploited a certain resemblance to Natalie Wood, wearing a lot of mascara to emphasize her dark eyes and her dark hair in a ponytail. Red lipstick on her pouty mouth. Her tops were always one size too small. She and Sonny shared a long-necked bottle of Narragansett and a cigarette. The radio in Hallie's truck was on—Lou Christie, "Lightnin' Strikes," with the falsetto chorus a tomcat yowl in contrast to the sticky verses.

"Nice diving form," she smirked.

"You're the expert," he said and ducked her mock angry feint.

Sonny was astonished at Reuben's temerity. "That's a nice thing to say."

"Nice thing to do," he pointed out, unlocking the wrecker. He rolled down the window and flicked the ignition key. "Lemme know next time you two go skinny dipping and I'll return the favor."

Joyce slid off the hood into Sonny's arms.

"Hey," Sonny said, "you should thank me. It was great advertising."

With a laugh and a shake of his head Reuben threw the wrecker into reverse.

* * *

The garage was cool and dark as the lake. He turned on the radio, flopped onto his mattress and picked up one of the books on his summer reading list.

A rap at the side door woke him with a start. Both radio and scanner were putting out static. He wondered groggily if he had missed a call. It hardly seemed possible—nobody had car trouble and there had been no accidents. Yawning, half asleep, he groped his way through the darkened garage. He yanked the low-wattage light just over the door, and the widow slipped in when he cracked the door as fluidly as a cat. She reached up and tugged the string and they were in the dark again.

The same taste of bourbon was in her mouth; it was like drinking it, the way it hit his blood. There was a familiarity, a recognition of half-remembered sensation, covering her body with his, yet it still had the thrill of a roller-coaster ride. When she ran a nail down his spine he seized her wrists and forced them down against the mattress. Her eyes widened. He felt the tremor in her diaphragm and then she arched under him.

She stayed all night, through his leaving three times on calls. Each time he threw down the wrecker keys and kicked off his shoes and dropped his coveralls it started all over. The first call caught them working each other up for a second go, and he went out with a stand and no shorts under his coveralls. It was a single-car rollover into a shallow brook, and he helped Frank Haggerty—it would be Haggerty at the scene—and an ambulance crew removed injured passengers. He felt like an accident himself. He was sure she would be gone, but she was still there.

Haggerty was at the second call too, a fatality—the elderly

driver of one of the three vehicles involved in a crossroads tango. It was a messy extraction that made Reuben sick in the bushes. He wasn't alone—nearly everybody on the scene lost it. But he could hardly wait for the widow's bourbon to wash out his mouth.

The third time he met Laura's father was in a roadhouse parking lot, where the cop watched him revive four vehicles suffering the usual parking lot failures—the dead battery, the keys locked inside, a frigged-up ignition, the ever popular home-repair job choosing the usual fortunate moment to crap out.

"What a night, huh?" Haggerty remarked congenially.

Reuben blinked away sweat. "Fucking A," he muttered.

She was still there, drowsy and wet, in the back room and they went at each other again. He felt like he was in an undertow.

When in the predawn he realized she was gone his first reaction was near panic. He jerked up on one elbow, listening intently as if for a prowler. The air in the room was muggy with sex. His head ached almost as much as his balls. Hungover not from the jar he'd shared with her but from screwing.

The sedan was still in the bay. She'd come by foot through the woods and returned home the same way. That's why she'd been wearing long sleeves and jeans—to keep the bugs from eating her alive. He could imagine that return hike, tripping and staggering half loaded from tree to tree. In his mind he saw her fall to her knees, give up, collapse, turning her head to rest against the duff. The dry needles imprinting a crosshatch on her cheek.

* * *

In shades, a butt hanging on his lip, Sonny jerked the wheel of the '57 Mercury Turnpike Cruiser and made racetrack squeals and revving noises. He paused to relate the tale of his acquisition of the Merc from Rita Schott.

"Back in '57 Rita had a boyfriend was a banker. Bought his wife one, so he had to buy one for Rita or maybe it was the other way around. She showed me a picture of it when it was new and she was on the hood showing off her legs. She had tits like—never mind what they was like, thinking about'm's getting me worked up. She ain't had no boyfriend since she could afford to spring for a new set of wheels. She's buying a Plymouth on time and the trade-in was piss poor, so she put an ad in the paper."

Push-button drive, loaded, a bagful of cute tricks—once upon a time it was hot stuff. Sonny's bad luck and worse judgment, this

particular Cruiser was a dog. Too many years of bad roads, salt
and snow and potholes. It was as banged out as its former owner.

"Sonny," he said, "it's beautiful."

Sonny's grin vanished. "Shit. Piece of crap, isn't it?"

"An opportunity."

"More money after bad," Sonny groused.

"What else you got to spend your money on? Besides Joyce?"
Sonny laughed.

"I know something you don't," he said.

"If you're gonna tell me it's got hair on it you told me that already," Reuben said. "I think we were in the fourth grade? It's
wicked ugly, I seem to recall you telling me—"

"Ha-ha—"

"Laura's got a job at Needham's. Saw her mother drop her off
this morning."

Deflated, Sonny pumped the Merc's horn rudely. "Here's your
chance. You can see her every day and Frank can't do doodly-
squat."

Reuben wandered back to the pit by way of changing the subject.

Sonny bailed out of the Merc to trail after him. "The hell with
ya, then. You won't get no sympathy from me she winds up going
with somebody else. She went to the junior prom with that
Haskell creep from Greenspark, didn't she?"

"Hey, Sonny, she's not interested in me."

"That's not what Joyce says."

"Also her old man told me to stay away from her. I got work
to do, Sonny."

"You always got work to do."

"Yeah, well, I do."

"Right," Sonny agreed in disgust.

VII

Pink Lace Ribbons twisted through the pale plume of
Laura's ponytail. Her uniform was pink too and outlined a sweetly
modest brassiere and her half slip. She wore light pink lipstick and
nail polish, and Reuben thought she must smell pink. Apple blossom or maybe candy apples with a touch of cinnamon. Sometimes
he saw her waiting outside the diner in the morning for Roscoe
Needham to open up. Sometimes she waited outside in the afternoon after her shift for her mother. Mrs. Haggerty would slide
over and Laura would take the wheel, giving Reuben a glimpse of
her legs. Once in a while she would catch him watching her and
look right back with a little wink of a smile.

He went to the diner two or three times a week to have a cup
of tea and eat a piece of pie—anything more was an extravagance
he couldn't afford. He considered taking up attendance at the
Catholic church in Greenspark. Too obvious an attempt to impress the Haggertys, he finally concluded and besides, he might
not be able to keep a straight face through all that Roman hocus-
pocus.

Over his pie and his tea he could at least exchange the time of
day with her. They could chat about the last ball game or the
next—she came to all of them, always in the safe company of her
friends. Once with Leon Haskell, who was one of those bland
blond choirboys who bald early and wind up selling insurance or
teaching high school math. Laura held his hand; he kneaded hers
nervously. With the same hesitation he tipped his chin at Reuben,
who returned the gesture only more faintly and without a smile. It
was a cautious acknowledgment of each other's existence on the
axis of Laura Haggerty. From Laura on that occasion Reuben received a cool, defiant smile.

The widow slipped into the garage several nights a week. He
never knew from one night to the next whether she would turn up

again. In the meantime she required nothing from him but a hard-on in exchange for a warm, wet place to ejaculate. Neither could he stop looking at Laura. Every time she looked back at him he seized up like a balky flywheel. The widow would not be flattered to know when he was with her, he often imagined he was making love to Laura.

* * *

Like a feral cat the widow's boy prowled the fields and woods, the roads, the trails around the lake. How the kid stood the bugs Reuben couldn't imagine. Every busted window, every fence broken between pastures that loosed livestock to roam, kicked-over gravestone, every petty theft—which were sometimes no more than someone misplacing something—and every dirty graffito that summer was credited to him. In at least a few instances David was almost certainly the guilty party. Reuben personally doubted any of the neighborhood hooligans knew how to spell *cunnilingus* or *fellatio*—he had to look them up himself in the big dictionary at the library to be sure after they appeared on the side of a boarded-up church. *Eat me* was more the local style.

If David had been local, something might have been done about it—at least questions asked. But he was summer people and they were a law unto themselves. Short of someone catching him redhanded he was his mother's lookout. Still, people talked, as always, and said he was neglected.

Reuben argued silently with himself in her defense. To the best of his knowledge she didn't beat the kid—admittedly a low standard. It looked to him as if she rarely disciplined David at all and then ineffectually. Maybe David was just one of those independent kids, loners and authority bashers from babyhood. Reuben was close enough to being a kid to know kids have their own lives, their own agendas that might overlap but were not identical to those of their parents.

The hours of the night he was with her he wondered uneasily from time to time if David was out roaming—not that it was any of David's nevermind whose bed his mother was in from half past midnight to half past three any given night. He locked the side door after she arrived and hoped the kid was at home. If not, maybe David was out breaking windows in an empty house or ripping off a car radio in someone's driveway. Or diving in the quarry. Just so long as he wasn't tailing his mother to Rideout's.

* * *

In the gloom of a rainy day the public library was as cozy as a houseboat. He often saw the widow's children there when he dropped by to return a book or pick one up that Mrs. Madden was saving for him. If David wasn't sprawled over a chair in the adult reading room, he was stretched out on the carpet in the children's room with his glasses on the end of his nose, reading aloud to the little girl. She used his stomach for a headrest, and once in a while he absently caressed her hair with one hand. He was a good reader, and if there were other kids there they listened too.

It was on one of these occasions, arrested by the expressiveness of David's voice, that Reuben happened to notice the patch in the little girl's eye—a wedge of gold in the blue, itself a familiar blue—and almost dropped the book he was taking to the desk. As Mrs. Madder checked it out for him the quick peek he meant to take at her eyes turned into a stare—the same color, the same splinter of gold in the left one. Gussie Madden—Augusta Nevers Madden, Joe Nevers' kid sister, the town librarian—shared the identical, significant and uncommon flaw in the color of her eye as the little Christopher girl. India, whom David called Indy. Now Reuben saw it the facial resemblance was striking. The little girl could easily be Mrs. Madden's granddaughter.

There must be a familial connection somewhere back between the Neverses and the Christophers. But if there had been surely he would have absorbed some knowledge of it. A town this small, everyone knew everyone else's ties. The Madden family was as familiar to him as his own. Bright-eyed, flyaway Gussie had always been kind to him.

And Gussie's daughter Elizabeth had been his sister Ilene's best friend. In sudden clear memory, Elizabeth, in baby doll pajamas, danced with Ilene to a record on her suitcase record player.

> *you women have heard of jalopies*
> *you've heard the noise they make*
> *well let me introduce*
> *my new Rocket "88"*

She must have been sleeping over—he had a vague idea at one time there had been a lot of that. And then Elizabeth had run away from home and never been heard of again. The story of her running away was legend, more real to him than most local legend because of Ilene's friendship with Elizabeth. His mental picture of Elizabeth clarified suddenly: her eyes—that same patch of gold in one eye.

For an instant Reuben lost track of Mrs. Madden's asking whether he liked the last book he had borrowed. Answering her distractedly, he sought to recall Joe Nevers' eyes in detail—Joe Nevers' left was flawless, he was certain. Tucking his book under his arm, he walked along the main road from the library to Rideout's with his head abuzz. From the evidence at hand he could deduce two things: that odd bit of contrary pigmentation in the eye was familial, specific to the females in the line. But the widow had no such mark; her daughter must therefore have acquired it along with her notable resemblance to Augusta Nevers Madden and to Gussie Madden's daughter Elizabeth from the man who fathered her.

Gussie and Nate Madden's only son had died in Korea a decade before the little girl's conception. The sole surviving male in the line was Joe Nevers. Reuben tried to recall Joe Nevers as he had been a decade ago   merely middle aged then. Even now a vigorous man. Not that age much mattered. He himself was testimony to an old man's potency. And he could speak as well to the widow's trap.

For an instant he could think of no other explanation, and it hit him like a blow to the solar plexus. Joe Nevers suddenly revealed as a figure in a farce. He coughed and the stopped breath burst out of him in a choking laugh.

Ah Jesus it was a ludicrous old world. And he was in no position to judge, was he? He laughed until he had a cramp in his gut and had to wipe moisture like spit from his eyes. Sweet Jesus the lot of them. Joe Nevers. One of the town fathers. Become a literal father by bastardy. The widow, taking young men and old into her bed as she pleased and foisting another man's child on her husband. Last and not least himself. In books they had a word for guys like him—callow. He'd looked it up and wondered if it applied to him. Now he knew it was practically his middle name. Idiot—dizzy—grateful—at the enormous good luck of an adulteress's favors.

Though he had rejected belief in a biblical deity since the Sunday school class treating the God of the Old Testament's demand of the sacrifice of Isaac's son, he nonetheless believed—with the gut-quivering conviction of personal experience that such behavior—lust, adultery, fornication, deception—was sin and corruption. They were all lesser people for it. Only the child, the little girl, was innocent. He'd never breathe a word to anyone concerning the child's likely paternity. It was the least he could do. For her, for Joe. He couldn't help wondering if anyone else had noticed. Mrs. Madden must have, but of course she was the one other person in town who'd want to keep the secret.

Fits of laughter kept coming back on him like ripples from a pebble, until Sixtus Rideout snarled at him.

"What's so cussed funny, buck? You got money in the bank?"

"No sir," he replied and pulled a long face, but a moment later, like a window shade snapping up, he was laughing again.

＊ ＊ ＊

August was steamy as the widow when she let him have the Cadillac to do the body work. The two nights he had it in the bay he had her too on the back bench again. Then the last coat of paint was dry and buffed and the ark gleamed like the lead car in a funeral procession. When he phoned to say it was finished, she instructed him to bring it to the house in the early afternoon, with the promise she would ferry him back to Rideout's.

The housekeeper's wagon was gone. The widow called to him from the deck when he knocked at the back door. Bourbon in her voice. The house was secretively silent as he passed through it to the deck in the lake side and he knew they were alone. She had managed it, of course, and he was immediately aroused. She was his to fuck for the moment and he was full of himself, taking what was offered with the same cynical insolence it was offered.

She was on her stomach on a chaise on the deck. Black two-piece suit with the top undone underneath her. Within reach, a coffee mug with a finger of bourbon left in it. He looked out at the lake and it was wonderfully deserted. Not a soul in sight. He knelt between her calves, lay down on top of her, cock nestled in the crack of her ass, and slipped his hands beneath her to cup her bare breasts. Low in her throat she made an amused noise.

"Want to see the car?" he asked.

"Only if I can see it from the bedroom."

But she didn't give it more than a glance as she dropped the bottom of the suit.

"Where is everybody?"

"Kid down the lake's having a birthday party. I'm allergic to kids' birthday parties. They're Bea's job."

Unsurprisingly her mouth tasted of the bourbon, as it did so often it was an aphrodisiac to him. She bit his lip. More startled than hurt, he bounced her into the mattress and trapped her wrists the way she liked. He fucked her hard and then withdrew abruptly to belly-flop her unceremoniously, yank her to her knees and jam her roughly from behind. All of it exactly what he'd learned she liked. All of which was intensely pleasurable to him too.

A spray of wet, cold droplets tickled his back. Starting, he withdrew in haste from her and rolled onto his side.

From the bedroom door David pointed a squirt gun. Behind his sunglasses his face was unreadably still.

"Shit," said the widow.

Reuben flipped the sheet over her. How long had David been there watching?

The boy turned on his heel and was gone.

Reuben reached for his pants. "I thought you locked the door."

"He knows better than to open a closed door without knocking."

Likely something he learned early with her for a mother.

Picking up his shirt, he went after David.

From the rocks at the edge of the beach the boy stared at the blankness of the lake. He opened his mouth to point the squirt gun at it and shoot water down his throat.

"I'm sorry," Reuben said.

"For what? Fucking my mother?"

"For not locking the door."

David smiled. "Very nice distinction. You needn't bother. You're not anything new under the sun. She likes young stupid guys with dirty hands."

Oh, she's nothing like that exclusive, Reuben stopped himself from retorting.

And wondered all at once if David was the doctor's son. Maybe David, like the little girl, was a bastard, gotten on the widow by one of her casual lovers—some teenage grease monkey dazzled at his good fortune. He saw no one he knew or had ever known in the boy's face—only David's mother—her eyes, her bone structure, her mouth.

"However you want to take it, I still mean it, I'm sorry."

"Oh, fuck off."

He nearly carried it off. Reuben was sick to his stomach for this white-faced kid trying so hard not to give a shit.

Naked at her vanity, the widow was pinning up her hair. He found his socks and shoes and sat on the bed to put them on. Her eyes followed him in the mirror.

"What's he doing here?" he asked.

"He's allergic to parties too. He wanted me to take him to the public beach today. Obviously he came home on his own."

"That door should have been locked."

"For Christ's sake, you're mechanical, you could have locked it."

After a pause he muttered, "Right."

Her gaze in the mirror broke from his and she stared into her own eyes. She drew herself straight and took a deep breath.

"You're fired," she said.

For a moment he sat there looking at her.

"Much obliged," he murmured, with a quick touch to his forehead, and then he left.

* * *

The relentlessly dismal Red Sox occupied Reuben as he scraped his face next morning. He was up in time to catch yesterday's scores on the radio. The thought the current slump had been going on eight years deepened his low mood. Meeting his own eyes in the mirror, he lifted his lip scornfully and promptly cut his cheek. Swearing, he let the blood flow and the air sting. He'd been a punk full of the certainty he knew the score when all he'd known was he had a hard-on. He didn't know whether to admire the widow or be angry with her for giving him the boot before he had the backbone to quit.

Joe Nevers pulled up to the pumps and leaned out to talk. "Sorry to tell you—ah, somebody, ah, did a job of work on Missus Christopher's Cadillac last night. You want to come over and look at the damage?"

Though it was nearly the last thing he wanted to do, it was his trade. He couldn't think of a credible lie to duck it, nor could he give Joe Nevers his reasons.

Sixtus was still struggling down the path from his house.

"Soon as Sixtus is settled in," he told the caretaker.

A quarter of an hour later, Joe Nevers pulled aside at the top of the driveway to the summer house, and Reuben edged the wrecker past, down the hill and behind the Cadillac.

It was still where he had parked it. He could smell the bourbon before he dismounted the wrecker. The shards of a Wild Turkey bottle mingled with the splinters of the windshield. After pitching the bottle into the windshield, *Ah-Somebody* had taken a baseball bat to the sedan. There wasn't a whole piece of glass in it or an inch of body unmarked. It had taken time to do and it must have been noisy.

"Why didn't somebody stop him? They must have heard him going at it."

Joe Nevers shook his head. "Maybe they were scared. Just a couple of women and a little girl in the house."

"There's nothing to him, nothing but bones and nerves and snot. The housekeeper's got to go one-sixty. Between her and his mother they could have put a stop to it."

Joe Nevers grinned mirthlessly. "Must have been a sight to see. Well, they not only won't own the boy did it, they're not reporting it to the cops."

"It'll have to go to the dealer," Reuben said.

The caretaker's gaze snapped from the sedan to Reuben's stony face. "Naw. It's just the body."

"I can't do it."

Joe Nevers blinked.

"Sheer destruction like this makes you heart-sick," he muttered. "I'll tell the missus."

"Would you?" Reuben returned politely. "I'd be obliged."

Late in the afternoon the caretaker stopped again at Rideout's to inform him the widow had decamped to Falmouth three weeks early. He seemed relieved. And by the by Reuben might care to know Missus had decided to trade the Cadillac.

Reuben let it go with a preoccupied nod.

Joe Nevers hesitated. His shrewd eyes were cloudy with speculation. But whatever question quirked his mouth stayed there. He sucked at his front teeth and lit the cigarillo and then took his leave.

* * *

In the ebb of August there was a trickle inside Reuben, a kind of sneeze on hold. The sweet purple milkweed going into feathery seed held his eye, and the Queen Anne's lace drifted high in the ditches with the electric blue of the chicory and the hot fuchsia of swampfire. The sudden cooling of the nights signaled the turn of the season.

His last year of school commenced. He was there only as long as he had to be. His real school was in Sixtus' books, his tutor a wheezing garrulous irritable cripple with bad dentures, bad sinuses and body odor, who could barely contain his exultation at finding a kind of heir. All the decades of Sixtus Rideout's grease-stained life acquired a new dignity and significance in the value Reuben assigned to the garage, to the old man's knowledge of how to run the business.

Hunting season opened, and Sonny and Hallie began to wake up before God to drag Reuben into the woods. Fine being up and out—early mornings in the woods a blessing on the senses—but otherwise his greatest motivation was the possibility of dropping a significant portion of the winter's meat budget with a single load. Still, it was always a relief to hand the gun back to Hallie. Carrying that shotgun reminded him forcefully of guys who had once played ball with him for or against Greenspark and graduated to the jungles of Southeast Asia. The odds were high he would be there himself by the next hunting season.

At the time, though, it seemed a stroke of luck when Joe Nevers got him out of another early morning trip with the Lunts by asking to borrow him to help him replace some shingles on the roof at the Christophers'. A morning's work out of doors on a fine day and business was a little slow anyway—Sixtus waved him out the door with the remark he would be pulling the afternoon and evening at the garage and he never thought he'd say it but he wished he could climb a roof these days.

Joe seemed as surprised as Reuben was to find the widow and her children in residence. Fortunately, the children were a distraction—David surly, India bubbling with excitement at going out in a canoe to fish, as children under twelve were allowed to do unlicensed and in all seasons. Still, as Reuben spidered over the roof, he wished Sixtus had been less generous.

VIII

Under the Roofless Sky of a November day as diamond-sharp and dazzling as a rime of ice on a dead leaf, the red canoe drew a curving thread across the still indigo plane of the lake. From the tree beam of the summer house, the three in the canoe—mother, daughter, son—were reduced to small versions of themselves, as if they were framed in a snapshot taken at a bit too much distance. Of the two men watching from the beam Reuben's young sight was country-sharp, and the older eyes of Joe Nevers, though faded in color, were yet undulled by age. Despite the distance, through the clean, flawless lens of crisp autumn air the features of the canoers had a three-dimensional clarity.

Lifting his gaze from his hammer and the nail head he was about to drive flush with a shingle, Reuben felt the roll of the heavens over him, the spin of the planet beneath him. For an instant he experienced a slight dizziness, the sensation the world was spread in devastating temptation beneath him. As he tightened the grip of his thighs upon the massive solidity of beam, the flutter of unease in his chest echoed weirdly in a crash of panic in the woods below. The three on the water waved at the two upon the roof.

The yearling doe emerged from the woods to leap through the brush into the lake like an image from the Song of Songs. At the perigee of her jump she crumpled with the sound of gunfire and staggered heavily into the shallows. Down upon her knees she lowered her head to the water and died. Darkness like the shadow of Mount Washington when it loomed between the lake and the western sun bled out of her and into the water.

Even as the doe leaped out of the woods the girl child in the canoe rose from the middle seat between her mother and her brother. She waved and her mouth opened to call the name of the caretaker upon the roof. The gunfire crackled again and something pushed her head back, spotting her white knit cap with a single dark blot. Her pupils opened, darkening her eyes from hazel to black in a fraction of an instant, and she fell backward out of the canoe and into the lake.

As she dropped, her brother's face was suddenly in Reuben's line of sight. Again it struck him how much David had his mother's looks. Confusion clouded the boy's mercurial eyes and fear twisted his mouth.

The canoe rocked as the girl's body flipped over into the water and the mother moved, reaching for her. Letting go his oar, the boy threw up his arms as if to catch hold of the air and then the canoe went over, taking the boy and woman with it. It all happened in fractions of seconds.

The mother's keening wail hung in the air as Reuben slid down the roof to the ladder. Joe Nevers swung his leg over the roof beam and followed, but being both long and young Reuben gained the ground well ahead of the caretaker. Picking up the old wooden canoe that lay cobwebbed to the wall of the boathouse, he threw it into the water and pushed off, leaving the caretaker upon the shore, struggling with his heavy shoes.

The red canoe bobbed upside down upon the water. Slick and imperturbable as a pool of mercury even now, the lake was no more disturbed than if a pebble had skimmed its surface. The woman's head broke the surface, she took air and disappeared again before he could reach her, but when David came up Reuben was ready. He hooked him one-handed.

Mostly arms and legs, the boy was slithery as a bass. David clawed and bit and beat at him as if Reuben were dragging him down to drown. At last the boy sagged into the boat. He hunched in misery, with his eyes never leaving the place alongside the red canoe, where the caretaker and the woman still dived and searched while Reuben rowed him ashore. His eyes were pits of darkness in his face, and the veins and vessels of his skin were visible in his colorless skin like the mottling in marble.

Standing on the beach, he kept his watch, ashiver, while Reuben raced to the house to call for help. Without a word he wrapped himself in the blanket Reuben brought.

Reuben kicked off his shoes and stripped to his shorts. "Help's coming. Soon as they get here you have to tell them what happened. You stay warm and out of the water. Your mother's going to need you when we get her ashore."

The boy's lips were blue. He nodded.

What Joe Nevers and the mother were doing was hopeless. In November the lake was fixing to freeze and the cold was killing. The caretaker surfaced first.

Reuben grabbed him by the forearm. "She's dead. This water's going to kill you too if you don't get out of it."

If they hadn't been treading ninety feet of glacial water and him already half frozen, Joe Nevers might have hit him. Face suddenly bleak, the caretaker made a choking sound. The woman came up and they both caught her.

"She's gone," Joe Nevers told her.

All of a sudden she went limp and they almost lost her for real. She didn't have anything left, Reuben thought.

Blue-lipped and shaking, the three of them crawled out of the lake. Years later David would write a poem about it, comparing them to the first sea creatures struggling onto the ragged, empty shore. But in the raw moment he showed no reaction. He stood there like a little wooden Indian in his blanket, his face gone unreadable as the lake that took everything beneath its surface.

Sirens closed upon them.

Huddled in the blanket, the woman squatted on the sand, her eyes fixed on the red canoe that still bobbed there like a balloon fallen to the water. Otherwise the lake was perfectly still again, as still as the boy. As motionless as the glass wall of their house that rose like a blank slate over them. She made no gesture toward her son, though he turned slowly toward her and his gaze came to rest on her.

Reuben's hands fell upon the boy's shoulder, turning him toward him. For a moment David stood like a wet stick. Then he began to shake and Reuben gathered him up.

* * *

The babble of organized rescue began outside. David's joints were rubbery as an infant's as Reuben dressed him in the warmest things that came to hand from the boy's dresser—a pair of long johns and socks. He zipped a sleeping bag up around him like a cocoon. David looked like something out of *Alice in Wonderland*: a blue-quilted nylon worm with the face of a young boy. Blue shadows around his eyes made him look a Victorian consumptive.

A low murmur of women's voices came up the stairwell—the ladies' auxiliary arriving.

A wave of shivering shook David. He reached up to touch a

baseball card pinned to his wall. The rectangle of cardboard was furred gray along the edges, the photograph with that odd, flat quality the cheap printing sometimes gives, of a badly done painting: Sammy Koberg's faded, raggedy rookie card. Koberg's crewcut head was shaped like a bullet and his eyes looked like bullets too. Reuben vaguely remembered reading Koberg was doing time for a botched liquor store stick-up in Denver.

There were other pictures pinned to the wall, snapshots of some kind. Faded black-and-white pictures of ordinary things: two perch on a flat rock; a peony dripping petals in a vase, an old bottle on a window with a lace curtain; a section of a birch tree's trunk; the widow, sunbathing facedown on a chaise. Some were just shapes and shadows.

Reuben asked what they were.

"Abstractions."

"What's that?"

Impatience hardened David's thin, androgynous features. "Pieces of ordinary things broken down into patterns. I was just fooling around."

"You took these?"

"Yeah. With pinhole cameras. I make 'em out of matchboxes. Stupid, really. But I like the way they make these soft images. That's one on the bookcase. Take it apart if you want."

It really was a matchbox, wrapped in electrical tape. Reuben peeled what appeared to be the end of the tape back and found there was indeed a pinhole in it. The tape came off like the peel of an apple. Inside the matchbox was a single frame of film, instantly blackened by exposure to light.

"How do you develop the film?"

"In a darkroom with chemicals like any other film. It's just like boiling an egg or baking a cake."

"You learn this in school?"

"They don't teach you anything really interesting in school. I read about it in a book and taught myself. I got the guy who sold me the film in the camera store to rent me his darkroom. He walked me through the process once. Since then I do it myself."

Other kids his age traded baseball cards and rode bikes. He built homemade cameras out of matchboxes and played around in a darkroom.

"David, you know it wasn't an accident, don't you?"

David stared at him through a long silence and past him into bitter distance.

"Yes," he whispered.

* * *

Milky as a cataract the dying light strained through the window glass. The sun cast the shadow of the mountains most of the way across the lake, and the woods about the house were a tangle of cross-hatched black and gold, a mysterious wall between day and night. The boy stared out the window a long time.

"It's beautiful," he said. "The sun setting."

He shut his eyes tight and thrust his face between Reuben's arm and chest as if trying to crawl into some burrow. Reuben held him in that peculiar headlock while he sobbed. After a while the tension went out of him and he fell into a shallow, exhausted sleep.

After tucking him in, Reuben went down to the kitchen, where the women were putting out the coffee and doughnuts. Nothing happened in this small town without coffee and doughnuts.

Outside, a flock of powerboats dragged the lake.

"I give her the strongest shot I could," Doc MacAvoy told him with a defeated little roll of his chubby hand in the direction of the mother.

She wandered along the beach, Joe Nevers' hand upon her elbow ready to restrain her from entering the water again. By the light of the dying day and with shock as well etching the caretaker's features, Reuben saw how Joe Nevers would look in old age. It was the first time he really understood that someday the caretaker, who had been eternal in his life, was going to die. As his father had died. Oh, not by his own hand necessarily, though Joe was as capable of that act as the old man had been, but nonetheless inevitably. One day he would be gone.

He watched the mother's vigil a moment before going up to her to put his hand upon her wrist. She was just a little woman, shaking with cold and shock. For an instant he felt a weakness for her, a guilty desire to hold and comfort her. Then the anger came back like the bile of indigestion and not just because of the boy abandoned to the suffocating weight of his grief and shock.

"India's dead," he said.

Even as he spoke she lowered her head and shook it no, denying the truth.

"David isn't," he continued.

A little gasp came out of her mouth and with it a bubble of spit like a glass pearl as her head jerked up to stare at him.

"David isn't dead," Reuben repeated.

She jerked her wrist away.

"Jesus Christ, Reuben," Joe Nevers protested.

It was the only time he ever heard the caretaker take the Lord's name.

"Jesus Christ has nothing to do with it, Joe," he said. "Does he?"

Joe Nevers' blue eyes widened and fixed upon him; his jaw slackened in astonishment.

"The boy needs her. Try to get through to her, will you?"

It took a moment but then the caretaker's gaze seemed to drift and Joe Nevers nodded in acquiescence.

Whatever Joe Nevers said she didn't hear it. She never did leave the beach until it was full dark and they gave up the search. They carried her off it.

* * *

There was of course a great deal of talk but the most remarkable thing was what didn't get said. Let the papers speculate about a panicky hunter struggling to balance his conscience against a potential manslaughter conviction and public disgrace. The folk on the Ridge all knew it was no accident—the doe mere window dressing by a deadly shot. The state police investigators admitted the odds of an accidental between-the-eyes shot was astronomical, but they had two witnesses to it.

Joe Nevers was suddenly gray and haggard. Never talkative, he barely managed the ordinary terse civilities. When he entered the post office or the store or the diner, conversation trailed away. It was as if the caretaker was a member of the family.

He was, of course—and Reuben thought now that almost certainly someone else on the Ridge besides himself and Joe and Gussie Madden must know it. Someone who had decided to play God and take a child in sacrifice—for something. As payment for some offense or as proof of their own omnipotence—it was more than he could contemplate without becoming sick to his stomach. The little he knew was too much; he would give anything not to know it.

* * *

I was so much older then when I was young, Eric Burdon lamented down an echoing tunnel of guitars. The lyric stuck like a burr, irritating in its regret for a youth still being dissipated. Still it was seductive—heavily textured with cymbal surf, the marriage of Burdon's vocal and the tomcat guitars, built on a steady barrage of drum. It was past suppertime and the bay was wide open to the early May evening. Reuben thought he recognized the signature rumble of Sonny's Merc underneath the music. Then somebody turned the radio down.

Sonny's shitkickers appeared on the cement and he knelt next to the decrepit Dodge to peer at Reuben under it.

"Shoot me for a goddamn idiot, ol' hoss," Sonny said. "Joyce is knocked up." A few inches away his face hung like a sick moon over the horizon of the pitted cement floor. He wasn't joking.

"How'd that happen?"

"That's the stupidest question I ever heard," Sonny snarled.

"Right. You going to get married?"

Rocking on his heels with his head in his hands, Sonny moaned in despair.

"I thought you were in love," Reuben said.

Sonny crept under the Dodge to get closer. "Being in love isn't the same as being married. Ain't you ever heard women stop putting out after you get married? And then there's the kid. Hoo-eee. I mean, they're great, I just didn't figure on being a daddy at eighteen. Accidents run in the family. I could be a grandfather before I'm forty." Then he looked up at what Reuben was doing. "Think that'll work?"

"For a while. Guy can't afford to replace the whole thing, and Sixtus can't afford to extend credit to somebody with more bills already than he can pay. But he won't be paying any of'm, he can't get to work."

It was all high finance to Sonny. "Gotta go home, tell the folks. Pa's gonna kick my ass up between my shoulders." A sudden thought lightened his hangdog expression. "Hey, we're gonna have a hell of a blowout, huh?"

"I guess."

"Don't tell me you gotta work, neither, you morose son of a bitch."

Morose. Exhausted was more like it. At least school was nearly done. Trying to finish school and work full-time—there were not enough hours in the day. And a winter of too many nights Reuben couldn't sleep or was plagued with nightmares. Sometimes he woke in so much distress he vomited. Even self-comfort often failed—he had trouble raising an erection long enough to jack off. Sonny probably had the right idea for once. A blowout might actually be just what he needed. Seeing as how what was done was done, they might as well have a good time.

* * *

Joyce and Sonny got married in the chapel of the Catholic church in Greenspark. Under the circumstances—one of the many euphemisms meaning the bride's pregnant—it was not a fancy wedding. Reuben was grateful not to have to rent a monkey suit—even more so when he held Sonny's head over the toilet to puke later that evening.

The reception at the meeting house in Nodd's Ridge was prodigiously wet. Folks he had never seen more than pleasantly lit drank that night as if Prohibition was being reinstated on the morrow. The lone abstainer was the caretaker. Joe Nevers circulated from table to table, having a word here and there. His wife had taken ill and he was alone in the same detached, withdrawn mood that had had him in its grip since the death of the little girl. Before Reuben got too loaded to notice much of anything, he was aware of Joe observing them all, seemingly bemused at the folly of his neighbors.

He doubted himself he would ever forget Tiny and Hallie dancing to the local band doing pop covers. It was like watching a pair of ocean liners coping with rough seas.

Laura had a date—good old Leon the Bible-pounder. Rat-faced, weedy little bastard. The more Reuben tried to ignore the two of them the more it ate at him. At some point he had enough dutch courage in him to cut in on them. Leon smiled and made a little bow.

"Twink," Reuben muttered.

Laura cocked her head. "What?"

"Nothing," he told her.

She was giggly and flirtatious—been into the spiked punch too, he thought.

Leon was keeping an eye on them from the sidelines. So, Reuben noted, was Frank Haggerty.

He tightened his hold on her and she gasped in surprise and then she giggled.

Leon was lurking at the last note and cut right back in, and this time Reuben was the one who smiled. He didn't make any mocking little bow, though.

He went punch-dipping awhile and watched Laura, and when she disappeared in the direction of the ladies', he started drifting that way. It was in the vestibule under the stairs to the balcony, and he intercepted her as she came out.

Her eyes widened and he caught her by the wrist and tugged her toward the stairs. She came willingly, with a breathless little giggle, and he hustled her around the turn of the stairs to the first landing. Hand in hand, they faced each other there. She tucked her face shyly, but when he sought her mouth she responded with a heavy-lidded sigh and parted quivering lips. They necked passionately for several moments. He was drunk enough to be clumsy, and when his hands wandered she caught them and held them, twining fingers distractingly. He got one hand loose of them, got hold of her skirt and pushed it up her thigh, and she gasped and tried to drag it back down.

"Laura?" Leon's voice quavered from the vestibule.

Reuben clapped his hand over her mouth and her eyes widened over his fingers. Her face was flushed and she looked glorious to him, like a wild lily. She stared up at him, fear and alarm suddenly stiffening her features.

He felt her quivering inhalation under his hand. She jerked back from him and fled down the stairs with a sharp clatter of heels that came to a sudden stop.

"Laura," Leon said, clearly relieved.

When Reuben turned the angle of the stairs, Laura was accepting Leon's helpful hand at the bottom step. At the sound of Reuben's footfall Leon's head snapped back and he stared up the stairwell. Tore his eyes away to sharply examine Laura, whose eyes were downcast, and then Leon released her hand.

"What's going on?" he asked, his eyes shifting back and forth between Reuben and Laura.

"Nothing," Laura said quickly.

For an instant Reuben doubted his ears. Then the denial sank through his intoxication and he was furious.

"I wouldn't call it nothing." He kept on coming down the stairs and Leon began to shrink back in alarm.

Now the color rising in Laura's skin was not from excitement or drink either, it was anger and embarrassment.

"Stop it," she cried. She stamped her foot. "You're drunk, Reuben."

Leon puffed up suddenly. "Leave her alone."

Reuben ignored him. He pushed past him to reach Laura. She wouldn't look at him.

"You're making a fool of yourself," she whispered. "And me. So stop it."

He was confused. She had gone up the stairs with him and swapped spit furiously with him. Now she was choosing the twink over him. He didn't understand. He walked away from it, back to the punch bowl. Somewhere along the way to total numbness he tossed the wrecker keys into the bare branches of the maple tree at the edge of the parking lot.

And woke the next morning in the back room to Grace Slick bombing him from the Airplane, according to the homicidally cheerful DJ, with "Somebody to Love." Church was letting out across the street from the meeting house, providing an audience of the elderly and respectable while he climbed the maple tree to retrieve his keys. He couldn't reach them; he had to shake them down. They finally plummeted into a puddle. Wearily he fished them out and dried them on his pants.

He remembered more clearly than he wished what had happened with Laura and it added to his nausea. He was doing something wrong, he guessed, but he didn't know what it was. He didn't understand her. He didn't know what she wanted of him.

IX

"She Wants You to Fight for Her," Sonny advised Reuben. "Knock his front teeth out."

"Haskell?" He laughed.

Sonny was mistaking Laura for Joyce. From the start Joyce had used flirting with other guys to keep Sonny in a nearly constant state of rutting rage. Most guys backed off in a hurry, but enough had locked horns with him to satisfy both of them.

It was possible Joyce was whispering strategy in Laura's ear. If that was Laura's game, she had a surprise coming: he wasn't Sonny. He had no intentions of pounding the piss out of a mug who probably fainted every time he cut himself shaving.

"Nothing makes a girl hotter than a fight over her," Sonny insisted.

Reuben reholstered the gas gun and spun the Merc's cap into place. "It ain't happening. I'm not playing any games. She better make up her mind."

Sonny spread a fan of singles and Reuben plucked three of them.

"You sort it out," Sonny said. "It's none of my nevermind."

Sonny and Joyce settled into playing house in her parents' camp on the lake and invited Reuben to supper. When he arrived, the Haggertys' wagon was already there. His irritation at being set up dissipated as quickly as it flared. He could and would be cool. Laura'd gone to the senior prom with Haskell. No money for that kind of date, he'd told himself, and the little matter of her father's continued opposition saved him spending a lesser and more reasonable amount on an ordinary outing to a movie or a dance.

Sharrards' camp was just that—an old-fashioned, unglamorous little cottage with tiny rooms, no cellar, no furnace and no insulation, basic plumbing, cast-off furniture, a fireplace, a screened porch and a clothesline permanently hung with faded bathing suits and raggedy towels. It was near the Narrows and had very little beach, so everyone sunbathed on the float anchored a hundred feet from the shore.

Joyce and Laura were on the float. Sonny whistled wolfishly and the two girls raised their heads, giggling, and waggled their fingers. Hair shorn off in a boy cut like Mia Farrow, Laura wore a two-piece bathing suit as close to a bikini as the local girls ventured. Joyce's swollen breasts and belly required modest coverage: a maternity bathing suit, waisted under her bosom and falling in a little skirt to the top of her thighs. Reminded of snapshots of his sister, Ilene, in various stages of several pregnancies, it struck Reuben that the clothes of gravid women exhibited an odd quality of childishness about them. Joyce's bathing suit was like a little girl's romper.

He and Sonny had another beer while they changed and then headed for the water. Because the girls were watching, Sonny played the fool, prancing around Reuben snatching at his borrowed, saggy bathing trunks—Hallie's, by their size—until Reuben picked him up bodily and threw him into the water and they raced to the float.

Joyce blocked the ladder.

"Go drown," she ordered.

Sonny clutched the side of the float and began to rock it. The girls shrieked obligingly. Reuben rocked it too. The girls kicked at them to make them let go until Sonny and Reuben grabbed at their ankles. The girls retreated, still shrieking, to the center of the float. On the count of three Sonny and Reuben gave a huge heave and the girls dived off the float as it turned turtle.

The girls came up under the boys, snatching at their ankles to pull them under water. For an instant they were in a whirlpool of bodies. Sonny caught Joyce from behind and pulled down the top of her suit. Contracted by the cold water, her nipples were dewed with tiny bubbles. He covered her breasts with his hands.

Reuben kicked upward, breaking the surface at the same time Laura did, only inches away. For a few seconds she trod water and sucked in air. Sonny and Joyce came up together, struggling and laughing. Joyce hung her arms around his neck and they started kissing. Laura kicked up onto her back and stared at the sky. Over Sonny's shoulder Joyce looked at Reuben with mockery in her eyes.

"Take it off, Laura!" Sonny called. "Show us your tits!"

Laura went scarlet.

Reuben nudged her. "Race you in."

Rolling over, she bulleted away to the shore.

Inside the camp she changed behind the curtain while Reuben lighted the fire in the grill. Then it was his turn to change. For a few seconds he was naked there, shaking out his shorts, and he saw her through the small bedroom window, clipping the pieces of her bathing suit to the line. With her blouse tied under her breasts she showed skin to the waist of her shorts. Her body was still damp and glowing from exertion in the cold water. Hastily he stepped into his shorts and reached for his jeans, but he was already getting a boner.

He turned on the bedside radio and found the ballgame starting and listened while he finished dressing. Conigliaro was back from Army Reserve duty and hitting day after day, and Yaz was doing the same. But it was only June. The Sox had months yet to go limp.

He checked the grill again. Laura was setting the dinette table.

"Don't mind Sonny," he said.

Laura slapped down a fork. "I hate the way they crawl all over each other all the time."

"They haven't been married very long. It's a big deal, right now."

"How big a deal can it be? They've been doing it for a couple years at least."

Cultural revolution reached even to backwaters like Nodd's Ridge. Human sexuality wasn't supposed to be a dirty secret anymore. Nevertheless Reuben had to force himself to make eye contact with her. She looked away, lower lip atremble.

"You and Joyce took P.E. together all through high school. You girls saw each other naked in the shower."

"That's different, it was just girls. Tonight she did it in front of guys."

"One of whom has seen her topless before."

"She *embarrassed* me."

"And me too." Reuben was anxious to change the subject. "Never mind. Don't let it spoil your good time. How long have you and Joyce been friends?"

Her mouth softened as she glanced up at him. "Since junior high. Boy, it's so weird, thinking of Joyce having a baby and being married."

"What about Sonny being a daddy?"

She laughed.

From the screened porch they watched the lake in the changing light. The surface was restless with rings of light worming over pocks of silver and graphite. Sonny and Joyce were on the float, making out, oblivious to them, to passing boaters, to the sun's splendiferous recession behind the mountains.

Laura looked about fourteen with her cap of damp, fair hair. Her skin had a dewy quality; everything about her was very fresh and soft, juicy as a new peach, perfect as the petals of a newly opened rose, velvety and delicate as a raspberry ready to let go of the stem. Her eyelids seemed to be continually at half mast, but it was not a look so much of shyness as of secretive observation. Much of the time her face was preternaturally still and impossible to read. Because of it and her diminutive perfection she had a doll-like quality. In some lights she had the untouchable serenity of the plaster Madonna in the Catholic church in Greenspark, the girl-child Virgin Mother, her stony eyes blind with the vision of the angel only she had seen, her small ears stopped and her slightly parted rose-tinged lips sealed with the secret only she had heard and the consent she had given.

But Laura was not a plaster statue illuminated by a dusty column of light in a silent barn of a church. She was warm and breathing, flesh and blood. The cold lake water had raised the buttons of her nipples in her bathing suit top. He couldn't help imagining her breasts as Joyce's had been, freed from gravity by the water to assume their most perfect form. Glancing up, she caught him looking at her.

"The wedding reception," he said.

Her eyes widened, pink blooming on her cheekbones.

"I had too much to drink."

She looked away from him, at the lake.

"It's all right," she said quickly. "I had too much to drink myself. I don't know what came over me. It didn't mean anything."

"But it did," he said. "To me it did."

Immediately her eyelids dropped again, hiding her reaction. She was having a reaction. That was good.

He ought to do something. Touch her, kiss her again. Only it hadn't worked. "I shouldn't have . . . grabbed you—"

"It's all right," she said, smiling with her little chin lifted high. "Lee was just looking out for me."

"You really like Haskell?"

She examined her nails, frowning at a chipped edge. "He's . . . a gentleman."

"A pansy," Reuben joked.

Laura didn't smile. "No," she said, "he's a normal guy."

That was exactly the assurance he hadn't been seeking, but he guessed he had it coming.

There was commotion on the lake beyond—Sonny and Joyce splashing each other on their way out of it.

Laura came to her feet, facing him, her body an inch from his. He could smell her hair, damp and mineral-scented from the lake.

"Who'll be the next in line?" asked Ray Davies from the radio.

Reuben asked his own question. "You still dating him?"

Laura blinked and for a moment she seemed to consider her answer.

"No," she said.

* * *

The draft board invited him within a month of graduation to explain why he should not serve his country.

The examining physician lingered over his ears.

"How'd your eardrums get punctured?" the doctor inquired at last.

Reuben was giving serious consideration to throwing up. He shrugged.

The doctor picked up his clipboard. "Well, they're a mess. I've never seen such a collection of scar tissue. You're a real disappointment, son. Look like a prime specimen but you've got a sloppy heart valve and if that wasn't enough, there's your eardrums. I'm going to have to cancel your ticket to Southeast Asia. And by the way, you need corrective lenses."

It was like having a sentence lifted. He should feel good but his ears were throbbing hotly.

"The bad news," the doctor went on with a volubility to match his examining style, "is twenty, thirty years down the line, your hearing's likely to be affected. A lot depends on how much further trauma your eardrums take. If I were you, I'd avoid any kind of work that exposes you to really loud noises—blasting, say, or jet engines."

He could work blind more easily than he could deaf, Reuben thought. He had to be able to hear how an engine was running.

Reading glasses would correct his vision, the doctor assured him, and the heart valve was only a problem in case of septicemia—blood poisoning. He suggested antibiotics before dental work and conscientiousness about tetanus shots.

"Four-F," Reuben informed Sixtus.

"Saints be praised," Sixtus said. And then twitched with worry. "You're a damned ox to look at. What is it?"

"Couple minor things—eyes and ears. 'Preciate you keeping it to yourself."

Relieved, Sixtus agreed. "Oh, sure." Thumped his walker. "Nothing to be ashamed of it, buck. There's fellas wearing lace drawers to get out of it."

"I'm no better. I don't want to go either," Reuben said abruptly.

Taken aback, Sixtus recovered quickly. "Be an inconvenience for me too, buck."

* * *

Business was good enough to justify hiring Sonny's younger brother, Charlie, to pump gas and incidentally give Reuben an occasional evening off.

He saw Laura every day. At nine-thirty, after the breakfast rush was over and there was no one left at the diner but the old bullshitters done up on caffeine, he would wander in and buy a cup of tea. They would pass a word or two. One or two afternoons a week she would stroll into the garage on her afternoon break with the last piece of pie or cake she'd made herself, and they'd have a cup of tea together. He began to give her a lift home from the pickup games at the town field. Fridays she began to meet him at the garage after work, and they would go to Sonny and Joyce's together.

She was eighteen now. Though still vaguely disapproving, her parents could do little as Laura and Reuben drifted into becoming a couple. No doubt they comforted themselves with the thought that once she was off to junior college in the fall she'd meet more suitable boys.

On the weekends Reuben closed the garage at nine-thirty or ten and took the wrecker to the party that was inevitably going on at Sharrards' camp. He would leave the scanner running and the possibility of a wrecker call gave him an excuse not to drink, while the wrecker's presence in the driveway encouraged his drunken friends to let him drive them home. Over the summer determining who was drunkest became a kind of game with the reliably sober Reuben as the arbiter. Later on they could turn to him for confirmation that they were as shitfaced as they claimed on this or that occasion and he could assure everyone they were. It was a cheap enough price to pay for not having to hose their blood from the pavement. Even off duty he confined himself to a couple beers. Morning came early and he had the Haggertys to impress with his sobriety.

On Wednesday nights he would take Laura to the movies. It was miles, just the two of them alone, to the various theaters in Greenspark or North Conway. She talked about her day, her job, their friends, and he would listen, liking the sound of her voice, her laughter. In the darkened theaters they held each other's hand. She began to be comfortable with his arm around her waist, to kiss him quickly for joy and slowly at the end of the evening. Only a few of the movies they saw had any impact on him—he was far too aware of her hand in his, her closeness to him, and often looked away from the screen to check that she was really there or just to look at her. On the way back to the Ridge they had something to talk about: he liked *The Dirty Dozen* and she liked *The Jungle Book;* neither of them much cared for *Bonnie & Clyde.* He was restless throughout *The Graduate* and when Laura said, after a long silence, that she was revolted by it, he quickly agreed and they consigned the subject to oblivion.

That it was a decorous courtship for the times did not go unnoticed or unremarked. Joyce made sure both Laura and Reuben knew that by summer's end they were the subject of wagers among their friends: when would they Do It?

Reuben took care not to press Laura. She had confused him, calling Haskell a gentleman and in the next breath a normal guy. He wasn't sure he was ready to discover whether that meant Leon Haskell had said please and thank you while relieving her of her virginity. If that was the case, there was nothing he could do about it, of course; it was done. He was in no position to judge. Exactly. His own experience restrained him. License had brought gratification but also a world of literal grief—humiliation, disillusionment and, when it was over, a depth of inadequacy and self-doubt. This was a fresh start and real love with Laura, not a stained mattress in the back room. Whether she had given her virginity to Leon

Haskell or not, she was a good girl. She'd be a good wife, a good mother; he wanted to be worthy of her. When the time was right they would know it.

* * *

Playing house got old for Joyce as she began to grasp what she had lost—her figure for one and with it her ability to turn heads. And with her enlarging belly, the romance, the scandal, the thrill, had gone out of being a shotgun bride. There was a lot of disconsolate weeping and Sonny sleeping on the couch. Their parties were marred by her tantrums. She accused him of pursuing other girls or drinking too much or just ignoring her. And as soon as she suggested it he took it up.

Sonny's normal good humor flagged visibly. He referred to Joyce as the old ball-and-chain. And Hallie confided to Reuben that Sonny was in trouble at work—too many hangovers, tiffs with his co-workers, a backhoe nearly ruined by his carelessness.

Friday came around again and Sonny skidded in and parked sloppily at the side of the garage. He stumbled red-eyed through the open bay, signaling he was headed for the lavatory. It wasn't nine o'clock yet and he was skunked.

Reuben took the keys from the Merc's ignition. August had turned the corner the way it did into cold nights that tarnished the trees with the first splotches of colors. He breathed it all in while he was outside, clearing his head and his blood.

Emerging from the lavatory, Sonny clapped a hand on Reuben's shoulder. "Shut this hole up, ol' hoss, we got some drinking to do tonight."

"You've got too much of a head start, Sonny."

"Whole night to catch up, dear. Come on." He made a sloppy pass at a salute. "Isn't every day your best friend enlists."

"Say again?"

Sonny grinned happily.

"You didn't."

"I did."

"Oh fuck," Reuben groaned. "All right, I'll have a beer at your place after I drive you home."

"The hell you will."

His answer was to dangle Sonny's keys in front of his nose and then out of his reach.

Sonny scowled. "Party poop. Okay, drive me home. Let's just

stop at the Waterin' Hole for a couple on the way, okay? Another couple ain't gonna make no difference. Might even be a mercy. Maybe I'll be passed out when Joyce takes the stove poker to me."

"Wait'll I close up."

But once he had Sonny in the Mercury, Reuben headed straight to Sharrards' camp.

"Hey." Sonny squinted at the passing scenery. "This ain't the way to the Hole."

"You're already in the hole far enough."

"Shit! I shoulda figured you'd punk out on me, you sullen son of a bitch. You wouldn't know how to have fun if it sat on your face. You been taking Laura out the whole frigging summer and you ain't had a finger in her, have you? Tell me the truth—you ever got it wet even once in your sorry life?"

"Shut up, Sonny, you're bombed—"

"Thank God."

No point in arguing with a drunk. Wiser to let him be. The Mercury wallowed at the turnoff from the main road.

"When will you have to go?"

"Dunno yet. Pretty soon. Can't be soon enough to suit me. I go through basic and come home on leave before they ship me out."

"You're going to Vietnam?"

"Asked for it."

"Jesus, Sonny. Why?"

Sonny cocked a pugnacious chin. "I'm sick of all the goddamn draft dodgers. Not just the fuckin' hippies either. Half the guys we went to school with are looking for an out. It ain't right."

"What about Joyce?"

"Jesus H. Christ, what about her? Maybe over in Vietnam I can get away from it for five minutes to a time. Fuck her, anyway. She'll be able to sit on her ass and eat chocolates the whole time, my check'll take care of her."

The sound of the truck brought Joyce to the screen door. One look at Sonny and she exclaimed, "You lost your job, you bastard, and you're drunk!"

Sonny stumbled up to her and threw his arms around her. "Baby, I signed up. Now I'm Uncle Sam's drunk bastard."

Her dark eyes widened. She looked like a toddler whose tantrum has been interrupted by a sudden frightening scream from Mommy. Her eyes begged Reuben to tell her it was a bad joke.

He shrugged. It didn't matter if he delivered his lines or not.

Sonny groped his way into the camp.

Tears streaked Joyce's face. For a moment she choked back sobs and then she followed Sonny. She moved like a drunken sailor herself.

Reuben tucked the keys under the floor mat of the Mercury and headed back to the garage on foot. At the juncture of the Main Road and dirt camp road he met Hallie Lunt.

Hallie ground to a halt to lean out his window. "Joyce called me, says Sonny's enlisted."

"So he says. He was skunked when he showed up at the garage. I drove him home."

"Get in. I'll take you back to the garage. Joyce and Sonny can wait a few more minutes for me to get into the middle of it." He was silent for a moment as he turned back toward the village. "Thanks for driving him home."

"No problem."

"You know I was almost relieved when he knocked up Joyce. I'd been waiting so long for it to happen. I figured it was the worst he could mess up, short of jail. Onced he was married, I thought he'd be off my hands. I know she ain't been no picnic lately, but she can't be as bad as a jungle full of Vietcong."

"Maybe he won't pass the physical."

Hallie snorted. "Popsicle's chance in hell a that."

X

At Work Again, he reconsidered the evening ahead. He was supposed to see Laura later. The plan was to meet at Sonny and Joyce's for a late swim, but obviously that wasn't going to work. Maybe Laura could be persuaded to go to the beach at the Narrows. Make out under the pines. All at once he was horny. It seemed like it had been years. He felt like a milkweed pod, a brittle shell ready to burst wide open.

Sonny had put beer on his mind, so he had a couple as he worked. It was officially Sixtus' beer in the icebox, but since Sixtus was unable to lift anything heavier than a single bottle Reuben fetched what he required from Partridge's store. What he drank of it was all he took for keeping Sixtus' house from falling down around his ears. He had also gotten Ruby Parks in to clean regularly, make most of Sixtus' meals, and ferry him back and forth to medical appointments.

He caught a glimpse of Hallie headed home, mouth bowed down at the news he was taking to Tiny. He turned on the radio to listen to the ballgame and uncapped another beer to go with it. Half an hour later, the phone rang—Laura, to tell him she was at Sharrards' with Joyce. Sonny had taken the truck and gone out again. Joyce snatched the phone from her.

"You have to go find him," she sobbed.

The hell I do, he was about to say when Laura came back on the line.

"He's just out boozing," he told her. "He's not halfway to the South Pole and eating his sled dogs. I'll check around for him, but if he doesn't want to come home, there's not a lot I can do about it. I brought him home once. I'm not going to sit on him to keep him home."

"Joyce is so upset."

"He's probably at the Hole and he'll probably stay there until he falls down. He'll be a lot easier to keep home if he's passed out."

"I'm counting on you," Laura said.

The irritation Reuben felt with Joyce immediately included Laura. He didn't understand why she let Joyce wind her up. Locking up again, he pointed the wrecker at the Waterin' Hole—Sonny getting his way after all. For a few minutes he followed the ballgame on the radio; it was a lot more interesting than his current errand.

Though he saw its parking lot every weekend he had never been inside the place. Sonny often got lost there on his way home from work. Sure enough, the Mercury was in the parking lot. He couldn't recall ever seeing so many vehicles jammed into the lot. Parking the wrecker on the edge of the road, he dismounted reluctantly, resentment kindling hotter at having to miss more of the ballgame.

The Hole was just that—a squat single-story cement-block building with a single window framing a dense montage of neon. Its entrance was a pair of double doors, matching a fire exit in the opposite side of the building, flush with the flaking pink wall. From the sound of the band and the crowd, the fire doors at the back were open—the proprietor's concession to the accumulated heat and cigarette smoke of a couple hundred people.

Sonny was propped at the bar. The proprietor no longer even bothered to ask to see his fake ID, let alone pretend to believe it.

Sonny blinked at Reuben and then grinned and tootled a cavalry charge down his fingers. "Joyce called, heh? Now you're here, you better have a beer."

Reuben was met with a wave of greetings—a good many of his high school classmates were present—and the barkeep shoved a draft along the bar to him. Collecting it up with one hand, he looked around. The place was packed with summer people who weren't fussy where they drank, as well as with locals. The harried waitresses couldn't keep up. The band was local, meaning Lewiston, and if it was any good, there was no telling over the din to which it contributed.

A tall, mannish woman pushed through the crowd to the bar. Miss Alden. A history professor who owned a place on the North Bay, she habitually costumed herself in a turban with trousers, shirts and boots. Sometimes she used a cane, but he didn't know if it was arthritis or what. He'd sold her a battery for her truck in

July. They nodded at each other and he saw she had one wrist in a cast.

"Sprained my wrist chopping wood," she explained.

He picked up a packet of the bar's matches to fire her cigarillo for her and the flame lighted her face, a long white mask with a great Gallic nose like Charles de Gaulle's. Kohl ringed her eyes. She had enormous lids like garage doors. Her mouth was almost lipless so her red lipstick—almost black in the light—bled into tiny vertical creases. The bartender slid a tray with several glasses on it to her.

"Carry that for you?" Reuben offered.

Miss Alden hesitated, then nodded.

He followed her through the mob to a corner booth. One of the occupants was Miss Alden's friend, the faded little woman who had lived with her for years—Miss Betty was all he could recall. The other occupant of the booth was the widow.

* * *

By smoke-bleary bar light it was like seeing her again in the back room of the garage. A cave of stippled, melting light and shadow, flutterings and murmurings and sudden explosive strikes by hunters in the night. He felt haunted. With the barest of smiles she took her drink. Wild Turkey. Her hair was the color of its highlights, the very color of the amber pendant she wore that winked with the familiar translucent petrified fire. The smell of the bourbon was heady. Her mouth had so often tasted of it.

"You know each other," Miss Alden said, a little dryly.

The widow said nothing but she looked him over as if he were a side of beef. His ears and face grew hot. Angered and humiliated, he retreated to the bar.

Hanging an arm over Sonny's shoulders, he indicated the door. "Let's go, soldier."

Sonny's protests were loud and obscene. People started to look at them and laugh at Sonny. He listened to Sonny briefly, then slung him over his shoulder in a fireman's carry and headed for the fire doors on a wave of raucous cheers and applause. Too surprised at first to resist, Sonny was squirming by the time they reached the exit. It was hard work holding onto him. He threw Sonny through the open doorway into the parking lot. Sonny yelped as the gravel bit like a bed of dull nails. Moaning, he rolled over to vomit.

Hallie and Charlie came pushing through the crowd, surging to the fire doors to watch.

"What happened?" Hallie asked.

"He puked. You better take him home."

A gleam in his eye, Hallie nodded.

In the wrecker Reuben paused to crank the volume of the ballgame. Lonborg was still pitching his way into the Hall of Fame, but Conigliaro had taken a ball in the eye a few days earlier and was hurtin' for certain. Until that had happened the Sox had looked like making first in the standings by the end of the month. He paused to listen for the score. Come September, he promised himself, soon as the summer season was over, he'd drive to Boston some Sunday, sit in the bleachers and see his first major league game in Fenway.

The widow came strolling up out of the night. She was wearing those tailored shorts. Lion-hunting shorts. The black silk of her shirt flowed like inky water over her breasts. Shivering as if chilled, she crossed her arms under her bosom. Her hair was up. He wanted to take it down and see it flow again, over the black silk and over her creamy skin. She looked up at him. Her face was calm as the lake in its secret moods.

"Ditched the Caddie again?" he asked out the window of the wrecker.

Startled into laughter, she was suddenly younger. She shook her head.

He opened the door and reached out to take the hand she offered. She pushed off on one leg and he caught her by the waist. She dived over him onto the seat. Rolling over onto her back, she giggled breathlessly.

Sprawled on the bench with the soles of her tennis shoes against his thighs, she was the gleeful wanton of that first time again. He slammed the door to kill the dome light and obscure her in the shadows of the cab. Light from outside the truck still gave him a little of her features, enough to see the skin under her eyes was as translucent as fine porcelain.

"I should throw your ass out into the parking lot too," he said.

"Dare you. Double dare you."

He closed a big hand around her ankle threateningly. "Tempt me."

"Sure."

He fingered her ankle, held it carefully as if he were weighing it. Head reeling, half drunk, though he had had very little to drink. He looked over the wheel into the August night and thought about it a moment. Surely nothing worse could come of it than already had.

"Where's your car?" he asked.

"I gave the keys to Alden."

Once they were away from the bar she moved closer to him and put a hand on his thigh. He was hard already. She touched him and her breath quickened and she laughed. He drew her closer and fumbled for her breast. At the garage he brought the wrecker inside the bay. Her mouth was on his. His fingers groped around her for the keys in the ignition but, once there, fell away. The ballgame went on around them like the stars reeling overhead.

∗ ∗ ∗

The taste of blood made him cough. His tongue was bleeding, his lower lip too.

She curled up against the door and drew curlicues through the steam on the window. Her hair was down in tangles and her shirt open, her bra torn too but still on her, hanging around her in black ribbons. Her thighs bore the welts of his fingernails and marks that were both grease and new bruise.

"Are we going to stay here?" she asked.

With a sigh he pulled himself together while she found her shorts. In the back room he turned on his radio, tuned it to the ballgame and stretched out next to her.

"David's camp is over tomorrow," she said. "He's probably suffering through some corny campfire right now. It's amazing he stayed. I thought he'd find a way to get kicked out the first week."

To shut her up he kissed her and deservedly, he thought later, lost track of the game. He was only brought back to any awareness of anything else by the ringing of the phone. It was Laura, he was sure, wanting to know where the hell he was. The widow raised one eyebrow in question. By way of answer he took her hand and put it on his cock.

Things got rough again, though not as violent as the first time. He was listening to the game, he recalled, and groped dazedly for the volume button on the radio. Next to him the widow caught her breath.

A sudden curiosity distracted him again from the game. "Did you plan on picking someone up tonight?"

She laughed. "It's always a possibility."

"Why me? Why not somebody different?"

"You're an easy lay," she said.

He laughed too and pulled her down on him.

And someone knocked at the office door.

"Be quiet." He grabbed his coveralls.

Sixtus wouldn't knock—he'd unlock the door and let himself in and be slow and noisy about it. Likely it was Sonny on the loose again at the door—or Hallie maybe with the late news on Sonny's rampage. The widow blew him a kiss.

He grinned. Outside, the streetlight silhouetted familiar forms—Maureen Haggerty's station wagon and Laura, hugging herself, peering in through the window of the door. He nearly froze. But she had seen him and he had no choice. Laura's hands fell away from her sides and she was smiling, a little nervously but hopefully too. Somehow he reached the door and slipped out quickly to forestall her entering.

A breeze ruffled what was left of Laura's hair. She looked like a novice who had escaped the convent and still found the outside world frightening. "I thought you'd come back to Sonny and Joyce's. There wasn't any answer when I rang, so I figured you were out on a call."

He wanted to tell her something, anything, to make her go away. He couldn't think. Couldn't speak. His jaw ached.

"But you're back," she went on brightly.

And still he said nothing.

Laura cocked her head. "So invite me in." She laughed, excited by her own daring. "I won't stay long enough to ruin your reputation."

She actually took a step forward; he blocked her way. Puzzlement clouded her eyes and her smile faded.

"You can't come in." It sounded as desperate as he felt.

She blinked.

And then her breath hitched and her eyes widened. Looking past him. He knew before he glanced behind him—the widow had appeared behind the night glaze of the window of the darkened office. In his undershirt, a white blur on her pale skin, with her disheveled hair on her shoulders, she looked like she was floating underwater. She studied them with ironic amusement.

He watched Laura with a sense of witness—this slight girl moving blindly backward, whirling around to run away from him. And her face a moony blur behind the windshield and the wagon fishtailing on the pavement.

When he turned to go inside again, the window was empty. She lolled on his mattress, his undershirt her only garment.

"Get your clothes on."

She raised an eyebrow. "That sounds like an order."

"Do what you like. I'll take you home bare-ass."

She began to dress calmly. "Your girlfriend?"

"Not anymore, thank you very much."

"You're welcome," she smiled, her eyes crinkling at the corners.

* * *

A nice dirty job waiting first thing in the morning allowed him to spend most of the day underneath a Ford flatbed. It kept him below the line of sight of the pump customers Charlie was covering, as well as Partridge's store, the diner, the post office and the firehouse. Below the line of sight of pink skirts.

Come evening Sonny rolled in, driving as if he felt every crack and pebble in the pavement. From the stubble on his face the razor hadn't been worth the risk. In the effort of moving from truck to garage he moved more than a little like Sixtus.

"Want a beer?" Reuben asked.

"That ain't funny. 'Course I do. Maybe I disremember but I could swear you mopped the parking lot at the Hole with me last night."

"Don't know what came over me—"

"Aw shit," Sonny grinned. "What's done's done. You'll look out for Joyce, won't you?"

"Sure."

He worked a cigarette out of a pack. "Anyhoo, I ain't the only one around here with shit on my shoes. Just as soon as Joyce give it a break from bawling, Laura turned up and started in." He scratched his neck and then an armpit. "You been a bad boy, I hear. Who was it?"

"Who was what?"

Sonny pushed his face forward and spoke in a stage whisper, "The one Laura caught you banging last night, choirboy."

Reuben looked at him a moment. Then he turned back to the bushings on the workbench. "Laura didn't recognize her?"

"Nope—said she looked familiar but she couldn't come up with a name."

"Do me a favor?"

"I dunno—hey, I guess I will take one of those beers, see if I can raise a little spit."

While Sonny uncapped a cold one and wet his throat, Reuben worked on his own beer.

"Tell Joyce something—"

Quick to conspire, Sonny came closer.

" tell her I was drunk and so was the woman and it didn't mean anything, it was a one-night stand—"

Sonny nodded encouragingly. " 'Course it was."

Reuben washed down the lump of the lie in this throat with the rest of his beer and went to the side door which stood open for the air. He stared a moment at the trash of woods behind the garage, and then he pitched the bottle into them and listened to it shatter in the darkness. Joyce would tell Laura and maybe it would do him some good, though in truth he was ashamed enough of himself to think he deserved to lose her.

Sonny idled a little while longer in hope of salacious detail, but Reuben was unforthcoming and after a while he sloped off home.

* * *

August went humid and hazy. Water stood spooky in the air on the utter stillness of the lake and whited out the mountains. The thunderbumpers would roll in around four and let loose with a slashing downpour, soaking the earth with the water the sun would draw out of it into the next day's haze. Reuben worked shirtless, running sweat, filthy with grease and oil.

Some nights the widow favored him; she got a considerable kick out of the way he took it now. Resentment and despair and self-loathing freed him from restraint. He exhausted them both.

"I was a virgin 'til I was twenty-three," she told him one night.

She'd been hitting the jar more heavily than usual. Not *fargone* exactly but getting there. Disheveled, face blurred with booze, she was showing her age, her losses. Witchy. Lilith.

"It spoils a woman to wait so long," she maundered on. "You always feel you missed something. That you must still be missing something because it's nothing, there's no way it can be anything to what you built up in your longing. Why do we make such a big deal out of it anyway?"

She was just talking, drunk. It was awful and he felt sorry for her, poor sad sorry bitch. You could still see what a beautiful woman she had been and brainy too—what the hell had happened to her to make her destroy herself? He couldn't put it down to the murder of her little girl; she'd been hell-bound before that. Maybe it went back to the death of her firstborn, but he didn't know. It was a shame. He wished he could do something for her, something decent for her, that would make a difference. He was more than a little drunk himself, and his eyes filled up with tears for her, for himself.

"If I'd known you when you were fifteen," he said, "I'd have fucked you."

She laughed until she had to wipe tears from her eyes. She was in that state where the laughter turned to tears quick. He wondered if she was safe to get herself home, but when he offered to drive her she wasn't having any of it.

"I know those woods shitfaced better than I do sober," she said.

He was staying overnight at the garage—had been since she started coming around again. Next morning when he went to unlock the door, he found David huddled on the stoop. The boy had grown taller and looked strong and healthy. But tired. His skin was drained white except for the shadow of exhaustion around his eyes.

"Want some tea?" Reuben asked.

David nodded and followed him inside. Reuben gave him a cup of tea. When he looked around the boy had disappeared. He discovered him asleep on the mattress in the back room. He called the widow to tell her David was at the garage and was going to sleep awhile.

"Good," she said. "We had a screamer. He took off. Now I know where he is, I'm going to try to get some sleep myself."

On Sixtus' arrival Reuben held a finger to his lips and indicated the back room. The old man peeked in and he snorted in amazement, his eyebrows dancing like a pair of woolly caterpillars.

At midday when Reuben looked in again, the boy was staring at the ceiling, one bony arm behind his head.

"Feel better?"

"This room smells like her."

"Like Wild Turkey, you mean. Come have some tea."

David shook his head no. He found his sneakers and wandered away.

That evening Reuben played baseball.

"Mud's my name," Sonny told him, "yours too. We're the Mud Brothers. Have a beer, brother Mud."

As Reuben raised the bottle he saw David sitting alone on the hillside, hugging his knees. The bill of his baseball cap was pulled down to shade his eyes against the sliding sun.

The widow let herself in the side door that night. She had bourbon on her breath and in the way she moved. When the lights washed over her they lit up a spectacular shiner.

"What happened?"

She shrugged. "Walked into an open cupboard door."

He touched the bruising lightly and she winced. Impulsively he kissed it, just a brush of his lips. She tried to turn away. He kept at her, chasing the bruised side of her face with the tip of his tongue. She slapped him and he captured her wrists and held her at arm's length while she tried to kick him. He got a knee between her legs and his weight on her and held her there, letting her buck and writhe and snap at him like she was rabid until suddenly she stopped resisting. A little while later she ceased to work with him and merely lay there under him. He looked down at her; her face was turned to the side, a gleaming mask, a track of tears running from closed eye to the corner of her slack mouth. Withdrawing, he ejaculated on her stomach. There was no pleasure in it, only a numb release. She watched him wipe his semen away with a dirty undershirt, all that came to hand, and then she got up and dressed and left. She said nothing to him. He said nothing to her. He didn't think she would be back.

The first night she and the boy were gone, back to wherever it was they went, he could not sleep. He found himself following the paths through the woods to the lake. Looking down, as the horizon tipped toward the sun, spilling red light into the waters, the lake looked mixed with blood. The empty summer house was a red-gold mirror, twinning the lake and mountains and sky. It was as if a wall had been breached and the whole world flowed without limits into the hole of that glass sheet.

XI

His Living Was in Summer but he was glad to get his town back in September. But this year the town felt smaller and emptier. Drained. Laura was gone without a word. Sonny would be soon.

For the first time he looked about himself at his neighbors who had lived their whole lives in this out-of-the-way place and tried to imagine his future beyond the goal he had set himself of owning the garage. A wife and children, he supposed, and someplace to house them. He had no interest in any other local girl than Laura of sparkable age, not for marriage. And when he realized in the wake of Laura's departure that this girl or that one was smiling at him wide-eyed by the pumps, flirting, he felt only the slightest twinge of interest. And did nothing. Beyond recalling each incident that night and embroidering it into a usually unsuccessful jack-off fantasy.

The widow had left him limp as a slack inner tube. A dead short in his shorts, he mocked himself, but the joke was more painful than funny. Guilt, he guessed and tried to face it—he'd hurt Laura and he'd hurt the widow and he was afraid he'd hurt David again too. He thought it likely the name of the cupboard that gave the widow her black eye was David. Of the three of them—the widow, David, himself—he was the one who had the least excuse for his behavior. This time especially he had known all the complications when he went to bed with her again.

He had put in a garden for his mother the previous spring and enjoyed the odd hour in it. He could see it becoming a hobby, growing larger, accommodating an increasing interest on his part in irises or glads, to make occupation for himself. A garden took you through the seasons and blurred the passage of years. He imagined a deepening awareness of what time it was and how he might begin to set the limits of his day and slow down to fill the hours and make them feel full. Dawdle in the diner for the company, linger at the library to draw out conversation from the librarian. An occasional drunk to relieve the tedium. A rural bachelor, half queer with his own dull company. It could happen. He could name a dozen right there on the Ridge.

His chief distraction was the Red Sox—number one in the standings. The fantasy of sitting among the sell-out crowds at the Fenway and watch a real baseball game was constant. He debated driving or taking a bus. He checked weekend game times against the bus schedule. Next weekend, he told himself, or the weekend after.

* * *

Laura got the jump on him at Sonny's going-away party. Knowing she'd come home for it he made sure to arrive later than usual, with intentions of making a token appearance and ducking out. But she was in the middle of *bobbieheidijoycejanice*, just inside the kitchen door, like a stop sign at a five-way intersection. Or a red light, from the fury that flashed in her eyes at the sight of him. She was different too—older and sexier. At first he thought she'd changed her look, naturally, to be more like the girls at her college. Then he recognized the skin-tight jeans and skimpy top she was wearing. He used to see them on Joyce before her pregnancy swelled her out of them.

And she had had her ears pierced. Laura's lobes were very small—almost not there. At the point of puncture the baby-soft flesh looked red and hurt. Another thing different was the beer in her hand. From her flushed skin he guessed it wasn't the first. He couldn't remember her doing anything more than sipping at one and putting it down half finished since Sonny and Joyce's wedding reception when she'd gotten lit on doctored punch.

Though the night was cool the number of warm bodies in the cottage necessitated opening the windows and doors. The floor was an inch deep in spilled beer and from the smell, the toilet was backed up. Sonny was already incoherently drunk—the point of this blow-out after all. The real trick was going to be to make his way to Sonny to shake his hand without falling on his ass in the lake of spilled beer on the floor. Waving blearily at him, Sonny pitched him a can of suds. Reuben caught it, ripped it open and let half of it foam out onto the floor, to a burst of applause and laughter that continued as the rest went down his throat. Feeling he'd done his bit to celebrate Sonny's idiocy he went into the bath-room and fixed the toilet. Martha, he thought. You're turning into that poor biblical drudge Martha. Oh, bullshit. There was no mis-taking Sonny Lunt for Sonny Jesus. And anyway my-girl Mary was a whore and that whole yarn had a taint of tough-shit-Martha, you're an ugly wench anyway and no goddamn fun so why don't you just shut up and go whip up the onion-soup-and-sour-cream dip.

Joyce leaned in the open door as he was washing his hands. In a bright yellow maternity dress cut low in the front and hemmed above her knees, she looked like Natalie Wood with a big belly. Her full breasts had a wonderful jiggle. Her legs still had their old elegant turn that made him want to slide his hand along them to see if they were as smooth as they looked.

"You can come to all our parties if you'll keep the john work-ing," she said. "Hey, everybody, Reuben fixed the toilet."

The announcement raised him a round of applause and whis-tles.

He didn't see Laura anywhere.

Joyce laughed at him. "Looking for somebody in particular?" Then she took pity on him. "She just went out the back door. Said she wanted some air."

Laura stood in the spill of house light down the dock. She glanced around at him and pointed her chin defiantly and turned back to the lake. There was nothing to see out there but the edge of light dripping off the dock into the water, but the wind sent the lake lapping at the pilings. As she tipped a long-neck back and drained it, her lips were dark in the frayed light. The dangling ear-rings caught the light as they twisted and swayed with her every motion.

"What do you want?" she demanded.

He'd come that far. "I'm sorry."

She snorted. Wheeling around to stalk past him back to the house, she snagged a heel in a gap in the planks and wobbled. He caught her by the waist. It wasn't just a gap in the wood. She was tight. At first she grabbed onto him to stay on her feet and then she realized he had his arms around her. She took a deep, shaky, beer-scented breath as he drew her close.

"You've had enough to drink," he said in one ear. "Let's sit and talk awhile and get you sobered up a little and I'll take you home."

She rested her head against his chest. A tear slid out from under her lashes, beaded with mascara. The dirty tear streaked down the inside of her nose to the corner. She twisted out of his arms in one step to face him, and for a long moment she stared at him from under her half-raised lids. Then she drew back and slapped him across the mouth.

Lower lip split, he was still trying to absorb the fact she had hit him—hit him hard—when she did it again, this time catching his left ear. In the immediate burst of white-hot pain the blow produced he brought his left hand up to protect the ear from further assault, checked her at shoulder level with his other and shoved her back an arm's length.

"You bastard!" Her voice shook.

Gently he took her by the shoulders and guided her, with only token resistance in a stiff-necked shrug, down the dock and the driveway to the wrecker at the end of it. He boosted her into the cab and held her while the heater kicked on. She did a lot of sniffling. He fumbled tissues from the box on the floor and wiped her face before daubing his own lip. His ear was hotter than hell and glowing red when he glanced at it in the rearview.

She swiped at her eyes, smearing her mascara all over. "I must look terrible. How could you do it? I couldn't believe it. I thought I knew you and then you . . . act like you did." She cried some more and thoroughly dampened the shoulder of his shirt. Then she blew her nose and sat up. "Joyce says it's my own fault."

"Joyce should mind her own business."

Laura peered into the rearview. "Oh God—" She went for the tissues again, trying to clean her face of the mascara runoff. "I hate you."

He'd apologized. Trying to explain was just excuse making. He groped in his jacket pocket for his keys.

"I'll take you home."

She sniffed. "I left my jacket and bag inside."

When he returned with the required items he half expected to find her on the far side of the wrecker's cab, but she was still sitting in the middle and she didn't move when he got behind the wheel. She stayed right there with her hip a few inches from his.

The woods were thick and dark on either side as they headed to the main road, and they did not speak or look at each other until Laura broke the silence.

"I hate school."

His ear throbbed. "So quit."

"Daddy would kill me."

"For quitting college?"

"He doesn't want me hanging here, around you—" She stopped and dug into the tissue box.

"Never mind," he said. "I don't care what your father thinks of me."

Her hand tentatively touched his forearm. He covered it with his own and squeezed it.

"Tell me about school."

Laura detailed a violent case of homesickness. She missed her horse, her mother, her own room—even him, though it about choked her to admit it and he didn't deserve it, she snapped, briefly furious again. Everyone at school was a couple, except for the geeks. The kids who went to the four-year college in the same town looked down on the ones at her junior college. She felt like a complete hick. She didn't know anything. Her clothes were wrong, her hair too—every other girl was wearing it long and straight. She had been laughed at for enthusing about her horse. The classwork was okay, but the teachers made fun of her country accent. She hated it, hated her roomie, a slut and a pig who smoked marijuana and borrowed her favorite cashmere sweater without asking.

Recounting her woes undammed more tears and she cried until she was hiccuping. He put his arm around her and stroked her arm. And in her parents' yard when he took her by the waist to help her down, she wrapped her arms around his neck and planted her mouth full on his. She stuck her tongue in his mouth. It was an electrifying event.

A screen door slapped open; they blinked into her father's flashlight. Laura staggered against Reuben, clinging to him to stay on her feet.

"Reuben," Frank Haggerty said. "This is a surprise. You're home early, Laura."

Laura stumbled toward her father, who grabbed her at the door and got a whiff of her breath.

"Jesus."

Jerking away from him, she lunged into the house.

Haggerty stepped outside. He came close to Reuben and sniffed; Reuben exhaled for him. The beer on his breath was faint indeed compared to that on Laura's.

"All right. How much has Laura had to drink?"

"I don't know. I didn't get to Sonny's until after eleven."

Haggerty nodded. "She got a head start."

"Yessir. The car's at Sonny's."

"It can stay there until tomorrow. I thought you two weren't seeing each other anymore."

"No sir. We haven't been."

"So why are you necking in my yard?"

Reuben scratched behind an ear and laughed.

Haggerty smiled thinly. "You wouldn't take advantage of a silly girl who'd been drinking, would you, Reuben?"

"No sir. But you can ask Laura."

Haggerty snapped off the flashlight. "Don't get shirty with me, Reuben."

"Sergeant Haggerty, I brought her straight home."

A tight nod of dismissal. "Thank you, then, and good night."

* * *

In the morning Laura called, wanting him to ride with her. Exercise and fresh air would cure her hangover, she said.

He wasn't much of a rider, but the horse she offered him, her father's gelding, was old and well trained. And it was a beautiful day. Getting more beautiful by the instant. It was as if he had given a grievously tight knot a tug and had it come neatly undone.

When he arrived at the Haggertys' the secondhand Plymouth her father had given Laura to take her back and forth to school was in the yard again.

"Daddy made me go with him to pick it up," she told him as they saddled the horses. "He gave me a lecture on the way over. Seems it was a miracle Someone Didn't Take Advantage of me."

Someone else might have, he thought, if he hadn't shown up and she'd kept on drinking.

"You should listen to your father."

Swinging into the saddle on her gelding, Elvis, she shot him an arch look. "On the way home, I got another lecture on finding myself a Better Class of Friends."

She took the lead and guided Elvis across the Haggertys' fields toward the bridle paths through the woods. His ear thrummed like he had something caught in it. The sway of the gelding's gait made him feel vaguely seasick. The smell of horse was rich and nauseating in the summer sunlight. It took him back to the horse barn.

"Anyway, I haven't met anybody at school," she went on.

She glanced back at him. He pretended to blink in the sunlight.

"You should go out. You'll be an outsider there if you don't."

She looked back again quickly with alarm draining the color from her face.

"I'm an outsider there, period. You could come and visit some weekend. We'd have a good time."

It came to him then he might be a kind of social security for her. The Boyfriend from Home. The shock of immersion into college life had somehow made anything familiar, even a guy she had caught with someone else, look safer to her. It made him a little light-headed. Between that and riding he felt sunstruck.

In an abandoned orchard they dismounted to let the geldings nibble a few crabbed falls. He pulled her into his lap at the base of a tree. She let him tongue her ear, feel her breasts through her shirt. Immediately he was aroused; he wanted her to touch him, but when he tried to move her hand to his crotch, she scrambled away from him and sat back on her heels. Her face was flushed as she straightened her shirt.

"Let's not get carried away," she said.

"Why not?"

She pushed his hands away. "Don't be silly."

Jumping up, she scooped up a couple of falls and offered them to Elvis. The gelding lifted his head to be fed. She put her hand on his neck and stroked gently.

"I know who she was now," Laura said without looking at him. "That rich bitch. She must be forty if she's a day. You must have been drunk to screw her."

He thought about things he could say before he decided not to say anything. The leaves rustled in the trees, saddle leather creaked, and the horses chomped and snorted. He watched Laura grasp the reins and swing her leg over her gelding's saddle.

And then, with a sigh, he rose to his feet.

* * *

The closest he came to Fenway in '67 was the radio. Two days after Laura went back to school Sixtus called him querulously from his bed in the middle of the night. Couldn't breathe. It was pneumonia and the old man was laid low with it for weeks. Then Charlie fell out of an apple tree and broke both wrists. The Cards ended the Red Sox run at the world championship in Boston. Next year, he promised himself. It was a young team. Next year it would surely go all the way.

Business slowed with the change of seasons. The pump business fell off and he cut back Charlie to the weekends. Pete Buck's arthritis swelled his fingers past moving, and he had to give up maintaining the fire engines. The job fell to Reuben. Joe Nevers was already leaning on him to take the fire-fighting course.

Laura was home nearly every weekend. Often she kept Joyce company, but sometimes he picked her up on his way to answer wrecker calls and afterward they necked on the back roads until he was dazed. She wouldn't let him inside her blouse, wouldn't touch him and jumped at the slightest contact with his erection, but she would let him kiss her for hours. She tasted, invariably, of Crest toothpaste. He fixated on her mouth, got hard at the first kiss because he knew kissing was what he was going to get. When he started getting hard brushing his own teeth, he switched from Crest to McLean's. At evening's end, their mouths were swollen and bruised. And his crotch felt about the same way.

Laura's parents somehow knew—no matter how far down the camp roads he parked the wrecker—but could do little except lecture Laura. Which they did, she informed him, her little chin defiantly high. Frank Haggerty's jaw turned to stone whenever he and Reuben crossed paths. But Haggerty remained scrupulous with his authority and instigated none of the myriad legal hassles he might have.

XII

As the Curate Spilled Holy Water over her forehead the baby's body jerked reflexively and she wailed, eyes squinched shut in terror. Brandi Marie Lunt. Right store, wrong aisle, Reuben reflected: beer would be the most apt name for Sonny and Joyce's little girl.

Joyce had not only burdened her infant with what the curate had explained patiently was a noncanonical name—by which Reuben understood not a saint's moniker—but she chose in Reuben a non-Catholic godfather. Brandi's godmother, Laura, was at least a card-carrying mackerel snapper. Saints be praised. Solemnly, on his own heretical soul, Reuben had promised to see the kid raised Catholic.

Soon after the baby's birth Joyce began to call regularly to announce ironically that she needed her battery jumped. The third time she pulled that stunt Reuben arrived within half an hour and went to work, converting the light fixture over the back door into an outlet and installing an engine block heater on the Mercury. He showed Joyce the outdoor extension cord to connect the heater to the outlet.

"Plug it in every night," he told her, "it'll keep your engine warm."

"I bet it will. Want a cup of coffee?"

"Take a cup of tea."

The sink was full of dirty dishes and the camp stank of unwashed diapers and sour milk. Joyce was still in her pajamas. Brandi fussed and gurgled in her crib. Joyce picked her up and juggling her onto her shoulder, lit a cigarette.

"I would have to have a colicky baby. Let that be a lesson to you. Don't get into the backseat of a Mercury if you ever want a decent night's sleep again."

She did look tired.

"Poor Joyce."

"Really. Thanks for rigging that heater. It's bad enough to be down here in the middle of nowhere in the middle of the winter with a baby, but when the car doesn't start it drives me nuts, I feel like I'm in prison."

Reuben took Brandi off Joyce's shoulder and arranged her belly down over her knees. She quieted right down.

Joyce laughed. "Minute she's on a man's knees she's happy. Must be my kid."

"Laura said she's going to stay with you this weekend."

"She wants to drool over Brandi."

He rubbed Brandi's back. She farted once and then cooed happily.

"You're good at this. Want a babysitting job?" Joyce asked.

He grinned. Just what he needed.

"I can't figure you and Laura out. What do you do to keep from going crazy?"

"I don't know what you're talking about, Joyce."

"Yes, you do."

"Laura and I are doing just fine. Nobody ever exploded from frustration."

"I'm going to." She puffed out her cheeks.

Reuben couldn't help laughing with her. It's either that or put her head under the faucet.

"I have to go." He returned Brandi to her crib.

"No, you don't, you're just chickenshit." Joyce drew his hand to her left breast.

As his thumb rolled over her nipple he remembered the way her breasts looked in the water, the summer day she'd slipped her top. Ruefully he took his hand away.

"Bye, Joyce."

She pouted. "Guess I'm not old enough or rich enough."

"Guess again. You're married. Sonny's my friend."

She stuck her tongue out. But she smiled when she closed the door.

* * *

Only Laura's Plymouth was in the driveway when he went to the camp after closing the garage Friday night.

"Joyce went out to a party," Laura explained. "She really

needed to get out, she was going nuts. I don't mind babysitting, really."

While she finished some homework he did chores, shoveling a better path from the driveway to the house and fixing the toilet, which was stopped up with a soiled diaper. After he tightened some loose connections on Joyce and Sonny's secondhand set, he and Laura tried watching television. He took up so much of the couch she had to lie in his arms—fine with him. Unless it was a sportscast or an old movie, television usually put him right to sleep. True to form, by midnight he was dozing, Laura tucked up next to him.

When the baby started to cry he eased himself off the couch carefully so as not to wake Laura. Brandi was wet and hungry. He undid her clothing and studied how the diaper went together. He washed her inflamed bottom with soap and water and succeeded, after a couple of false starts, in pinning her into a clean one. Draping her over one shoulder, he found the bottles, heated one to room temp and fed her in the rocking chair by the fire. She took a lot of burping up; he heard the gas in her stomach quite clearly. When she was sleepy he took her behind the curtain and stretched out on Joyce and Sonny's bed, with the baby arranged on his chest. She seemed to like it there.

The Mercury crunching down the driveway broke in upon shallow, confused dreams. His watch read almost three. He got up and returned Brandi to her crib. The noise of Joyce entering woke Laura.

"Wow," Laura was groggy, rubbing her eyes, "it's three o'clock."

"No shit." Joyce kicked off her shoes. "I hope you don't mind. It was a great party."

Rattling the curtain as she went into the bedroom, she threw herself onto the bed with a groan.

Laura was almost asleep again. He kissed her forehead, checked the fire and left.

✳ ✳ ✳

Laura's father intercepted Reuben as he arrived at Haggertys' to go riding with her one Sunday afternoon.

"Hand with the goats," Haggerty said. As they emptied a bag of feed into a trough he got down to his real business. "You and Laura are all alone down there at that cottage, aren't you?"

"Yes sir. With the baby."

"I don't think much of it. A blind man can figure it out. That girl's out playing around while her husband's overseas. I've spoken to Laura about it. It isn't right for you two to take care of her kid while that tramp plays around."

Reuben thought Joyce would be "playing around" if she had to do it at home. His Friday nights with Laura at Joyce's were a warm place in his week. Laura claimed to be happy with the arrangement, which allowed her to get her homework done. They were both attached to the baby too; it would be a wrench to give her up.

There was an unspoken cost to himself—dreams in which Joyce returned to the cottage as she usually did, under the influence of something, with her clothing and hair disheveled. She strutted in, bright-eyed, makeup smeared, hips swiveling as if she'd recently had ball bearings installed. And Laura wasn't there. Just Joyce and him.

But when he was actually around Joyce he didn't feel any special attraction to her. Joyce in the flesh sat at the kitchen table in her bathrobe with her hair in rollers and a butt dripping off her bottom lip. He didn't have any trouble resisting her come-ons— even to her they were a species of joke. Nothing was going to happen between Joyce and him. Except in those dreams, the kind of dreams he couldn't help having.

"What does Laura say?"

Haggerty snorted. "Won't hear a word against Joyce, you know that."

"Somebody needs to be there for the baby."

"Let her hire a babysitter. She manages to find one the nights you aren't available. You're Sonny's friend, his people have been next thing to a family to you. How do you think it makes them feel to see you and Laura give aid and comfort to that tramp?"

Reuben wasn't going to tell Laura's father about the night in July he had gone out to the Hole in the Wall to separate a couple of cars that had tangoed in the parking lot and seen Hallie crawl out of the backseat of Rita Schott's Plymouth with his fly undone. Drunk as a lord Hallie had been, but not too drunk to do whatever he and Rita had done that required unzipping his fly. Nor too drunk to realize Reuben had seen him.

"I don't like it either. I'll speak to Laura about it again, but she's Joyce's friend, you know. She's very loyal to her. She thinks Sonny ran out on Joyce."

"That's no excuse for how Joyce is behaving—"

"It's none of my business."

"Bullshit. God put the power of judgment into us for a reason, son. You may not enjoy having to exercise it, but you know damn well it's necessary. You do it every day in your business, don't you? If your friends' bad judgment does damage to you, you've got an obligation to protect yourself." Haggerty glared at Reuben. "And I'll tell you something else. As long as you're courting my daughter, you damn all had better protect her and that includes from the consequences of her own bad judgment. Now, you've had a tougher go than Laura, it's made you older in experience and maturity. I expect a lot of you, Reuben Styles, because you're capable of it. You hear me?"

Reuben nodded.

"Try and talk some sense to Laura, then."

But he might as well have been Frank Haggerty himself for all the good that did. He was coming to understand it was a big mistake to get in between Laura and her father when they got into a head-butting contest.

He stopped at the Lunts'.

"Why, darlin'," Tiny said, "I'd rather have you and Laura there looking after Brandi than anyone else but me. You promised in church to look out for that baby and so far as I can see, that's what you're doing. Don't you fret, now. Joyce'd be out, carryin' on, anyway." She waddled to the stove and flopped tea bags into cups and tipped the kettle over them. "Sonny had his fun, put her in the family way, she's Sonny's lookout. I allus knew she wasn't much. My poor Sonny, he's a natural-born poor man, you know. He's always gonna pay twiced as much as anything's worth and get half the value. He gets it from the Lunts. The only good bargain Hallie ever made was me and he don't even know it."

From the angry glint in Tiny's eye, it was a safe guess Joyce and Sonny weren't really foremost in Tiny's concerns at that particular moment.

* * *

The wind bansheed in the chimney and Laura jerked awake, eyes wide and fearful but with that sleepiness in them that fasci-

nated him, as if there were inside her a girl who still slept. His un-
awakened princess.

"It's all right," he said.

"I wish Joyce would get home."

It was well after three. The night had been still when they fell
asleep around midnight. Reuben listened for the baby; Brandi was
quiet in her crib. Laura shifted against him and touched him inad-
vertently. And snatched back her hand as if she'd gotten a fistful
of bramble cane.

"Oh, for shit's sake, Laura, it's just my dick," he said. "It hasn't
got teeth and it's not poisonous."

"You don't have to be crude."

"I'm sorry. I can't help it. It gets hard in the night, they all do.
Your father's docs."

"Reuben!"

"Ask your mother!"

She burst into tears. "You don't understand," she sobbed. "I'm
afraid of getting pregnant."

"No chance of that," he said and then apologized. "I'm sorry,
I'm sorry. Laura, I don't want to knock you up. I'm not spending
time with you just to jump your bones—I mean I do want to, but
I want to marry you."

"You do?"

"If you want to wait until we're married I can live with that."

Still weeping, she allowed him to hold her and they stretched
out again under the blanket.

"Only let's get married soon," he said.

"What? Mom and Dad will be furious with me if I don't finish
junior college."

"College students get married all the time and still finish."

"You mean I'd live in the dorm and come home on weekends?
Where would we live when I was home?"

"With my mother. The house is half mine. You like my
mother."

"I don't know. I'm not sure I'd be allowed to live in the dormi-
tory if I got married."

"Don't worry about it, we'll work it out."

"It seems really silly to get married and then only live together
on the weekends."

"It's only until you're out of school. I wasn't thinking about it
as a permanent arrangement."

She giggled.

In a moment they were entwined. When an entirely uninnocent hard-on reared its head she touched it gingerly, as if it were a potentially rabid dog. He put his hand over hers. Her eyes widened again as he guided her, like the blind men feeling the elephant, over it. She didn't like it much.

He released her hand. "See, it likes you."

"It's so gross," she said in a choked voice.

He closed his eyes. "Sex is like driving a car, you know. You get a license and pretty soon you're cruising around, not even thinking about it."

"You can't get pregnant from a driver's license," she said.

"Oh yeah?"

She giggled but it was an uneasy, tense little sound.

Bad joke, he thought, she'd probably never get into the wrecker with him again. However many months it happened to be it was going to seem like a very long engagement. He could hear Sonny's raucous laughter all the way from Vietnam. All he could hope was that getting engaged would relax Laura a little bit and nature would take its course. He could wait until they were married. If he had to. Nevertheless he would tuck a rubber into his wallet.

They were prepared for resistance and discouragement from Laura's parents. Reuben thought there was real possibility Haggerty might even attempt to forbid it entirely. And indeed, when they made their announcement a little moan of despair escaped Maureen Haggerty, as if she'd just heard Laura were going to run off with Charlie Starkweather on a tri-state kill spree. But Frank Haggerty's reaction caught them both by surprise. Laura's father couldn't see them married fast enough to suit him.

Reuben didn't know who to kiss first, Laura or her old man. Then the set of Laura's mouth registered.

"I'm finishing school first."

"What'd you need to do that for?" her father said. "You've learned enough to do Reuben's accounts for him, haven't you? You don't need a degree."

"I want one."

Reuben tried to catch Haggerty's eye, but all Frank could see was Laura.

"All right, then," Haggerty continued, "I'll pay the tuition, help you two out. What's the problem? Why don't you go ahead and get married anyway?"

"Fine with me," Reuben said and Laura rounded on him.

"It's not fine with me! I'm not having everybody in town saying I had to get married because I did it in a hurry."

"They'd know different quick enough," her father put in. "People always figure a couple engaged very long are sleeping together anyway. And right they are, most of the time."

"Frank, don't be coarse," Maureen Haggerty scolded. "Laura knows her own mind. It's up to her."

"What about you, Reuben?" Haggerty said. "You just part of the furniture?"

By then he might as well have been. Laura was stonily unmovable. Thanks a bunch, Frank.

* * *

Winter gave way to mud and blackflies, and Reuben swapped a new transmission with a local rock hound for a chunk of locally mined amethyst. He made a trip to see a fellow on the coast who polished and set the stone in a handmade band for a surprisingly reasonable fee. Laura was tied up with exams that late May weekend, so Reuben kept on going, driving south on Route 1 all the way to Boston. He'd never seen the like of the traffic in the Hub, but a sympathetic cop got him to Fenway and at long last he saw his first major league ballgame. He wished Sonny could have been there with him to drink beer and admire the leather-lunged jeers of the bleacher crowd.

He gave the ring to Laura on her birthday, the second of June. Tears sprung to her eyes. On the pretext of taking a walk she took him out in the horsebarn and kissed him with more ardor than she had ever before revealed. She did more than kiss him, she put his hands inside her shirt and bra and ground pelvises with him until he was so aroused, he was numb.

The Friday after he gave her the amethyst was the first hot night of the season. The heat made Brandi fussy and he walked her a lot early in the evening. She finally went to sleep and he joined Laura in front of the television. Soon they were making out. When they started to slide off the couch he picked Laura up and carried her into the bedroom, sending her into a fit of nervous giggles.

Her skin was rosy with excitement. He took off his shirt. Placed his wallet on the nightstand in easy reach. As he unbuttoned her shirt she closed her eyes. She let him unsnap her bra. He tugged the straps down her arms and over her hands, and she shivered and looked down at her bare breasts with a kind of shy surprise. She had extremely small nipples and almost no areola shadowing them. But they had come up to hard points and when he touched them she swallowed and arched her torso.

The back door crashed open and Laura dived for his shirt. High heels clattered across the floor and Joyce ripped back the curtain.

"Oops!"

She was more than drunk. She was high. Reuben had smelled grass on her before, but this time it was as strong as an old lady's sachet.

Laura scooted off the bed to snatch up her bra and her own shirt.

"Joyce," a man's voice said, "where the hell'd you get to?"

The man thrust the curtain aside as Reuben was swinging his legs over the side of the bed. He was one of the innumerable Spearin clan from Grant—if Reuben had the right one, he drove a seven-year-old Ford pickup with a homemade muffler on it. He had not bothered to remove his wedding band, as Joyce had. The image of two little boys, twins or maybe Irish twins, looking out the back window of the pickup, came to mind. Spearin had a jug of cheap wine by its neck and pretty much of a skinful.

Laura was trying to hook her bra but her fingers weren't working and Spearin took a look at what he could see, which was quite a lot of the little she had.

"Don't let us interrupt your party," he said.

"Laura, toss me my shirt," Reuben said.

She flung it at him and struggled into her blouse. She was incandescent, as if she had a bad sunburn.

Joyce laughed uproariously and flopped onto the bed between Laura and Reuben.

"Brandi had a bottle at ten," he told her. "She spit most of it up. The heat, I guess."

"Hey," Joyce said, "I feel like shit, throwing you two out of bed. You can have the couch if you want."

"Thanks, Joyce. You've got a heart of gold."

Laura slammed out the door and drove away while Reuben was pulling his shoes out from under the couch.

XIII

Laura Wouldn't Go Back to babysitting at Joyce's, which meant they had to find something else to do on Friday nights. If there was no party they had little else they could do but the movies. Leaving Charlie to cover the pumps was one thing, but it made Reuben unhappy to traipse off to North Conway or Greenspark to the movies—if something went wrong at the garage it was miles to return. And it was money out of pocket. Babysitting had had the virtue of being a cheap date.

Several mornings a week he stopped at the cottage to see the baby. As young as she was it wouldn't take many days for her to forget him. Consequently he saw as much or more of Joyce than anyone. Once she got it through her head that he wasn't there to be seduced, Joyce seemed pleased that he troubled himself over her child.

She coped nicely with the change by making the camp party central. It had gradually been transformed. The couch was gone, replaced by a double bed covered with an Indian cotton throw and piled with cushions. It was better for lazing around, watching TV, listening to music or playing with the baby. All of the Sharrards' duck prints came down and the walls were papered with black light posters and there was a strobe light to go with them. Joyce had taken to parting her long hair in the middle, gold loops in her ears, and wore bell-bottomed hip-huggers or long Indian gauze skirts and no bra under her tie-dyed T-shirts. The decor amused Reuben. He wished Laura would take up going braless too.

Joyce's taste in music had changed too but not improved. Reuben listened patiently to the sitar-tinkling, twinkle-toed, tie-dyed hippie-dippie phlegm passing as rock 'n' roll and wondered if she and her friends got stoned in order to enjoy it, or had to, to endure it.

Not a word of it did Reuben mention to Sonny in the postcards and notes he sent to him. Mostly what he wrote was about Brandi. He could tell Sonny she was unmistakably a Lunt, fair and cherubic, inquisitive and good-tempered, when she wasn't colicky. Always he wondered as he wrote his mundane notes if Sonny, who'd qualified as a sniper, was even still alive.

With Laura waitressing again at Needham's he saw her every day and most of the long summer evenings. They went to an occasional party, even a few times to Joyce's—but less to socialize than to find places—and there were always places, boathouses and barns and empty bedrooms—to be alone. The town was a map of make-out spots and they used most of them. About the only place they didn't go was to the back room of the garage. It wasn't so much delicacy on Reuben's part but Laura's distaste for the garage. She hated the way it smelled and was always fearful of staining her clothes with grease.

Reuben was not always the one who started it. It encouraged him that she seemed to want to be aroused. By August he had gotten her out of her jeans and was working on developing a fetish for rearranging her panties. He got his finger into her. His own pants stayed on. Laura wanted his thing kept behind a good, stout brass zipper. She never touched him below the waist on purpose. He thought she must have known when she let him dry-hump her that he was coming in his pants, but she never actually acknowledged it. He looked into her eyes and sometimes he thought there was another eyelid there, a nictitating membrane, like a dusty transparent veil, a film of mercury that was as impenetrable as her hymen. The rubber in his wallet was looking a little shopworn.

* * *

Dope was in the air at Joyce's. As he parked the wrecker he could see the glowing end of the joint Joyce was passing to Laura. He had only to open the door to provoke a burst of giggling. The remains of supper still on the table included an empty wine jug.

Brandi was in her crib, sucking a pacifier. Her little limbs pistoned at him and he picked her up.

"You want a glass of wine? Beer?" Joyce asked.

Reuben took a beer. With Brandi on his hip he put it away and then poked around in Joyce's records and found a Temptations 45. As he rocked Brandi in his arms, singing "My Girl" to her, she bashed excitedly at his mouth and nose with her tiny palms.

The glowing end of the rope as the girls passed it was like a single eye they were sharing. They were weird sisters, languorous as whores waiting for business. Their eyes were full of a kind of smoky contentment, like a cat with a gutful of fresh kill. Joyce's fingers rolling another one, the tip of her tongue on the edge of the paper, her eyes crinkling with nameless glee, were all suddenly intensely interesting. Taking in breath in the vicinity of the burning pot, he was smoking it too, he realized. No wonder he felt so spooky.

Laura poured herself another glass of wine out of a jug sitting on the floor, held it up to the light and squinted at it, drank half of it and lay back on her belly, with the glass held to her navel. She was wearing a little vest that stopped an inch or two below her breasts, exposing her belly to the top of her denim hip-huggers. The way the cloth wrinkled at her crotch made his throat close.

Joyce was a dream from an old painting, a cloud of dark hair, peaches and cream skin, lips and eyes heavy with the revelations of grass. My girls, he thought, and wondered how the dope was affecting Brandi. Was it making her world all sweet and sexy the way it was his? How could anything be sexy to an infant? His brains must be in neutral.

Putting her back in the crib, he stirred the mobile above it. She stretched after its brightly colored shapes. He watched her a moment, then gave her a quick kiss on the top of her head.

He took Laura's wrist and brought her to her feet with a good solid tug. She swayed and almost fell against him.

"Whoa," she said.

Joyce nearly fell out of her chair laughing.

He led Laura out to the wrecker. As soon as he was behind the wheel she snuggled up against him. He stopped at Partridge's for a case of beer and then it didn't take long to put them down a tote road on a patch of paper company land that hilled up over the North Bay of the lake. The scimitar of the moon looked down on its own image in the dark pool of the water. He drank another beer, dropped the empty on the floor of the cab and put his hands under Laura's vest. Half a sweaty hour later she was moaning and thrusting against him, in nothing but her panties.

"Now," she said, "now."

Her sudden capitulation took him by surprise. The most he'd hoped for was a dry hump. He started to reach for his wallet on the dashboard and stopped. If he knocked her up they'd be married in two months at the outside. It wasn't right, he knew it wasn't, but he had waited so long. She couldn't say it was all his fault.

Praying she wouldn't change her mind, he got her panties down to her ankles. He'd felt her and fingered her until he could have drawn it from touch memory alone, and he wanted a good look at her curly muff and the pinkness of her little notch but she hung on his neck and all he got was a glimpse. Still she put it right in his hand and he marked his place with his pointer and forefinger. She was as wet as he could wish and engorged from his rubbing her through her panties. One-handed he unzipped. Laura sagged against him and hitched her breath.

"Oh God," she sobbed.

Then she threw up on him.

She puked a lot, mostly on him. It was red wine puke, looked about as bad as anything he had ever hosed off blacktop after accidents and smelled worse. And it stained too like no other kind of puke. There was no question of taking her home.

At the cottage Joyce came to the screen door with her head canted like a curious bird. She sniffed the air and burst out laughing.

He dumped Laura into the shower stall and turned on the water. She yelped and moaned as the water soaked her hair and ran into her eyes. She looked like a wet kitten and was about as cooperative. It was as difficult to get his T-shirt off her as it had been to get it on her between her bouts of vomiting. He uncapped a bottle of shampoo and applied the stuff liberally to Laura. She whined about soap in her eyes and he told her to shut up and she cried and he was brisk as hell. He lathered shampoo into her bush and in between her legs and she got mad and flailed at him but she was too loaded and slippery and she just fell all over him. He turned the water cold to hear her yelp again and also to try to deflate the boner that had revived as soon as he was naked in the shower with her. Then he rolled her into a towel and handed her out to Joyce to bundle into bed. With the shower to himself, he skinned out his wet, red wine puke-stained jeans and turned the water hot again. He used the shampoo to kill the smell of the puke on his skin and then, in desperate need of relief, to jack off.

When he came out of the bathroom, Joyce was sitting at the kitchen table. It was still uncleared from supper and looked like staying that way until breakfast. Joyce was smoking a Tareyton and giving Brandi a bottle.

"You look cute in that towel," she said.

"How's Laura?"

"Passed out. I called Maureen while you were in the shower and said she was staying over. What about you? Hang your clothes on the line, they'll be dry in the morning."

"I'd better go home. I'll wear my clothes wet."

"Sleep with Laura," Joyce said.

"Can't."

"Why not?"

He thought about telling her the truth since she had to be so nosey: he couldn't share the bed with Laura now and not fuck her, and he wasn't about to fuck her for the first time when she was semi-conscious—or within Joyce's hearing. But even that was telling Joyce more than she had any right or need to know. He gave her an alternative truth.

"She's going to wake up with a righteous hangover, Joyce. I doubt waking up in the same bed with me and bucky-ass to boot is going to improve her mood."

"I'll find you a pair of Sonny's pajama pants to wear. Don't tell me you two didn't do it. What do you think she got plastered for?"

"Are you serious? She threw up first."

Joyce clapped a hand over her mouth to smother laughter.

"Was this your idea, Joyce?"

"For Laura to puke on you? No. Come on, babe. She's scared shitless. I thought a little wine, a few tokes, would relax her enough to get her by the first time. It works for the rest of the world, for shit's sake. Most people manage not to throw up, at least not with their pants down. I never saw puke zipped up before."

And she hunched over the baby, her shoulders shaking, eyes leaking tears of laughter.

Still wearing the towel, wet clothes in his hand, he went outside to try to clear his head, which had begun to ache like a forecast of the hangover Laura was going to wake up with. He draped his things on the line to let them drip. Then he retrieved Laura's clothes—she had managed since she was out of them at the time to avoid puking on them—and a clutch of beers from the cab of the wrecker. One, he thought, just one would be a help with the headache. He handed Laura's clothes into Joyce, who told him not to be an idiot, to come inside and spend the night, and once again he declined.

She paused and then she looked at him with a challenge in her eyes.

"Sleep with me," she said.

He glanced past her and then back to her and then he brushed past her without reply. She shrugged and went back to the kitchen table to burn a Tareyton.

From the kitchen he fetched a bucket of soapy water and scrubbed out the cab of the wrecker. Undoubtedly the stench would linger awhile. Then he rewarded himself with another beer and sat on the dock to drink it. The lake smelled clean. He looked at his wet jeans on the line and thought about having to skinny back into them and smell them on the way home. He untied the towel from around his waist, tied the beer into it and slipped into the water, swimming out to the float with the knotted ends in his teeth. With a light breeze keeping the bugs off the water he stretched out and listened to the loons and emptied the brews into him.

On the gently rocking float, unmoored by two six-packs of Carlson and a contact high, he fell asleep. He dreamed of Joyce, Joyce walking upon the water, her skin and her wondrous inky cloud of musky-smelling hair dewed with the water, Joyce riding him, moving with the easy motion of the float.

✳ ✳ ✳

The soft purr of a nearby motor woke him. He cracked an eyelid and there was Joe Nevers in his skiff, with a fishing rod in his hand. The caretaker nodded and idled on. Through a scree of hangover Reuben became aware he had a prodigious, numb hard-on. He raised himself to his elbows. Through a sun-dazzled squint he saw several more boats. A number of the early rising fishermen and women waved. One of them raised a little camera, presumably brought along to snap a shot of the loons. He rolled himself off the float and into the cold water, which cured his hard-on as fast as anything could.

The shock of the cold water also cleared his head to an almost painful clarity. Or maybe it was only the raw nerves of hangover. He had only rinsed his clothes and they were not only still damp, they still reeked. He put them on anyway. The cottage was quiet and the girls still asleep when he let himself in, but the baby was awake, playing quietly in her crib. She held out her arms as soon as she saw him. Predictably, she was soaking. In his damp, sour jeans he felt a kinship with her.

Laura was in the double bed in the living room. In the August heat she had kicked off the covers and bared her legs to the curve of her hip, where Joyce's borrowed nightdress had ridden up. She shifted restlessly and he caught a glimpse of her pale feathery bush against her white skin.

He took a long deep breath and then carried Brandi into the bathroom to bathe her. She sat up well in her bath and splashed the water with the flat of her palms. Her bottom was inflamed, as usual. Her baby sex made him think of a zipper in a cushion cover, the rounded velvety edges making a straight line that hid the actual works. She kicked when he plastered on the thick, fishy-smelling ointment and then she smiled at him, so he supposed it soothed her. All she would need in the heat was her clean diapers and an undershirt.

When he came out of the bathroom with the baby, Laura was asleep again, her breasts outlined against her nightshirt. There was no point in waiting for Laura to come around. She'd be hungover too.

* * *

His mother's mouth tightened at the first whiff of him as he gave her a peck on the cheek in passing. She was up, of course, lingering over her toast and tea. When he came downstairs in fresh clothes and with a clean jaw she had breakfast on the table for him.

"Stayed at Joyce's last night," he said.

She sniffed.

"I slept on the float, Joyce and Laura slept in the house, Ma. Take it easy."

"Easy is how it sounds. Come home stinking of vomit. It's bad enough making a drunken pig of yourself but with those girls? What will Laura's parents think?"

Reuben swallowed a mouthful of toast and pushed his plate away. "Whatever pleases 'em, I'm sure. It's not my puke, Ma. Laura had too much wine and threw up on me."

"Well, I'm sorry if I accused you unjustly but good heavens, what are you and Laura doing, going around with people like that

Joyce? Can't you find any decent young people for friends? A nice
girl like Laura wouldn't be drinking too much if it wasn't being
around that Joyce. It's just not like her."

Wait'll she found out a select group of town fathers and summer people had seen him bucky-ass on Sharrards' float with a neat
parade line of empty beer bottles and a hard-on. He could hear the
witticisms at the diner and the post office now. Wait'll Frank
Haggerty found out.

"Ma, the world's changed. The kids I went to school with drink
by the keg, they smoke dope, they sleep around with less discrim-
ination than Barney. All of them, okay? I only know one suregod
virgin in my entire graduating class and that's Laura. So give me
a medal and get off my back."

"Oh, that's not true, I don't believe it," she said and then she
repeated she didn't believe it. Maybe that made it truer to her. She
meant she didn't believe Laura was the only virgin he knew, not
that she didn't believe Laura was. Then again, considering how
close he had gotten to terminating Laura's virginity, it was probably a moot point.

He slammed out, got as far as the wrecker and trudged back to
the house to apologize.

"Way to go," he muttered to himself. It would be so much sim-
pler if Laura would just marry him.

* * *

Not a word from Laura all day but evening brought Frank
Haggerty to the garage. The ballgame was on the radio; Yaz was
chasing another batting title in a field where everyone was struggling red-faced to hit above three hundred. Out of uniform but
wearing his cop face, Haggerty stalked into the bay, where he was
at the workbench.

With a glance past Haggerty toward the front, where Charlie
was tending a customer at the pump, as a hint he was working, he
said, "Frank."

Haggerty spat on the floor. "What the hell went on at Joyce
Lunt's last night, mister?"

Reuben looked at the spittle on the floor, then at Haggerty.
"Laura had too much to drink and threw up. I put her to bed at
Joyce's. That's all—"

"So how did you wind up bare-ass on the float?"

"I had too much too." Reuben cast aside a shim and went burrowing in a box for another. "Do you think I would have been out there if I were sleeping with Laura?"

Haggerty thrust his face into Reuben's. "Think? What I know is the whole town's talking about you and my daughter and that tramp—"

"She's Laura's friend—"

"You're down there every day, everybody knows it—"

"Everybody knows shit."

Reuben threw down the shim he was holding and headed for the icebox. He pulled out a beer and tore the cap off it.

"You get her in trouble," Haggerty said, his voice suddenly strained and hoarse, "I'll knacker you with a rusty razor—"

"Go away, Frank," he interrupted, "this is my place of business. I've got work to do."

Haggerty glared at him a moment longer and then stalked out.

"Knacker me," Reuben muttered to himself. "With a rusty razor." He laughed ruefully and turned up the radio to let the ballgame flow over him.

* * *

She came across the fields on Elvis as he was filling the woodbox for his mother. He walked out to meet her and she slipped out of the saddle and into his arms.

She kissed him shyly. "I told Daddy he was ridiculous. I think he's embarrassed now."

Reuben ruffled her hair. "I can handle your old man. Outrun him anyway." He grinned. "Joyce said you got wrecked the other night to work up your nerve to have sex."

"I didn't mean to get sick. It was that wine, it made me queasy to start with. Joyce said if I won't sleep with you, you'll sleep with someone else."

"You listen to Joyce too much."

"You did before," she blurted.

As he stood in stunned silence Laura turned away from him and touched her forehead to Elvis' neck and started to cry. Blowing, Elvis rolled mad eyes at Reuben, as if to ask what it had done in a previous life to condemn it to standing around in the heat, drooling green foam, being nibbled by flies and missing its testicles. He felt a sudden sympathy for it and had to remind himself how often the beast had tried to step on him when he was handing Laura up into the saddle.

He hesitated, afraid to do or say anything. Then he put his hands on her hips and kissed the crown of her head.

"It won't happen again," he said.

XIV

"Brown-Eyed Girl" on the Radio and Joyce at the kitchen table in a bathrobe, spooning cereal into Brandi, seemed just right to him one morning when he stopped in. She took her cigarette out of her mouth and put it in a saucer doing ashtray duty.

"Hey, look who's here," she said to the baby.

Brandi pushed cereal back out of her mouth with her tongue. She grabbed the lip of the cereal bowl and dragged it away from Joyce, tipping it over the tray of her high chair and onto herself. Joyce laughed.

Reuben held out his hands to Brandi, and she seized a couple of fingers eagerly and tried to boost herself up. When he scooped her out of the chair she shoved her sticky fingers into his hair and climbed up his chest like a little mountaineer. He hauled her back down again and took her to the changing table to strip off her dirty overalls.

"I just put those on her," Joyce said.

"She's wet too."

He was changing the baby when a naked man carrying a bath towel opened the screen door. Reuben had seen Freddy Cape in the altogether in high school locker rooms too many times to be fooled by his shoulder-length hair and a neat beard. The sight of him made Freddy pause on the threshold.

"Oops." Freddy gave Joyce an anxious look.

"It's okay," she said.

Brandi giggled and Reuben rolled the crown of his head over her naked belly and she shrieked happily.

"Da!" she hooted. "Da da!"

The baby had started calling him Da, and Joyce encouraged her when she saw it embarrassed him. He had gotten used to it and even a little bit proud of it.

Still dripping lake water, Freddy kept a close eye on him. "Hey, Reuben, long time, no see."

Reuben nodded at him.

"The water was great," Freddy told Joyce. "Woke me right up." He patted himself nervously with the towel. "You got something going on you forgot to mention?" He grinned at Reuben. "He acts like he's to home. Making like daddy. Maybe I've blown too much dope, but I could swear the guy you took the vows with that time was Lunt. Why's the kid calling him daddy?" Without giving her a chance to answer, he addressed Reuben again. "No offense, man."

"Shut up, Freddy," Joyce said and poured him a cup of coffee.

"I'm just keeping a list for Sonny," Reuben said.

Freddy laughed uneasily.

"You shit." Joyce blew smoke at Freddy. "He's teasing. He's got a warped sense of humor."

Freddy looked from Joyce to Reuben and back again. "Hey, I'm a lover, not a fighter."

He went into the bedroom, where they could hear him rummaging around.

"Here, pantsy," he cooed, "here, little shirty."

"Win some, lose some," Reuben advised Joyce.

She made a face. "Up yours. He's a lot more fun than you are. Why don't you mind your own business?"

"Why don't I?" Reuben put Brandi into her crib.

"Thanks for changing Brandi," Joyce said.

"You're welcome."

"And so are you, you sanctimonious shit." She picked up a crumpled cigarette packet from the table and tossed it at his head. He pulled it out of the air. "If it weren't for you, the goddamn car would be broken down all the time, the toilet wouldn't work, this place would be down around our ears. No wonder my kid thinks you're her daddy."

Reuben hugged her and she sniffled on his shoulder.

Emerging with a pair of sandals in his hands, Freddy paused at the sight of them. He had covered his nakedness in the height of counterculture anti-fashion and tied his hair back into a ponytail.

"Sit down," Joyce said, "I'll make some breakfast. You want some, Reuben?"

"Eaten already, babe. Got work waiting."

"Nice to see you again. Love to shoot the shit with you, Reuben, but I'm headed back to school tomorrow," Freddy said.

"Still dodging the draft at Columbia?"

"Fuck you," Freddy said. "My old man didn't think it was worth blowing his brains out to make me the old lady's sole support."

Joyce flicked her cigarette at Freddy. "Shut up, you shithead."

Reuben was already at the screen door. "See you around, Freddy."

"You don't have to say hello to Lunt for me, you see him before I do," Freddy called after him.

"Shithead," Joyce said, and Freddy said, "Fuck, stop that, quit hitting me." "Shithead," Joyce repeated, "I can't believe you said that."

In the wrecker Reuben shook his head and laughed.

* * *

A cool night foretasting fall brought a blank sky and an oppressive atmosphere to his mother's birthday, the twenty-fifth of August. Reuben went to work early. His rest had been troubled by a bad dream about his father. Though now infrequent, they left him sweating and on the edge of vomiting. He'd come straight to work to get his mind on something else.

At the time he had considerable old tin out back, having picked up several from summer people who'd simultaneously come to the conclusion the old heaps that they'd had for years just for tooling around the Ridge weren't worth storing another winter. Among them was an abused '59 Eldorado Biarritz, its once gleaming black skin blistered and scabbed with rust the color of dried blood. A parts dealer in North Conway had a customer for the engine, and Reuben knew he could dispose of the other parts that were salvageable. The tires weren't worth an empty potato chip bag, the body had all the integrity of a beer can after five years in a ditch, but the interior was well preserved, everything under the hood was in good shape, and the radio sounded better than the one in his wrecker. It was the first thing he pulled. He was lifting the engine when the phone rang inside. With the rattle of the chain fall he thought he had probably missed the first couple rings and was surprised there was anybody there when he picked it up.

There was a great hitching breath on the other end, and then Joyce's choked voice. "Brandi's not breathing."

He knew he told her to call an ambulance, that he was on his way. He knew he had keys in his hand before he dropped the phone, that the receiver fell off the cradle and he didn't pick it up. He knew he walked out of the garage, leaving the door unlocked and standing open behind him, and the register unlocked, and drove the wrecker to the cottage at some ungodly speed. But the next thing he was really aware of was going through the screen door at the cottage hard enough to tear it half off its hinges and finding Joyce holding the baby.

She gave Brandi up to him with enormous gentleness. The baby was cold. He felt the cold pass into him and through his bones into the middle of him, with the shock of immersion in the lake. The baby was limp, her lips cyanotic, no pulse, no breath. Dead for hours probably, some doctor would say. It wasn't up to him. She wasn't breathing: it was necessary to do CPR. He had done it on a doll. Cradling her in his arms, he went through the motions with Brandi, knowing it was as likely the CPR doll would ever take breath as she would.

"Do you want to tell your wife?" the emergency room doctor asked.

It took Reuben a few seconds to sort out who his wife was supposed to be and then he nodded.

Joyce was just outside the little room where the doctor had pronounced Brandi dead. Reuben didn't have to say anything. Joyce was pale and sweating with shock. There was a nurse at her side who helped Reuben get Joyce to her feet. The doctor asked if they wanted some time alone with the baby, and Reuben realized the man didn't know Brandi's name. Inside the little room Joyce held the baby again. She stared at her as if she were trying to memorize her face.

"They have to take her now," Reuben told her.

Her fingers relaxed and the nurse quickly took the baby's body from her and turned away to put Brandi down on the examining table again. He took Joyce by the hands and started to draw her away. She was quiet, trembling a little, but when they reached the door she faltered and looked back. Her breath started to hitch. Reuben had his hand between her shoulder blades and felt her suck in an enormous breath and then she twisted around, arms flailing, and let it out in one long, agonized shriek that took her whole body to produce. For an instant he thought she was going to tear herself apart, and he clamped his arms around her.

* * *

The cottage was silent, the crib achingly empty.

"I should change," Joyce said, plucking at her T-shirt.

She disappeared behind the curtain into the bedroom.

He felt helpless. He had to do something. He gave the screen door a tug and finished taking it off its hinges. The wood was ripped up. He couldn't put the door back on without replacing part of the door frame. He propped it out of the way.

When he came back in Joyce was rolling a joint at the kitchen table. She'd changed into black, a gauze blouse and full skirt that fell to her ankles. He supposed it was all she had for mourning.

"I woke up late," she said. "The days your truck isn't the first sound I hear, Brandi wakes me up, fussing. When I looked in the crib, her lips were blue. I saw right away she wasn't breathing."

She ran the tip of her tongue along the edge of the paper. Her hand shook a little, and she didn't get a very even seal on the joint.

Reuben reached for it and she batted his hand away.

"In a few minutes this place is going to be full of people. I'll have to sneak out to the boathouse for a hit."

He watched her light it and suck the smoke in and hold it, with her eyes closed.

She offered him the joint. He looked at it and then he took it. It was harsh, like catching a lungful of grass-fire smoke. Other than the irritation of smoke in his lungs and eyes he didn't feel anything right away. Joyce obviously did. She got that cat-on-catnip look in her eyes and she took the joint back eagerly. They smoked about half of it before she put it out and away in a little tin box for future consumption.

By then he wanted some music. He shuffled through Joyce's records until he happened on "My Girl." He put it on and stood there listening to it until Joyce came up and circled his waist with her arms. They moved slowly to it, not quite dancing. It was like being on the float again, being rocked by the water. Putting his hands in her hair and tasting the tears on her face and the smokiness of her mouth seemed perfectly natural. The record stopped. Her body against his was warm and womanly, and he wanted to weep and he wanted to make love to her. The sound of Hallie's truck in the driveway broke the long, deep kiss. Blinking tears, Joyce smiled up at him and moved away.

* * *

Laura came running from the diner to the garage when he pulled up on the apron. She clutched her elbows as she ran, as if she were cold. Exertion brought pink to her face that matched the crystalline pink of her uniform. Her eyes were wet and when he reached out to embrace her, she leaned forward as if to protect her vitals, and covered her mouth with one hand. He held her head against his chest.

"Is it true?" she said in a hoarse whisper. "Charlie says his mother called."

Charlie Lunt leaned against the pumps and wiped his nose with the back of his hand. Sixtus thumped to the open door and stood there with his mouth open, the better to hear. Down the road at the diner a black Cadillac sedan squatted placidly, taking up as much space as a bad parking job could manage. Reuben could feel the heat of the wrecker's engine as he stood next to it.

"They're all at the cottage, you want to go down there," he said. He patted her head and gave her a little nudge toward Charlie. "Take her down there, Charlie."

The boy's face worked with confusion, and he stuck his hands in his pockets and checked his balls.

Laura clutched Reuben's hand, digging him with her nails. "Reuben?"

"Go down to the cottage."

"Come on, Laura," Charlie said, "I'll take you."

"G'wan," Sixtus said. "Leave him alone, girly. He don't want to be down there with a lot of bawlin' women."

"Reuben, what are you going to do?" Laura demanded.

He glanced back at her. She was trembling.

"Go down to the cottage," he repeated. "Leave me alone."

He didn't mean it the way it came out. All at once he was exhausted, not in his body but in his mind, in his heart. Inside him was a big black poison egg sac getting ready to burst and swallow him. He didn't want her to see him come apart.

She crossed her arms again, only now she was tight with anger. She lowered her eyes and stalked to Charlie's old bomb, with Charlie shuffling behind her.

Sixtus had his mouth turned on as Reuben passed him in the open bay. "Gimme a turn. I come in this morning and the door's wide open for anybody to come in to rifle the register and nary a soul to stop them. It's Ede, I says to myself, and rung the house and who answers but herself so I didn't have a clue." He scratched his head. "Turned up the scanner and heard Tiny calling Hallie and that's how I found out you'd taken the baby to Greenspark. Didn't make it, eh? Poor thing."

"Crib death," Reuben said. "That's what the doctor said."

Sixtus clucked.

Reuben looked down the road at the black Cadillac outside the diner. That's right; camp would be out. She'd be back to pick up David, spend the last week or so. Tires looked soft as Sixtus' satchel-ass, and the rear bumper was dented from another parking lot kiss-and-run. What was she, the goddamn angel of death? She came to town and kids died. Her kids, somebody else's. Maybe David was a miracle, maybe just surviving her was a goddamn feat. No wonder she boozed. He didn't know why he hadn't seen it before. Maybe he just needed a headful of smoke for it to become obvious.

There was something wrong here, something that needed fixing. As his gaze moved restlessly over the familiar environs of this place he had made his own, he saw the solution propped against the wall next to the desk: his own thirty-eight-inch slugger. He loved the heft and stroke of the thing, a simple junk of ashwood crafted into a gorgeous tool.

He went out the back door with it and took the windshield out of the Biarritz in one clean swipe. Then he popped the side windows, quick easy licks, and after that the rear with both hands and overhead, bash, and the curve of the glass collapsed neatly, still hanging together.

Sixtus clumped to the doorway to watch.

Sweat trickled down his forehead. Dope was supposed to mellow you out. He didn't feel real mellow. Maybe Joyce'd gotten stiffed, got a nickel bag that was half oregano and something else, some kind of locoweed. Then again, maybe this *was* mellow and it didn't bear considering what he'd feel like with the edge still on.

"Son," Sixtus said and Reuben handed him the bat. Relief slackened the old man's features and he rested the bat against the inside wall.

Reuben turned back to the Eldorado, took a running jump and landed on the front bumper. It tore away at one end. He jumped on the other end and it clattered to the weed-knotted ground. The body of the car bounced up as he fell off it. Picking himself up, he lifted the hood, bounced it experimentally a couple of times and then on the third uplift put himself underneath it and drove it up and back toward what had been the windshield. The hinges screamed and tore. He ripped sideways and the hood broke free and he flung it aside.

The sound of breaking glass and shearing metal had begun to draw some attention. Earl Partridge in his apron appeared next to Sixtus and then David's wraithlike figure slipped past the two old men. The diner apparently emptied out—a little fringe of watchers formed at the corner of the garage, Joe Nevers, George Partridge, Walter McKenzie, regulars at the bullshit table. Roscoe Needham was moved to abandon the diner's grill. Ruby Parks' Alf crept up, with a cidery, incredulous grin on his face. Miss Alden and Miss Betty and the widow herself.

He opened a door, planted a foot on it and kicked it off. Then he took off the other three. It took some out of him and he staggered when the last one fell to the ground. He hunkered down a minute to catch his breath and knuckle sweat from his face. He wished Sonny was there so he could tell him smoke does hurt your wind.

David crouched in front of him and plucked at his forehead. Wet trickled down Reuben's face. David showed him a bloody chip of glass that must have bit him when he smashed the windshield. It disappeared into one of the boy's pockets, and then David ducked past Sixtus and came out with the bat. He took aim and stroked it neatly into the rear fender. The rust-eaten sheet metal crumbled and broke. With a deep bow he presented the bat to Reuben. Reuben shook his head. Solemnly David pushed his glasses up his nose with his middle finger.

Coming to his feet, Reuben went straight up the back of the car and trampolined on it. The brittle metal crumpled as readily as the rest of the body had. He kicked off the rear bumper and started tearing out the seats.

He didn't know how long it took to tear the Eldorado apart, but it was down to the chassis and looked like it had been chewed up by a train when rain started to run down his face. He dropped the electrical harness he'd been tearing out to wipe the blur in his eyes with his hands. At first he thought it was just more sweat or blood, and then he saw the water beading on the dashboard and looked up at the sky. He let the rain come down on him until he was soaked and then he went inside. Sixtus and Earl and Joe and the others who had had sense enough to come in out of the rain made way for him. David, who didn't, brought in the bat.

Reuben slumped on the stool and Earl handed him a Coca-Cola. He drank it off in one swallow. Earl handed him another. Along with the sweet relief of the tonic came the burning of alcohol.

"Feel better?" Sixtus said.

Except for his hands—bloody raw meat, three or four nails gone—Reuben felt fine, physically, his body happy the way it used to be after dominating a game of basketball or after he had just put in a good hard day's work. Almost as good, he thought, tasting the bourbon in the Coke, as he used to feel after a weekend slamming the widow into the mattress. Maybe she would turn up later and extend her generosity one more time. He knocked back the doctored Coca-Cola, and a hard, tiny, buzzing knot untied itself between his eyes.

The spectators were dispersing, resuming their interrupted business or hurrying to tell someone, anyone, what they had witnessed. Down the street the black Cadillac sedan was gone from the diner parking lot.

David followed his line of sight. "My mother cut out soon as you stopped. She gave Sixtus her glove box fifth for you."

Sixtus shoved the bottle at him. "If you're all done blowing off steam and ready to get shitfaced, I'll just shut this place up. You want to go down to Sharrards' camp?"

Reuben shook his head.

"Don't blame ya, I'd rather drink alone m'self. I'll call Ede, tell her you're staying here tonight. You, you four-eyed little peckerhead," he said to David, "what are you hanging around for?"

"Nothing else to do," David said, "just like you, you six-legged old dink."

Sixtus stuck his tongue in his cheek and faked a fist at him. David laughed. The old man thumped to the phone.

"You want company?" David asked.

Behind the Orphan Annie circles of his lenses, his eyes were sunk in shadows like bruises and his face was colorless. He looked like he'd been on a binge. He was taller but thinner than ever. Needed a haircut again.

Reuben shook his head no.

David walked out into the rain, held out his arms and raised his face to the downpour.

" 'Oh, what a world!' " he shrieked. " 'Oh, what a world! I'm melting!' "

But it was the Scarecrow's dance he did, falling-down, loose-limbed and boneless, to the Wicked Witch's last lines. It was both funny and mournful, like the scree of a fingernail on a chalkboard. He wobbled down the road, jerking himself about by invisible strings until he was just a watery blur bobbing on the other side of the window.

XV

Closed in Respect of Lunt Babby read
Sixtus' arthritic hand-lettering on the sign he was propping shakily
in the window as Reuben came out of the lavatory. It had been
torture to clean the glass cuts on his face and wash his flayed
hands, but Reuben had forced himself to do it, with the help of
several gulps of the widow's glove box fifth.

When he offered it to Sixtus the old man shook his head. "Ain't
got the kidleys n'more. Couple lousy Nastygansetts gets me out a
bed six, seven times a night. You want company?"

"No," Reuben said.

Sixtus nodded and patted his shoulder and let himself out.

Reuben watched him all the way to his door in case he should
fall on the wet pavement, and then he went into the back room
and turned up the radio, crawled onto the mattress, and worked
on the glove box fifth until his hands felt like they belonged to
somebody else. He moved on to the beer in the icebox after sucking the fifth dry.

✱ ✱ ✱

A bright, flat band of midday light burned through his eyelids.
When he tried to sit up, the pain in his head made him roar and
then he crawled to the toilet and yakked until his gut ached. His
hands were on fire. He couldn't look at them for long, they made
him sick. He sat against the wall in the lavatory, thinking, *Oh Jesus this is going to be a long goddamn day.*

David peeked in the half-opened door. "You alive?"

"Uh-huh."

He crawled up the wall to a more or less upright position. He
was trying to remember if the widow had visited last night. He
propped his face against the wall over the john and fumbled for

his cock, and that way he didn't have to aim, he was hanging right over it. No, he decided, there wasn't any skin gone off it.

Sixtus was at the desk. He looked up and grunted at Reuben and then flapped his newspaper theatrically and studied it over his bifocals. Outside, Charlie was pumping gas for Miss Porter. He was moving like he had a head himself.

Reuben made it back to the mattress in the back room. David followed him in and handed him a beer. Reuben could hardly get a grip on it.

"Go on," David said impatiently, "it's the quickest cure, every alcoholic knows it. It's against my principles, but I'm making an exception under the circumstances."

"Too kind," Reuben muttered.

Just ripping the thing open hurt, from his fingers to his head. But it did help once it was inside him.

"You ought to eat something now, believe it or not. It might come up again, but some of it will probably stick. Right now you're poisoned and dehydrated and starving. Let's go to the diner."

"I stink," he said.

"No kidding." David rolled his eyes, pinched his nose. "Want to wash first?"

"It might hurt."

"It will hurt. The whole day's gonna hurt like hell, you know that. You knew it when you got started on it yesterday. It's the principle of urtication."

"Urti-what?"

"Old folk cure. Whip the hell out of yourself with nettles and you won't know what it was that ailed you anymore. Come on."

"Say it again."

"Urtication."

"Just the word hurts."

The water felt like it was made of little chips of safety glass. Or nettles. David handed him clean coveralls.

"Want a shave?"

He was in no condition to put a blade anywhere near his throat. Just shaking his head made him nauseated.

They went across the street to the diner in the glaring light, and he thought he knew what Dracula must have felt like when the vampire hunters trapped him in the scald of day. Laura wasn't there—must be off comforting Joyce. It was too early for the lunch crowd, too late for breakfast. The old farts were still there, running the town from the bullshit table. When Reuben came in they fell silent, needing all their concentration to observe the damage accurately.

David made him drink orange juice and strong hot tea and then eat a full breakfast. He ate a couple of breakfasts himself. The summer was on him, days of sun reflected in the glow of healthy young skin, the swimming muscle in his neck and shoulders and his lengthened legs.

"How old are you now?" Reuben asked him.

"Almost thirteen. India'd be eleven now, the age I was when she died."

It must have been on his mind, the baby's sudden death tearing off the scab. Reuben foundered in the backwash of memory, one little girl cold in the lake, the other cold in her crib. Somehow it suddenly seemed important that the war would be over before David came of draft age.

"What are you going to do?"

"Today or with my life or what?"

"You know."

"Go to med school."

"Be a doctor like your dad."

David made a face. "I hope not. The quack killed my brother."

"How was camp?" Reuben asked.

"Sucked. No, it wasn't that bad. It was okay. I'd rather be at camp than with my mother when she doesn't want to be with me. She can only take me in small doses."

A couple of times during the meal Reuben had brief moments of feeling better and then his stomach would go weird again or his head would flare up. It was a relief to pay up and get out of there. Six of one, half a dozen of the other whether he was going to make it to the toilet to toss breakfast or if the bushes on the other side of the building were going to have to take it. Stepping into the garage, though, into cool and dark and the comforting smells of oil and grease and rust, he felt a little better. And he also felt like he'd better lie down again for a while.

Sixtus had sent Charlie in to gather up the empties. Reuben collapsed onto the mattress. There was a little silence and he realized David was still there, crouched next to him.

"I'm sorry about the baby," David said with a curious formality.

Reuben raised an arm over his eyes.

"I'm sorry about your father too," the boy went on. "I never told you that, did I? I don't remember mine that well. I used to be able to remember my brother better, even though my father died after Tommy, but now I don't remember Tommy very well either. All I can remember anymore is playing catch with him and Joe one day and everything else is gone. I remember India, though, I remember stuff about her every day."

Reuben could feel himself getting ready to be sick again.

"Go away," he said faintly. "Please."

David touched Reuben's temple with his pickpocket's fingertips, and the hair on Reuben's head rose and he shook all over. And then the kid was gone, with a quick squeak of his sneakers and rustle of corduroys like dry leaves spinning in a cul-de-sac. Reuben groped his way to the lavatory again to spew a slightly used breakfast.

Late in the afternoon when he came to again, he got Sixtus to help him bandage his hands. He did some work for the sweat and went home for supper. His mother said nothing—she didn't need to. She fed him up in cold silence. This time his stomach was more welcoming. He went back to work and put in a few more hours. He undid the filthy bandages, used the razor he kept in the lavatory and washed up again. After changing into clean clothes he'd brought from home, he went to Joyce's.

It was late enough so everybody had gone back home and she was alone. She was doing a joint by candlelight at the kitchen table, her face half hidden behind a veil of dark hair and smoke. The crib was gone—all the baby things were gone—and the cottage seemed half empty.

"How ya doing?" she asked. "Got over your head yet?"

"Been over my head for a long, long time."

Her laughter was like the secret, soothing tumble of the water on the lake shore in the dark.

"I meant your hangover."

She looked like hell, worse than he did. When he stepped behind her chair and bent down to kiss the top of her head, she reached up and took his hand and squeezed it. She felt him wince and glanced at his hands and sighed. He was taken by surprise when she lifted her chin and tipped her head back against him. He hesitated, then kissed her, a quick, soft brush of lips.

"Nobody's been able to reach Sonny. He's in the jungle, or

something. It doesn't matter, of course. He wasn't here when she was born, he's never seen her except for snapshots."

She let go of his hand and reached for the smoke. She held a toke with her eyes closed for a long moment.

Reuben shook the kettle, refilled it and set on to boil. He pulled out a chair at an angle to Joyce's and turned it around to straddle it.

She wiped wetness away from her eyes with the tips of her fingers, took a deep shuddery breath and tucked her hands between her knees.

She tried to laugh. "You took apart a Cadillac yesterday with your bare hands, I heard. Wish I'd seen it."

"It was stupid—"

Reaching for his flayed hands, she cradled them gently. "Do you think it's my fault?"

"What?"

"The baby."

He had no way of knowing and didn't want to know anyway. "No."

She returned his hands to the back of the chair and sat back in her own, her face blank. Then she put her head on her arms.

He made tea and put a mug of it in front of her.

She lifted her head to stare blearily at him.

"Go away, will you?" she said. "I gotta bawl again and it makes me ugly."

He stopped on his way out to kiss the top of her head again, but she had her arms crossed and her spine stiff against him.

She was so sedated—or stoned—at the funeral, he thought she could hardly know she was there. She looked as if she were hollow inside and would shatter if she were dropped. Laura held her hand the whole time.

The mourners had left the cemetery before Joe Nevers and Reuben lowered the small box into the small hole in the ground.

"I'll do this if you want," the caretaker said.

Reuben shook his head. He took the shovel and filled up the hole himself, though his hands had stiffened up and using them was a misery.

The cottage was overflowing with mourners. Laura was at Joyce's side. She looked right through him. He supposed she had a right to be bent out of shape at him. She was having to put up with all the talk about his reaction to the baby's death. He was sorry if the speculation caused her humiliation, but she knew the truth—Brandi had been Sonny's get. But he couldn't bear her touch or to touch her smooth, whole skin with his flayed fingers.

Hallie followed him out. "They caught up with Sonny." He breathed beer fumes on Reuben. "If he takes compassionate leave now, he just has to go back and finish the last six weeks of his tour, so he's not coming home. It's the practical thing, isn't it? I mean, coming home ain't gonna change nothin', 'tis it?"

Reuben shrugged. He didn't give much of a shit if and when Sonny got home. He pinched the bridge of his nose to stop himself dissolving right there.

Hallie didn't seem to notice. "What's the matter with Joyce? She drunk?"

"Stoned."

Hallie frowned. "No shit. Tripping or what?"

"That's LSD. She's a pothead."

"I can't keep up with the slang."

"You'll live just as long, Hallie."

"You spend a lot of time down here, you smoking it too?"

Reuben's head hurt again and he hadn't had so much as a beer.

"What about you and her?" Hallie persisted. "You tried it on like every other punk in town?"

"You're drunk, Hallie."

"What if I am?"

"You're living in a glass house, that's all."

Hallie's eyes brimmed suddenly. "Sonny should be here, shouldn't he?"

Then he turned away and went back into the cottage, his broad shoulders hunched against the answer.

* * *

Laura spent her time with Joyce before she went back to school. He went to Joyce's as little as he could, though he rang every day to check on her.

Once school was in session again Laura did not come home every weekend. Some of the faces on campus had become familiar; she began to call some of them friends. Reuben suspected her new-found willingness to take a social toke opened a few doors for her but he didn't ask. It was her bag; this year everybody had their own bag, their own trip, and it was impolite to so much as raise an eyebrow over someone else's bag. Or trip. He was in his own bag and it was deep and black and airless.

The first weekend she did come home, she was the one who couldn't wait to go parking. She let him dry-hump her and then she cried and wouldn't tell him why. Increasingly she flared at him over small things until his gut tightened at the sound of her voice on the phone or the sight of her car at the pumps when she stopped on her way home. He told himself to be patient, the year was spinning away, June coming when they would get married and it would be all right.

Yaz won his title, but the Sox finished fourth. It felt like Lucy yanking away the football every time Charlie Brown tried to kick it.

Sonny's tour was shortened a few weeks by way of compassionate leave. By the time Reuben arrived at the welcome-home party Sonny was already loaded and had taken on someone's fists with his face. Laura wasn't there; it was one of the weekends she didn't make it home. The party itself had a strained feeling; it was going to end ugly. When Reuben took early leave Joyce followed him out and hung on his neck and stuck her tongue in his mouth. For an instant he was running on all cylinders and could have screwed her right there. But common sense got the better of him, and with a rueful laugh he peeled her off and patted her bottom and sent her back to the party.

The Sunday morning after he was breaking a cord of wood in the yard when Sonny tacked the Mercury up the driveway. Wearing sunglasses over the worst of the bruising around his eyes, where the color of the skin was like an oil slick on a puddle, Sonny also sported a puffy lip. Lucille, the Labrador pup Reuben had acquired in a barter, danced up to him on her long legs and wagged her tail passionately.

"Hey, you're cute," Sonny said, kneeling to scratch behind her ears and rub noses.

Reuben rested his mallet and wedge long enough to shake Sonny's hand.

"Ol' hoss," Sonny said. "Nice little bitch."

He found a stick and flung it and Lucille raced after it. He picked out a stump and lit a butt. Reuben resumed reducing the cordwood to fire-box size.

"I looked up Friday night and you were gone. You didn't stay long enough to wet your whistle."

"On call," Reuben said.

Lucille bounded up to Sonny and dropped the slobbery stick at his feet. He pitched it for her again. "Makes me feel really funny, knowing you knew my baby better than I did. You actually held her. I never did, not once." He honked his nose between his fingers and flung the snot away. "Shit," he muttered. Lucille dropped at his feet, the stick in her mouth. He patted her head but declined to throw it again. "What about you and Laura?"

"Still on for June."

With his ruined lip Sonny's grin was gruesome. "I heard you been a wild boy. Bullshit table at Needham's still debating whether you coulda sailed that float if you'd tied a sheet to your pecker and cast off. I'd loved to have seen that—say nothin' of seeing you demo that Eldorado down to the frame with your bare hands. I heard that, I knew you wasn't getting any. You gotta tell me sometime why you want to spend the rest of your life with a woman who thinks sex should be licensed."

Reuben broke a piece of wood in one blow, and it teetered around the blade and then fell off the stump. He stooped to pick it up and fling it onto the woodpile. "Mind your own business, Sonny."

Sonny, unfazed, belched contentedly. "Oh, I like minding yours better, seeing as I'm not real good at my own. Shit, man, I knew when I lef' there was gonna be hell to pay. What could I do about it? Pay her back. Which I did. I figure we're about even. 'Bout the first words out of Joyce's mouth was she wants another baby right away. I can't oblige on account of having a wicked case of clap. Which is how I got my lip busted and my eyes shined. Man, she was pissed."

"Jesus, Sonny."

"Get a grip on it, hoss. A hero like you is few and far between. Most of us is just everyday sinners and baby killers."

Reuben stood still and stared at him. "If you got a genuine bitch against me, spit it out."

Sonny looked up from tussling with Lucille. He blinked rapidly. "Sorry," he said, his bruised face collapsing into hound dog mournfulness. "I been beat up nonstop since I got home—Joyce, my old man, the old lady, my goddamn in-laws. I guess I had to beat up on somebody else."

Before he left he pressed Reuben to go hunting with him and Hallie and Charlie and to spend an evening at the cottage.

Reuben had Sixtus covering Charlie's hours to free Charlie for hunting season. And Sixtus was almost useless for anything except gossip and change-making. Everytime Reuben had to stop a job to pump gas it meant longer hours. The volume of business tended to shrink steadily through October, and November was always lean. He turned nothing down, worked every after-hours and Sunday odd job he could find and tried to take comfort in the idea he didn't need to be paying out Charlie's salary anyway, not for standing around picking his nose and moaning about the size of the buck he would kill if only he was in the woods where a man belonged in hunting season.

Saying no to Sonny took a lot of energy—getting a word in edgewise, to start. He did it, though. He had no taste for finding himself in the middle of an ugly marital brawl between Sonny and Joyce once the booze inevitably loosened Sonny's tongue at both ends. He couldn't solve their problems. He had all he could do to tend to his own nets.

XVI

The Rain Was Almost Cold Enough to be
snow and it took Laura longer than usual to drive home on Friday
night. She stopped only briefly at the garage so Reuben would
know she was back. He worked all day Saturday and most of the
night too, when the fire alarm summoned volunteers to the diner.
It was fully engaged and all they could do was contain it, but it
kept him out until five. Frank Haggerty had also worked the night
shift—he'd been at the fire scene—and he invited Reuben to stop
for breakfast on the way home.

Maureen was shooing the younger children from the table to
finish their dressing for church. Frank decided he had better
shower first and change to go with them.

"Make yourself some tea and toast," Maureen instructed Reuben. "I'll be right back down to make breakfast for you and
Frank."

While he was making himself tea Laura came in from the barn,
color high from the cold air and the exertion of mucking out. She
gave him a quick peck on the cheek.

"Joyce wants us to come eat with them Friday night."

"Can't," he said. "I'm working every weekend this month, remember? So Charlie can spend the month with Sonny and Hallie."

"She said we could eat late if you were working."

He made a mental note to strangle Joyce at the first opportunity. "That's nuts. It's Friday night, I'm open 'til eleven."

"So close early."

"November's skinny enough as it is."

"Two hours is going to make or break you?"

"It's my business, Laura. I take off any time I feel like it, it
won't be for long. I don't want to go down there, okay?"

"Why not?"

"Because I don't need an evening of breathing Joyce's dope

smoke and watching Sonny crawl in the bag and pull it over his head."

She pushed herself off the counter. "Oh, come on, grass is harmless."

"I'm not going to debate it with you. You go smoke pot with Joyce Friday night and I'll go to work."

"Maybe I will."

Maureen came bustling into the kitchen. "Reuben, you're making Laura late. Go on, Laura, your father's out of the shower and you're not going to Mass smelling of horses."

Laura rolled her eyes. "See you later."

Late in the afternoon, Reuben knocked at the kitchen door and let himself in. Laura was at the table with a notebook spread open. Her kiss was absentminded. She took him through the pages. Halfway through her detailing of the enormous June wedding she and Maureen were concocting he covered the page with his hand.

"This is starting to sound expensive."

"Daddy's paying."

He thought about it a minute while she watched him, an edge of impatience curling her lip.

"He's putting you through two years of college and he's got three other kids to educate and marry off."

She conceded the point graciously. "I'm sure he'll let you pay for some of it."

He reached for her hand. "Laura, you've worked my books with me. You know I don't have the margin to throw away money on extravagances."

Her face tightened with every word. Something shut down behind her eyes. "So our wedding is an extravagance?"

"It will be if you stick to this plan."

"Why?" she demanded, her voice rising.

He didn't like the way this was going. He put his arm around her shoulders and tried to draw her closer. She resisted.

"We don't need to fight about this. Let's find a compromise."

Shrugging off his arm, she slapped the notebook shut. Tears tracked her face.

"For God's sake, don't cry," he said. "Talk to me about it, we'll work it out."

She snatched up the notebook and threw it at him. He caught the notebook with one hand, which only infuriated her more. She grabbed the first potential missile she saw, the coffeepot. Dropping the notebook, he ducked and used his hands for cover. He succeeded in knocking the percolator off its course toward his head. It impacted on the floor and the contents exploded out the top and out the spout, spraying a slurry of hot coffee and grounds over him. Only his hands, held up in self-protection, got scalded. Laura, farther away, jumped backward instinctively and was unharmed.

Frank Haggerty lunged through the kitchen door. Reuben came out of his defensive crouch and thrust his hands under the cold water tap.

"Everything all right here?" Haggerty asked, his eyes moving rapidly from Laura to Reuben and back again.

Laura was panting. She had a child's angry guilt in her face and tears on her cheeks as she bolted past her father and out of the room.

Haggerty glanced at Reuben's cherry red hands. "You okay?"

"Yeah," he muttered.

Laura's father picked up the scattered parts of the percolator and took out a mop.

Reuben kept his hands under the cold water. "What do you think of these wedding plans Laura and Maureen are making?"

Haggerty shoved the mop around for a minute before he answered. "That what you were fighting about?"

Reuben nodded.

"It's what she wants," Haggerty said.

"It'll cost a frigging fortune."

"I said almost exactly the same thing to Maureen. She says, 'This is the most important day of your daughter's life, Frank.' "

"I hope not."

Haggerty scratched his head. "Come again?"

"I'd planned on life after marriage. I don't see why either of us has to beggar ourselves to do it."

Haggerty hung up the mop. His Adam's apple climbed and fell a few times. "Be nice to keep the thing under control, son."

Reuben found Laura in her bedroom. She was sitting on her bed, wiping her eyes with a clutch of tissues. He sat down next to her.

"I don't want to talk about it," she said.

Then she changed the subject. She climbed onto his lap and

planted her mouth on his. She wriggled around. In a moment they were wrestling on her bed.

"If we go to Sonny and Joyce's Friday night," she murmured, "we can stay overnight, Joyce said we could."

He sat up. "What are you going to tell your folks?"

"That I'm staying and you're going home. On account of your mother being alone."

"And what are you going to tell your old man when he shows up at two in the morning?"

She giggled. "Oh, he won't—"

Reuben relaxed against the pillows and let her wriggle on him. Her tongue was in his mouth again and his hand was between her legs, feeling her through her jeans. Soon he had her out of her jeans and her T-shirt up above her breasts. He slipped a forefinger under the edge of her panties and into her notch and she made a strangling noise. He clapped a hand over her mouth. She stared up at him. He lifted his hand and put his tongue in her mouth. Her eyes clenched shut—she had been from the start an adherent of the if-you-keep-your-eyes-closed-it-doesn't-count school of petting. His free hand drifted to his zipper and undid it. He eased his cock between her thighs. First contact had an electrical effect: as she registered his penis against her vulva, she slapped his left ear hard enough to make his eyes water. In shock, he ejaculated.

"Oh, my God, what are you doing?" she hissed, battering his chest. "Oh, yuk."

He slid to the floor in a daze. Head on his knees, he closed his eyes. He could remember sneezes with more bang to them.

Kleenex rattled from the box on her nightstand. "Oh, yuk, I can't believe you did that on me."

Reuben pinched the bridge of his nose.

She sat on the edge of the bed and slung her legs over his shoulders. She slid forward, practically sitting on his head. If he turned, she'd be sitting on his face. Another time that would have excited the hell out of him, but just then he didn't feel the least bit sexy. His ear was hot and painful. He crabbed away and she crawled after him.

"Cut it out, Laura."

"No," she giggled.

He pushed her away and got to his feet, zipping himself up. She climbed him like a monkey on a banana tree, and he caught her wrists behind her and dropped her back onto her bed. She pouted and then she reached for her jeans.

"I can't do this Friday night sleep-over, Laura," he said. "Not if you're going to let me get all worked up and leave me hanging."

Laura heaved a huge disgusted sigh. "I like making out. Why isn't that enough? We used to sleep on the couch together and you were happy with just kissing."

"Laura, what just happened? I don't have an infinite amount of self-control."

"I guess not."

"Come on, Laura. It hurts, after a certain point, just stopping, do you understand that?"

"Oh, that's too bad, isn't it? I guess if it hurts, I just better spread my legs."

"Shit," he said, "I'm outa here."

She jumped up and stood between him and the door with her arms crossed. He put his hands on the door on either side of her and bent to kiss her, but she turned her face away. She smelled of horses. She fingered his shirt buttons.

"I just want a nice wedding."

"I just want you to love me," he said. "It's not like you're not gonna give it to me anyway, right?"

"You're a sex maniac," she said in a hoarse whisper.

He licked the hollow of her throat and she giggled. He pushed his fingertips between her legs and rubbed the soft warmth of her pudendum.

"Please," he said.

"Pig."

He made a snuffling noise in her ear and she laughed.

"Maybe we could make a deal," she said.

He closed his eyes. For a fraction of a second he let himself think, all right, that's reasonable. Then sanity reasserted itself. Two thousand dollars to screw a girl he had already promised to marry? If he paid for her fancy wedding, did she mean she would let him fuck her once before the wedding, or twice, or anytime she wanted? The idea made both his ears *and* his balls ache. Maybe he'd been going at this all wrong. Maybe he should have demanded a handjob every time he took her to the movies.

"No way," he said with an immediate sense of relief.

"You cheap shit," she said and burst into tears.

* * *

He let her cry. He went downstairs and into the yard and set about changing the oil in her Plymouth. He was adjusting the timing on it when she came out of the house. She had pulled an old black watch cap of her father's over her hair and wore a faded plaid jacket and a flannel shirt over her T-shirt and jeans. The edge of handknit wool socks topped her mucking boots. She strode past him toward the barn. When he had the timing corrected he followed her.

The light was already failing and the cold strengthening. In the barn with the big doors wide open it was like being out of doors. Their breaths—Elvis', Laura's, his—hung visibly in the air. Laura's color was high and she sniffled against the cold and put a huge effort into ignoring him.

Elvis showed him teeth big enough to mark graves. He gave the gelding an apple and it slobbered green foam over his fingers. Just in case the beast thought it would be amusing to take one of his fingers off, though, he held its head, which made it shift from one hoof to another and blow cidery breath at him.

Letting go of the gelding's head, he moved behind Laura and circled her waist. She stiffened. She shook her head against him nuzzling the nape of her neck and then she let him. Immediately jealous, Elvis lifted its tail and shat mightily on the barn floor.

"I'll tell Sonny we'll be there at seven, if Charlie turns up on time to cover the evening hours."

She spun around and flung her arms around his neck and kissed him hard.

* * *

An unfamiliar Studebaker with bald tires and a wired-on muffler was parked at the side of the garage, next to Charlie's piece-of-shit Dodge. The windows framed an empty office and permitted a glimpse into the empty bay.

Laura yelped and grabbed the dash as Reuben spun the wheel into a sudden turn. Yanking on the parking brake, he threw himself from the truck and flung open the door to the office. The cash register was open but unrifled. The radio in the back room was emitting "In-A-Gadda-Da-Vida." Crossing the garage, he jerked the door open and looked down on Charlie's pale hairy ass, pumping energetically between the legs of a chubby blond girl to the unintelligible lyrics of Iron Butterfly. The girl screamed as Reuben loomed over them. Startled, Charlie had an unfortunate mishap.

The girl's scream rose to a teakettle shriek, and she pummeled Charlie around the ears. "You promised to pull out, you creep!"

Mercilessly he grabbed Charlie by the heels and hauled him off her. Charlie scrabbled at the pants cuffing his ankles. Reuben propelled the interrupted lover, tripping over his pants, out into the garage bay.

"You left my cash register wide open, you piece of bugshit," he shouted. "Why didn't you put up a sign that says *Steal This Cash* while you were at it. Were you just in too much of a hurry to get your end wet? Iron Butterfly, I'll iron your butterfly, you hard-on with ears!"

"Oh Jesus." Charlie clutched his crotch. "I think you ruint me."

"Ruint you? That's the half of it." He bellowed toward the back room. "Little Miss Muff, Goldilocks, whoever the hell you are, haul up your drawers and vamoose, pronto."

The girl crept out just as Laura entered the garage, her curiosity having gotten the better of her.

Charlie squinted up at her shyly. "Hi, Laura."

"Hi, Charlie." She blushed hotly and tried to find someplace safe to look.

"Pull your pants up," Reuben told him. "You're embarrassing Laura."

"Sorry, Laura," Charlie said.

He grabbed Charlie's dick and brought him to his feet the fast way.

"Oh Jesus," Charlie moaned, "I'm sorry, Reuben. Please don't tear my dick off." Following the line of Reuben's sight to the register, Charlie nearly fainted. "Please don't close my dick in the drawer," he whispered.

It was a close thing. Reuben let him go.

While Charlie fumbled with his pants, Reuben went into the lavatory, washed his hands and breathed deeply a few times. When he emerged Charlie was modest again and miserably hangdog.

Reuben asked Laura if she'd like a beer.

She nodded.

He busted a six out of the icebox.

"Charlie, you know the rules," he said.

"Yessir." Charlie squinted with effort. "Don't leave the register open and unattended, no buddies hanging around during working hours and no chicks neither, no drinking during working hours, no dirty magazines in the toilet, and no credit, free Cokes, butts, gas, oil, parts, tools or rubbers for my buddies, don't be late to work, nobody picks up a vehicle without the bill's paid, and if there's any question, see you about it, I get'm all?"

"Think back, Charlie. Which rules did you forget tonight?"

"No chicks, no drinking, don't leave the register open and un-attended. Am I fired?"

"I'm thinking about it. Get out of here. Just looking at you pisses me off."

Charlie nodded. "I'm sorry, honest, I got carried away." A fond memory presented herself. "That's her name," he said, "Carrie." Charlie grabbed his jacket and headed for the door. "Or Kelly," he said.

Laura choked on a mouthful of beer. She managed not to howl until Charlie was behind the wheel of his Dodge beater, frowning with the realization his mother was going to want to know why he was home from work so early.

Reuben closed the register drawer and then liberated another beer from the holder. Laura hadn't finished her first.

"Sorry about that," he said, "Charlie's timing's always been a little off."

She grinned. "I couldn't believe how fast you moved out of the truck and then Charlie came out of the back room with his pants flopping around his feet like clown shoes and you grabbed his thing, oh my God, I thought you were going to tear it off. Who was that girl—Carrie?"

"Or Kelly." He shrugged. "She looked like a Schott."

The laughter died out of the air. The room seemed chillier. The fire in the stove was dying, thanks to Charlie literally fucking off. He filled the firebox and opened the draft.

"I'll close up long enough to take you to Sonny and Joyce's. You can get Sonny to run you home or wait there and I'll be by later after hours."

"You're going to work?"

"I have to, Laura. I can't be closed on a Friday night."

Her cheekbones reddened.

"You promised!"

"I can't help it," he said. "It's my business."

Her face was dead pale, her eyes aglaze with tears. Blindly she reached out for him. He stroked her hair.

"That's all you care about," she sobbed, "your stupid till and your stupid garage. All you want me for is to screw."

He lifted her face and tried to kiss her. She turned her face away, but he pursued her mouth and all at once she was kissing him back. From the road the horn of a passing vehicle jeered at them, and they realized in the lights of the garage it was like they were on stage. He locked the door.

The mattress in the back room was still warm from Charlie and the blonde. Laura closed her eyes and let his hands roam at will. She was perfect. She made everything else in the world seem coarse and badly made. For once he prayed no one would come along wanting service for at least an hour.

When she was naked except for her panties he reached for his zipper. He looked at her on the mattress and she looked at him and she didn't say stop so he shed his jeans. The bulge in his shorts embarrassed her and she looked away hastily. He took them off. He tugged her panties down and they were both naked. He closed her hand around the rod of his penis. Her fingers were damp with nervousness. He put his hand between her legs and she trembled; she was as tense as a drawn bow. She was gripping his penis like she thought it was a life line. It hurt. He peeled her fingers off him.

"It's all right," he said and put his knee between her legs and half covered her with his body. He put a finger inside her and she shuddered. He sucked her nipples and she moaned. He kissed her navel and stuck his tongue in it and she giggled, but it was a nervous giggle, just a reaction to being tickled. He looked up at her and grinned. Her eyes were blank as a wall. She didn't grin back or even try to smile.

He rolled over on his back and stared at the ceiling. Chambers Brothers on the radio: *"Time—tink tock—time—tink tock—time."* It was all wrong. She was scared out of her mind and she didn't really want to do it; it was just to keep him, to get her goddamn expensive June wedding. He'd have given in too, the instant he got inside her, he'd have been babbling, telling her to spend five thousand on it, invite the pope to be her maid of honor and Ho Chi Minh to be the flower girl. He had to bite his tongue to keep himself making the offer now.

His hard-on throbbed. He looked down at it, jutting out over his belly. There was a bead of semen leaking from it, and he wanted to fuck so bad he could cry. Cry or fuck, he thought. He could roll over on Laura and ignore her tears and fuck her and have done with it. Only he couldn't.

Laura didn't move. She opened her eyes to look at him curiously. At his face. She didn't look at his body, didn't look at his cock. She tried to be solemn, but there was a tiny flicker in her occluded eyes she couldn't quite hide. Relief.

XVII

A Fist Hammered on the office door.

Reuben muttered an imprecation. He pulled on his coveralls and stuffed his bare feet into his shoes and leaned out the door of the back room to see who it was. Frank Haggerty's flashlight aimed through the front window nearly blinded him.

"It's your father," he told Laura. Her face went white with panic as he closed the door on her.

Haggerty stood impatiently outside while Reuben worked the locks.

"What are you doing here?" Haggerty demanded. "Where's Laura? You're supposed to be at Sonny and Joyce's. I saw the truck and the lights on and nobody around, I figured I'd better check."

"Charlie had an accident," Reuben said. "I sent him home."

Now was the time to say Laura was at Sonny and Joyce's. She could hear him; she wasn't going to come crashing out of the back room and contradict him. He stood silent for a moment, thinking it over. Haggerty's gaze roamed the garage, looking for Laura-sign. Then he moved forward, past Reuben to fling open the door to the back room. Haggerty caught Laura barefoot, trying frantically to zip her jeans. She blushed incandescently.

"What the hell is going on?"

"Nothing, Daddy—"

Haggerty grabbed her by the shoulder and shoved her out of the room.

"My boots!" she cried.

Her father gave her another violent shove toward Reuben, who caught her as she stumbled and held her close.

"The hell with your boots. You think I don't know what you were doing? You were diddling—"

"Daddy!" Laura blurted in shock.

"I'm calling a spade a spade."

Reuben put his arm around Laura's shoulders. She hid her face from her father against his chest.

Haggerty glared at them a moment. Then he gestured to Reuben. "You come outside with me." He stalked out.

Reuben squeezed Laura's hand. She jerked it away from him and knuckled her eyes with her fists.

Outside on the apron Haggerty stomped his feet next to his cruiser. "I'd like to bust your face for you. I'd put a stop to you marrying her right now if I could. You're going to marry her, all right, and pronto or I'll know the reason why." He sagged suddenly as if the weight of it all was suddenly too much for him. "Take her home. I'm calling the house in fifteen minutes and she'd better be there."

Laura was in the back room. Crying. The way she usually did, her head down, intent on doing something else—this time putting on her boots. It wasn't something she ever just stopped and did. Tears were like sweat to Laura, flowing out of her almost unnoticed. They filled her eyes thickly and overflowed without restraint.

"Oh, this is just *great*," she sniffled. "Now my father thinks I'm a slut."

"I'm sorry."

Her little chin jutted fiercely. "I don't care what he thinks."

"He told me to take you home."

Wiping her eyes with the edge of her hand, she nodded. "If my mother says one word—" The space between her fine eyebrows knitted in a little white chop mark of defiance.

"He wants us married in a hurry."

Laura laughed. "Bet that makes you happy."

"What's really funny is he doesn't want us married at all." Reuben grinned. "I'm a bum and you're a tramp and we have to get married to punish us."

Laura glowed red with embarrassment again and she blinked back tears but she was laughing too. Her eyelids were puffy when she looked up at him and her mouth was wobbly. "I'm a tramp and you're a bum. We didn't even do it. It is pretty funny, isn't it?"

"Yeah." He stroked her hair and kissed her. "I love you."

Laura took a deep breath. "I'm not giving up my wedding. Daddy's wrong. I'm entitled to white and I'm going to be entitled to it in June."

"You'd be entitled to it in December," he said quickly. She looked at him pityingly.

After returning her to the Haggertys' he came back to the garage and opened up again. He knocked the cap off another beer, wet his throat and dialed Sonny and Joyce's number.

" 'S me," he said. "We're not going make it over tonight, something came up."

"We figured that out already," Sonny said. "Is it still up?"

"Very funny. I caught Charlie banging some girl in the back room. He wasn't doing it well enough to pay him for it, so I sent him home."

Sonny roared. "I wisht I'd seen it."

Reuben rang off and tuned the radio to a rock station, adjusting the volume so he could hear the scanner. Then he brought a Chevy inside that had been sitting out back waiting for a brake job.

He glanced at the old clock hanging on the wall above him. CADILLAC SERVICE, it read. Sixtus claimed to have picked it up from a bankrupt dealership in the forties. The hands lurched from hash mark to number. It wasn't broke, just dragging, like the works were glued up with the gunk of decades. It didn't give the correct time, not even twice a day, but stayed a minute or so behind. Time. *Tink tonk.* Kept was a funny word to use about time when keep was the one thing you couldn't do with it. Even telling time was tricky. Just because the clock was correct didn't mean it was the right time for something. As soon as he had time, he decided, he was going to fix the clock.

* * *

Full of apologies and eager to make his worth apparent, Charlie turned up early for work. Reuben had already decided not to fire him—this time.

Laura called first thing and asked in a subdued tone if he would come see her at lunchtime.

She was exercising Elvis in the paddock when he got there. He leaned on the fence and watched her. Cooped up during hunting season, the gelding was restless and touchy, but Laura didn't cut him any slack. It always amazed Reuben that such a fragile little woman could so completely control that huge, willful beast. As Elvis had gotten on in years, what passed for his personality had not become any more lovely. With everyone but Laura and her father he was outright nasty. Reuben kept him in line by sheer muscle power, and Elvis paid him back in sneaky kicks and nips.

Frank's old gelding Smokey, which Reuben used when he rode with Laura, stuck his head out of his stall and whickered, hopeful he'd take him out.

Laura brought Elvis to the fence. Exertion and cold had raised the color of wild roses in her cheeks. Her eyes, though, looked sore.

"Daddy told Mummy. She cried all night. I didn't sleep very well myself."

"I'm sorry," he said.

Laura's jaw worked. She stared off over the fields toward his house. Elvis shifted restlessly under her.

"I've changed my mind. I think we should get married right away."

Reuben took a deep breath. "If it's what you want."

She wiped her swollen eyes with the arm of her jacket. "I don't want to come back here again. I'll stay at Joyce's if I have to."

He put his hand on her knee and patted it.

"It'll be a nice wedding," he promised. "The best we can make it. A white wedding."

*　*　*

The most lucid, peaceful mornings are winter ones. After a night of scant rest he looked from his childhood bedroom over the white valley of the frozen lake, toward what the old books call the White Hills. In the near distance of the Haggertys' pasture Laura's gelding danced in the snow, snorting, blowing, tossing his head, around the stolid, indifferent Smokey.

His mother was up and making tea. He kissed her forehead and with his arm still around her told her of the change in his and Laura's wedding plans.

She clapped her hands together. "Oh, good. That reminds me. When you two are married I want you to have the front room. It's bigger and it's right next to the bathroom. I expect you'd like to have a new bed, and that's what I'd like to give you for a wedding present."

"I'd feel as if I were throwing you out," he said.

"Nonsense. I've thought for a long time I'd like to have Ilene's room. It's cozy and has such a nice view of the orchard in the spring. I like it being right next to the back stairs so I can come down in the morning and not wake anybody else, getting up as early as I do. I'd like a smaller bed, too—the old one feels too big and empty, just me in it."

He hadn't thought about the adjustment she'd had to make after decades of sharing the bed with his father. Giving up her bedroom to them, his mother signaled a willingness to cope with having a daughter-in-law in what had been her domain.

Through Laura's eyes he had seen the place anew, the faded, outmoded wallpaper and furniture, the general dinginess and deterioration. They didn't have central heating. Since his father's death he'd renewed the roofing and the old clapboards had sucked up a coat of paint thirstily but the plumbing and appliances were antique.

"Wednesday, would you like to go to North Conway and look for wallpaper and a new bed?"

Her eyes twinkled behind her glasses at the suggestion.

As his father had isolated them increasingly from the community after Ilene left, his mother's life must have been excruciatingly lonely. The old man's death had allowed her to renew her contacts with the town, but it had also left her alone in the house even more, for Reuben was abroad early and late and often did not sleep at home at all. Dutifully he had seen to her immediate needs—firewood and so on—but what did it total? Days and weeks passed when he barely saw or spoke to her and always with his mind on the next task. He had gotten the bitch to keep her company, and as much as she and Lucille loved each other, a pet was a poor substitute for a son. No wonder she looked forward to a Wednesday night's outing to Greenspark, to her church activities—no wonder the prospect of a daughter-in-law living under her roof pleased her when another woman might have been threatened.

* * *

The word got around and early next day Joe Nevers turned up with a very old dress box under his arm. Setting it on the desk, he hauled out an enormous handkerchief and blew his nose vigorously.

"My mother's dress." He tucked the hankie away. "Found it in Gussie's attic. Gussie wore it when she married Nate, but her oldest girl took after the Maddens and was too big for it, and then 'Lizabeth, well, you know. If she's still alive she's probably already married anyway. So there's nobody with dibs on it. I asked Gussie if you could have the dress for Laura, if she wants it, and no hard feelings or nawthing if she don't—well, she was tickled at the idea. We'd both be pleased to see it used again."

It was the longest speech Reuben had ever heard Joe Nevers make. The gesture moved him. Among the pictures Joe kept on his living room mantel was his mother's wedding photograph, Josie in this very dress. It raised goose bumps to see the reality of it, lovingly folded in tissue. Glistening like ice on the lake, the silk was the color of moonlight. It made the woman in the photograph real in a way she never had been before. He remembered how the dress had fallen straight from Josie's shoulders and the square-cut neck, in a column of beads and silken fringe, to her elegantly turned ankles in silk hose. She'd been slim and straight as a beeswax candle, her unveiled hair dressed up in a billow, begging to be released from its pins into some man's hand. Whoever had hand-tinted the photograph had faithfully colored the splinter of gold in one blue eye, the mark she had passed to Gussie and Elizabeth. And India.

"Makes me think of Elizabeth, this dress."

The caretaker started. "Took the thought out of my head. Don't say so to Gussie, if you please. You remember 'Lizabeth, do you?"

"Sure—she was a friend of Ilene's."

He didn't promise the dress would be used. That would be up to Laura.

* * *

Come the day, the Friday morning, he saw Joyce off to fetch Laura from school. He worked until one and then left Sixtus to keep the place open another hour. He would close for a couple of hours and then Sixtus would open up again and keep the garage running for the weekend. Charlie Lunt, serving another day of his second year as a senior at Greenspark, would cut out of school early to come to the wedding and would go on to work the evening at the Texaco. Reuben had had a word with Hallie, and Charlie was going to have a surprise visit from his old man to make sure he kept his pecker in his pants and his mind on the job.

Reuben went home to bathe and shave and put on his wedding clothes. All he had had in his closet was one of his father's suits, altered by his mother, but it was both noticeably outdated and shabby. He had had to buy a suit and stand still for alterations, which were at least included in the price. He supposed he would get the wear out of it at other people's weddings and at funerals and going to church once in a while with Laura. What with the cost of the new suit and new shoes and a tie and a proper coat to go over them and the antique pearl drop earrings matched to the borrowed dress he had bought as a wedding gift to Laura and the rings and this-that-and-the-other thing getting married required, he had blown quite a little bit more than the two thousand bucks she had wanted for the June wedding. He didn't doubt it was a bargain, though; the running total on this wedding had only confirmed his suspicion that her budget had been the tip of the iceberg. As he shaved after breakfast he was struck with how much he had come to resemble the old photographs of his father.

Laura's roommate Suzy came floating past. She wore a kind of gypsy rig, big gold earrings and velvet and ribbons plaited in her hair. She looked just the thing for a highwayman to carry away. She threw her arms around his neck and gave him a smacking kiss right on the mouth.

The female contingent of the wedding party was organizing itself in a side room to the chapel. Strange girls who had come with Suzy from Laura's college peeked out first at Reuben and then to check the house. Their incessant giggling seemed to raise the temperature of the room.

"They're all higher than the pope's hat," Hallie advised Reuben. "Joyce said they was having a champagne party when she got to the dorm."

The pews of the small chapel filled up and the priest came out. The priest nodded to Reuben and looked at his watch. They would have only the traditional Mendelssohn performed by the blue-haired lady organist who had been doing it for a couple generations now. The old Catholic standards were foreign to Reuben, and he had not heard anything that appealed to him at the weddings of high school classmates, which had featured bad solo guitarists performing contemporary ballads. What he'd wanted was a good tape of Aretha Franklin's "Baby, I Love You" as a processional and "Do Right Woman, Do Right Man" to go out on but the priest had rolled his eyes and Laura had been embarrassed.

As the girls began to assemble in the foyer he glanced back at the pews. It was an awkward time, three o'clock on a workday afternoon, but the town had done its best by him. Joe Nevers and Gussie Madden. The Lunts overspilling two pews. His mother bright-eyed and with high color on her cheekbones she owed to no rouge. Maureen Haggerty stiff and furious ushered to her seat by her oldest boy, Terry. She glared at Reuben as she sat down. Her younger children pogoed restlessly in the pew beside her, poking each other and whispering.

The music commenced and everyone quieted and turned toward the foyer and Suzy swished up the aisle, and then Joyce did and then Laura on her father's arm. In Josie Nevers' wedding dress. It was a little big for her and with her boy-cut short hair it made her look very young. But the creamy white of the fabric made her skin petal pale and the cloth flowed over her body. Her face was touched with a blush of rose. Excitement plus champagne with the girls, he figured.

His mouth was suddenly dry.

Her father, wooden faced, handed Laura over with an air of relief—perhaps it was only a normal discomfort with ceremony, an eagerness to be quit of his part in this traditional bit of theater. Laura kept her eyes on Reuben as this act was performed, but as Frank Haggerty stepped back she shot her father a look of triumphant defiance.

Reuben squeezed her hand and she turned her attention to the matter at hand.

Laura whispered her vows as if she had laryngitis. When the priest bent his ear evocatively, there was a murmur of laughter from the wedding guests. It made Laura crimson extravagantly; Reuben was reminded of the creams and rubies of an exotic lily.

He was nervous, he was exultant; his chest was tight and he was sweating in his new suit. Standing up with him, more or less, Sixtus wheezed and chuckled. In a few moments it was over, a mercifully simple, brief business that left them married almost before it began. He felt like he'd cut a knot, not tied one.

* * *

"Do you think Father Dan thinks I'm pregnant?" Laura asked as they escaped the reception at the meeting house.

Reuben shrugged. He had let the priest draw his own conclusions about the haste to cut the red tape. Of course, he was obliged in return to take some kind of instruction from the priest on his commitment to see his and Laura's children raised Catholic, but he had been going to do that anyway.

She blew her nose. "Everybody will, getting married in a hurry like this."

"It won't be long and they'll know different. Next summer, would you like to spend a week on the coast?"

"Really? You'd take the time off?"

"Are you kidding? I'd love it."

She sat back and stared at the ceiling of the truck and sighed. "Married. I can't believe we did it."

Reuben reached for her hand and rubbed the ring on her finger as if it were a magic lamp.

XVIII

The Short Light of a Winter's Day was already draining into dusk when they crossed the state line. He'd made a reservation at a two-story intown motor inn, within walking distance of the shops, restaurants and movie theater. Now it occurred to him perhaps Laura would have rather stayed right in the mountains at some place that had views out of the windows of something besides the bus stop and the 2000 Salad Bowls sign.

Unlocking the door to the room, he prayed silently that it wasn't a sleazy pit. He was relieved to find it looked okay, though it smelled a little of disinfectant and old cigar smoke.

Laura didn't seem to react at all. Hands in her pockets, she looked around disinterestedly before saying, "Where's the bathroom?"

He pointed her in what he guessed was the right direction, and she disappeared around the corner into it.

When he came back from finding some ice she was sitting on the bed, looking doubtful. Under her coat she still wore the antique dress, which with its ankle-length hem and relatively austere design was more like a cocktail dress than a wedding gown.

The same day he'd found the pearl earrings in an antique shop in this same town, he had bought a bottle of champagne at the back door of a fancy French restaurant, after asking the proprietor what was appropriate. Even wholesale the price had been astonishing for something he was going to change back into water. He had told the guy bluntly for that kind of money the label ought to read *Cana, A.D. 30,* and the man had laughed—well, he might, considering he was coming out ahead in the bargain. The fellow had thrown in a couple of fancy glasses he had called flutes, not so much out of shame at what he was charging, Reuben thought, as in unspoken horror that the bumpkin groom might drink the stuff from a jelly glass with Wile E. Coyote chasing the Road Runner around the rim—or possibly straight from the bottle. He stuck the champagne into the ice and sat down next to Laura.

She cleared her throat. "What do we do now?"

He glanced at the clock on the nighttable as if it would tell him something he didn't already know or possibly had some marking on its face authorizing an official bedtime for them.

"It's too early for supper. We could go for a walk."

Her shoulders relaxed and she breathed deeply and then gave him an ironic smile that said she knew she was being silly but—

Friday night, the shops on Main Street were full. Hand in hand they looked in a lot of windows but nothing fetched her. They adjourned to the restaurant where he'd dickered for the champagne and ordered a meal she didn't eat, though she put away a couple of glasses of the wine the proprietor picked out for them. He put a hand over her glass after the second one, and she giggled and rolled her eyes at the reminder of the last time she'd pulled a drunk on him.

On their return to their room, Laura twisted her rings nervously while he worked the key in the lock. He opened the door and she hesitated. It was not, he knew, any expectation of the corny gesture that stayed her at the door, but he did it to distract her—he swept her off her feet and over the threshold. It seemed to work. She giggled.

Setting her on her feet, he kissed her and she kissed him back. After a few moments necking, he turned her gently around and undid the hooks that closed the back of her dress. She took a deep breath and held herself very straight. If he had his choice of wedding pictures, he thought, this is the one he'd like to have framed in silver: Laura in the sheer layer of her slip, stepping out of the dress, intent on not letting it slide to the floor where it might be soiled. The coolness of the room or friction with the fabric or perhaps awareness he was watching brought up her nipples against the thin material.

When she had the dress hung to her satisfaction, she found her handbag and went rooting in it. Hiding her hands behind her, she asked him to pick one. The childish trick made him laugh and he reached around her with both arms and seized her fists. She relaxed her fingers and let a foil package drop into his hands. He peeled a corner of the foil to confirm it contained a neatly rolled pair of joints.

"Wedding present from Suzy," she said.

"Suzy'd like you to spend your honeymoon in jail, would she?"
Laura groaned. "Don't start."

"Come on, don't you ever think about how your father would
feel if you got busted?"

"I didn't notice you giving any thought to my father," she said,
her voice rising hotly, "when you were trying to screw me in my
room."

Reuben held his finger to his lips and she reddened. He picked
her up bodily and dropped her gently onto the bed. She bounced
and that made her giggle. Pouring a glass of champagne, he sat
down next to her.

"This is legal," he said, "and so are we."

She snickered at the tickle of the sparkling wine, breathed
deeply and closed her eyes, relaxing against the pillows.

Reuben went into the bathroom, took off his shirt and shaved
for the second time since daybreak. When he came back to the
bed, she had crawled between the sheets. Propped against the pillows, she turned the empty champagne flute, studying the light
breaking along its rim. He sat down on the edge of the bed again,
took the glass from her and turned her hand over to trace the lines
on her palm.

"We'll go slow, okay? We've got all night."

She peeked at him from under half-closed lids and made the
slightest of nods.

The silk stockings and garter belt she was still wearing were
something different for them, so he made the most of them. She'd
had enough to drink to loosen her inhibitions a little and slowly
she became more responsive. She tensed when he put his hand between her thighs and more at the first slight intrusion, the stroke
of his thumb, and yet more at the direct insertion of another finger.

"We've done this," he reminded her.

She nodded but her nails dug into his arms and her upper lip
was wet with perspiration. And after a while she pushed back and
got wetter and more open.

At the touch of his penis on her bare thigh she flinched. He
caught her wrist and placed her hand on it. It leaped to her touch
and she jerked her hand out of his grasp.

Trying to lighten the mood, he joked, "It's alive."

She blinked nervously.

He took both her hands and drew them down against some resistance to his penis in the hope of breeding a little familiarity.

There was a tremor in her voice. "It's kind of, ah, big."

He bit his lip but she must have felt the tremor of laughter
shake his diaphragm. Her body stiffened under his hands.

"Don't worry about it," he said. "It's just standard issue. Mil-
lions do this every day, you know, and it's amazing how well the
parts work together."

"Don't make fun of me," she whispered, her eyes brimming.

He retreated. He kissed her, nuzzled her, tickled her, did everything he could think to soothe and distract her. Twenty minutes
later he had a knee between hers and he started to lift himself over
her onto it.

"Wait a minute," she gasped, "what about the thing?"

"Thing?"

She pushed up against the pillows, with a tremor of little tits.
"I could get pregnant."

"I heard that too. I think it's only if you soul-kiss."

"Stop teasing. We didn't talk about this."

"Talk about it," he said, touching the tip of her right breast. "I
could swear I promised not five hours ago to raise our get to be
good little mackerel snappers. I wasn't just talking through my
hat."

"Don't be silly. You know I was going to go on the Pill in
May."

He pulled her down next to him again. "Trust me, baby. I
knock you up, I'll marry you, I promise."

Her mouth twitched delicately, signaling confusion and disarray. Staring down into the depthlessness of her eyes, Reuben had
the sense she had gone away from him, like something dropping
rapidly beyond sight or recovery.

"Oh, what's the odds?" she muttered.

He wasn't surprised she didn't seem to know. When they'd been
reading the pamphlet the priest gave them together he could tell
from the bored glaze in her eyes she wasn't paying attention. It
would be okay, he calculated; by the time school let out she'd only
be six months gone.

But she tensed and her breathing quickened. He waited another
moment, keeping his fingers inside her, his glans against the hollow of one thigh. Withdrawing his fingers to their tips to open her
labia around the glans, he pushed against her gently a couple of

times, and felt her tensing again. When he pushed forward he met a total resistance, as if despite the evidence of his fingers she was not ready. Her breathing rapidly labored and he rolled over onto his back and held her.

"Easy," he murmured, but her face was wet with silent tears.

He poured them both another glass of champagne and then he started at go again. When again she seemed ready he took her hands and lifted himself onto her and tried once again to get into her. It was like trying to screw the blast door at NORAD headquarters. Her breath hitched and she dug her nails into the backs of his hand and thrashed under him.

"Oooh," she moaned, "it hurts, it hurts," and then she screamed and he got off her in a hurry. "I told you it wouldn't fit," she cried, "it's too big!"

On his stomach, his hard-on withering with painful rapidity and his balls aching, he clenched his eyes closed and smothered a spasm of something between laughter and a scream.

She curled up on herself, sobbing wholeheartedly. When he tried to hold her she pushed him away. He yanked the champagne out of the ice and took a couple of good swallows straight from the mouth. He considered Suzy's pot. The last time Laura had mixed a goodly quantity of alcohol and pot she had tossed it all up. Likely it had just been the cheap wine, but he wasn't really up for an experiment. When he stretched out next to her again she let him hold her and the crying subsided.

"I think we need some lubrication," he told her. "You don't have any hand lotion or face cream with you, do you?"

"No," she said.

It was the one detail he hadn't considered. He thought of the Vaseline in his cargo box in the truck but it was dirty, tainted with black grease and oil.

He bent over and kissed her navel and then kept on going and she grabbed the hair of his head and yanked.

"What are you doing?"

"Going down on you. It'll get you wet and you might even like it."

He hadn't ever done it before and wasn't even too sure how to go about it but had had a serious interest in it for some time. He'd heard it asserted in more than one bull session that women who didn't respond to anything else went off like rockets from oral sex.

Her voice rose again. "Oh no you're not. And don't even ask, you're not sticking that thing in my mouth!"

"Look, maybe we should just do it. I know it hurts right now—"

"Damn right it hurts!" she snapped.

He slid out from between the sheets and grabbed his pants.

"Where are you going?"

"I've got Vaseline in the truck."

Laura moaned and turned her face away.

Sockless in his shoes, shirt misbuttoned and shirttails flapping over his pants, he went out the stairs and out to the truck. Uncapping the Vaseline in the cargo box, he grimaced at the muck in it. But he hurried it back to the room.

Laura was staring at the ceiling.

He went into the bathroom and opened the jar of lubricant again. He made a little nest of toilet paper in the trash can. Fingerful by fingerful he scooped goop into the paper until he was nearly at the bottom of the jar. And then he bore the pristine remnant to Laura.

He used it all the time at work. After having heard countless witticisms in shop classes referring to its uses as a venereal lubricant—handy, he remembered someone announcing, while jerking a fist suggestively, very handy stuff, and of course queer jokes by the dozens, he'd tried it once as a jacking-off aid and not much cared for it—probably too used to his already established habits. But now it felt wonderful, cool and slick on his deflated erection, which in response snapped to painfully ready attention.

"Yuk," said Laura at the sight of his greased cock.

Lying there in a tangle of sweaty bed sheets, hectic with stress and mascara smeared around her puffy eyes where she'd rubbed them, she was so vulnerable that it took his breath and his spit away and, for an instant, stopped his heart. Or so it seemed. As if the second hand caught on something and dragged through that particular fraction of time.

The touch of the jelly when he applied some to her made her start. She closed her eyes and he slid his fingers into her again. A few minutes later, with both of them gritting their teeth, he finally got into her. It was slow and painful and not just for her—she was indeed a very tight fit and it wasn't just the adamant tension of her muscles against him. He lifted her bottom and pushed hard and then he was fully inside her cunt for the first time. He had imagined the luxuriant, slick heat of it, her skin against his, their bodies as close as they could be countless times. But the reality was shockingly unpleasant. It was humiliating as well; he felt dog-locked and had to fight the impulse to break free at all costs. She was crying silently again.

"Push against me, Laura," he whispered.

She moved very tentatively and for an instant there was a kind of relief, her silky cunt hugged his hard cock and it felt good and he was so grateful and it was going to be fine and he loved her limitlessly. Then she stopped. Trying to help, he moved her bodily but for all the times he had dry-humped her she didn't seem to understand there was a rhythm to it. After a while he stopped trying to get her into it and just fucked her and she didn't do much except wait for him to finish. He tipped her face and tried to see into her eyes, but she had them clenched closed.

"Look at me," he begged.

Her eyelashes fluttered and her eyelids twitched, but she wouldn't lift them to more than half mast. He wanted to see what he had seen, not always but often, in the widow's eyes, a glitter of passion. But Laura's eyes were blind, blind with silvery tears. If she saw him at all, he thought, it was from under water and as a blur.

It felt as if his balls were tied in a knot, like a knot in a sneaker lace, only a hell of a lot bigger and tighter, and he wanted to come and be done with it but he couldn't. He was numb. He pounded her pretty much into the mattress—not that there was much difference between her and the mattress except she was marginally wetter—and he was intensely aware she wasn't having a good time and he felt like a jerk and a failure and resented the hell out of her, just lying there, blind and unreachable. This is fucking awful, he thought, and when he finally came it hurt from the top of his head to his toes, with an excruciating spasm of pain in his balls. He was running with sweat when he freed himself from her limp body. They lay there silently for a long moment while his breathing evened out.

"I hate you," she said abruptly.

"Thank you very much. That was wonderful," he said, regretting the sarcasm the instant it left his mouth.

She sat up very stiffly and tried to stalk into the bathroom and then winced and sort of hobbled. She slammed the bathroom door behind her and a second later the shower shooshed on.

She wasn't the only one who was sore. His dick felt like it had been through a wringer. He rolled over, reached for the champagne bottle and knocked back a long, cool swallow. Going down his throat, it made him realize how thirsty he was. The room *was* shabby when you got right down to it and now it reeked of fucking. What he most wanted to do was change to his everyday clothes and pack up and go home. Take Laura to her folks and then go back to the garage and spend the rest of the night on the mattress in the back room. And possibly never leave the garage again except to take care of his mother. After a while the talk would die down and he'd be just another one of the town's considerable population of eccentrics—*oh, that's Reuben Styles, who was married to Laura Haggerty for one night that turned them both into old maids. Good mechanic, though.*

He straightened out the bed linen and lay back on the bed with one arm under his head to finish the champagne. Laura came out of the bathroom wrapped up in a towel. Her eyes were red from crying. She pulled a flannel nightgown out of her overnight bag and jerked it over her head with shaking hands. After she had gotten into bed and turned off the light, he tried to take her hand but she jerked it away.

"Still mad at me?"

"I'm bleeding," she said.

"A lot?"

Reluctantly she shook her head.

"Then it's just normal, isn't it?"

Her only answer was a long, angry silence.

"I'm sorry," he said.

She was crying silently. He put his arms around her and at first she was stiff and angry but after a while she was just crying, in an exhausted way.

"Do you want me to take you home?" he asked her.

Her body went rigid again and her face in the dark was white and drawn with shock. "What?"

"Do you want to go home?"

"I don't understand," she whispered.

"Maybe you can get an annulment."

Amazingly, she started to cry again. He didn't know where she was getting the water from anymore.

"We did it! They only let you have an annulment if you've never done it," she sobbed.

"I'll swear we never did," he offered.

"They check," she snapped, suddenly angry again.

"Well, what do you want to do? Some Catholics do get divorced."

She wilted and her eyes overflowed again. "They can't marry again, and what if I'm pregnant?"

He wasn't sure it mattered, since if she was he would have to take care of her and his child—his child, it felt so strange to even think the phrase—whether they stayed married or not. The idea of knocking her up promptly now seemed spectacularly stupid. But maybe it would be all right, maybe that was just what they needed. Closing his eyes, he drew her closer and held her while she shook and wept. After a while she fell asleep with her head on his chest.

He stared at the ceiling. It'll get better, he told himself. It has to. How the hell could it get worse?

XIX

The Rattle of Water in the shower woke him—Laura in the bathroom again. Bright sun leaked around the edges of the curtains and he closed his eyes against it. He was aware of the not unpleasant pressure of a full bladder and a thickened cock. He was still sore; he supposed Laura was more so. Probably that's why she was bathing again. The shower stopped. She emerged in a rush of steam. She was wonderfully pink and moist, except for her eyes. They were a mess, hugely swollen as if she'd been stung.

"Come back to bed," he said. "I just want to hold you."

A little reluctantly she dropped her towel and slipped in next to him. She closed her eyes and bent her head so her forehead was against his chest. She made little fists between them.

"I'm really sorry about last night," he told her.

She didn't say anything. He waited awhile, thinking she was working out something to say, but the silence just went on.

Finally he asked, "Are we still married?"

She rubbed her forehead against him in assent.

He closed her tight fists inside his hands and worked his thumbs inside them. Slowly she relaxed the fists she had made.

"It'll get better," he promised.

He had to leave her to drain his bladder. When he came back she was out of the bed, had on her panties and was hooking her bra.

They went to breakfast, then wandered around the town again and he was permitted to buy her a nightgown that wasn't flannel on the grounds that she couldn't go back to the dorm from her honeymoon without some slightly scandalous lingerie. While she was looking at wallpaper books he ducked into a pharmacy and bought a tube of K-Y.

Laura admitted to being tired. He asked her if she wanted to go back to the motel.

"Could we just put our feet up and rest?" she asked.

He agreed they could.

In the somnolence of the motel at midday Laura fell asleep. He read a novel he'd been dragging around in the truck with him to fill the odd waiting moment. It was a short book about an old man trying to catch a big fish. It was possibly the best book he had ever read, but it was very disturbing because the story had such a core of sadness to it. He thought it wasn't really about catching a big fish so much as fighting the desire to eat a load from a shotgun, which the man who wrote it had, and of course that made him think of his father. Every turn of a page seemed very loud in the quiet.

Laura slept heavily and woke in a cross mood. When he tried to kiss her she pushed him away.

"I've got studying to do," she said in a sulky voice.

He went out and walked the same short streets they had already mapped, and in the course of his trek conceived a dislike of the place he would never shake. It would always be cold and lonely, a place where he felt like a refugee, far from his own country. He drank a cup of tea in a café, picked through yellowed paperbacks in a secondhand bookstore and poked around in various other shops until he found a sturdily made carpet bag for his mother, to replace her old frayed one. He watched the sun go down in the abrupt way it does at the foot of Mt. Washington. Suddenly there was a scatter of snowflakes in his face, little shocks of cold that were the best part of the day.

When he came back to take Laura out to a movie and dinner, she was weepy and headachy. He felt for her. Neither her honeymoon nor the reality of life after marriage was meeting her expectations. She was still Laura and he was still Reuben and everything else was pretty much the same. Her homework still needed to be done. She had given up her virginity in pain and awkwardness, only to discover intercourse was as gross and sticky and sweaty and invasive and effortful as she had feared. He suspected it had dawned on her this was going to continue to go on between them *for years*. So far it had been about as much fun as having her teeth filled without Novocaine. What if it didn't get better? What if she had to go having the gross Thing shoved into her every night, only to be rewarded with it flopping wetly on her thigh afterward, like a smelly, drooling old dog?

The cold air helped clear her head a little. She chose the movie—*The Odd Couple*—with an ironic laugh.

"Somebody made a movie about us," she said.

But he was relieved to hear her laughing hard at the comedy.

"I'm Oscar and you're Felix," she whispered.

He squeezed her knee and took a calculated risk to make a sexy joke. "I don't think they've ever been to bed together, do you?"

"Oh, yuk," she giggled.

They went to the French restaurant again, and the proprietor made Laura a special dessert or at least he said he had made it special and she liked the idea enough to believe him. Reuben managed not to wince over the bill.

She was nervous about going back to the motel, but all he did was kiss her and hold her, to her obvious and unflattering relief. When she was asleep he went into the bathroom and jacked off, imagining for himself a hot, willing and dry-eyed Laura.

* * *

The snow-pearled countryside seemed brittle and ragged to Reuben as they traveled the miles back to Laura's college. The skies were blank and the miserly light seemed to be sucked down into the snowy fields and frozen watercourses and diluted there. Laura was mute, withdrawn from him since she had turned her back on him to dress before breakfast. When he offered to stay to take her to dinner somewhere, she said she had more studying to do. And she shouldn't come home next weekend, not with exams starting the Monday after. After insisting her finishing school was no problem he could hardly make an issue of it. He had to work next weekend anyway. In order to free himself for this one he'd had to swap his fire department shift and the tow-call rotation as well.

He headed back to the Ridge, his mind filled with what was to come. Christmas break was only two weeks off. He had given his mother an air ticket to Oregon to visit Ilene, as his Christmas gift to her. She had seemed delighted.

He would have plenty to keep him busy in her absence and Laura's—wallpaper to put up, the bed to install, things Laura wanted moved from the Haggertys'. Not the least of those items was Elvis. Frank was willing enough to keep the beast while Laura finished school and Elvis was used to him, but taking the gelding was a gesture on Reuben's part to Laura. Loathe the bug-eyed monster as he did, if its presence in the barn made Laura feel at home with him, Reuben would shovel as much shit as the bastard could produce.

Stopping at the garage first, he did the minor chores that Charlie always seemed to forget. It was still chilly when he installed his recently prescribed reading glasses on the end of his nose, pulled out the gloves from which he had scissored the fingertips—he thought of them as his Bob Cratchit gloves. He opened his books.

* * *

The limbo of December with its day-long twilight that felt like premature burial bore heavily upon him. The days passed in slow motion, the very brevity of daylight a weight that defeated him with the sense another page was gone from a finite calendar but without any real accomplishment. A sin to wish away time yet he did wish it away and with a black panic hard in his chest at the thought that when Laura returned the same disaster would occur.

When she stopped at the garage on her way home from school two Fridays later she was nervous—so was he—but she only stayed long enough for a quick kiss before going to her folks' house to visit her mother. At five Reuben left Charlie at the garage and met her at the house. First they visited Elvis in the barn and only then, after she had nuzzled the horse much more enthusiastically than she had him, did she go into the house and upstairs to look at the bedroom.

The room was on the bare side, the new, lighter paper enlarging it visually, the old dark draperies removed and the windows left with only the lace sheers. His mother's dark oak pieces had been removed to the room that had been Ilene's. The new bed, mattress, spring and Hollywood frame stood headless and footless in the center of a pale field of oak strips once hidden beneath braided rugs.

Pleasure lit her face as she stood in the doorway, and she squeezed his hand. "I never thought it could look this good."

She let him pull her down onto the bed on top of him, first just kissing, and then when she tensed, he tickled her and they wrestled like kids. He was excited from the start. They were alone in the house for the first time, and he pinned her to the bed and she stopped giggling. He let go of her wrists.

"Please," he said.

She tucked her body into a curl and turned her face away.

"We have to try again sometime," he said.

She sat up and silently undressed and he watched her, telling himself there was nothing wrong with watching his wife take her clothes off but he still felt guilty because she was so clearly reluctant. As she took her jeans off he sat up abruptly and unbuttoned his shirt. She was in her panties and she looked at him, and he went to her and wrapped her in his shirt.

"It'll be better," he said.

She nodded.

Then he slung her over his shoulder and spun on his heels and she shrieked and he did it until they were both dizzy and collapsed on the bed.

Panting, she sat up on her elbows and blinked at him. "You are so weird."

It was better. He had greased his cock to a faretheewell. She moved a little. Then he surprised her and himself, rolling her over so she was on top. Straddling him on her knees, she started to rise away from him, but he had her firmly by the waist and his cock was so tightly jammed into her he thought they were probably going to need a hosing to break apart. After a while she moved on him tentatively and then more surely and then her eyes went wide and glassy. She worked at it for a bit and then shook her head, and he rolled her over again and let himself come.

Tucked up inside his arm afterward, she was very quiet and still for a long time.

"You almost made it, didn't you?"

She blushed hotly and hid her face. "I guess."

She didn't know. She never had. He wasn't surprised, exactly—in all the making out they'd done she'd never given any sign or signal she was coming. He blushed himself, thinking what a callow prick he'd been, so caught up in getting what he wanted he'd never concerned himself with her satisfaction. Well, he could fix that. Would fix it. When they had started horsing around on the bed he'd liked the way it felt, having her on top of him. Putting her in the superior position had been pure impulse, and he was as surprised as she was at the result. It was a relief too to know that given time and patience, there was hope of her learning to enjoy it as much as he did.

* * *

Shivering in the chill, he groped sleepily for his nice warm bride and found her side of the bed already cool. There was cold light but the sun was still below the horizon and the clock's hands were both on six—an hour late for him, the result of two late wrecker calls. No problem: Sixtus had tipped him a wink the previous afternoon, assuring him he would come to open the garage Saturday morning so Reuben would get his rest.

Rolling over, he looked out the east window and saw the first combers of pink cloud rolling before the sun. When he passed the window on the landing that showed the southern view, he saw Laura on Elvis, moving slowly along the fence line toward the lower fields. He supposed he'd have to buy or barter another nag if he wanted to keep her company. Twice the amount of horseshit. Next time he married, he decided, he would find himself a woman who was allergic to four-footed shit machines.

It was strange to come downstairs and not find his mother. Lucille must have missed her too, for the dog slobbered all over him and was only distracted by filling her dish. Hers was the only breakfast prepared at the house. A note on the table said Laura was going to ride to her mother's to eat breakfast and he was invited.

Elvis was visiting Smokey in the paddock when he got there.

Frank and Maureen were at the table and Laura was leaning against the counter, eating a piece of toast. Her cheekbones were a drift of wild roses and she glowed. Reuben boosted her to the countertop as he had often done and kissed her toast-buttery lip. She pushed him away.

"You better have something to eat," Frank said, "you're light-headed."

"I'll cook it," Laura said, slipping past him.

Maureen's face was red and her cup rattled disapprovingly on her saucer.

As Laura set a place for him at the table he hooked an arm around her waist and mock-bit her blue-jeaned bottom, mostly to keep Maureen's water boiling. Laura's mother stood up stiffly and left the room. Laura batted his head smartly with a napkin and he let her go. He didn't need to keep his water boiling, he had to go to work in short order and the hard-on he had felt like the all-day kind.

Laura followed him to the truck but not to give him another one of those open-mouthed soul kisses. He didn't really expect one, not with her crossing her arms over her little girl's bosom and refusing to look him in the eye.

"What's the matter?"

"You shouldn't be so fresh in front of my folks. It's embarrassing."

"Laura, I think they know we're sleeping together."

She stamped her feet. "This is serious. Maybe I don't like you pawing me in front of my own parents, maybe I felt like a piece of meat, like you don't respect me enough to treat me like a lady, I'm just something you own now. I hate it."

He was stunned. It hadn't occurred to him she might take it that way.

"I'm sorry. I didn't mean to do any such thing. I love you, I want you, I didn't think there was anything wrong with letting it show."

She wiped her eyes. "I just want you to be more discreet. More grown-up. I don't want to be like Sonny and Joyce, crawling all over each other in public, okay?"

"I've got to go to work," he said.

She closed her eyes and raised her face, he hesitated, their dry lips met glancingly and he went to work.

The two weeks of Laura's Christmas holiday were busier than he ever expected. The hours he worked, they were separated—Laura never spent more than ten minutes at a go at the garage. Sometimes when they were together he was called out on one thing or another—wrecker calls, of course, and it was fire season too. Laura occupied herself—she rode every day. She went Christmas shopping with her mother as well as one Wednesday evening with him. She saw her high school buddies.

And she settled into her new home. The bedroom was a beachhead where she could safely depose her own things without displacing anything of his mother's. There seemed to be a lot of clutter and clothes thrown about in her moving, and she was slow to tidy her things into place. He remembered uneasily how her bedroom at home had always been. She didn't seem to be able to use the toothpaste without strangling the tube. He put a sliding clip on the tube that pushed out the toothpaste evenly and showed her how to use it and she laughed with delight at it. But she didn't use it. The toothpaste went on looking as if Lucille had gotten at it. Small change, he told himself. Pride in her own home would eventually get her picking her clothes up.

Still they had more time together than they'd had since the summer and a lot of it they spent making plans.

The newest appliances in the house were the washer and dryer he had bought for his mother shortly after his father's passing— their cost had come out of the estate. The wood stove had to stay, since they could not presume to ask a woman his mother's age to learn to cook on an electric range, but Laura wanted something a little less antediluvian for herself. It wasn't urgent until after she was out of school, but he was definitely in the market for a range. And a refrigerator. His mother's Kelvinator was a museum piece. The house had but one bathroom, an old-fashioned installation of claw-foot tub, basin and john, islanded in a former bedroom. They decided to turn the small room that had once been a nursery next to their bedroom into a full bath and to install a second full bath downstairs, off the kitchen, in what was a cold pantry. The present upstairs bathroom would revert to bedroom. And so on and all with due concern for his mother's feelings and advice.

Sooner or later, though, they ran out of conversation about the house and had to go up to bed. Once there Laura's immediate silence was intimidating. Always he had to weedle her out of her pajamas. At first she was reluctant about assuming the superior position, but after a particularly frustrating bout with him on top she climbed onto him of her own accord and succeeded in coming, to his great relief. After that they nearly always did it that way. It wasn't surefire but it was the only way she seemed to be able to come.

Once as she was drowsing off he slipped his hand between her legs from behind her and found her still lubricious. She murmured sleepily into the pillow. With an arm around her waist he drew her back against him. It wasn't until he wedged his cock between her legs that she understood what he was doing and moved against his restraining arm. By then he was inside her.

"What are you doing?" she said as he lifted her to her knees.

"Making love to you," he said and tugged her hands back between her legs to touch the root of his penis.

She jerked away from him, causing him considerable discomfort. From the way she winced it must have hurt her too. She rolled over on her back and lay rigid with fury.

"Don't you ever do that to me again," she hissed.

He tried to tell her there was nothing all that unusual about the position. He really didn't understand what the problem was. It was just a different angle, but she was reacting like he'd screwed her in the ass.

She didn't get her period in late December and he knew it but she didn't tell him. The second Saturday in January, he woke to her weeping. Clutching herself, she rocked on the edge of the bed. As he reached to comfort her she bolted for the bathroom. He found her huddled over the john. He washed her face for her and carried her back to bed to bundle her up and hold her.

He tried to joke her out of her blues. "It's okay, I said I'd marry you."

She burst into tears again.

Suddenly having a baby had a direct physical cost, one he wasn't paying and Laura was. Deliberately knocking her up on their honeymoon struck him then as incredibly callous. He couldn't begin to apologize but he tried.

She wiped her eyes and blew her nose. "It's my fault for not making you use one of those things."

"No, it isn't."

"What?"

As he made his stumbling confession her eyes went blank and her face, already pallid, became almost transparent except for two thin red lines from the corners of her nose to her mouth. Before he had completely finished she boxed his ears. The pain blocked out everything for a minute.

When she had calmed down again she insisted she didn't want to tell anyone just yet—she didn't want to be teased. She meant everyone would assume she had been pregnant when they got married and she wouldn't have any proof otherwise until the baby was born nine months from their honeymoon. Given her morning sickness, it didn't take his mother or hers very long to suspect the pregnancy. All that was said when Laura finally admitted she was, at a Sunday family dinner in March, was *How wonderful!* from his mother, a tight *Congratulations* from Frank and then Maureen blubbered and gave Reuben one of her how-could-you, you-beast looks.

He'd never much liked Maureen, but now she was his mother-in-law, he was surprised to discover the true depth of his loathing for the woman. She was Laura's mother, he reminded himself, and it was ridiculous to live inside a mother-in-law joke. He'd just have to rise above it.

XX

Earl Partridge Went to Bed with a bad headache one February night and didn't wake up. His wife, Alma, had had a series of bad winters, plagued with bronchitis and pneumonia, and she wasn't up to trying to run the store without Earl. So she shuttered it and hung a *For Sale* sign on it and sat down at her kitchen table to wait for a buyer or the Grim Reaper, whoever came first. Much to her surprise, there was no immediate interest from anyone meeting the description of either party.

Rotated to West Germany, Sonny got busted back to buck for insubordination and then wrecked a jeep under the influence of pruno and glue. It wasn't his first tangle with the MPs or the first black mark on his record. Shortly thereafter he found himself abruptly returned to civilian status, with a large good-of-the-service boot print on his rear end.

To Reuben Sonny confessed he counted himself lucky not to be in Leavenworth or worse—there was some business involving the sale of some grenades and handguns that weren't, strictly speaking, his, to a West German woman who had picked him up in a bar and turned out to be a student radical—but apparently that was embarrassing enough to rate a cover-up, and just then the military justice system had a lot more badasses than him to chew up.

"Drugs," he told Reuben. "You wouldn't believe the goddamn drugs. You want to know why we can't win this fucking war, it's on account of the whole goddamn outfit's on the nod. And there's so much money in it—they're stuffing stiffs with smack like turkeys to smuggle it into this country. Some poor fucker bought it out there in jungleland gets his dead ass used to bring the junkies their shit. And then there's the ever popular race riot—here you got the gooks killing each other left and right, and we're supposed to be stopping it and our own guys are at each other's throats all the time, fuck you dinge and honky motherfucker—shit"—Sonny crumpled his beer can in disgust—"it's all a big fucking joke. I'm glad to be out of it."

* * *

On a raw spring night that would have passed for winter in more kindly latitudes, Reuben came home from work to discover Elvis had jumped the paddock fence. The gelding had knocked down the top rail in going over and fallen, leaving a patch of churned-up mud where he'd gained his feet.

With Lucille he tracked the gelding across rotten snow and half-frozen mud. Elvis had moved slowly at first, picked up speed, then slowed again on entering the woods. In among the trees, knee deep in the beginning of a dead cold fog, they heard the gelding scream. Lucille went into a frenzy and then tore off and led him right to the gully where the beast had finally come to grief. Through the tatters of fog Elvis rolled a ghastly eye and then screamed again.

A scramble down the gully later the beam of Reuben's flashlight, diffused by fog into an ectoplasmic smoke, revealed the stricken animal. After plunging over the steep edge Elvis had fallen among boulders and onto a slash pine. It was a granddaddy of a white pine, recently fallen, and its wood was green and hard. The boulders that had broken its fall had also broken the limbs of the pine, turning them into jagged, dangerous spears. Elvis was impaled on some of them. Bone had ruptured the hide of its right front leg and both hind ones, and there was bleeding from every orifice. Reuben went back to the house with the horse's shrieking still paining his ears.

His mother waited in the doorway. "You found it?"

"It fell into that gully near the north line." He took down the four-ten from the gun rack and broke it open. It and the twenty-two were the only arms left in the house; he'd sold the rest.

She sat down slowly. "You be careful with that gun."

"Don't worry, Ma."

"Poor beast," she said. "Poor Laura."

He went to the barn and found an old tarp. Lucille followed him again as he made his way back to the gully. Again he shined the light down on the beast on his side at the bottom. The gelding was wet with the sweat of agony. Its mouth was full of bloody foam, its eyes wild out with the madness of pain.

He let himself down carefully, working his way close to his

head. When he reached out to touch it the gelding jerked back its head but he came in slowly and the beast relaxed a little. He put his fingertips on its nose and then along the side of its jaw the way Laura always did and Elvis quivered. Then he moved back and up the side of the gully, aimed the four-ten at its right eye and fired. Lucille yelped and skittered away. The huge corpus jumped at the impact and gave a massive shudder before collapsing.

He spread the tarp over it in a feeble defense against the predators of the night. When he reached the top of the gully Lucille was waiting, but she cringed from him. It was a slow trudge back to the house. He handed the gun to his mother when he came through the door and went upstairs to wash the blood and tissue off his face and hands and out of his hair.

His mother put a mug of strong tea into his hand while he waited for Laura to come to the phone.

She was breathless, having run downstairs to the phone booth.

"Laura," he said, and stopped to clear his throat.

"Am I glad to hear from you. Wait'll I tell you what happened today."

He listened while she burbled she hadn't been able to zip her size-four jeans, even lying down.

"Laura, something's happened. Not your dad."

He could imagine her twisting the phone cord in sudden anxiety.

"It's Elvis. Elvis got loose and fell. It was bad, honey."

"He's dead? Elvis?"

"Yes."

She wailed. The receiver thumped against the wall. He could hear her far away and he called her name but she didn't answer. There were other voices, concerned ones, and then someone picked up the phone.

Some girl he didn't know asked, "Who is this?"

"Laura's husband. She's upset because her horse had an accident and had to be put down."

"Oh? She's pretty hysterical. Maybe you ought to come be with her?"

"Try to get her to talk to me again, okay?"

"Okay, whatever."

A distant murmuring and then Laura was back on the line, still crying.

"The vet did it?"

"No. I did. I didn't call the vet."

"You didn't call the vet? Why?"

"Elvis fell into that gully near the north line, do you know which one I mean? It looked like green-stick fractures of three legs to me. He was bleeding from his mouth, from everywhere, I'm sure there were internal injuries."

"But you don't know. You should have had the vet."

"Elvis was in Christ-awful pain, Laura. I'm sorry, honey, there was only one thing to do."

She was sobbing again, unable to speak.

"Do you want me to come be with you tonight?"

"No," she said at last, "I can't talk anymore."

She hung up abruptly.

Next day he took her father to the gully. Frank winced when Reuben exposed Elvis and he saw the extent of the injuries. It took two horrendously messy, smelly hours before they succeeded in winching the dead horse from the gully.

"Jesus," Frank panted when they had him out of it, "did you have to use the shotgun? Why didn't you come to the house and get something that wouldn't make such a goddamn mess?"

"Didn't think of it," Reuben admitted. He didn't want to tell Haggerty how much it had hurt his ears hearing the sounds the gelding made in its agony. It had been difficult to think clearly with that going on. He hadn't slept all night with the headache. "I just wanted to stop it hurting anymore. It was my twenty-two or the Winchester, and I wasn't sure the twenty-two would do it quick enough."

"I was you," Frank said, shaking his head, "I wouldn't keep that Winchester anyway. Makes me nervous knowing you've got it."

"I keep it so I won't forget."

Frank shook his head again.

Laura came home that weekend and wept over the grave in one of the Haggertys' fields, and then he took her to the gully and they looked into it.

"You should have taken better care of him," she said. "I don't know how you could have done it."

She stalked away to press her forehead against a tree and cry again.

✳ ✳ ✳

In memory of his boy, Earl Jr., one of the two local boys who hadn't come back from Korea—the other being Harry Madden, Elizabeth's older brother—Earl Partridge had bequeathed funds to the town to build tennis courts, a basketball court and a playground. So far it had been too cold and wet to use the new basketball court behind the library, but Reuben had his old high-tops and a ball ready for the first opportunity. May came in the open bay door one Sunday morning with the distant bop of a ball on the new court and overpowered him. With the glee of truancy in his heart he locked up and jogged down the main road.

As he came around the corner of the library, David was in midair, slamming a ball through the net. He was a spindle, man-tall bones on which the substance of the man was being spun. In a ragged sweatshirt from which the sleeves had been torn, his arms and chest had muscle but his face was still beardless. The androgyny was emphasized by his hair, tied in a ponytail, and by the small gold ring that pierced one earlobe.

For a moment Reuben was distracted, remembering the boy David had been the day his sister died. Had India died that long ago? He was unprepared for David's molting from that boy to unfold into the butterfly man.

David dropped the ball and crossed the court, snatching off his glasses to wipe them clear before setting them on the end of his nose and reaching to clasp Reuben's hand.

"You're early," Reuben said.

"You're late," David answered. "I've been here a quarter of an hour."

Reuben flicked his ball off the ends of his fingers into David's stomach. They knocked around on the new court for a few minutes, playing one-on-one, goofing. Sonny and Charlie showed up. Then church let out and pretty quick they had enough guys for a game—a couple of kids still in high school, one of whom actually played varsity, several volunteer firemen, the grammar school phys ed teacher, a brace of carpenters and the minister, an ex-Peace Corps-divinity school-draft dodger with a wicked outside shot.

As in the pickup baseball games there was a high level of foolishness punctuated by moments of intense competition. Sonny insisted Reuben's team take David as a handicap to Reuben's height and size. Playing forward, David made Sonny regret the gratuitous insult almost as much as the hangover Sonny was trying to sweat out. Sonny got more and more pissed as the ball kept disappearing from his hands and reappearing at the ends of David's spidery fingers as if attached by invisible rubber bands.

David had a lovely hook, but when he shot from the outside, the ball would typically run around the rim like water going down a drain. Sometimes it would drop through, other times would wobble off. He knew his weakness and set up the plays so the minister or Reuben could make the shot, while he controlled the ball from one end of the court to the other.

Reuben could see Sonny was pushing himself too hard to keep up and tried to joke him off the court but got nowhere. The game ended abruptly when Sonny fell to his knees at mid-court and blew his cookies over the ball.

"Thanks, Sonny, that's my ball," Reuben said.

David couldn't resist temptation. "Some play, Lunt."

"Blow me, faggot," Sonny retorted, tossing the ball at him.

David cat-stepped out of the way and watched the ball bounce harmlessly to the fence line.

The minister tried to make peace. "Please, gentlemen."

"You can blow me too," Sonny snapped.

"Sonny, Sonny," David sighed, "is this an impulse or a confirmed habit?"

Sonny lunged at him and Reuben stepped between them.

"Come on, Sonny, that's enough. Charlie, why don't you take Sonny home?"

"Yeah, Sonny," Charlie urged, "let's go home. You don't look too good."

All the rage had drained out of Sonny's face as another spasm of nausea took him.

"What'd you do last night?" Reuben asked Sonny. "Drink the world?"

"Close. I'm gonna kill that little faggot."

"Cool it," Reuben advised. "Go on home and sleep."

David was washing Reuben's basketball at the hand pump behind the library. He tossed it to him and then passed his hands through the water and shook them off. He picked up his own ball and put it under his arm.

"Sonny okay?"

"He'll live to sin again. It's the length of your hair and the earring irritating him."

David flicked the gold in his ear. "Shit. All the hours I spent picking it out, just for him."

"I'm hungry," Reuben said, "but my mother and Laura are cooking Sunday dinner, so I better not spoil my appetite. How does crackers and peanut butter sound?"

David kissed the tips of his fingers.

"You stink from outside," Reuben told him as they walked down the edge of the road to the garage. "It's a millimeter off every time."

David jammed the ball of his thumb into the bridge of his glasses. "Double vision. My lenses don't correct it perfectly."

At the garage Reuben put the kettle on the hot plate and the Ritz crackers and jar of Skippy out of the old bread box under his workbench. They tipped back a couple of chairs next to the cold stove and started dipping crackers into the peanut butter.

"Saw Laura riding yesterday evening," David said. "Nice seat. What happened to the nag she used to ride?"

"Had an accident."

"Did you?"

Reuben raised his eyebrows.

With his hands David made a belly in front of him.

"You're drawing conclusions on insufficient evidence," Reuben said, "not that it's any of your beeswax anyway. What did you do with your winter?"

Licking his fingers, David stretched his ever-longer legs and stared at his raggedy sneakers as if he hadn't noticed those weird appendages at the bottoms of his ankles before. "Nothing so earth-shaking as baby making, señor. I got myself bounced out of school in November and went to Belize with my mother."

"Belize?"

"British Honduras. Heaven on earth. She was working. I fucked off. Six months of reading paperbacks on the beach. Played some basketball with the local missionaries, baseball with the local kids. Sailed, did some diving, some deep sea fishing." That explained the deep color in his skin. "Payback's camp this summer and a real school in the fall. I don't care. I've never minded studying, it's the fucking haircuts and neckties and ass-kissing that burn me."

"Why didn't you just tell your mother you wanted a transfer?"

"Where's the fun in that?"

"How is your mother?"

David leaned forward to scoop another crackerful of peanut butter before he answered. "Mean as a fucking snake. She had to put up with me all winter. I mean she worked, it wasn't like I was in her face all day, but she couldn't go off and lose a weekend, which is how she usually manages to stay dry on the job. She found a young guy to screw"—he looked up at Reuben from trailing a cracker through the peanut butter to see how he was taking it—"local boy, didn't have a word of English but he spoke fuckee, fuckee just fine. Still, there's nothing like bourbon to keep a girl happy, you know. It's been a long, parched winter for her, she's sick of me and I'm sick of standing between her and the next jar."

He handed Reuben a cracker larded with Skippy, and Reuben washed it down with tea.

"You think she'll start drinking as soon as you're at camp?"

"She's been going to AA since we got back in the country, but she's been in and out of it before—how the hell do I know? Butch is around, they're old drinking buddies, I wouldn't be surprised she fell off the wagon."

"Butch?"

"Alden."

Reuben snorted. "You call Miss Alden Butch?"

"To her face. Sometimes I call her Douglas, sir, after MacArthur. You oughta hear what she calls me. It's okay. We're just ranking each other. You know how soldiers are, rough and crude. She taught me how to shoot. Fortunately, bullets are more efficiently designed to hit their targets than basketballs are, and I can close one eye when I'm shooting. Butch respects good hand-to-eye coordination almost as much as she does running the trains on time."

"You really think your mother's an alcoholic?"

He gave Reuben an incredulous stare. "Sweet Merry Jesus."

"Come on, alcoholics are stinky old men who sleep under bridges. Your mother doesn't drink all that much more than a lot of people I know."

"You know a lot of alcoholics, then. My mother's a fucking drunk, sometimes literally. As you well know."

Reuben shook his head.

"Anyway," David said, "the hell with my mother. I don't care anymore. As far as I'm concerned she doesn't need to stay sober for me. She wants to so she can keep on working, that's up to her, but please mother darling don't do it for me. Fuck it." He shook the empty cracker box. "All gone. Tell me about you and Laura. Thought you were getting married this June and I was going to be one of your bridesmaids. What do my wondering eyes behold but Laura who appears to have swallowed a basketball."

"We got married in December. Didn't Joe send you a clipping?"

"Yeah, but it didn't say the rabbit died. Feature you a dad. Makes me feel old."

"You make me feel old. You're bolting up like spinach in a hot spell."

David grinned. Rocking the chair forward, he stood up and stretched. "Hey, thanks for the chow. I'm glad about you and Laura. Keep her pregnant, she looks good in the bigger cup."

Reuben watched him lope away, dribbling his ball down the middle of the empty road.

XXI

Broody after a Bad Night, Reuben let himself
into the garage by the office door. He flicked on the office lights,
the pump switches, unlocked the register, a sequence so automatic
he was barely conscious he did it. Raining whispered softly on the
road and the roof. The place was dark and quiet around him. Going to unlock the back door, he found it open. He couldn't believe
he'd left it that way. Disgusted with himself at this inexplicable
lapse, he turned toward the lavatory to make sure it was ready for
the day and saw David huddled on the cot in the back room under
the old blankets. For a second he froze, waiting for David's chest
to move. Then it did, in a long, slow rise. He stepped into the
room and laid two fingers over David's carotid artery. A long slow
strong pulse. The boy's eyelashes fluttered on his cheeks.

"Am I still alive?" David whispered.

"Very much so."

"You're early."

"No, you're late," Reuben answered.

He left David rubbing sleep from his eyes and went to fill the
kettle. He was putting it on the hot plate when David, wearing the
blankets as Indian robes, shuffled from the back room to the lavatory. Reuben turned on the radio and the Animals greeted him
with "When I Was Young," which only added to the melancholy
grayness of the day.

"Want some breakfast?" he asked when David emerged from
the lavatory.

The boy nodded. Reuben lent him an old jacket and they
slogged through the rain to Partridge's old store, where Roscoe
Needham had reopened the diner. David was shaking as they sat
down at the counter.

"I'm not used to this cold anymore," he said.

"What cold?" Roscoe snarled as he shoved utensils across the counter at them. "How come you got that ring in your ear? I see the goddamn hippies wearing'm on the TV. I was in the Navy, the ports was fulla old-time merchant fleet swabbies had a ring in one ear. They wasn't guys you'd want to run into in a dark alley. Them fellas chew one of your goddamn hippies up for breakfast and they wouldn't be nothing left to spit out 'cept the goddamn earring." Roscoe began to chant, " 'Tom, Tom, the cabin boy, he was a naughty kipper, he lined his ass with broken glass and circumcised the skipper.' "

David blew him a sour kiss, then proceeded to tuck away enough of Roscoe's dubious chow to stop his shivering. Reuben stoked some himself, just to keep him company.

A little anxiously Reuben asked, "I didn't leave that back door open, did I?"

"No, I picked it. I didn't steal anything. You into ugly women? I found a skin magazine tucked behind a box of toilet paper, but it was Skags International. I didn't know women could be so ugly. Kinda thing not only instantly cures horniness, it's an adverse threat to a person's sexual fix."

"Looks like it was printed on cigarette paper? That'd be Charlie's, he usually hides one there."

"Charlie is a sick man."

"Just indiscriminately horny. Charlie'd look at pictures of sheep if he could find the right publication."

"He graduate this year?"

"Finally. Only took him 'til nineteen."

"Great timing. What's his lottery number?"

"Number seven. But I don't think he can pass the literacy test. He's still not sure how many t's there are in tit. Thanks to his flawless timing, he's going to be a father end of September, same time I am, but he's way ahead of me, 'cause he's also going to be a father again in December. Neither girl thought it was worth the effort of marrying him, though he was perfectly willing to marry both of 'em at the same time. He has me take twenty bucks a week out of his check to give to the girls."

"You're a public servant." David grinned.

"All comes out in the wash. His mother fed me a lot of venison meatloaf when I was younger. You want a ride home?"

David shook his head.

Reuben wondered if he just didn't want him anywhere near his mother. The kid might even have slept in the back room last night to make sure she didn't.

He worked a key to the back door off his key ring and handed it to him. "This is for any time you need a place to sleep or get out of the weather for the night. Nobody but you. No buddies, no girls, no cigarettes, booze or dope. Eat or drink anything you can scrounge if you're hungry. Be careful of the fire in the stove."

David's fingers closed around the key. "My mother have one of these?"

"You're holding it."

"Thank you."

"Take care of yourself, David."

Reuben watched Sixtus shuffle over the pavement under a blue plastic tarp that draped his walker as well as his bent form, so he looked like a fat old mailbox that had been knocked over too many times. He opened the door for him and urged him out of the wet.

"See you going down to Needham's with that rapscallion. Little shite's getting tall, isn't he? I see a ring in his ear. Next thing he'll be wearing a tutu. Early, ain't he? I don't mean today—'tisn't June yet. How come he ain't in school?"

"Bounced."

"War goes on awhile longer, he can try gettin' bounced outa the military."

"By the time he'll be draft age it'll be over. Besides, they don't draft rich kids, they just send 'em to college."

"Don't draft pansies either. I bin thinkin' about it watchin' the TV every night. It's not sensible sorting out the healthiest young stock you got and using it for cannon fodder. Take a kid like that long-hair little twist and send him. Smart like he is, you could train him to fly and let'm drop them napalm bombs. He'd have the best time of his life burning up them straw villages over there fulla cows and them black pajamas. He gets blowed away it's all to the good—one less nutcase in the world."

"We oughta make you Secretary of Defense," Reuben told him.

"Joint Chief," Sixtus said, "I want to be Joint Chief. Always liked that title."

"I gave him a key to the back door."

"Eh? The Joint Chief?"

"David."

"You taken leave of your senses?"

"He slept here last night, didn't do any harm. Some nights he needs a place out of the weather."

"What about that palace on the lake? Ain't that a home? Ain't he got a mother? Oh hell, now I bring it up I guess you could argue the point. Well, it's your business, but I tell you what, the day you come in here and find the register empty, I'll laugh my cracked old ass off."

"I'm not worried, Sixtus."

Not worried about David stealing except as a lark. But worried about the kid—yes. Reuben would be working late and there David would be squatting against the wall drinking a Coke and watching him. And there he'd sit like a stain on the floor until all of a sudden Reuben would realize there wasn't anyone there anymore, just an empty bottle with a little film of dark puddled at the bottom. More mornings than not he found David sleeping in the back room when he opened up. It crossed his mind more than once he ought to have a word with David's mother, but always the mere thought was enough to put him off. She never stopped for gas or anything, had taken her custom to Maxie Sweetser in Greenspark and that suited him to a faretheewell. Then David went off to camp and it was all moot.

* * *

June brought Laura's graduation. After the ceremony they packed her things into the Plum to return to the Ridge. She came up onto her knees passing the driveway to her parents' house and twisted around like a little kid to wave at them as Frank and Maureen turned off into it. When she slid back down onto the seat, her waif's face was tight and clouded. She was such a little thing there wasn't any place for the baby to go but right out front, and she really looked like she belonged in a home for unwed girls.

Reuben's mother came out with Lucille to greet them. After the old lady hugged Laura, Laura knelt down and hugged the dog. Reuben picked up Laura bodily and carried her to the barn. First she protested and then she laughed and waved at his mother and Lucille trailing along behind. She stopped laughing when the sound of Lucille's barking brought the palomino gelding, its eyes bright with curiosity, forward from the shadows. Reuben set her on her feet and she held out an unsteady hand to the youngster.

"It's just two," he told her.

"Two? Too much," she said, "it's gorgeous."

She ran her hands lightly over its head and along its spine and walked all around it. She leaned against its neck to smell it, and her hands moved over the long arc of the neck and into the mane. The gelding stood still while she grabbed a handful of mane and swung herself with a small boost from Reuben onto its bare back. She gave a gentle squeeze of her knees, and they moved easily into the yard with Lucille dancing behind them. The young gelding moved like a dancer, and Reuben could see the delight in Laura's face. She'd been riding Smokey when she was home, and the aged beast wasn't much fun anymore.

Laura put Elvis Two on the palomino's papers, but it was always known as Two.

He didn't have the wedding or the gelding paid off, but Reuben took her to the coast for the third week of June anyway. It was strange not to be working, strange not to see the mountains in the morning and not to know the people in the streets or on the beach or in the restaurants where they ate.

Because this was supposed to be their real honeymoon Laura allowed him to make love to her, but when she had painful contractions, she panicked. He took her to a doctor, who assured her everything was fine but advised going easy. To her easy meant no intercourse at all. They reverted to an early stage of dating—hand holding and a little deep kissing. He wasn't allowed even to touch her breasts as she said they were too tender. He couldn't help noticing how much less tense she was around him, how much oftener she put her arms around his neck, snuggled up to him and kissed him when she knew it wasn't going to lead to intercourse. It was just the pregnancy, he told himself; it would be different after the baby.

* * *

"That little punk cribbed here every damn night 'til he went to camp," Sixtus informed him. "Ate all your crackers and peanut butter so I bought him some more. Guess he ain't really a fairy. He lef' a couple dirty magazines on the mattress onced."

"Thanks for looking out for him."

Sixtus harrumphed and put on a show of disgust.

Joyce stopped one day, ostensibly to buy gas. She thrust a couple of parcels wrapped in baby paper at him and peeled out. One was a new photograph album, one of those baby's-first-year things. Pasted inside the front cover in a glassine envelope was a copy of a snapshot of Brandi. The other package contained a Brownie Starshot like the one Joyce had used to take pictures of Brandi. That night he handed them wordlessly to Laura. She paled at the picture of the baby.

"Get rid of it," she blurted. And with a sudden quaver in her voice tried to explain herself. "It's bad luck. Please." She gave him a scared little laugh. "I can't help it. It must be being pregnant. All of a sudden I'm superstitious."

Reuben took it to the garage to burn but wound up burying it at the back of a file cabinet.

One night in mid-August Reuben's mother called him at the garage to say that Laura's water had broken. It was too early, but her contractions were regular and strong. She delivered the baby within ten hours. Frankie was only five pounds, without nails or eyelashes and with most of the top of his skull still soft, but he was sound of lung and heart—just a little unfinished.

Everybody who'd assumed they had had to get married counted their fingers and winked significantly, though Maureen must have recited the circumstances of the baby's premature birth thousands of times in a vain attempt to set the record right. Since in her heart she didn't believe Laura hadn't been pregnant before the wedding, she never succeeded in convincing anybody else of it.

With his son in his arms Reuben couldn't imagine wanting or expecting more out of life. Except maybe a World Series championship for the Sox. He was intensely grateful to Laura. With her the whole time, he was overwhelmed with the physical feat of birth—Laura had worked as hard as he ever had in his life. Now Frankie was the center of her existence. He didn't mind; Frankie and Laura were the center of his.

It would be nice, though, to get ahead of the bills. He was bartering hay and feed with George Partridge for rent of a couple of fields, so Two wasn't expensive to keep, bar the vet's bills and the blacksmith. But the medical bill for a two-week hospital stay for Laura and the baby and the cost of all the baby gear was more than he'd succeeded in paying off on the wedding and the trip to the coast. Laura wanted so many changes in the house, and even with him doing the work, there were fixtures and materials to buy or barter. As much as he wanted to be around more to help Laura with the baby, the financial burdens meant if he had the work he was at the garage early and late most nights until ten or eleven and most of Sunday too. Some weekend nights he slept there. He was glad Laura was wrapped up in Frankie; it kept her from noticing how worried he was about just holding onto the garage.

* * *

The whisper of a turning page alerted him to the presence of an overnight guest when he arrived at the garage one morning in the last week of August. He stuck his head into the back room.

" 'Morning," David said, peering over the top of his glasses.

He closed the book around a finger and threw off the blanket. He'd slept in his clothes. Shivering, he groped for his sneakers.

"Laura hatched, huh?"

"Yeah. When did you get back from camp?"

"Last night."

David gave his laces a jerk and one broke off in his hand. He examined the shredded end, then stuck it in his pocket. When he stood up it was apparent the rush of growth hadn't slowed since he'd left for camp. He ran his hands through his hair and smiled.

Please God, Reuben thought, no son of mine should ever be so beautiful. No daughter either.

"Couldn't stay home one night?"

David shook his head. "She's on some fucking tear."

"Want some breakfast?"

He grinned. "Always."

They walked down the road to the diner. It was a dewy late summer morning—a little chilly, the odd rust of red and yellow in the trees, the exhaust of passing trucks standing in the air. The vegetation had begun, as it always did in the wane of summer, to look rank and weedy. The world was rolling on toward October to World Series time. Tony Conigliaro was back in the lineup; Rico Petrocelli was hitting homers. Reuben hadn't gotten to Fenway this year, but maybe he would in October.

"How's it feel, being a father?" David asked.

"Okay. I pick him up and it feels right, but sometimes I'm amazed, I feel like I should give him back to his real parents."

David laughed.

He put away the meal wordlessly, but Reuben was aware of him taking in the conversations going on around them with a cool reservation beyond his years. So much about David was beyond his years. But something was eating him, chewing on him worse than usual. Outside again, the boy paused to spill it.

"I hate her," he said softly. His jaw worked. "My mother." He spoke the word in an agony of contempt.

"Don't," Reuben said, "don't go home." It came out of him in a rush with no time to stop and consider the complications that might ensue. "You can stay with us, we've got room at the house. I'll call your mother and tell her where you are. She might be glad to have you off her hands."

David smiled. "I bet your wife would love having me as a house guest. I could go to Greenspark Academy. Thanks for the offer, boss, but it's only ten days until school starts." David grinned and clasped his hand. "Don't worry about me. I'll get by."

Reuben watched him drift down the road and off it, across a field where three horses grazed among Queen Anne's lace. Cattails were standing in the ditches and there was blue chicory like flowers on wallpaper in the high grass that was mauve with seed head. David stopped to feed a hank of grass to a mare and play peekaboo with a shy red foal. The mare shook her head and snorted at him. Long legs akimbo the little one bucked and kicked. David loped and feinted and frisked, his long limbs rubbery and loose in his scarecrow's caper.

* * *

Lounging on the mown grass at the ballfield, David was there before Reuben that evening. He tucked his paperback into his hip pocket and helped Reuben set out the bases. It was the last game of the season, a perfect day for it, and they were not alone for very long. Laura arrived with the baby, taking him out for the first time. David peered into the carrier for a long, intense moment. Then there were other players and their wives or girlfriends, and Laura took the baby to show off.

David picked up a bat.

"Mamacita's not nursing," he said, swinging the smaller one. "Too bad—it's better for the baby and her to nurse."

"How d'you know?" Reuben asked.

"Baby smells like cow's milk."

"No, I mean how d'you get to be an expert?"

"School I got bounced from last spring? One of the faculty wives was nursing a baby. She told me all about it. I used to watch her do it—she did it in front of the kids all the time. It's natural, isn't it? She figured it was educational. The little sucker used to go for her nipples like a Doberman for a burglar's throat. He'd start off whimpering and sort of searching around with his mouth all trembly like a little fish and get frantic and then he'd glom onto her. He'd bite her, you know. She had nipples the size of your thumbs, and when she was really full of milk it would spray out. Shit, I'm getting a boner thinking about it."

Reuben laughed.

David twirled the bat and laid it down.

"It was thin but very sweet," he said.

Reuben gave him an incredulous look. "This lady was letting you all have a suck, too?"

"No, just me—one Sunday afternoon when everybody else was whooping it up at an anti-war teach-in on the library steps. The baby was fussy, so she took him off into the stacks where I was reading. We got talking while she changed him and she was going to nurse him but he fell asleep. She said she was so full she was uncomfortable. I took the head off for her."

Reuben shook his head. "I don't know whether to believe you or not."

David twitched the front of his shorts uneasily. "Suit yourself. Mamacita nursed, she'd keep those nice tits awhile longer."

"My wife's name is Laura," Reuben said, "and you mind your mouth."

"Yessuh, boss." David was unperturbed.

A six-pack in either hand, Sonny rolled toward them.

"You ain't playing with us," he told David.

David flung his arms around Sonny and kissed him on the mouth. Sonny threw him off and wiped frantically at his mouth. David picked himself up and danced away, leaping and pirouetting and blowing kisses.

"Faggot," Sonny muttered.

Reuben rested a heavy arm on Sonny's shoulders. "He's as tall as you are now."

"I could break the little fucker in two with one hand. This game's for grown-ups," Sonny protested. "We don't need any more players anyway."

"Royce's gotten too fat to play left field. Next summer let's put the kid out there and see what he can do."

On the hillside David was talking to three girls. Reuben had seen them here and there during the summer. They were help at one of the lakeside inns. Long-legged, athletic college girls in Phys. Ed. Dept. sweatshirts from one of the Seven Sisters, they were otherwise chiefly distinguishable by the size of their breasts and the color of their hair.

Sonny nudged him. "The brunette in the short shorts. I hope she sits where I can see her from third."

"I hope she doesn't. I'd like you to pay attention to the game."

"Them three was playing the bases, I'd be sliding all the way home."

David was making himself comfortable among the three girls. He rested his head in one girl's lap and she ruffled his hair. Another one was feeding him cherries. The other took his sneakers off to play piggies with his toes. They were all giggling and chortling and having a high old time.

For a moment Reuben was surprised by unexpected relief and then a mix of regret and envy. Kids grew up on you. They became what you might have been but were too shy too poor too ungifted too unlucky to venture. They made their own lives. He supposed one day he would feel much the same thing about Frankie.

XXII

The Lamplight Cast a Soft Gold Veil over Laura and the baby in the bed. In his sleep Frankie's little hand rested on her breast. His mouth was a rosebud from a graveyard cherub. Laura's eyes were closed too and she looked like a Madonna.

Reuben, fresh from the shower, tied his pajama pants and bent over her to kiss her ear.

She opened her eyes.

He cocked his chin at Frankie and she nodded. Carefully he moved the sleeping baby to his cradle.

When he came back to the bed Laura was on her side, up on one elbow.

"That kid," she said. "The one who was looking at Frankie—"

"David."

"Right, I drew a blank on his name. He's weird."

Reuben lifted the sheet and got in next to her. "He's just a kid."

"Joyce says Sonny says he's a fairy."

Reuben grinned. "Sonny's been calling anyone smarter and better-looking than him a fairy since he was in the third grade."

A smile quirked her lips. "Yeah, I guess he has. Except you—I guess he doesn't dare." She picked at a French knot on the embroidered border of the top sheet. "All the same, I don't like that kid hanging around Frankie."

"He wasn't—he just looked at him, just like everyone else did."

She was silent a moment, still plucking at the French knot. And then she raised her eyes to his. "I know who he is, you know. He's her kid. That woman. He looks like her."

Reuben put his hand on her hip. "I haven't spoken to the woman in a couple of years. I'm married to you. I love you. Let it go."

Her gaze went back to the French knot. "Why do you let him hang around—"

"I don't. Laura, he's just a kid. He's lost everybody but his mother, and she's got other fish to fry—"

"Does he know about you and her?" Laura interrupted.

Reuben took his hand off her hip and flopped onto his back to stare at the ceiling. "Yes."

"It's sick."

He sat up abruptly. "What's sick? A lonely kid who lost his brother and his father and is groping around for some kind of family? He knows I don't have anything to do with her anymore. I'm one of the people who was there when his sister died. He trusts me. I don't see anything wrong with being his friend."

Laura gave up on the French knot. She narrowed her eyes. "You don't have to be ugly with me about it."

He let himself down again, slowly this time, trying to recall his tone of voice, the words, to spot the ugly in them. He might have been ugly. He was angry at her, bringing up David so she could make him feel guilty. About that woman. That Woman. Jesus. He closed his eyes, feeling the bed shift as she did, and they were lying side by side, both of them silent as the dead.

* * *

After a night that was like sleeping in a graveyard the possibility David might be at the garage never crossed his mind until he was unlocking the door. David was awake, reading among the tumbled sheets and blankets. The back room was redolent of sex.

"Hi, boss," he said. "You need a new left fielder."

"Next year. Did you have somebody in here?"

David closed the book and flung it aside. "Sorry, it was too buggy for the woods last night."

Reuben grasped the lintel of the door frame and lifted himself idly. "I don't give a shit. I made a rule."

"Which is why I broke it. It's nothing you didn't do yourself."

"Don't yank me around, punk. I'm not your mother. I don't want somebody I don't know wandering around in here after hours. And you're underage. Somebody's screwing an underage kid on my premises."

David sat up and groped for his clothes. "Nobody did any wandering. Nobody's going to make any complaints. She's eighteen—you think she's ever going to admit to anyone she let a sixteen-year-old screw her?"

"You're not sixteen. You're not even fifteen."

"She thinks I am."

"David—"

"Don't sweat it, man. I won't bring her here tonight. She's going to sneak me into her room." David shoved his feet into his sneakers. "You want your key back?"

He thought about it. "No. I worry about you."

"Why? I notice getting laid didn't stunt your growth any."

"It's not without hazards, either, is it?"

"Everybody's on the Pill, boss. And nobody cares anymore who sleeps with whom. Or what."

"I don't think my wife would be too keen on me cavorting with one of those girls."

David laughed. Refusing breakfast, he took off.

Maybe the girl didn't quite dare to sneak him in or maybe he just had to flaunt it but he was sleeping in the back room when Reuben came in the following morning and he'd had company. Reuben didn't say anything, just hauled him out of bed and held him under the shower, running dead cold water over him. David thought it was a terrific lark. It was impossible to be angry with him.

The following morning he had rigged a bucket over the door to shower Reuben when he opened it. Reuben retaliated by filling the sheets with crumbled Saltines. Tasted just fine off a girl's skin, David informed him. And filled the cash register with peanut butter, a prank that wasn't nearly as amusing to Reuben as it was to him. Reuben made him clean it out and eat the peanut butter, which he did quite cheerfully, on Ritz crackers supplied by the management. While Laura was at her mother's that evening Reuben spent an hour with her sewing machine, stitching the sheets together. The next morning when he turned the cold water tap in the lavatory basin to fill the kettle, it spurted in his face. He found a shim jammed up into the faucet.

"I surrender," Reuben told David. "I can't think of a payback."

"Nancy's going home today anyway."

"Next year why don't you get yourself a girlfriend with her own accommodations? I can't take this level of excitement."

"It's the ambience here that gets me."

"Ambience?"

"Italian for unwashed sheets. You want me to take them to a laundromat?"

"Never mind. I'll do it. Beat it, twerp, some of us work for a living."

One Sunday afternoon a month he did the laundry generated at the garage, separating it to avoid getting grease on the domestic laundry. It had always been his job—he had not cared to add to his mother's burden of housework—and knowing Laura's aversion to the griminess of the garage, he continued to do it after their marriage. He didn't get around to taking the sheets home for a while after David went back to school. And then he was called out on a predawn chimney fire and stopped to shoot some hoops with the younger volunteer firemen and didn't get home again until nearly noon. He went straight down cellar to the laundry room, meaning to run the load while the baseball game was on. Laura was emptying the bag.

"Yuk," she said.

"Let me do that," he said, but she was in the middle of it, separating the sheets from a tangle of coveralls and she just smiled at him.

She shook them out. And like a black bird, something flew free. She dropped the sheets and stooped to pick up a pair of black bikini panties.

"You bastard!"

"I didn't do anything!" He stopped himself on the verge of telling her about David. He couldn't defend letting a precocious fourteen-year-old use his premises for a knocking shop—especially not this one. "It must have been Charlie," he lied, his face flaming with it. "I haven't been near anyone else."

It wasn't out of his mouth before he knew she knew he was lying and naturally would assume about all of it. Another thing she knew, he thought with a flare of resentment at her outrage, was he'd had exactly nothing from her since June. The doctor had said they could resume relations, but she had kept him at arm's length. Too tender still, too tired, not in the mood, headache, the baby due for a bottle, too busy, getting, got, still had her period. She had lost her prescription for the Pill and the replacement was yet unfilled. She had good reason to worry about his stepping out on her.

She bolted upstairs. He loaded the machine with the sheets and started it. His mother was sitting in front of the game and the national anthem was playing. Frankie slept soundly on his stomach on the couch next to her.

"Where's Laura?" he asked.

His mother poked a knitting needle at the ceiling.

In their bedroom Laura was sitting in the rocking chair, her hands between her tight knees. Her face was streaked with tears.

She looked up at him in the doorway.

"I want to go home," she said.

It hit him like a blow to his stomach. For a moment he thought he was going to vomit. He hadn't done anything. Suddenly something let go in him, like a belt breaking and whipping free.

"All right," he said. "I quit. Go home. Go running back to Daddy and Mummy. Maybe you can find some other fool willing to work sixty hours a week to pay your bills for the privilege of sleeping next to a frigid bitch." He meant it too, with his whole heart. It felt like jumping off a cliff. Scared shitless and thrilled and free all at once and it didn't matter much if there was rock or water waiting below. Sonny and Joyce had done it, cut each other loose in one hellacious weekend of drunken recriminations. Other people did it. There wasn't any lock on the exit door. You just banged through it when the bell clanged.

She flinched. Her eyes filled up fast, but behind the glaze something was happening. He couldn't tell what, though. Now she was the one who looked ready to throw up. He watched her throat work, her mouth open and close. She was trembling all over.

"Go home," he said in a near whisper. "I'll find a woman who wants me."

She stared at him a moment, and then she made an inarticulate little cry and threw herself facedown on the bed to sob.

As he watched her heaving shoulders, his gut and his fists unclenched and he was swept with a hot shame. He turned away and leaned against the door. He couldn't believe he had said those things to her. He remembered her bravery having Frankie. His baby, his son.

Slowly he turned back and made himself cross the room to her side.

"I'm sorry," he whispered and then he said it more loudly, hearing his own desperation.

The convulsions of her grief only grew more violent. He sat down on the edge of the bed and tentatively touched her hair. He expected her to recoil but she didn't.

"Please," he said. "I didn't mean it. I was just so thrown by you accusing me of something I didn't do."

Her sobbing trailed off as he spoke and she curled up and knuckled her eyes, peeking at him between swipes. Hesitantly he kissed her and she let him and then she looked at him questioningly. His heart leaped. Everything would be all right if they made love. They could choose not to destroy everything. They didn't have to be Sonny and Joyce.

He got up and closed the bedroom door and locked it. He turned on the radio by the bedside to cover any noise they might make. Laura refused to look at him as she began to undress. Watching her unbutton her blouse, he took off his shoes mostly by feel. He wanted to undress her, but his throat was almost too dry to speak and he was already hard. He stood behind her and drew her back against him, and she was pliant and shivering as he finished the unbuttoning.

"Do you have a thing?" she asked.

"I'll pull out," he said.

She nodded.

He managed to hide his amazement. Assuming he wouldn't be able to go more than a moment or two and needing moreover to be able to withdraw, when he thought she was ready, he got on top. He fucked her for several moments before he realized he was in the same condition he had been on their wedding night, his orgasm tantalizingly just beyond achievement. She clenched her eyes tight and her fists too. He couldn't do anything about it. The pressure of imminent orgasm was too great, the pleasure of her body so intense after so long without. He tried to get her to move, but she stiffened more, punishing him by refusing to work for an orgasm with him. But after a while the resistance in her seeped away and she clasped her hands at the back of his neck and he became aware of her breath quickening. She had softened and she was slick all over with their mingled sweat and she rolled with him and at last began to seek release. The sudden surrender was too much for him, and he pulled out and came on her stomach.

"Oh, yuk," she moaned.

She wriggled out from him and bolted for the bathroom. When she emerged, she started dressing immediately.

"You did that on purpose. I was that close."

"I'm sorry. You don't want to get pregnant, right?"

"You got yours." She looked over her shoulder at him. "If you were so desperate, why'd it take you so long?"

"Laura—" He reached out for her but she evaded him. "That's why, all right? Look, I'll get some safes and we'll do it again tonight until you come twice, okay?"

"Just leave me alone," she said, and took the rest of her clothes into the bathroom to finish dressing.

* * *

She wouldn't talk about it, would hardly speak to him at all. He had desperate thoughts of bribing Charlie to go to her and confess to an amorous encounter with one of his females on the mattress in the back room and leaving the incriminating panties. Charlie likely would do it for free—would happily have confessed to killing JFK if Reuben asked him to do so.

He filled her prescription and brought it home to her. She held the little plastic box in her palm for a moment, and then she threw it at him and burst into tears. He tried to comfort her, and for once she didn't twist out of his arms.

"What is it? What's wrong?"

"It's wrong," she said. "It's a sin."

He was flummoxed. "What?"

"The Pill. Birth control. I thought I could do it but I can't," she sobbed. "I can't go to confession and pretend I'm not committing a sin."

For a while he rocked her in his arms until the sobbing let up and then he tried to reason with her. She wasn't buying. It didn't matter the majority of Catholics in the country were ignoring the Vatican on the subject of family planning. It didn't matter that her own high school friends who were Catholic had no qualms about using the Pill.

"It isn't even the Pill," she confessed. "The thing is, I *want* to use it, I don't want to have eighteen kids—"

Nor did he make much progress by reminding her the Church taught the pleasure of marital relations was in itself good.

In desperation he went to the priest in Greenspark and obtained a new pamphlet on the rhythm method. They worked their way through it until he thought they both had the hang of it. She was supposed to record her menstrual cycle. There would be two weeks a month they would be able to have relations in relative safety. Considering they weren't having relations at all, it looked like a huge improvement to him.

But Frankie was almost three months old before Laura slept with him again, after they got drunk at her parents' twenty-fifth wedding anniversary party. It wasn't a safe time, but he pulled out. And they got away with it.

In January they went to Heidi Robichaud's wedding. Laura began to get tipsy early on at the reception. He paced himself and started coming on to her, taking her out onto the dance floor, using everything he had ever learned about what turned her on. In the parking lot outside the Legion Hall in Greenspark, where the reception was being held, he pulled her close and they necked furiously. She was drunk enough to be really responsive for once, and he got a couple fingers inside her and kept them there all the way home. He carried her upstairs with his hand over her mouth so his mother wouldn't hear her giggling. He didn't wait for her to undress. She was a little too plastered to be aware he didn't withdraw. She was the most uninhibited she'd ever been. It was worth having to hold her while she threw up all those margaritas later on.

Laura woke up with a paralyzing hangover. He dosed her with aspirin and took Frankie to work with him so the house would be quiet and she could sleep.

When he brought the baby home at noon, Laura was just out of the shower. Sitting at her vanity, she was brushing her hair at a zombie pace, as if the roots hurt with every stroke. He kissed her shoulder and took over the brushing for her.

"I drank too much," she said.

"A little."

"We did something last night, didn't we?"

"It was great. Thank you."

"It must have been, I can still feel it."

He put the brush down, bent over her and kissed her, sliding a hand down the front of her robe.

She pushed him away. "You never get enough, do you?"

"Let's have another baby."

"Are you out of your mind?"

He tugged her toward the bed. "Time for a nooner."

"Don't be obnoxious, I can hardly move."

"That's okay, I'll do the moving."

"N-O, no."

Then she missed her period. She locked him out of the bedroom. For the first time, though hardly the last, he slept on the couch. She rushed to have a test and it came back negative, to her relief. Then she started sicking up and had it again and it was positive. The doctor said the first test was just too early.

She had the last laugh on him. One of the rewards of being pregnant was a whole pack of unquestionable excuses for not having sex. He spent a lot of nights on the couch, a lot of nights working late so he'd have the excuse of sleeping at the garage. He'd turn up very early to do the chores, help with Frankie, have breakfast with his mother. If Laura got the chance she made some snide remark about what he was doing at the garage overnight. He managed never once to snap back, *Jacking off.*

* * *

It was the first summer David didn't go to camp. Most mornings he shot hoops behind the library first thing, and sometimes Reuben stopped and shot a few with him. Though David didn't have much to say, there was something reassuring in his turning up there day after day. As in years past Reuben caught glimpses of him very early and very late, seemingly wandering again. David still made an occasional visitation to the garage, drinking a Coke while he watched Reuben work, and then disappeared again.

In other ways David seemed to be sorting himself out. The years of going to camp had cut him off from the other kids who summered on the lake. That summer he organized a chess club to meet at the library on rainy days and also volunteered to read to the younger children at story hours. Ignoring his mother, isolating himself from her, he constructed an almost normal existence with friends his own age and all the physical outlets in sports he could manage. He also pursued girls.

"I thought I was a horny kid," Sonny groused to Reuben. "I'll tell ya, he plays with us, I check my glove every goddamn time I pick it up in case he screwed it in passing. I'm just glad I ain't got a wife anymore in range of the little hard-on." Sonny had a new reason every day why he was glad he didn't have a wife anymore. Occasionally one would directly contradict the one he had claimed the day before. They all seemed to carry equal weight with him.

A couple of times a week David played left field and batted lead-off. He was fast and nimble, and when it counted he threw bullets. At bat he was a switch hitter who'd rather bunt than hit line drives or homers, kissing off the ball every time instead of slugging it. And he was a compulsive base stealer, provoking Sonny to screams of outraged profanity when David threw away runs because he couldn't resist making a try at the next base.

"You like it in the dirt, you little faggot!" Sonny would scream, jumping up and down and throwing down his catcher's mask. "You'd eat dirt all the way to home if you could!"

One evening Reuben tried David on the mound.

"I knew it," Sonny said, "a goddamn screwball pitcher. Look at that bastard sink. I'll be goddamned if I'll try to catch it."

After that Reuben used David to spell himself and played catcher for him. It was fun watching David work batters into frenzies, as the tendency to hit the batter for which the unpredictable screwball is notorious sent them into spasms of flinching and cursing. On several occasions he beaned Reuben or the umpire, and once a batter connected with one of his sinkers and drove it into Sonny's crotch. At the end of the season, over Reuben's objections, the rest of the team voted to bar David from the mound.

Of David's mother Reuben saw very little, no more than in passing. Rumor had it she was on the wagon and he took it to be true, mostly on the basis of David's not crashing in the back room. He didn't know who did her maintenance and figured from the way the ark sounded when it passed it wasn't getting any. He knew how that felt, he reflected.

XXIII

When the New Baby, Karen, was about three months old, Reuben encouraged Laura to take a part-time job keeping the books at an automobile dealership in Greenspark. He thought she needed to get out of the house and away from the babies. And they could use the money. There was an immediate return: she was much sunnier. She kept some of her earnings besides what he already paid her for helping with his books. When she blew it on clothes and having her hair and nails done, he was proud of how beautiful and stylish she suddenly was. The portion of Laura's income she gave to him provided a little financial breathing room. He liked having the excuse to drag Frankie around with him and sometimes Karen too. But the biggest payback was having Laura soften toward him. All at once she was frisky; she invited him to make love to her again. He thought they'd turned a corner.

Immediately they had a pregnancy scare. It shook Laura enough to bend her conscience. She gave the Pill a trial and her blood pressure went through the roof—and she seemed relieved when she had to quit it. Next stop was a diaphragm. Laura found the idea less objectionable than the Pill—Reuben's impression was the riskier the method, the less morally troublesome it was for her. At first it was awkward and she hated it and wanted to give up on it. He offered to help her with it, and after a while it was just something he took care of for her like her car.

But gradually she cooled off. He didn't know what to do about it. Maybe it would pass. Weeks and then months began to separate their lovemaking. On their fifth anniversary he took her to North Conway to Jean-Claude's and gave her jewelry—silver and turquoise earrings that year, to match the squash blossom necklace he had given her on their previous anniversary—and she drank enough to get amorous. He was already inside her when he remembered her diaphragm. The hell with it, he told himself; they'd agreed to have another baby anyway and maybe she wouldn't catch on. Suddenly she started struggling. At first he thought maybe she was coming, saints be praised, and he let himself come and she slugged him one in the ear hard enough to bring tears to his eyes.

"My diaphragm!" she cried. "You forgot!"

Six weeks later she picked up the molded salad at suppertime and threw it at him. The old lady was speechless. Frankie laughed gleefully at this sudden domestic outbreak of the kind of slapstick that so fascinated him when he watched old *Three Stooges* episodes with his grammy. Karen, who was sitting in Reuben's lap while he fed her, reached up to slide curious fingers around in the gooshy stuff cascading down his face.

Laura burst into tears and Frankie stopped laughing and Karen started crying.

"What's wrong, dear?" his mother asked Laura anxiously.

Laura lifted a tear-stained face. "I'm pregnant again, that's what's wrong. He did it on purpose, too."

Awkwardly the old lady patted her hand. "Now, dear."

Laura cried harder.

Reuben stuck Karen in her high chair and his head under the faucet. It didn't do much good and he realized he was going to have to use some shampoo. He had the goop inside his clothes too. Full shower and change.

Laura had stopped sobbing and was just sitting with her head in her hands while his mother quietly cleared the table. He hoisted a kid under each arm and took them upstairs, cleaned them up and turned them over to his mother and then scrubbed himself. When he came out of the bathroom Laura was on the bed with her eyes closed.

"I'm sorry," he said, putting on his shorts. "I guess the timing's bad."

She turned her head and opened her eyes to glare at him. "You don't have to go through it, you shithead. You don't have to be sick every day for weeks, and get fat and ugly and constipated and have the pain and have it half kill you at the end."

He sat down next to her and brushed her hair back from her forehead. "I'm sorry, I'm really sorry. Do you want to get rid of it?"

"Yes, yes, I do. I don't want this brat, I don't want any more of your kids, I don't want your thing inside me ever again."

He was stunned. He'd asked her the question only as a way of underlining the fact of the baby's conception, trying to get her to accept the reality. Despite their use of a method of birth control the Church forbade, she was still a communicant. She took the kids to Mass every Sunday with her parents. But it was a leap from contraception to abortion. He couldn't imagine the process of squaring it with her conscience.

He got up and finished dressing and went downstairs. His mother had rocked Karen to sleep. When he stretched out on the couch Frankie dropped his Tonka truck and climbed up next to him.

"How's Laura?" his mother asked.

"Miserable."

"I can remember feeling so low with the morning sickness. She always has it so badly, poor dear. When she gets over it she'll start looking forward to the baby, you wait and see."

Frankie's fingers locked around Reuben's and they played Chinese handcuffs.

"She's not going to have the baby, Ma."

The creak of the rocker stopped abruptly. "I don't understand."

"She's going to get rid of it."

The old woman's face paled and tightened. "You can't be serious."

"She's serious, Ma."

"And you're going to let her?"

"She doesn't want it, Ma."

"She should have thought of that when you were making it."

"Accidents happen."

"And people cope with them, it's the price of having relations."

"It wasn't an accident really," he confessed. "I did it on purpose. I took advantage of her when she was drunk, and that's how I got Karen on her too."

"Oh, what foolishness! A man can't take advantage of his wife drunk or sober. This birth control is the trouble, you know. In the old days you had to take your chances, take what the good Lord sent your way. If you couldn't afford another child you controlled yourself. It made people appreciate their marital relations more. It meant something besides a tussle in the backseat of an automobile. I don't make a practice of interfering between you two, but if you allow her to kill that baby I'm leaving this house."

He tucked Frankie under his arm and then took Karen from her. "Sorry, Ma. It's not your decision or mine, it's Laura's."

While he tucked in the kids he heard his mother's and Laura's voices raised. He went back downstairs to the couch again, but he didn't sleep even after they both stopped bawling and went to bed. In the morning after his mother came downstairs he went up and rapped at the bedroom door. Laura looked as if she hadn't slept much either.

"Do you want me to make an appointment?" he asked her.

She nodded.

"When?"

"Right away."

He would do it. He supposed he was betting she wouldn't go through with it. But if she did he would live with it. It would be a fair punishment for his forcing the baby on her to start. He wouldn't let himself think about the baby. It was a blob still. In any case the argument over abortion was a useless one to him. Follow the antis to the logical extreme, and you might as well be a Christian Scientist leaving it to the Deity to cure your kid's peritonitis, or a Buddhist unwilling to sacrifice a malarial mosquito for a human life. Follow the pros to the end of their logic, and you'd be leaving handicapped infants and old folks out for the wolves. Add time to the equation and in the run of things you never knew how anything you did or didn't do would turn out for everyone. Probably most of what people did amounted to a fish fart in the water. It came down to doing the best you could. She didn't want the baby. It was her body. He couldn't force her to endure the process, the risk or the pain at the end.

Laura and her parents were going at it when he got home. Frankie and Karen were wailing in terror. Ignoring his furious wife and in-laws, he picked up the kids and carried them upstairs to Frankie's room. He wiped Frankie's nose for him and Frankie ran straight to the nearest of his Tonka cranes to start excavating invisible dirt. As soon as Reuben thrust a bundle of plastic keys into her hands Karen forgot the tears still wet on her hectic face and started smiling.

The row downstairs subsided.

Frank Haggerty called Reuben to the head of the stairs and met him on the landing. "How can you let her do this?"

"This isn't any of your business or Maureen's. Do me a favor and take Maureen home."

"I guess it's my business my daughter does something like this. I blame you, you selfish bastard. She didn't want another child, you should have taken care not to get one on her."

"Lower your voice or you'll scare the kids again, Frank. You're right to blame me, so go home, will you? And take Maureen with you."

"For Christ's sake," Frank said, "you're her husband. Stop her."

Reuben didn't say anything.

Frank literally threw up his hands. He hustled Maureen out of the house and they drove away.

While Reuben was bathing the kids Laura came out of the bedroom and stood in the bathroom door. "You didn't have to tell your mother. You should have known she'd tell my mother."

"You told Ma you were pregnant. I think she would have noticed if there wasn't a baby to show for it sooner or later."

"I was going to tell her I lost it."

"Left it on the bus?"

"Very funny. Ha ha. Now she's shut herself in her room and won't speak to me, and my folks are ready to disinherit me. If you think they can pressure me into having it, you've got a surprise coming."

He bundled Karen into a towel and handed her to Laura. "She's starting to wrinkle."

Laura took Karen away and he dried Frankie and shoveled him into his Dr. Dentons. Frankie promptly went fishing around inside them for his penis.

"That's right, get a grip on it early," Reuben said, but he took Frankie's hand out of his pajamas and stuck a soapy miniature Corvette in it.

✳ ✳ ✳

The house fell tensely silent except for kid noise. Reuben's mother stayed in her room. Laura followed her normal work schedule, and Reuben went to work and came home. He took care to fall asleep on the couch, a library book on his chest and the television running. At the end of three days he was still on the same page—maybe it was the six-pack of Miller he was using every night as a sleeping pill.

The night before the appointment Karen put most of her supper in her hair and on the tray of the high chair. He noticed she seemed warm to the touch when he bathed her.

"This kid's feverish," he told Laura.

She finished snapping up Frankie's pajamas and found the thermometer. Karen was furious at the intrusion, almost as disgusted as Laura was at having to use the thermometer.

"She's so pissed off, her blood pressure must be through the roof, never mind her temp," Reuben said.

"Just hold her still," Laura snapped.

"Right."

He got to read it; the kid was running a hundred.

"That's not too bad," Laura said. "She's got a runny nose, she's just getting a cold."

With some liquid cough medicine and rocking, Karen finally corked off. It was time for his own liquid medication. The television glowed and he stared at his book for a while and killed the six.

Laura bundled up her embroidery, stood up from her chair and yawned. It seemed to him her breasts were a little bigger. As she passed the couch he caught her by the wrist. She looked down at him.

"It's okay," he said.

"No, it isn't," she answered.

He dropped the book and pulled her down on top of him. It was like kissing a sapling. He let her go. She sat up, fixed her clothes, stood up.

"Your tits are bigger," he said.

She slapped him and stalked upstairs.

He wanted to tell her he meant they were pretty, he loved her, but it just came out all wrong. She was right, though, it wasn't okay.

Karen's crying woke him. It was about one in the morning. He tripped over Lucille and a shoal of empties on the way to the stairs, but he managed to reach Karen's crib before Laura did. The baby was shrieking. Her ears were bright red and she was much hotter. He picked her up as Laura came in, blinking and rubbing her eyes. His mother was on Laura's heels.

"I think it's an ear infection," he said. "I'm going to take her to Greenspark."

Laura nodded. "I'll get dressed."

He bundled the baby and his mother took her while Laura dressed and he went out to warm up the truck.

Five minutes later they were on the road to Greenspark. Normally Karen fell immediately asleep as soon as she was in the truck, but this time she wailed the whole distance.

"Nasty old ear infection," pronounced the P.A., "of the one in the a.m. variety."

Either from an immediate response to the shot of antibiotics or out of exhaustion, Karen fell asleep on the way home. As they stood over her in her crib at home, Laura started to cry. Reuben put his arms around her.

"It's okay," he said. "She's going to be fine."

"It's not," Laura sobbed. She pushed away from him. "You win."

He followed her to the bedroom, where she kicked off her sneakers and pulled off her jeans with jerky, furious motions.

"I win? What? The encyclopedias or the trip to Hawaii?"

"I can't go through with it. I'm not having the abortion, okay?"

"I win. I *win*. Laura, have the goddamn abortion so you can win. I don't want to win."

In her T-shirt and panties she stood in the middle of the room and stared at him, her eyes brimming. "What do you want?"

"I want you to be happy. I want you to love me."

She closed her eyes and tears flooded from under her lashes and her shoulders shook. What was he supposed to do? He held her. She let him. He took her to bed. And in the aftermath she remained in his arms. They had never before enjoyed a simultaneous orgasm.

As he held her it came to him if she'd gone through with aborting the baby he would have left. Not divorced her. That option he had long since given up, not because of some blinding illumination or conviction but from the day-to-day process of fatherhood. He had seen enough divorced fathers to know a man who left his marriage nearly always lost his children too. So that was out of the question. He'd have lived at the garage and supported her and the kids and tried to be a good daddy to them but never slept under the same roof with her again. Never troubled her for her favors again. They were hard thoughts that brought tears to his eyes. He didn't sleep for a long time, but when he did the old nightmares wracked him like a hurricane.

But in the morning it was like the calm after a big storm. The air was cleaner and sweet, and he thought maybe they had weathered the biggest crisis they ever would.

＊ ＊ ＊

Laura had her own way to find. Flirting with the mortal sin of abortion brought on tremendous guilt. After recovering from Sammy's difficult birth—worse in its way than Karen's—she began to attend Mass on a nearly daily basis. She became more active in Church organizations. She developed an interest in charismatic Catholicism and became a lay reader, a position only recently opened to women.

A woman with whom Laura worked invited her to attend a service at a Protestant church in Grant. Reuben wasn't sure why Laura accepted. Some sense of ecumenical noblesse oblige maybe. Whatever her motivation she went to that service with her friend from work. It wasn't an immediate conversion; she brooded awhile. And she kept going to the services, and suddenly she was reading the Bible before she went to bed. Soon she was no longer going to Mass but attending services regularly, several times a week, in Grant.

And taking the kids.

He hunkered down and waited for the inevitable shitstorm with the Haggertys to be over. Laura and her parents went at it hammer and tong in the centuries-old tradition of Christians and religionists the world over. In the end Laura went to her church and they went to theirs and they all prayed their knees raw for each other.

Rumor had come his way about Laura's new church, but he had no solid information. It seemed to espouse a hard-shell fundamentalist Protestantism unaffiliated with any of the mainstream fellowships. At the time there was a lot of that going around. The social revolutions of the free-wheeling sixties and seventies had thrown many folks into a panicky reversion to a hard-eyed, exclusive form of white man's salvation they called being born again. A lot of people—Laura among them—seemed to need to submit to the paternal authority of righteous, rigid men who knew all the answers, knew who would be saved and who cast into the flame.

He visited the priest in Greenspark, who listened patiently and told him he'd made a solemn promise to the Church, not to Laura, and he was obligated to keep it. The priest seemed to think what Reuben really needed was a further commitment to the Church, some good solid time on his own knees in the shadow of the stained glass to find the moral resources not only to get his kids to Mass but to bring Laura back to the Church. It wasn't particularly helpful since what Reuben most admired about the Catholic Church was it had given up using the rack and burning suspected heretics and witches. So he proposed a compromise: Laura could take the kids to daily services at her new church, and he or her parents would take them to Mass and CCD classes.

"They won't know whether they're coming or going," she snapped. "It's a stupid idea."

"To hell with it, then," he said. "I'm not going to ruin every Sunday with a fight over who's got the skinny on Jesus."

"Your profanity simply reveals the weakness of your position," Laura said.

"Thank you very much, Laura. As always, you're generous to a fault." Reuben headed for the nearest beer.

Jesus, he thought, sitting on the back stoop with a long-neck sweating in his hand. Religion. He'd planted stiff after stiff in the boneyard hard by Joe Nevers' house and expected to lay his own bones up there. All the praying in the world wasn't going to get him out of it. It was a nice peaceful place. He figured it was all there was of eternity. You got your heaven and your hell while you had the nervous system to feel them. Heaven was as easy as a cold beer on a summer day or as impossible as fucking Marilyn Monroe in the owner's box at Fenway as Yaz grand slams the Sox into a World Series title. He thought a long time about what hell was. Looking in the mirror and knowing you weren't up to the job. Being scared shitless. Meanness just to feel for a moment a little less powerless. No, he suddenly realized, hell was your kid in the lake with a hole between her eyes. He shuddered and sucked a long draft of cold beer past the sudden stricture in his throat.

XXIV

On the Dashboard of His Truck one Monday
morning was a tract about the evils of demon rum. And then he
was awash in poorly written and worse-printed pamphlets on
flimsy pink and green and blue paper, left on the dashboard or the
breakfast table or in whatever book he was reading. He made a
collage on the wall of the garage of the most outrageous ten-point
type bullshit about the Humanist Fellow-Traveling Red Race-
mixing Papist Jew Lesbo-Feminist Homosexual Conspiracy
Against the Word of God. Passersby decorated it with smiley-face
stickers he saved from junk mail offers and with graffiti of their
own inspiration.

"Do you believe this crap?" he asked Laura once.

She had the grace to blush. "I'm not a political person. But I accept the fact that the word of God is the source of all truth—"

"Jesus Christ," he muttered.

Her mouth tightened.

A few days later he stared stupidly into the refrigerator. For an
instant he wondered if he had drunk that six of Miller and forgotten about it, which raised a little flutter of panic in his stomach.
And then he was sure he hadn't—his memory of the previous night
was clear—a meeting at the firehouse and after, tinkering with a
balky starter in one of the pumpers. He had had a six-pack of
Miller chilling in the fridge and now it was gone. He didn't even
want a beer that badly. It was just a reflex.

When he went out to the shed, where he'd left the rest of the
case, he found it filled with emptied bottles waiting for redemption. He hadn't drunk the beer; somebody—not hard to guess
who—had emptied them. It pissed him off so much he went
straight out and bought two more cases.

When he returned Laura and his mother were in the kitchen.

He liberated a bottle from the carrier and shoved the rest of the six-pack into the refrigerator.

"Laura," he said, "keep your pious mitts off my beer."

His mother looked down her nose at Laura, I-told-you-so triumph all over her face.

Laura bowed her head and started praying.

Ten minutes later as Reuben was reading a bedtime story to Frankie and Karen, he heard the bottles being smashed outside. His mother scuttled down the hall and slammed her door shut. He finished the umpteeth reading of *Where the Wild Things Are*—Karen's favorite book—and tucked in the kids.

In the kitchen Laura was reading her Bible. The refrigerator was emptied of beer and so was the shed. When he stuck his head out the kitchen door the air was tingly with the smell of it. Reuben went out and cleaned up the broken glass and then drove back to the village and bought two more cases. The fellow who waited on him asked him if he was having a party.

"Yeah," Reuben said. "It's my unbirthday."

Laura didn't look up from her Bible as he tucked a six into the refrigerator.

He leaned over the table and flipped it closed. "Laura, quit pushing me."

She looked up at him. She got up to walk away, taking her Bible with her.

"Quit it, Laura," he repeated. "Just quit it."

He got no answer except her back as she walked away from him.

When he came home from work the following evening there was broken glass all over the yard. Lucille had a hangover from lapping up puddles of beer. He cleaned up the yard and switched to cans, though he disliked the undertaste of metal and plastic. He went out and bought a secondhand refrigerator and installed it in on the back porch, with a padlock on it.

His mother took one look at it and huffed. "Oh, that looks so rubbishy. Next you'll be leaving some old junker to rust to bits in the yard."

"Talk to Laura about it. She's the one won't have the beer in the house."

His mother didn't get anywhere with Laura either. Laura got up and left the room if he came into it. Then she found out he was letting Frankie and Karen keep sodas in his beer refrigerator.

"They asked," he said. "They get a charge out of locking and unlocking the padlock. I thought it was funny."

"It's not funny, it's encouraging them to defy me."

"How's that? Is Coca-Cola against your religion now?"

It was time to put supper on the table and she was slicing a pot roast. She threw it at him. He ducked. Lucille glommed onto it.

"You win," he said mockingly.

She threw the butcher knife and he caught it blade first. The cuts weren't bad, but the sight of blood did give her pause. He put the blade in the sink and then he took the rest of the roast away from Lucille before she could make herself sick with it.

"Let's go out to that pizza place in North Conway," he said.

Laura was staring at his bloody fingers as he bandaged them. She cleared her throat.

"All right," she said.

* * *

The minister came to call. Reuben heard the heavy engine of his Cadillac and then the ting of the bell line. He was alone, occupied with replacing a smashed door on an old T-bird with a salvaged one. Business was slow and Sixtus had grown chary of his old bones, preferring not to put them at risk by venturing out in this kind of nasty weather. Reuben got a glimpse of the Caddie that had swung past his pumps to park outside the office door.

He watched the man's approach. He knew who he was—had seen his picture in the newspaper. Of middling size, he was nonetheless well knit and had a surprisingly tough look about him. A full head of dark hair like a crow's pate and dark, sharp eyes. A thin mouth and a strong jawline. He had been, according to the newspaper, a wild youth who had served hard time for armed robbery. Got Jesus in the joint, as it was said. There was no sign of the prison yard about the man now—he looked like a very successful real estate developer, the kind who regarded screwing people out of money as his constitutional right, not to say duty. The American way. He didn't wear a dog collar—too papist. From outside he smiled reassuringly at Reuben and raised his hand in something between a wave and a salute. He stepped into the office with his hand already outthrust.

" 'Morning," he said. "I'm Reverend Smart."

A firm, measured grasp but his hand was soft. Fingernails manicured, Reuben noted. The minister kept on smiling, and Reuben thought the man's face must get tired, keeping that up all day.

"Your wife asked me to stop in and have a word with you."

"She did." He wasn't surprised somehow.

Smart nodded. "She's troubled."

"Really. Well," Reuben said, "sorry to hear it."

"For you," the minister said. "She fears for your immortal soul."

"Pardon me. My immortal soul, if I have one, is my business. My wife is welcome to attend to her own."

The minister's eyes raked Reuben. And his smile shrank to a bad taste in his mouth.

"You look like an honest man," Smart said. "In fact, you have the reputation of an honest man in trade. Can you say honestly that you are happy with your life?"

"Again, that's something I regard as my own business—"

"Not your wife's? With whom you share your life?"

"But not religion. If she wants to discuss how happy or unhappy either of us may be, she doesn't need to call in a third party. In other words, it's none of your business." He spoke his piece carefully and without visible anger.

"Your business. Your wife's business. My business. It's all God's business, my friend," Smart said, his smile deepening with joy and enthusiasm. "I was myself a troubled man for many years. I know how a sick heart lies to itself and hides itself from—"

"I don't believe in God—" Reuben said.

"And that is the source of your trouble," the minister concluded.

"You ever let anybody finish a sentence?" Reuben asked.

Startled, Smart laughed but color rose in his face. "God comes to those who open their hearts to him, my friend."

"Catholic priest told me the same thing once. He told me if I wanted to believe sooner or later God would give me faith."

"Even a liar can speak the truth—"

"No shit." Reuben was deliberately crude. "You know what it sounds like to me? Like once you've got yourself convinced, you tell yourself God gave you the gift of faith."

Smart's mouth tightened up again. "You must prepare the soil to receive the seed."

"I've got a living to make. You'll excuse me—"

"You've got an immortal soul to save—and the wonderful thing about saving your soul is in doing it you will save your life. It's all so simple once you truly hear the Word of God—"

Reuben indicated the door. "Good day to you."

For a moment Smart hesitated, as if on the verge of one more argument.

Then he nodded. "The Lord cares more for the lost one than the ninety-nine saved. You're in our prayers."

* * *

He fingered his mustache in the mirror over the lavatory basin.

"Baa," he said. "Baaa." The mustache did have a sheeplike quality. He grinned at himself and zipped up.

Smart was a smooth customer, all right. He didn't look like a right-wing racist asshole. He just peddled that crap to a bunch of scared people who wanted a simple answer that would make them feel justified if not actually safe.

Simple answers. Faith. Gotta have a friend in Jesus. Reuben's personal favorite preacher was Norman Greenbaum, cheerfully enthusing about "The Spirit in the Sky," with a beat you could dance to behind him.

He meditated upon it as he hefted the salvaged door into place on the side of the T-bird. He didn't know—which he guessed was a good place to start. Maybe it was a case of the stopped clock. People fumbling after a God that really did exist and so managed twice a day to be right about Him. Or It or Her or They. Or maybe it was faith itself that was the stopped clock, right twice a day the way even Alf Parks arguing with the old farts at the bullshit table might be right there had to be a second shooter on the grassy knoll. And still be dead wrong about what kind of conspiracy was involved or just as full of shit about how he could cure finger warts by tying a rag around the finger for a month and then walking widdershins around an apple tree under a full moon. A liar can still tell the truth. If there were a devil he probably used that line twice a day.

What if Laura and her minister and her fellow believers were right, not about everything but maybe about what was more important? He knew goddamn well he didn't know everything there was to know. Undoubtedly he believed as much bullshit as anyone else. He could be wrong. There might be some simple answer that made everything right, and he supposed it was possible Laura and her minister had stumbled on it.

* * *

The suit jacket strained across his back as he whipped the tie around his neck and knotted it. He'd gotten thicker while the dry cleaner was busy shrinking the suit. About time for a new one, but he hated to spend the money.

"Baaa," he advised the mirror. "Baaa."

He had been shoveling horseshit in the barn and Laura saddling Two to go riding when he'd caught her off guard, asking if he could attend a service with her and the kids. She had to think about it for a minute. Tail end of winter and cold enough to make breath visible.

As Two danced over the barn floor, she strangled the reins and gave him a disbelieving glance. "Okay. I'd better not smell liquor on your breath."

As if a knock was the first thing he did on a Sunday morning. He never. It was disheartening to think she had come to have such a low opinion of him. He brooded, wondering if she didn't see himself more accurately than he saw himself.

"Yes ma'am," he said. "I'll be sober and my nails'll be clean."

Come Sunday, having satisfied her with his respectable appearance, he was allowed to drive his family to her church. It was bigger than he had thought in merely passing by, and surprisingly crowded. Every surface was thickly varnished and the floors deep-carpeted in a purple color that made him think of the inside of a coffin. The atmosphere was thick with hothouse flowers, banks of lilies and stiff fans of gladioli.

The faces in the church were familiar—some of them were high school classmates, some folks with whom he'd done business or worked multiple-alarm fires. Good people. And remarkably like himself. They were working men, their families living from paycheck to paycheck on the back roads in modest houses they built themselves because that was the only way they could afford them. He was a little ashamed of himself—the way he'd dismissed them all out of hand. They might be misguided, but they were his neighbors. He had his hand shaken endlessly and was repeatedly hugged by both men and women welcoming him into the Lord's presence before the service. Reverend Smart was cordial but spared him effusiveness.

The subject of the sermon was repentance, and Smart was unapologetically fierce in his preachment. There was no mention of political matters. Reuben was surprised at the man's skill as a speaker—Smart was charismatic, all right. The congregation was rapt. Even as Reuben doubted, he was moved by the man's conviction and the response of the congregation. When the choir sang he was swept by the voices—he let it wash over him, admitting ruefully to himself he was ever vulnerable to music. He could imagine sitting in this church week after week just to ride the storm of those voices.

Laura left him in peace on the ride home, sensing perhaps his quiet meant something. But that evening when he came in from a meeting at the firehouse she was curled up on the sofa reading. She smiled up at him.

"I waited up for you," she said in a soft voice that dispelled all question as to why.

The following Sunday he had tended Two and changed for church when she came downstairs, ready to go. And damn if he didn't get laid on Sunday night again. When he thought about it in the quiet of the garage he roared with laughter until he had to wipe tears away. If he'd only known—all he had to do was go to church.

"Baaa," he teased himself. "Baaa baaa baaa."

Imagined himself slung over the preacher's shoulder like the lamb in the old Sunday school tintypes. And then it hit him. It was the simple answer. Stop the clock. Never mind God. To make Laura happy all he had to do was exactly what she wanted him to do. He stopped laughing about it and just shook his head.

Without saying anything to Laura but knowing she was sure to notice, he stopped drinking. And was surprised by the relief he felt when he didn't crave it. He didn't miss getting plastered. As summer came on he let himself have a beer or two and found he could stop with a couple of beers on a hot day or after a baseball game. He could have two or three beers when he had a bad night, but that was all. Two or three did the trick.

Every Sunday he sat by her side in her church. He listened to the sermons and thought about them, engaging in long mental arguments that settled nothing for him except that he did not believe. He simply did not believe. At the minister's emotional orgies, when Smart wept and beat his breast and fell to his knees, he managed to keep a straight face. He held his tongue when Smart spoke of demonic possession and exorcism. More troubling were the political passages—he had thought he would be able to sit through those as a cynical observer, but the reality made him sick. There was a furious subtext of blaming folks who were somehow different for everything that might be wrong. Smart meant that shit. No one in the congregation challenged him. Laura's expression as Smart was handing it down was the one the Madonna wore in that picture that hung on the wall of the priest's study in Greenspark where he had taken his instruction in the Catholic Church. In it the Archangel handed her a lily that represented the word of God. She looked pretty much like she was coming.

He stared at her hand clasped in his in his lap. He closed his eyes with a feeling of vertigo.

Baaa baaa baaa baaa. Sometimes lambs got saved, sometimes they got slaughtered.

* * *

She nudged him and he realized she was passing him a five-dollar bill as the collection basket approached. He thought she wanted him to put it in for her and so he did and then she put in another five-dollar bill, in an unsubtle hint he should be putting his own money into the basket.

That night he got into bed with her and kissed her, and she turned her face away.

"Your mustache tickles," she said. "I don't like it."

He touched it. "I'll take it off tomorrow."

She smiled at him and her hand moved over his bare chest. "And next Sunday you'll put your own money in the basket?"

He stared at her. "No, I won't."

Her hand stopped moving. "Why not?"

"I can't support what the Reverend Smart's peddling, that's why. If he stuck to the golden rule I might consider it, but a lot of that money you give him is going for political shit. And honestly, Laura, even if I did believe in it, why should I give money to a guy who lives better than I do? He's driving a frigging Cadillac."

Laura sat up. "You're just cheap—you always have been."

"For Christ's sake, Laura, business sucks this time of year. I don't have money enough to give some preacher to wipe his ass on—"

She moved too fast for him to duck and caught his ear with unerring accuracy. He cried out and she slapped him again, this time across the mouth.

"Get out of my bed," she said.

He got out slowly, one hand on his ear, the other checking his mouth. In the bathroom he swabbed his lip with a damp washrag. He had a headache that made him want to weep, and he thought he might throw up. He washed down some aspirin. When he picked up the wet rag to put it back on his lip, he noticed the basin was crusted with toothpaste. The tube was in its usual disgusting state. He used the rag to clean up the basin. Then he headed downstairs, stopping at the linen closet for a pillow and a couple of quilts. He made himself an ice pack and laid himself down on the sofa, though he doubted he was going to be able to sleep. There wasn't a beer in the house.

He rectified that little problem the next day. She didn't speak to him all week long. On Sunday he stayed in his horse-smelling, greasy work clothes and she took the kids to church without him. He didn't take off his mustache. The stopped clock was back to showing the wrong time.

XXV

Laura Had a Birthday they marked with dinner at Jean-Claude's in North Conway. She opened his gift, smiling painfully over the antique strand of pearls as if they'd come from the five-and-ten. She murmured they were lovely before closing the box and setting it aside. He reflected on how much time and money he had invested in that string of beads. Next time he guessed he'd ask her if she had something in mind she wanted.

When they were home again she dropped the box on her vanity in the bedroom and started to remove her earrings. He picked up the box, took out the pearls and circled her neck with them. Despite a sudden tremor in his fingers he managed to join the barrel clasp. She thrust out her chin and touched the pearls with the tips of her fingers, admiring the way they looked against her skin. He kissed the nape of her neck.

"Just because it's my birthday," she said, "don't think you're going to get laid."

He straightened up and squeezed her shoulders and tried to be light, but it didn't come out that way. "Why not? It's a cinch I won't get laid on *my* birthday."

Rage darkened her eyes. Her fingers tightened over the pearls and she yanked at them violently. The string exploded in a spray of creamy beads, one of which found his left eye with an unerring malevolence.

With an icepack on his eye, he looked in on her before he went back downstairs to sleep on the couch. She was on the bed crying. When he reached out to touch her she jerked away from him, turning her face to the wall and closing her eyes. The oversized T-shirt she wore for a nightgown was rucked up around her hips. He tugged the hem down a little and then made himself take his hands away.

He couldn't figure out what he'd done wrong this time.

* * *

Sixtus went suddenly, with congestive heart failure. It hit Reuben hard and he found himself struggling in the old black bag. The booze kept the bad dreams at bay too—he had them but if he woke up with his head pounding with a hangover he couldn't think about them. He rarely drank to the point of passing out— just enough to ease him into a few hours of sleep. He tried to be home first thing in the morning for the kids. There were more nights it might have been a relief to crawl in the bag that he stayed sober and sleepless because he was on call for wrecker, fire or rescue service.

Laura was working full-time at Willis' and volunteering as bookkeeper for her church. They could go weeks without exchanging much more than scheduling information. Outside of town functions they didn't have a social life together. When they went out, they took the children.

What time and energy the kids and work didn't consume he sank into playing one kind of ball or another according to the season or into the fire department, the rescue service and in doing the detail work of a small town's daily life. The town was his larger family, in which he was a valued son. There was always something needed doing. The old women vied to fill his plate, the old men to tell him stories of the old days and the old characters. They made of his children, brought their custom to his garage, told his mother how lucky she was in her son.

He counted his blessings. Healthy kids. Three squares on the table and a roof over their heads. If there was a God, he was living in God's country. He was a grown-up now and he knew most marriages were a long shot from the twaddle in the movies and on TV. They weren't romances but partnerships, and sometimes people got along and sometimes they didn't. You didn't always get what you wanted, went the gospel according to the Stones. But sometimes you got what you needed.

And sometimes you didn't get that either. He courted Laura, asked politely, did everything but beg, and once or twice he did that when he was drunk enough. He never could figure out what would bring her to yield but she did, occasionally—often enough to encourage him to try again. Sometimes she evidenced some response to him and he would stay the night. Waking with her in the bed that was supposed to be theirs but was really hers, he would experience a sudden violent jolt of adrenal panic at the strange sensation he was in the wrong place with the wrong person and an angry husband was imminent.

If once in a while he succeeded in arousing her enough for her to make some kind of effort for an orgasm, mostly she just tolerated him. Invariably she got down on her knees afterward and prayed. It came to him at last she was submitting to him because her religion required it. She was offering her subjugation up to her God as a sacrifice. Submitting to him. He was revolted. But need drove him to her until at last he began to have trouble staying hard and then getting it up at all.

He listened to other men grouse about the coldness of their wives and speculated if he could be a fly on the wall in their houses, he might find out he and Laura weren't so different from everybody else. You were yoked and you had to pull together, but you didn't need to have a conversation to do it. It was your life. You lived it.

* * *

The last time he ever made love to her they were getting ready to attend Joyce's second wedding.

He finished shaving and went into the bedroom to dress. Laura was in her slip doing her makeup. The pearls he'd had restrung were on her vanity. With her eyes following him in the mirror he picked them up and put them around her neck and fastened them. She stiffened when he kissed the nape of her neck. He picked her up and took her to the bed and she did not resist. She let him caress her, though she turned her face from his kiss, and she let him insert her diaphragm and climb on top of her. Shortly he sensed her growing impatience, which immediately made him soften so he had to stop and wait, trying not to lose his erection. When he sought her mouth to kiss her, she turned her face away.

"For God's sake, hurry up," she hissed.

For a moment he didn't know what to do. Then he pulled out and rolled over on his back. Closing his eyes, he took his cock in hand and stroked it hard again.

Laura rolled off the bed and went into the bathroom. When she emerged he was still doing it.

"That's disgusting."

He spasmed into his fist.

She turned away to the closet, dragging her dress from its hanger savagely.

"Thank you, Laura," he said when he caught his breath. "That was unforgettable."

"You'd better get dressed," she said. "We're going to be late."

"This is Joyce getting married for the second time, Laura, not Prince Charles and Princess Di. Maybe sometime you'd tell me what the hell I'm doing wrong."

"Playing with yourself in front of me for starters," she said. "You're an animal."

He looked at the ceiling. He should do something about that longitudinal crack in the plaster, he thought, before the whole damn thing comes falling down.

"We're all animals, Laura."

"We have souls. We don't have to give in to animal instincts."

"Bullshit. There's nothing incompatible with having animal instincts and having a soul. That's like saying an automobile isn't an automobile anymore if it has a radio in it."

"I'm not going to argue with you—the universe is not a garage, thank God."

"That clears everything up, Laura. Tell me, what do you do?"

She zipped her dress at the side and dropped her heels to the floor in front of her. "What are you talking about?"

"Do you masturbate? Do you count getting off while you're riding as masturbation or lucky accident or what?"

Her cheekbones, he noted with some satisfaction, reddened instantly.

"Shut up," she said tightly, "shut your filthy mouth right now."

Unlike Joyce's first wedding this one was a very big deal—six bridesmaids in costume and the groom and best man in tuxes. The bride did not wear white or a full rigging of gown and veil. To make up for this inexplicable lapse in bad taste Joyce and her attendants wore extremely short black satin dresses that on first glance looked like slips. They wore black stockings, not panty hose, and their garters were visible when they sashayed down the aisle. They looked as if they were doing a spread for *Playboy*.

At the reception at a high-priced inn in Greenspark he dumped Laura at the coat rack and headed for the bar, thinking it was a goddamn shame Sonny wasn't there to booze with. He went straight for the hard stuff that he almost never drank. A stinging drop of the widow's poison, he advised himself, would be a great thing to go numb on. A few times he glimpsed Laura but kept the room between them. When she worked her way through the mob around the bar once and touched his arm, he brushed her hand off and walked away from her. He looked women over with red-eyed hunger and drank the bar-brand bourbon as if it were iced tea on a sweltering summer day.

By the time the band, which sucked, took a pause for the cause and somebody shoved a tape into the P.A. system, he was feeling very little pain. He had a dance with Joyce to Paul Simon's "Loves Me Like a Rock."

Later he came out of the men's room and met Joyce coming out of the ladies' and they wound up in the coatroom kissing each other in a loopy slow-motioned wet-mouthed way. He pulled down the front of her dress and he was so drunk he thought it was like seeing her tits under water again. He slid a hand up under her skirt and was amazed to discover no panties. He was fumbling with his zipper with one hand while she posted slick and juicy on three fingers of his other hand when Terry Haggerty pulled them apart.

"Jesus Christ," his brother-in-law said. "Jesus Christ, Joyce. Get yourself straightened up. You want your husband to catch you in here with this asshole? You whore, you just got married."

Terry shoved Reuben out an emergency exit and down some steps, where he jerked his knee into Reuben's crotch. Reuben folded up and fell into a snowbank. He rolled over and threw up on his shoes.

"You stupid drunken fuck," Laura's brother snarled at him, "what the fuck are you doing?"

"What's going on?" Laura called from the door.

"Reuben's shitfaced," Terry told her. "I'm taking him home. You go home with Mom and Dad." He bent over Reuben. "Gimme the keys to the truck, asshole."

Terry shoved him back into the snowbank, scooped up a hand-ful of snow and washed his face with it. Then he hauled back a fist and smashed it into Reuben's numbed face.

The next thing Reuben knew Terry was groping in his pants pockets for his keys. He couldn't get Reuben into the truck by himself, but Frank came out of the hall with a couple of other guys and they muscled him into the cab.

"Oughta strap the drunk son of a bitch to the hood like a deer," Terry said.

"What'd you hit him for?" Frank asked.

"Shithead was trying to screw Joyce in the coatroom. That slut was lettin' him too."

Frank reached into the cab, got a hank of Reuben's hair and lifted his head up high enough to drive his fist into Reuben's mouth.

"That felt good," Frank said. "I expect you're not feeling much of it just now, but it'll still have some flavor to it tomorrow and if you want some more, lemme know." He turned to Terry. "Want me to go with you?"

Terry shook his head.

Once his brother-in-law was behind the wheel, Reuben told him he didn't want to go home. He wanted to go to the garage.

"Fine," Terry said. "If you can't make it inside I'll just leave you by the pumps and maybe you'll die of exposure and good riddance. I suppose it's something in your favor you don't want your mother to see you like this."

"Not Ma," Reuben said, "Frankie. The kids."

Terry laughed. "You think he doesn't know what you're doing when you stay at the garage overnight? I heard him telling Karen just the other day not to be a pest on account of you had a hangover. Kids don't miss anything, you know."

Terry speeded up to take a pothole as roughly as possible, and Reuben moaned with the impact.

"Joyce fucking Sharrard, for Christ's sake," Terry said, "she's supposed to be Laura's friend. Thinks she's hot shit now on account of she's married somebody pisses indoors and everybody's gonna forget she used to be married to Sonny Lunt. You were screwing her back then, weren't you? What, was she throwing you a little fuck for auld lang syne?"

Reuben stopped trying to follow him. It was all pretty much the same idea anyway. Terry was disappointed when he made it into the garage on his own steam. But despite his earlier sentiment Terry was kind enough to build a fire in the stove before he left.

* * *

He believed he was dreaming. Laura was there and the children with her. Frankie. Karen. Sammy with his hand in Laura's. He saw them blurrily as if they were underwater.

Frankie's eyes were downcast. Laura jerked at Frankie's arm.

"Look at him," Laura said. "Look at your father."

Frankie shook loose of her and turned his back. Karen spun suddenly and ran out, the sound of her sneakers rubbery on the cement.

Sammy yanked his hand free of Laura's and ran to him. He crouched down and stared into Reuben's face, and then his fingers trailed softly over the prickle of his beard.

Reuben closed his eyes and everything spun around again and he fell through the hole in the world.

* * *

His eyes were slits in a face that appeared to be turning into an eggplant. He drew back from trying to peer into the mirror over the lavatory basin and stooped to splash a little cold water over his face and head.

It was Sunday, the garage closed. The day was mostly gone before the world began to coalesce for him again. In purgatorial misery he struggled to clean himself up. He discarded his ruined suit for coveralls. Then he had to mop up the vomit in the back room. He couldn't go home yet. He wasn't sure he could go home at all. He wanted to burn his suit—his wedding suit—but it would stink in the stove even worse than it did in the trash. Good riddance to the frigging thing anyway; he could buy a new one, he reflected bleakly, for divorce court. He made himself tea and sat hunched over it by the stove. There was no ducking it. He might as well go home and find out if Laura was going to fire him.

His mother barely looked at him when he came through the back door. Karen was in Sammy's high chair and his mother was circling it, frowning, with her hair-cutting scissors in one hand. Karen's hair was shockingly ragged, as if someone had gone at it with hedge trimmers.

"She decided to cut it herself," his mother said, "with nail scissors."

Karen raised a gap-toothed grin. "Nana's gonna make it all even."

"I'm going to try," his mother said with a grimace.

"Where's Laura?" he asked.

His mother gestured mutely toward the upstairs.

Frankie and Sammy were in Frankie's room, on the floor with baseball cards fanned out all around them.

"Hi," he said.

Frankie glanced up and then right down again. Sammy jumped up and came running for a hug.

"You still loaded?" Frankie asked, his strict attention on his baseball cards.

"No."

Another quick appraising glance. "You look like shit."

"I feel like it."

Sammy squeezed his hand.

"Well, you're in the doghouse with Mom," Frankie told him flatly.

He tried the door to his and Laura's room, but it was locked.

"Laura," he said.

Silence.

He went back downstairs and collapsed on the sofa. Seeing them made him realize it wasn't a dream about Laura and the kids. She really had brought them to the garage. Jesus. It was unbelievable. She had gotten them out of bed and made them dress and dragged them down to the garage so they could see he was stinking drunk. Why? He was already ashamed of himself. It was some kind of payback, he guessed. But Jesus. The kids. She ought to have kept them out of it. And then the shame deepened and crested—it all came back to him. He was the one puking in the back room.

He stayed there on the sofa with his eyes closed while they all came down to supper. He listened to them at the table, nothing but Laura giving thanks, a chorus of Amens and then polite requests for the condiments. And then they all went upstairs again, his mother last and slowly.

He spent the night there and after he'd taken care of Two in the morning, he knocked on the bedroom door. Laura was dressing.

"I'm not talking to you," she said before he could open his mouth.

It wasn't an outright dismissal. Maybe she hadn't made up her mind yet.

He stood there a moment staring at her as she perfected her makeup in the mirror of her vanity. She was as beautiful as she had been when they were teenagers and he loved her from afar. He still loved her, he still wanted her to love him. He had hurt her as much as she had hurt him.

He didn't know what to do. It was like swimming in a fog, searching for the shoreline, and not being able to tell where the water stopped and the land began. His throat was rigid as if he had been screaming for her to tell him where the shoreline was but there was never any answer. He could feel her slipping through his hands like the water and the mist. But if he had not been able to discover how to make her happy, he had made promises and vows and he would keep them as best he could so he could look himself in the mirror. Maybe someday she would notice. Quietly he closed the door between them.

* * *

"Goddamn," Sonny breathed reverentially when he stopped at the garage the following Friday evening, "I heard Frank and Terry cleaned your clock for you. You look like it was Ali cleaned your clock."

"It felt like Ali," Reuben said.

Sonny laughed and there was an edge in it, a nasty one he couldn't quite hide. Like he was glad somebody had cleaned Reuben's clock for the offense. "Did my heart good to think Joyce was willing to put horns on that jerk the day she married him. I give it three years and she'll take him for all he's worth."

Given the eagerness with which most people dish dirt on an ex-spouse, Reuben wasn't surprised Sonny knew about Joyce and the reception or that he found it hilarious.

"Do me a favor, Sonny, just drop it."

Sonny couldn't; it was too much fun. "Heard you were some fucked up. Hey, it's okay with me. She's been hot for you for years. Wonder you never tried it on before. Or maybe you did. You wouldn't be the first. Did it myself not six weeks ago. I ran into her having a drink after work. She tells me she's getting married again and we went right out in the parking lot and screwed each other silly. Cheered me up, I'll tell you."

"I'm not feeling very cheerful about any of it. What about Annie? You've been with her a couple years now. I thought it was serious."

Sonny made the effort to be mildly embarrassed. "Yeah, well, Annie doesn't know about it, she'd be wild if she did. You think I'm a jerk, I know. I really do care about Annie. It's just Joyce and I were together a long time."

"Hand me that torque wrench, will you? I'm hardly qualified to judge anybody, am I? For what it's worth, I never have screwed Joyce. Just come close in the cloakroom, that's all."

"She didn't have any pants on, did she?"

"Sonny, I was drunk out of my mind."

"Sure, sure. Ol' hoss, why do you stay with Laura? I mean, I know when two people are unhappy together, I seen enough of it. You two are miserable. Everybody knows she's thrown you out of your own bed and you sleep here most of the time. Why the fuck don't you cut loose from the bitch?"

"I got three kids—not that it's any of your nevermind."

"You think your kids don't know exactly how it is between you two? I ain't forgot myself what it was like when my folks'd be screaming at each other in the middle of the night when Dad came in stinking drunk with some tart's drawers around his neck. Yeah, he always ran around on Ma. When he was fifty he fell in love with one of his whores and started talking about leaving Ma for her. Never got around to doing it, did he? I'm telling you kids know when their mom and dad are bitched up. It just ties 'em up in knots. They'd be better off you split up and they didn't have to live with the fights and the tension."

"I'm not sure they'd think so if you asked'm and anyway, it's not going to happen."

Sonny opened another beer. "Wish I'd been at the wedding. Joyce says ol' baldy likes her to go around with no pants on; it gets him hot. I figure he's asking for it, he's one of them guys gets off watching other guys bang his wife, probably can't do it himself. Shit, I bet he told her to do it, they probably set it up between them."

"Jesus, you got a dirty mind."

"Shit no, I lived with her, remember? The last year we was married, we did a shitload of swapping." Sonny looked a little uncomfortable. "I figured you musta heard something about it."

Reuben had, the way he heard most things sooner or later, but he hadn't thought it was any of his business.

"She always wanted to get together with you and Laura, but I told her nothing doing, I wasn't risking my nuts between ol' Ironpants' thighs. No offense, you know Laura and me's like cats and dogs."

"Go away, Sonny. You're stepping on your own tongue."

"Ouch," Sonny said. "Makes me think of the time you threatened to jam Charlie's dick in the drawer. Guess I better split while you're still in a good mood."

XXVI

"I Don't Give a Shit," Terry said, "whether you've found Jesus or not—I'd like to be allowed to eat an occasional meal with my parents without you shoving religion down my throat."

"Terry!" his mother exclaimed. "Your language!"

At which point Terry's wife, Tricia, informed Maureen Terry was a grown man who risked his life every day as a cop, and if he wanted to say shit in his own house he could. And she was also sick of Laura's constant implications that everyone who didn't go to Laura's church was going straight to hell. Frank tried futilely to calm everyone down.

Reuben picked up his beer, left Easter dinner cooling on the table and turned on the tube to drown out the sectarian shouting with a football game. In seconds his kids were sheltering with him, Sammy sticking his fingers in his ears, Frankie and Karen rolling their eyes in disgust at the whooping and hollering.

On the way home from her brother's, Laura upbraided him for not coming to her defense.

"Since you bring it up and in front of the kids, why should I? I think you're damned rude about it, if you want to know the truth," Reuben said.

From the backseat of the T-bird Karen's giggle was cut short by Frankie's elbow in her ribs. A glance in the mirror revealed Frankie staring carefully out the window, Karen glaring at her brother and Sammy paging through a comic book with great intensity.

"May God forgive you for your unbelief," Laura said, closing her eyes and bending her head to pray.

"Right. I got a better chance of God's forgiveness than yours," he muttered.

Her lips moved in prayer. Reuben said a prayer of thanks himself that she'd belted up for a while. His ears had started to hurt every time she opened her mouth and the word "God" fell out.

* * *

Sundays kept coming around and on one of them shortly thereafter, he was wakened by Sammy's hand resting on his chest. He was on the sofa and he could barely open his eyes. The stench of piss cut through the fog of headache and nausea. He sat up and rubbed his face and got his eyes all the way open. The kid was standing there barefoot, his pajama pants hanging wetly around his sturdy legs.

"Jesus, Sammy," he muttered. "Again?"

He took him upstairs and showered with him and then changed the pissy sheets. Sammy went out with him and helped him tend Two. On the way back from the barn he was surprised by the sudden scrabble of Sammy's hand at his.

"Daddy," Sammy said, "Chu-chu-church is scary. Duh-duh-do I have to guh-guh-go?"

Reuben stopped himself saying of course not. "Why is it scary?"

Sammy stared up at him. His face was pale with strain and he sucked spit frantically and nearly strangled on what he had to say. "Th-th-the shh-shouting. The-th-the Re-re-reveren's angry at me fo-fo-fo puh-puh-pissing the buh-buh-bed."

Reuben grabbed him by the shoulders and hugged him. "Oh honey, I don't think so."

Blinking, he took Reuben's hand again. "You cuh-cuh-come with us, Daddy."

Reuben didn't reply immediately. His first impulse was to tell Laura the children wouldn't be going to church with her anymore. Remembering the extreme boredom of his own hours as a small boy parked in a pew, he had supposed it to be largely harmless. But it was obviously upsetting Sammy. He couldn't ignore Sammy's distress even if there'd be hell to pay.

Laura's face pinked under her blusher when he came downstairs in his good suit. "What are you all dressed up for?"

"Church," he said.

Sammy grinned from his chair at the kitchen table.

She couldn't say anything, could she? But she was nervous as a cat underfoot.

Reuben's reception this time was markedly cooler. He had the sensation of being watched by unfriendly eyes.

The preacher took the pulpit. Turning anthracite bright eyes on Reuben, he began without pause, " 'What man of you, having a hundred sheep, if he lose one of them, doth not leave the ninety and nine in the wilderness, and go after that which is lost, until he find it? And when he hath found it, he layeth it on his shoulders, rejoicing.' We welcome our brother on his return."

He smiled incandescently as the congregation murmured its approval. "The wilderness"—a contemplative expression shadowed the preacher's face and then he threw open his palms—"surrounds us—the ninety and nine. Any one of us is susceptible, any one of us may stray and become the one that is lost." A mournful hush filled the church. "Yet the Master will always come searching for us."

The observation evoked an immediate susurration of relief.

The preacher looked them over for a long moment, gaze pausing on this individual or that, and then he came back to Reuben. "We love the Master, we love the Good Shepherd's gentle hands that lift us to His shoulders to transport us back to our brothers and sisters."

"Yes!" cried a woman to Reuben's right, and a murmur of agreement swept through the congregation.

The preacher turned a soft smile upon the woman.

"Yes," he said. "Yes." And then his face darkened. "But the Master is also strong. He defends his flock against the depredations of the wilderness, against the wolf and the hyena and the thief." The preacher opened the Bible on the pulpit in front of him. He flipped ribbon markers and then he took a breath and read. " '. . . *There met him out of the tombs a man with an unclean spirit. Who had his dwelling among the tombs; and no man could bind him, no, not with chains; Because that he had been often bound with fetters and chains, and the chains had been plucked asunder by him, and the fetters broke in pieces; neither could any man tame him. And always, night and day, he was in the mountains, and in the tombs, crying, and cutting himself with stones. But when he saw Jesus afar off, he ran and worshiped him, And cried out with a loud voice, and said, What have I to do with thee, Jesus, thou Son of the most high God? I adjure thee by God, that thou torment me not.'* "

The preacher paused and the silence was tense with anticipation.

" 'Unclean,' " he said softly. "This man lived like an animal, naked and dirty, in the wilderness. He lurked in the graveyard. He had lost his sanity and his soul, and he was possessed by unclean spirits. Demons. Can you imagine this man's pain? He was living in hell! But his Master came seeking for him. '*For he said unto him, Come out of the man, thou unclean spirit.*' " Smart's voice was calm and commanding and he stared at Reuben. " '*And he asked him, What is thy name?* And he answered, saying, *My name is Legion, for we are many.*' The demons possessing this man heard and recognized the Master's voice and spoke out of the wretched man's mouth because they had no choice. They had to bow to the authority of the Master. It is ironic that the very demons of hell must bow to the Master's authority, and yet we, weak and mortal creatures, are free to defy Him."

Sammy was rigid, his hand sweaty in Reuben's. The congregation hung upon the preacher's next words, and Reuben himself was affected. It was fierce, powerful stuff.

"The demons knew they were beaten. They asked to be cast into the two thousand swine feeding nearby." He launched again into quotation. " '*And forthwith Jesus gave them leave.*' " He shook his head in wonder. " '. . . *Jesus gave them leave. And the unclean spirits went out, and entered into the swine, and the herd ran violently down a steep place into the sea . . . and were choked in the sea.*' And we are told, '. . . *him that was possessed with the devil, and had the legion,*' was seen '. . . *sitting, and clothed, and in his right mind.*' "

The congregation chorused amens and thanks-bes, and the preacher took a sip of water and wiped his brow.

"We all live in the wilderness. The demons assault us all. They name themselves rock 'n' roll music and the movies and TV and comic books, they name themselves pleasure and tell us we have earned them, we deserve them, they are but small indulgences that do us no harm. And so we take that beer and the demon of drunkenness enters into us and gives us its name. And we listen to that music or we let our children, our precious, pure children, listen to that music that corrupts them, exciting in them as it does in us the sexual urges consecrated only to our marriage beds. And the demon enters into us and gives us its name. And we go to the drive-in and watch those movies and commit in our hearts acts of adultery and self-abuse and uncleanness of all kinds, and our minds are clouded with the conviction that everyone commits these sins of carnality, they are of no import and little damage and the demon enters into us and gives us its name. And filth comes out of our mouths and we live in filth like that wretched, unclean man who cut himself with stones. We cut ourselves with our sins, unknowingly trying to cut the demons out of our sick souls. The strength of our demons is so strong that when our loving families and neighbors attempt to restrain our madness, we break those fetters of love and commitment and citizenship and run raving through the cemeteries and the wilderness."

The congregation sighed and there was sobbing and murmured amens.

"Reuben," he said.

A stir moved the worshipers and Reuben straightened in his pew as Smart's gaze came to rest on him once again.

"Are you ready to ask what the Lord Jesus Christ . . . has to *do* with *you?*" The question was put quietly, but the tension in the church racheted higher. "Is that why you have come here today? To give up the wilderness once and for all?" The preacher left the pulpit as if in a trance and came down the aisle with measured tread to stand directly before Reuben. He pointed his finger at him. "Are you ready to ask your Master to cast out your demons and make you clean?"

Reuben, shaken by the direct confrontation, began to rise. Sammy clung to his leg.

"Answer me!" the preacher suddenly roared. "In the name of your Lord Jesus, tell me your name? Is it Legion? Is your name Legion? Is your name Drunkenness? Adultery? Profanity? Unbelief?"

On his feet under the verbal assault Reuben was wrenched with the anger that once burned against his father. Sammy shook against him and Karen moaned softly. Frankie's face was totally white. Reuben stroked Sammy's hair and held his head against his chest.

"You're scaring the shit out of my kids," he said to the preacher.

His words carried calm and clear through the church.

"I mean to," Smart replied with equal calm. "I mean to scare the very devil out of them."

"They haven't got any devils in them," Reuben said angrily. "Nor have I."

Smart's gaze fell upon Sammy.

"Don't you dare," Reuben said through gritted teeth. "Don't you say another word."

Smart whirled about and strode to the front of the congregation.

" *'Give not,' "* he cried out, " *'that which is holy unto the dogs, neither cast ye your pearls before swine, lest they trample them under their feet, and turn again and rend you.' "*

Frankie and Karen pressed closer to Reuben. He picked up Sammy and smiled at each of his children reassuringly.

"I can quote the Bible too," Reuben said. " 'Beware of false prophets.' "

"Shame!" cried several worshipers, and outbursts of anger and outrage from all over.

" 'Know them by their fruits,' " Reuben continued, and the congregation roared like a wounded beast. " 'A corrupt tree bringeth forth evil fruit.' "

"Stop it," Laura hissed.

The preacher flung back his head. "See how bold he is! The devil comes right into our midst to dispute with us!"

"Baaa," Reuben muttered as he led Sammy out of the church. Karen and Frankie followed on his heels.

"Let us pray!" Smart cried out.

The congregation fell immediately into loud responsory prayer with the preacher.

Reuben noted at least some had the grace to lower their eyes as he passed.

They waited in the car for Laura. She did not emerge until the service was over.

"Have a good time?" he asked.

She gave him a murderous look and faced straight ahead in stony fury as they headed home. Eric Burdon was in mourning; he'd gotten the word there was "No more Elmore James." Laura reached over and turned off the radio. No more Elmore James, Reuben thought, no more Eric Burdon either.

" *'This train don't carry no gamblers, hoochie-cooch dancers or midnight ramblers,' "* he mocked.

Frankie whispered something to Karen and then began to imitate the preacher's voice.

"Rock anda roll is a Satanist Com-a-nist conspiracy," Frankie intoned, "ekaciting the seckshal urges of our young people to sin and per-version—"

Karen and Sam giggled nervously.

Twisting in her seat, Laura reached over the back to strike him, and Reuben seized her wrist. The children fell silent.

She fumed the rest of the way home. Getting out of the car, she struck Frankie on the back of the head with the flat of her hand and started pummeling him with her handbag. Reuben wrapped his arms around her from behind and lifted her right off her feet. He told the kids to go into the house, but they hung back for a moment and then Frankie evidently had enough and hustled his brother and sister into the house.

Laura fought furiously, hitting Reuben with her handbag until she unbalanced into an icy remnant of snowbank. Where she burst into tears. Reuben gave her his handkerchief. She struggled to her feet, slipped on the ice and sat back down again hard in the snowbank.

He helped her up again. "Don't whack the kids around, Laura. It makes them feel like shit. It scares Sammy."

"Frankie had it coming," she said. "You encouraged him to mock me."

"Not you, Laura—he was getting his own back at your preacher."

Her lips tightened and she hugged herself defensively. "You've no right to tell me what to do. Their moral welfare is my business."

"Tell me what's moral about striking children."

"You're a fine one to lecture me on morality."

"Just keep your hands off the kids and leave'm at home. You've had it your way long enough."

"You can't stop me taking them to my church."

"If they go, I go, and I'll stand up and answer every lie and piece of bullshit that falls out of that sanctimonious prick's mouth."

She blinked. It was like watching the blur of the flashcard images in the windows of a slot machine and waiting for the cherries to come up.

"You can't do that. You'll be barred from entering."

"I guess we'll find out."

"I won't forget this."

"You never do."

She stomped into the house and locked herself up in the bedroom while he saw the children to bed.

* * *

Laura went alone the next time she went to church. She prayed over the children every night when she came home from evening services. Then the church books began to keep her after services and took her out of the house on Saturday afternoon as well. Taking up the slack, Reuben tried to be home for meals and bedtimes. He resumed dropping the kids at the Haggertys' to go to Mass in Greenspark.

One Sunday morning he found his father-in-law sitting at the kitchen table in his suit and tie, staring into cold coffee. "Laura come by earlier and took Maureen with her. I don't understand it. All Maureen said was she could see Laura had found something important and she wanted to know what it was. I don't understand," Frank repeated. "No offense to you, son, or anybody else in this town who's Protestant—"

"I'm not even that," Reuben said, "I'm a heathen—"

His father-in-law went on doggedly, ignoring Reuben's mild joke, "—but my great-grandmother and three of her children starved to death because they wouldn't give up the faith for a handful of half-frozen rotten spuds. I've never thought of myself as a real devout Catholic, but I don't understand how Maureen can do it. Now she says the Church went astray in the sixties, but you know that ex-con ain't saying the Latin Mass over there, so what's she mean?"

Increasingly Laura and her mother lived their lives around their church. Frank retired at about that time and had far too much time to fight with Maureen about religion. Any attempt at a family gathering invariably broke down in a raging argument. Laura's brother and sisters and their respective spouses began to find excuses to do no more than drop off the birthday or anniversary acknowledgments and to find it was necessary to spend the holidays with the in-laws or at home.

When once she would have helped prepare it Laura now gave only a cursory reading to their income tax returns. Reuben never expected her to have a day-to-day interest in the business, but in earlier years at least she had stayed aware of the broader picture. Remembering how ill informed his father had kept his mother as regards the family finances, he wanted Laura to be as informed as she could be in the event of his sudden death. But it had become more and more of a chore to interest her in the nitty-gritty. When Frankie began to ask questions about how it all worked, it came as a relief. Since a toddler Frankie had loved wheels and motors, and now he asked after the business end with relentless curiosity. Reuben was pleased; Frankie was only a little younger than he had been when he started to learn his trade, and the signals were excellent that the sign that read Reuben Styles & Sons, Props. would one day be a reality instead of a hopeful announcement.

Then came Laura's sudden demand, one evening at the supper table, that they tithe his income as well as hers to her church.

"Are you shitting me?"

"You don't have to be vulgar. It's only money. It's the least you can do to save your immortal soul—"

"I'd like to save my mortal ass from a stretch in Leavenworth for nonpayment of taxes, if you don't mind."

He was struggling to survive a purge of independents by the distributor. It wasn't as if she'd put anything into the business, which produced most of the income, or into the property he shared with his mother, which brought in the rest. She kept all her own income—had for years—and did what she wanted with it. She'd been tithing that from the time she joined her church. He had heard stories about people in her church working three jobs to increase their tithes.

"The church does more than save souls, it feeds the hungry and—"

"And keeps the preacher in Cadillacs," Reuben interjected. He came to his feet and threw down his dinner napkin. "Are you out of your god-fuddled mind?"

Laura rose to her feet too. "I'm legally entitled to half of your income, and I can spend it on what I want!"

"Stop it!" Karen shrieked. "Just stop it!"

Knocking over her chair, Karen jumped up and ran from the room. Suddenly the table was abandoned: Reuben's mother, muttering, rose slowly against her knuckles and headed for the kitchen. Frankie shoved back his chair and stalked out. Only Sammy remained, staring at his plate while Reuben and Laura glared at each other over the meatloaf.

"You suh-suh-suck," Sammy said.

His eyes were squeezed shut to dam tears that leaked out anyway, slicking his face. His upper lip was smeared with snot. His fists were clenched on his plate, and mashed potato squeezed through his knuckled fingers as he dug his nails into his palms. Then his fists drove down onto the plate and it exploded into fragments.

There followed a week in which Sammy refused to come to the table and took his meals sitting in the bathtub with Lucille for company. He was mute even in school—the teacher stopped at the garage to talk to Reuben about it—and his sheets were soaked every night.

One night, watching Laura praying over her plate, Reuben abruptly picked up his and joined Sammy in the bathroom. Frankie followed and then Karen, rolling her eyes at the faint aroma of piss that was constant on Sammy, no matter how often he bathed. They sat there cross-legged on the floor with their plates on their knees, solemnly forking down salad, while Karen struggled not to giggle.

"Oh poop," she said finally and flicked a cucumber slice at Frankie.

He tossed her a cherry tomato and she caught it in her mouth.

They started bombing each other with vegetables. Sammy and Reuben grinned at each other and joined in. Reuben had a feeling there was a toothpaste war in the offing.

XXVII

It Started in the Usual Way with Sammy jumping from behind the shower curtain with a tube of Crest clutched in one hand and a berserker gleam in his eyes.

"Puh-perpare to duh-die!" he shrieked.

The object was to get as much of the stuff in each other's hair as possible. It allowed for an enormous expenditure of energy—running around the house, upstairs and down, vaulting over furniture, whooping and screaming and ambushing each other. Sometimes they got toothpaste on a ceiling or a light fixture; pastel smears and dried worms of it turned up even after the most thorough clean-up. Karen usually greeted these outbreaks with a scornful declaration that they were all too childish for words and then would come bursting out of a closet fully armed to ambush Frankie or Sammy or Reuben. Occasionally one of them took some toothpaste in an eye or incurred minor bruises or scrapes. This time Karen gave herself a floor burn skidding down the hall after Frankie.

When she called *Medic!*, Reuben threw her over his shoulder in a fireman's carry to be taken behind the lines for first aid. He plumped her giggling onto her bed and examined the minor abrasion on her shin. Then he kissed it, which made her giggle harder.

"Daddy! That's gross. You'll get germs in it."

The admonition inspired him to lick the scrape lavishly while she squirmed and squealed.

"Now you'll need rabies shots," he advised.

Karen giggled yet more. She was an inexhaustible giggler. Got it from her mother, he thought, recalling the giggling creatures that had made up *laurajoycejaniceheidibobbi*.

He went to the bathroom to look for a disinfectant. Rummaging through a drawer, he hesitated over an old tube of spermicidal jelly, the lubricant for Laura's diaphragm—it would be soothing at least. It seemed to him, though, that the last time he had used it to prepare the device the tube had been three quarters full. Now it was all but empty and looked as if the dog had had a gnaw on it. Laura was still hell on anything that came in a tube— toothpaste, glue, whatever. Maybe she had used it as a weapon in a spermicidal lubricant war.

Distracted, he stirred the litter in the drawer idly, congratulating himself at having resolved their differences over toothpaste. He had his own tube of toothpaste—neatly rolled from the bottom and cleanly capped—and she had hers that she maimed and mutilated and left drooling on the counter.

Something caught his eye. Slowly he nudged another, brand-new tube of the lubricant from behind the plastic clamshell that contained her diaphragm. And nothing seemed to shift inside the box. He knew by its weightlessness it was empty before he opened it. And he remembered abruptly Sonny Lunt mentioning in his loose-mouthed way seeing Laura on the road to Five Corners Pond on a Saturday afternoon when she was supposed to be shopping in Portland.

Maybe she had thrown it out. Rubber disintegrates. This particular bit of rubber had probably cracked around the rim and ruptured for lack of exercise. Possibly her church had had a bonfire of contraceptives to express their horror of the immorality of a world in which women were no longer eternally barefoot and pregnant.

If she were using it for what it was intended, had she inserted it herself? Touching herself intimately had always grossed her out. Lubricating the device and seating it had been his job. His armpits were suddenly wet and his guts aroil. It couldn't be, a God-fearing woman like Laura—she wouldn't be out test-driving her diaphragm in some motel? But why had she bought a brand-new tube of lubricant, and where was the damn thing now?

He dropped the diaphragm box back into the drawer. No—no mystery. She'd thrown it out, that's all. It was the devil's work, after all, even the pope knew it. What purpose she had for the lubricant he didn't know, but maybe she used it to keep her thighs from rusting together. And in the cupboard beneath the basin in a jumble of suntan oil and sunblock, he found a can of antiseptic burn spray and took it back to Karen with the announcement he had located the rabies kit.

After the kids arrived at a peace-with-honor and had their bedtime snacks, he tucked them in and went back to the garage to work until it was too late to go home. Next morning, though, he was unable to forbear temptation. In the bathroom to shave and shower before breakfast, he took the box out of the drawer and found the freshly powdered, perfectly flexible diaphragm neatly filling it.

He explained it to himself while lathering his jaw, "Took it to have it serviced, some shop in New Hampshire, adjusts the timing, replaces the rings, gives it a lube job. Whatever the manual calls for."

Opening the drawer again one-handed, he flicked the lid up. Still there—the magical now-you-see-it-now-you-don't diaphragm, a little disk of rubber on a flexible nylon ring like a miniature trampoline. Carefully closing the box and drawer again, he tried to concentrate on shaving, but his hand shook and he nicked his upper lip painfully.

It might be amusing to punch a pinhole in the rubber disk and sit back to see if Laura would—give it six weeks, two months at the outside—attempt to seduce him in order to slip a cuckoo's egg into his nest. He didn't think abortion was any kind of option anymore. Then again, she was also supposed to be dead-set against adultery, and that hadn't stopped her taking it up as a hobby. For a mad instant the thought of getting laid even by mutual and farcical trickery sparked his flat battery. The faint spark of lust like a whiff of ozone forced him to laugh at himself, which in turn helped steady his hand.

Still, he had to shake his head over her carelessness. She'd be skinning it, taking it out so quick. So maybe it had been an afternooner. Maybe she'd pulled up her drawers and rushed home to have chicken soup and biscuits with the family and then out to her prayer meeting while whoever's sperm died unrequited inside her, barred from her womb by the diaphragm. But it was also possible that Laura, despite her newfound facility with the device, had come in late last night from a post-prayer meeting bounce with whomever—one of her fellow Christers, one of those horny con men who faked working for a living at Willis', it didn't matter—and extracted her diaphragm prematurely. She had never liked having it inside her; he had always had to remind her not to take it out too soon.

The eyes looking back at him were amused. She had been careless about contraception in the dim, dead days when she had chosen to humor his delusions he was a married man; it would not be surprising to discover she was still careless. Laura and contraception were all of a piece with her strangled toothpaste tube and the swath of untidiness she left behind her—a piece with her sloppy personal income tax records, which exhibited a disarray in striking contrast to the meticulous work she did for Dale Willis. She was a smart woman who was good with numbers and yet was chronically inattentive to the vital details of her own life.

Why not? She had gotten the right husband. He kept oil in her T-bird's engine and gas in its tank and decent tires on it, remembered to pay excise and property and withholding taxes and kept her gelding from burying itself in its own manure. She had him pussy-whipped without actually having granted him any in years. He had believed in her chastity. He had had so much experience of it.

Peering into the bedroom, he found her still asleep, her face in shadows, her body slack and vulnerable as a child's. Though nearly thirty-five, in the dimness of the bedroom and the relaxation of sleep she didn't look a minute over seventeen. Waking, she would tense and look her age.

He could have gone to her then, disturbed her rest and crawled on top of her and she would have let him—it was her Christian duty according to her own repulsive dogma. It wasn't pride or scruples that stopped him but the simple fact he couldn't get it up even to jack off anymore. But at that moment he did desire his wife with an intensity he found nearly as shocking as she would have had she known. It was as if he had a sudden hard-on for some strange woman who'd pulled up to his pumps. Some perfectly respectable and unsuspecting woman who just wanted to buy gas or use the rest room or maybe get directions to somewhere else.

*　*　*

Called out to fight a fire, he didn't get home until breakfast time one morning and didn't come in until he had tended the gelding. It was several days after his discovery, days in which he had been afflicted with a headache nothing seemed to cut. Dressed and made up for work, Laura was at the kitchen table having coffee. He brought the funk both of the fire and the barn into the house with him. The smell of Laura's perfume mingled with the sweetness of the home-grown maple syrup on his pancakes and the stench of burning that was like breathing through sour ash. He must have soot still inside his nose—even with a mask it always managed to penetrate. It was like sand at the beach; it turned up places you couldn't imagine how it got there.

She caught him watching her. A natural color infinitely more delicate than her blusher had darkened her cheeks. Her hands flew to her hair and her ruffled collar swift as birds on the wing from the shadow of a cat.

"What is it?" she asked.

He rose wearily to his feet and from behind her he stooped to murmur in her ear, "You're so beautiful today."

Her body stiffened.

Putting the edge of his hand under her chin as if to chuck it like a baby's, he gently tipped her head back against him. With his free hand he brushed her hair back from her forehead, leaving a smudge, a fleck of soot. Nearly kissing her delicate lobeless little ear studded with the pearls he had given her on one anniversary or another, he whispered two words. *I know.* A tremor went through her. And he kissed the nape of her neck and took his hand from her chin and went to work.

When she went out after supper—avoiding his eyes with a persistence that piqued him—he thought about putting the kids to bed and going after her. He could take the anonymous Dodge wagon he'd just tuned up for the grammar school principal. Park in the shadows of the supermarket next door to Laura's church in time to catch the prayer meeting letting out. He could follow her wherever she might go next.

But he had done it already once, the evening after the toothpaste war—taken one of his customers' heaps out for a prayer-night test drive. Had watched her say good night to her fellow Jesus shouters and then walk to her T-bird—shiny and sleek as a water-polished river stone, he had restored it for her—and she had looked back at the preacher standing on the threshold of the church. The two of them, his wife and her minister, had met each other's gaze. It was the glance of a fraction of a second, unnoticed by the few lingering churchgoers exchanging pieties on the steps, but it was like a flash bulb going off in Reuben's eyes. And then she had driven away. He had waited. Almost immediately the preacher had followed her.

And Reuben had not. After seeing her look at that man, that vain peacock of a con man with his soft, thieving preacher's hands, the nails as conspicuously manicured as an undertaker's, that Bible-thumping, hypocritical Pharisee—the Reverend Matchbook Mail Order Bible School Richard Jailbird Cocksucker Smart—with that fever in her blue eyes with her lower lip wet and quivering—after seeing that, if he had caught them together he'd have killed them. Bare-handed.

He had been shocked at the strength of his own emotion—almost blinded by it. The idea of Laura cheating on him wasn't mordantly funny anymore. In that instant of revelation it had stopped being a huge farcical joke on himself. He hadn't been able to breathe; it was as if a giant had kicked him in the chest. The whole world had gone dark and hot. If he had been standing he would have fallen to his knees like a gut-shot deer. It had been no particular precaution to leave the old man's four-ten locked up in the gun rack at home. Keeping himself at home had been a precaution.

And more than she bothered to take. She couldn't be troubled to explain her hours, which increasingly approximated those of a night-shift nurse or a barmaid. Reuben wondered what the Reverend Jailbird told his missus. No doubt men of the cloth, like quacks and cops, had an infinite variety of reasons for being out half the night, all amounting to I-had-to-work. Didn't they know what a joke they were—the horny preacher and the church secretary? Once he was past the first shock of knowing, what could he do but weep, laugh or get loaded? The alternatives seemed much the same.

* * *

He set out to kill the case instead of his wife and her lover. By eleven-thirty the beer was drilling a black hole between his eyes, threatening to suck in his whole existence by an irresistible cosmic force. He groped his way upstairs. It was irrational; he knew the children were all right. His visits to their bedrooms as they slept were to comfort himself. Weaving in their doorways, it came to him then he ought to have gone to the garage. It had been a mistake to stay home tonight.

When he moved on to peek into her bedroom his mother peered over her glasses, pursed her lips and dropped her gaze immediately back to her book. She was angry at him for staying home to do his boozing.

He was drunk enough not to care overmuch. As she had

grown older he had habituated himself to the motions of a cour-
teous, indulgent affection for her, but it amounted to no more than
he would have extended to any elderly woman who might somehow have become part of his household. Her heart was as tight as
her mouth, he reflected, and wasn't sure exactly what he meant.
He was beer-stupid; if he had a bar to lean against he would be
boring the tits off some bartender as he wended his way to the ul-
timate wisdom of all drunks: *fuck it*. She was right, though. He
ought to have gone to the garage and left this business alone.

At midnight he heard the shuffle of the old lady's slippers down
the hall to the upstairs bathroom and then the click of her teeth in
the glass as she carried it back to her bedroom. Her door closed
decisively; the bedsprings shook and the lamp button snicked. In
a little while the odd wheeze or sucking breath or snort became
audible. Though she slept on an incline of pillows, she had begun
to work hard to breathe at night. She was solid and looked eternal
but her pump was clogging—so the family doctor had advised
him.

Then he was the only one awake in the house waiting for Laura
to come home.

✳ ✳ ✳

She crept up the stairs on tiptoe, pumps in one hand. He stayed
sprawled on the couch, eyes covered with his forearm as if it had
come to rest there in uneasy sleep. Above him the bathroom door
shut with a furtive click. He lowered his arm and came to his feet
with a grace that surprised even himself, his body remembering its
strength and coordination better than his mind. Raising himself to
the tips of his sock-clad toes in childish drunken mockery of her,
he followed her upstairs.

Theirs—hers—was the front bedroom. Both bedroom and bathroom opened on the hall and each other. Passing the hall bathroom door, he went into the bedroom. Her dress was flung upon
a chair. When he tried the door from the bedroom to the bathroom he was not surprised to find it unlocked. He opened it.

There she was, his wife, in some scraps of lace and satin—no
doubt they had names, French ones sounding the way they would
feel—but he had never seen them. Silk stockings and garters, sweet
baby Jesus. Panties puddled on the floor, she stood with one foot
on the ring of the toilet, one hand in interesting proximity to her
bush. The clamshell was open on the counter next to the basin.

Her eyes widened at the sight of him, and then her mouth twisted in defiant contempt.

Lurching toward her, he asked, "What are you doing?"

She did not understand what he meant. She raised her head, stiffening her slim neck pridefully. Eyes locked with his, she dug her nails into his wrist and drew his hand between her legs. She flinched when he thrust a thick finger into her sex—hot and slick, she was deliriously so and not just, he was sure, from her own melt. He tipped the rim of the rubber saucer and it slipped neatly out into his palm. She released his wrist and shoved his hand away from her.

"You really should leave it in at least six hours," he advised her.

Making a strangled noise, she crossed her hands over her satin-draped breasts—so small, Laura's breasts, that he had loved for their vulnerable inadequacy—in a curiously modest gesture. He pushed a lock of hair behind her ear and she jerked away from his touch. Pallid of face, she stared at him. Behind the immediate glaze of startlement and fear, her eyes were as opaque and reflective as a mirror. A one-way mirror through which she saw but which showed him only himself. He had the sense she saw right through him, saw him naked in his clothes, saw his bones clothed in his flesh, saw his soul that cringed and writhed in the trap of his bones. Her mouth curved downward with distaste, as if she had stepped in shit.

His mouth was dry. His thoughts felt suddenly thick. He couldn't think what to do next. He was drunk, he realized. Pretty drunk. The thread of his thoughts escaped him. He dropped the diaphragm into the toilet, flipped the ring and unzipped his pants.

Laura drew a sharp breath of disgust.

He unloosed a stream of piss onto the rubber saucer, driving it toward the outlet. As it spun neatly some very inebriated brain cells became fascinated with the slow spiral.

She stepped out of her drawers on the tiled floor and brushed past him to the bedroom.

Stupid pissing on her diaphragm, a soberer troop of brain cells informed him. He was just going to have to fish the frigging thing out to prevent it blocking the drain or the septic outlet. He zipped up and stooped to pluck her panties from the floor—a wisp of pleated satin—damp with a tidal scent that made his balls tighten and his dick stir and his head swoony. Though maybe the light-headedness was booze.

In the bedroom she had her dress on again.

He tossed her the panties. "Forgot something."

She flung them at him. He let them flutter to the floor.

Dragging an overnight case from the closet, she threw it on the bed.

"Going someplace?"

"I'm leaving you, you drunken son of a bitch."

She crowed it. He thought she must have rehearsed it many times to herself.

He went back into the bathroom and fished the diaphragm out of the toilet, washed it off with shampoo, dried and powdered it and stuck it back in its clamshell. He flushed the toilet and closed the lid. He washed his hands with inebriated care. He looked at the foozled fool in the mirror.

" 'I'm leaving you,' " he mouthed, " 'you drunken son of a bitch.' Baaa," he bleated. He fumbled the clamshell from the counter. "High-riding bitch," he muttered. "Go ahead. Piss-poor excuse for a wife anyway."

Laura was folding things from her dresser drawers—making up an outfit. She might be leaving him, but she'd turn up at work looking as if she had stepped out of a bandbox.

He tucked the diaphragm box into the overnight case. "Want me to get you a toothbrush too?"

She grabbed the clamshell and threw it at him. He caught it one-handed, spun around and slam-dunked it back into the bag.

"Two points," he said with a sloppy grin.

She didn't laugh. Never had much of a sense of humor, Laura. But this time she let the box be. She yanked the case's zipper.

"Don't go," he said abruptly. "At least wait until morning. Then I'll be sober and you'll have showered away that smear of come on your right thigh and we'll pray for guidance over the good book and forgive each our trespasses like Christians."

While he pled half-mockingly with her she jerked the case off the bed and then she drew back and slapped his face. The wet smack of her hand made him realize his face was wet. He was ashamed of his tears and of his mockery and everything else then. He was in a world of shame, he wanted to tell her, drowning in it, but his throat closed up. She began to waver and dissolve as if he looked at her from underwater.

Then she left, stalking down the hall past his old mother standing in the doorway of her room with the children clustered wide-eyed around her. Seeing them, Reuben realized at some point he and Laura had raised their voices and shouted at each other and the children must have heard.

Swaying on the threshold of his wife's bedroom, he had a series of fragmentary impressions. His daughter's breasts beneath the gathers of her flannel nightgown were bigger than his wife's. When had that happened? His mother seemed witch-like, clawed hands twitching on Karen's shoulders, nose narrowed to a knife edge, her hair hanging loose past her bony shoulders in a dry white fall like angel's hair. Frankie's mask of adolescent dignity was as askew as his cowlicked hair. Sammy's eyes were huge and empty as Little Orphan Annie's and one hand frantically squeezed his penis through his pajama pants. His sons wavered in his sight as if he were trying to make out their reflections in a weary, warped old mirror.

"Mum," Frankie said, "where are you going?"

When Laura hesitated, Reuben wondered if the question had really occurred to her before.

"To Nana's," she said with the decisiveness of impulse.

She smacked Sammy's hand away from his penis. Then her heels trip-trapped down the stairs and the front door slammed.

XXVIII

"*What's Going on?*" the old woman asked.

Her mouth, puffed out indignantly, gave a simian cast to the lower part of her face. Her lower lids drooped, making the whites of her eyes look like boiled eggs. Her skin was suffused with a gray shadow and her lips were blue.

"Frankie," he said, "get Nana's nitro for her."

A glance at his grandmother propelled Frankie to his task.

"Is she coming back?" Karen demanded.

"I don't know."

Karen sniffled angrily. Reuben gathered her into his arms, but when he opened an arm to Sammy, the younger boy backed away. Frankie reappeared with the pills and a water glass from his grandmother's bed side.

"Of course she's coming back," Frankie answered Karen. His face was stony. "She would have taken us with her if she wasn't."

Of course she was coming back. She'd never just abandon the kids. To Reuben in his inebriation it made perfect sense to extrapolate she would therefore never leave him—not for good. The idea she might not come back was a glass wall reaching up to the sky and going down into the earth all the way to China. He couldn't get around it. All it showed him was what already was—world without end.

With a sudden drizzle and patter Sammy was standing barefoot in a puddle of piss.

"You big baby!" Frankie exploded. "You retard!"

The younger boy stared at the floor. His damp pajamas clung to him. Mutely he pulled the waistband away from his body and let the pants fall to the floor.

The old woman gasped and clapped a hand over Karen's eyes.

Karen jerked away from her grandmother.

"I've seen his stupid cock before," she said. "It's just a cock."

"Karen!" The old woman was scandalized.

Karen flounced away to her room, chanting, "Cock, cock, cock."

"Reuben!" His mother turned to him.

Frankie stomped away to get the mop and pail.

Reuben ignored Karen's outburst and his mother's outrage. Sammy scooched to mop the floor with his pajama bottoms and then took Reuben's hand and allowed himself to be led to the bathroom. While Reuben tested the water in the shower and nudged him into it, the boy never took his eyes from his father's face. His sockets were deep and bruised with shock, but he didn't cry. Even as an infant he had almost never cried. Sometimes he had nightmares and wet the bed, which he did at school on occasion as well. The pediatrician insisted he would outgrow the wetting if it wasn't made into a big deal. Once in bed again Sammy yanked the covers over his head and was rigidly still. He was a firm believer in the protective omnipotence of his bedcovers.

Reuben checked on his mother. The gray-blue had faded from her face and nails. Her eyes were sunken under their hooded lids, and she looked as if she should know ominous details of the future.

"What have you done?"

He had to think about that for a minute and bite his tongue, finally replying, "Faced her down about carrying on with her minister, Ma."

Bright spots bloomed on the old woman's cheeks. "She didn't come in until after one the last few nights you've been on call. She snuck in as if she didn't want anyone to notice how late she was. You're sure?"

He nodded.

His mother made a disgusted sound in her throat. "Using churchgoing to cover it up, it's a scandal. I never have liked her church either. It's unseemly making such a public business of one's relation with the Almighty. Ignorant, low-class behavior, I always thought. Here I was relieved to have you marry a nice girl even if she was a Catholic. I never thought someday I'd wish she'd stayed Catholic." She sniffed. "You and your friends were all so sure your parents were all wrong and you knew it all, and look at the lot of you, can't stay married for love nor money and what are your children going to make of it?"

He kissed her forehead wearily. "Don't fuss too much, Ma. Try to get some sleep."

"You're drunk," she said. "Your father—"

"Treated his horses better than he did me," Reuben said. "My father drove my sister into a bad marriage to get away from him. My sainted goddamn father put a goddamn shotgun in his mouth and pulled the goddamn trigger, Ma."

He realized he was shouting at her. She stared at him with her mouth open, her hands crossed on her bosom. Her lips trembled and then she turned her face from him and stared at the wall. Suddenly light-headed and ill, he groped his way out, leaving her behind in offended silence.

"Way to go," he muttered. What other damage could he do with what was left of the night?

Frankie was sitting up in his bed, nervously rubbing the downy dark on his upper lip. A Styles in his heavy build, in the face he was all Haggerty, the image of Laura's father and brothers.

"You okay?"

"I heard Mum come in. She mad at you because you're loaded?"

"Didn't say anything about it. I braced her about coming in so late. She didn't take too kindly to that."

Frankie's gaze dropped and he picked at the knots on his quilt. "She's been coming in later and later when you aren't home." He licked his lips. "She gets phone calls, she closes the door so she can't be overheard. She got a boyfriend?"

Reuben nodded.

"What's going to happen?" Frankie asked.

He shrugged. "Whatever Laura wants. We'll have to figure it out, I guess. We'll go to Nana Haggerty's first thing in the morning to see her."

Frankie's fists clenched on the counterpane. "I hate this crap. If you didn't drink, maybe she'd stay home and she wouldn't have a boyfriend."

The anger in his son's voice hurt more than anything Laura had said or done. It was the kind of hurt that would get worse once the air got to it.

"I'm sorry." He patted the boy's leg under the quilt. "Best get some sleep, there's school in the morning."

Frankie tugged the quilt to his chin. "Basketball practice too,

Dad, after school. Will you wait 'til I get home to work on that four-wheel-drive transmission so I can watch?"

Reuben's throat tightened. "Of course."

He was on the verge of weeping. He didn't want Frankie to see him come all apart. On the threshold he glanced back and saw Frankie drop his forearm over his eyes to hide his own tears.

* * *

Like a haunted house the front bedroom loomed dizzily around him. The king-sized bed seemed large enough to sleep the entire family. The paper Laura had chosen to replace the old cabbage-rose paper of his parents' residency had itself darkened from cream to toast, its miniature blue sprigs of violets gone to steely spatters like squashed mosquitoes. A few of his clothes—the suit that had replaced the one in which he was married, a couple of dress shirts and ties—hung at one end of the closet and his work clothes filled up the drawers of an oak lowboy, but otherwise he had no presence in the room. It had become Laura's room, spooky with the ghost of her perfume, strewn with her peculiar disorder—clothes, makeup, jewelry and shoes abandoned like fingernail parings. He passed through it only occasionally to obtain some item of clothing he couldn't find in the clean laundry basket.

Her jewelry box was open on the vanity. Everything he had ever given her was all still there, spilling out of it along with the gaudy costume bijoux childish eyes and hands always seemed drawn to choose for Mommy. She was coming back or she would have taken the box.

Seized by sudden curiosity, he stirred the tangle of bracelets and pins and whatnots, but there was nothing there he did not recognize. Opening the drawers of the vanity, he studied the chaos of compacts and tubes and jars and brushes—how could she ever find what she wanted? He had never understood how she could live in such a welter of confusion, any more than he could figure out what was so difficult about squeezing a tube of toothpaste neatly from the bottom instead of strangling it until it ruptured and blurted sticky spurts and went half to waste.

He didn't know what he might find. Not a packet of love letters, surely—he didn't suppose anyone ever wrote such things outside of novels. A diary maybe. He shut the drawer abruptly. If she had such a thing he couldn't bear looking at it. It would be an invasion of something more intimate than her overheated little cunt with his finger.

He was sorry now he had done that. He had let her goad him into behaving badly. He ought to have turned the other cheek, a blind eye, a deaf ear, played 'possum, played dead, played it as it lay, or she lay—whatever it took—and maybe she wouldn't have left and the affair would have burned itself out. Except he had a pretty good idea she had wanted to leave. She was the one put his hand between her legs.

Wandering around the room like a blind man trying to make sense of an elephant, he picked up the discarded panties. The silk snagged on his callused fingers. He crushed them into his palm. They condensed to little more than the size of an apricot and were as weightless as an eyelash. Sinking onto the bed, he pushed the wad of material under the pillow, where it was only inches from his ear as he lowered his head to the pillow slip. The fresh linen bore none of Laura's scent, just the scorched breath of the iron his mother had used on it.

There was no sleep, only an uneasy, rocking suspension, as if he were on the float at the Sharrards' cottage again. He could almost smell the clean mineral bouquet of the lake and the complex green of the woods about, mingled with the stale beer dregs in the dead soldiers he had lined up along the edges of the float.

* * *

The dark wore away to a smudge and he gave up and got up. He took the case of mostly empties to the shed so it wouldn't be the first thing the kids saw, should they come downstairs by way of the front instead of the back kitchen stairs. Then he took his whirling head and sick stomach out to the horse barn, where he could vomit beyond their hearing. After dousing his head under the cold water tap in the tackroom, he saw to the old gelding.

A near ton of shit machine, he thought resentfully, an enormous dumb beast seemingly content with its fenced, neutered existence, waiting for Laura to harness it and put it through its paces every other day. Then again, the animal had always enjoyed more of Laura's disciplined love than he had so perhaps there were compensations. As he curried it he was only dimly conscious of murmuring to it and of the way it snaked its big head around to stare at him with liquid eyes. He leaned into its shoulder with sudden poisoned weariness. Two whickered and stood steady, as if understanding Reuben was on the verge of falling down.

In the kitchen his mother glared at him coldly when he came in, but he ignored her and kept on going. He stayed in the shower a long time. His hand shook too much to shave, so he went back downstairs and out again onto the porch and took a beer out of the refrigerator and drank it right there with the old lady looking at him through the window. Then he could scrape his face without cutting his throat, though he did nick himself a few times. Stooping to a knock before breakfast was something he rarely did, but it was important not to see Laura unshaven.

He got Sammy out of a wet bed and into the shower again. Coming out of the bathroom, he met Frankie bundling Sammy's sheets into the laundry chute. Standard drill.

"Maybe you should take him to the garage today," Frankie said as they shook out clean linen over Sammy's plastic-enveloped mattress and swiftly made it up.

Reuben had already considered it. On other occasions when he had offered to let Sammy spend the day at the garage with him, the boy had refused. Staying home to avoid embarrassment was shaming in itself.

What with his stutter and the episodes of incontinence, Sammy hovered on the edge of being a schoolyard butt. The size of him—nearly as big as Frankie already and Frankie at fourteen was man-sized—undoubtedly intimidated as many potential bullies as it attracted. A disarming smile and a placid temperament also bought Sammy patience from his teachers. Nor was Sammy just a big little kid. He had an arm on him and he had speed and nimbleness and there was talk he would be the finest athlete the town had produced since his old man. It all made for an odd offhand protectiveness from the other kids where there might have been persecution. Oh, they teased him—Frankie most harshly with fraternal privilege—but they wouldn't allow it from outsiders. Sammy might be a stuttering pants-pissing retard, but he was *their* stuttering pants-pissing retard. He wasn't, though, not even mildly retarded, the school had assured Reuben—slow normal—whatever that meant. *Retread,* Sammy muttered sometimes when he was angry with himself. *Retread. Retread.*

While the kids ate Reuben did some more chores and then he put them into the truck and took them to the Haggertys' down the road to see Laura. They could catch their buses at the foot of their grandparents' driveway. Though they tried with varying degrees of success not to show it, they were twitchy with nerves. When Sammy slid across the seat, following Karen out of the cab of the truck, he looked back at Reuben and smiled his mute angelic smile as if it were his father who required reassurance.

Frank Haggerty met Reuben at the door and spread a hand on his chest, pushing him back from the entry. "Laura wants a few minutes with the kids by herself."

Reuben looked down at his father-in-law's hand. Frank removed it.

"Christ," Frank said, "you been drinking already this morning?"

"Just one to steady the razor."

He grimaced. "You can't blame her, can you?"

Reuben didn't want to be angry with his father-in-law, not least because he didn't have the energy to expend. As Frank could well see he was hungover; he felt as if he had been suffering the attentions of a bad amateur taxidermist.

"She came in after one last night. When did that bunch of holy rollers start having midnight Mass? Or do they have all-night bingo games now? She must have had herself a hell of a set of cards."

Frank's face purpled and his Adam's apple threatened to go into suborbit.

"I just want her to come home," Reuben went on. "I don't care if she's moonlighting in a whorehouse—I mean, I care—but I want her to come home."

"Shut up. Just shut up. Not another word."

The door slapped in Reuben's face. It was a near thing, he thought, that it was not his father-in-law's fist. The truce they had cobbled was fraying rapidly.

Shortly the children emerged with his mother-in-law to be escorted to meet their school buses. Maureen drew back from Reuben as if he were a cootie-ridden bum. Karen threw her arms around his neck and kissed him. Frankie didn't say anything, but his eyes were narrowed and his jaw worked angrily. Sammy looked like he was sleepwalking. His father-in-law held the door open after them and gestured Reuben into the kitchen.

The heavy smell of boiled coffee sickened him with its faintly ammoniac undertone and brought back the time Laura had thrown the pot at him when they were fighting over how much she wanted to spend on the wedding.

She was at the table. Though dressed and made up for work, she didn't look as if she had slept any better than he had. She kept her hands around a mug of coffee to warm or steady them perhaps, and she didn't want to look at him. All at once he saw her as the very tense, tired woman she was, her age and her temperament in the lines around her mouth and eyes. She was leaving her youth behind, fading too soon into middle age, and her disappointment and desperation had worked on her like a constant, wrenching wind bending a tree into a hunchback. He was stricken with the sudden realization of how much their wretched marriage had wrung out of her too.

Frank loitered, clearly unwilling to leave them alone.

Reuben sank to his knees next to Laura's chair. He wanted to touch her but he didn't dare. Her hand fluttered from the mug to tug her skirt away from any contact with him.

"Come home," he began. "I mean it. This is tearing up the kids. I'm not doing too well either, and you don't look as if you're having a good time. Let's find ourselves a marriage counselor and put this back together, like we should have ten years ago. We can do it, Laura, we can make a new start."

"You've been drinking already this morning. I can smell it on your breath. That's a new start?"

The prudish tone from a married woman who was fucking her married minister struck him as vintage Laura; not knowing she really saw no contradiction, you'd think she had some brass. But he drove down the upwelling both of laughter and anger at her hypocrisy. He raked a hand through his hair, destroying the careful combing he had given it.

"I'm sorry. That was a mistake. I'll quit drinking altogether if that's what you want."

It was the first time he had ever offered that concession. Now he was desperate and nothing was too high a price to pay—not his balls, his dignity or his soul. And not the bottle, especially not that. What Frankie had said the previous night had hit him hard.

"It's too late."

"You could have just told me you wanted out. Why did we have to go through last night?"

A tear trickled to her chin and she wiped it away, smearing her eyeliner.

"I want you out of my life," she whispered. "I want a divorce."

I want a divorce. Is that any way to end a marriage? It starts with an *I*, moves directly to the *want*, and then drops the shit on your head, *a divorce, fuck you very much, goodbye asshole.* The way the Moslems did it, now, had a little more class—a nice, rhythmic *I divorce thee, I divorce thee, I divorce thee,* acknowledging there were two individuals involved, *thee* and *I*, separated by the severing verb, and with the repetition dignifying the significance of the act. Even that didn't cover what was really going to happen. Why didn't she say, *I want to tear apart the family?*

And then a spasm of rage twisted her mouth and she slammed the coffee mug into his left ear.

He spun away from her in an instant's explosion of silent agony. Hardly feeling the scalding spray of the coffee, he was stunned by the mortar burst of pain in the ear. Crouched on the floor, he held his head and waited for it to stop. He was only vaguely aware of his father-in-law's amazed bellow or of Laura bolting from the room. Something had happened to his vision and he couldn't see anything clearly anymore. Staggering to his feet, he groped his way out the door and down the steps to dry-heave into the winter-stripped lilacs until his sides hurt. The side of his head was wet. When he touched his ear, his fingers came away dripping with dark fluid.

Frank came out of the house, took a look at him and hurried back inside to fetch a wet hand towel. He daubed the torn ear and Reuben flinched.

"She surprised the hell out of me," Frank said apologetically. "I wouldn't have let her do it if I'd seen it coming. You best get some ice on it."

Reuben had had enough of the Haggerty clan. "I'll get some at work."

He left his father-in-law holding the bloody towel and shaking his head in distress.

✳ ✳ ✳

A gutted buck drooling its tongue hung at the corner of Needham's diner waiting to be tagged. The sight of it added to his queasiness.

Jonesy had opened up already. Reuben had hired him right out of the high school motor shop. Barely five feet six inches in stature but heavily muscled from a lifetime of manual labor, Jonesy was so shy people often took him for retarded. Still unmarried, though he had been courting a girl as absymally shy as he was for going on seven years, he lived in the house next door to the garage that had once belonged to Sixtus Rideout. Without heirs, Sixtus had left his house to Reuben, who rented it to Jonesy for a nominal fee. Jonesy kept a motorcycle in the living room, handy to work on if the evening's game shows weren't to his taste. He had a first name, but only his girlfriend ever called him Bruce.

Jonesy waved the doughnut he was munching in greeting.

Hooking a beer from the icebox, Reuben flicked off the cap with his thumbnail. He wet his throat and then broke ice from a tray, wrapped it in one of the raggy hand towels he used around the garage and held the makeshift ice pack to his ear. He put down the beer to check the cash drawer. Raising it for a second swallow, he realized Jonesy was staring at him with some concern in his eyes.

Reuben winked at him. " 'S okay, Jonesy. Wife clocked me one, that's all."

Jonesy smiled uncertainly. Laura made him nervous. Fortunately, she rarely made appearances at the garage.

Reuben built the fire in the woodstove that supplemented the small oil furnace heating the building. The place rapidly became a sweat lodge. Jonesy knew the routine. He shucked his shirt with a grin and plied Reuben with aspirin, water and orange juice.

XXIX

The Banker's Voice Shook with Anxiety.
It was shortly after two when the phone rang, and Reuben was
surprised by the voice of Piers Larsen. They'd been doing business
since Reuben first bought the garage.

"Reuben, I'm calling to ask"—Piers always said *aaaska*, in a
fine, fluting prep school bray—"if we've done something wrong.
Whatever it is, I'm sure we can set it right."

"Pardon me, Piers?"

The banker cleared his throat. "Mrs. Styles wouldn't specify
your complaint when she closed the accounts. Unfortunately, I was
in a real estate closing and didn't find out about it until a few minutes ago. If either of you had spoken to me personally I'm sure
whatever the problem is could have been cleared up instantly."

"Back up, Piers. Laura did what?"

"Oh dear," the banker fretted. "She cleared your accounts."

Reuben closed his eyes. His head felt like a grenade with the
pin pulled. "All of them?"

"Oh yes. Savings, checkings, CDs. Took it all in cashier's
checks." The firmness drained from the banker's voice and he began to plead. "She was authorized to make withdrawals. We
couldn't legally refuse her the funds—though if I'd been aware of
the transition as it was occurring I assure you I would have called
to confirm it with you."

Oh, it was legal as hell. Her name was on the accounts from
the early years of their marriage when she had worked on his
books with him.

"I thought you might have had some complaint," Piers bab-
bled.

"Say again," Reuben interrupted. "Laura came in and emptied
our accounts."

"That's right. At eleven-thirty."

The silence stretched while he tried to get his mind around the shock.

The banker cleared his throat again. "There's a problem, I take it?"

Reuben did some hasty mental calculations.

"There's a problem," he conceded. "I'm going to need some cash to operate on until I catch up with Laura and find out what the hell she's up to."

"Can you be here by one-thirty?"

"Ayuh."

"Gosh," Piers sighed. "I'm sorry about this."

"Not as sorry as I am," Reuben said.

Cutting the line to the banker, Reuben dialed the Haggertys' number but got no answer. Where the hell was Laura, and more important, where the hell was his money? He rang her number at work.

"Reuben?" The receptionist was puzzled at his question. "Laura called in sick."

Sure she did. Sick of him, he guessed. In a fever. From the ball-cutting pneumonia and the rip-off flu. She had had something else to do with her morning.

He needed a beer to fix the swarm of wasps rousting in his head. He actually walked the seven steps to the icebox and stared in at the almost untouched case of dewy bottles. No, he concluded; he was now too poor to go calling on his banker with beer on his breath. Slamming the icebox door, he told Jonesy he had to go to the bank. He remembered to tell him to save back the transmission job on the four-wheel drive.

Piers leaped from his chair and shook Reuben's hand with the enthusiasm of a politician in an election year. He forbore more than an appalled glance at Reuben's ear.

It took far too little time to ascertain how completely Laura had emptied the till. All she had left in the safe deposit box were the titles to the business and the farm and his and his mother's wills. He couldn't legally mortgage either property without Laura's consent, so he effectively had no equity. Piers gave him a high-interest short-term line of credit on his bank card.

"Pardon my intruding on the personal," the banker hemmed, "but am I to assume marital difficulties?"

Reuben smiled thinly. "Go right ahead."

Piers showed his big, uneven teeth in a mirthless grin, over the tips of his fingers as he tapped them thoughtfully together. "Well, you might want to cancel any credit cards that are held in both your names."

"The bank card. It's the only card we have in common. She has her own cards and I don't use but the one."

The banker whipped out another form, and Reuben removed Laura as an authorized signatory to the bank card.

"And," Piers advised, his eyebrows hitched significantly, "you'd better see a good lawyer right away."

* * *

Bright and painful, the sun still shone with a thin warmth like one of those little puddles of heat on the surface of the lake under which the waters remained frigid enough to shock the heart and burn the skin. There was not enough heat in it to keep Reuben's ear from stinging and aching in the cold, and he wished he had grabbed a watchcap to pull over his ears on the way out.

Terrane, Cape, Shumway and Bosque did business on the second floor of a fine old brick-and-granite edifice dating from the 1890s just down the street from the bank. Norman Bosque had handled Reuben's legal papers since Charlie Shumway had retired several years earlier.

The receptionist was Heidi Lasker, Laura's old chum. Back then she had been Heidi Robichaud. The friendship between Laura and Heidi had gone bust when Laura got religion and Heidi, like most of Laura's old friends, had declined to be proselytized. Heidi raised her plucked eyebrows at Reuben and fluttered heavily mascaraed lashes.

"Norman in?" he asked.

"In court," she said.

Heidi leaned forward so Reuben could look down the discreet cleavage of her silk blouse. Sometime since high school Heidi's tits had gotten dramatically bigger.

She flashed him a confidential smile. "It's a public-defender case. Norm's doing his bit to keep the scum on the streets. You in a hot hurry, Reuben?"

"Ayuh. How about Freddy?"

"How 'bout Freddy?" she grinned. Heidi's manicured nails hovered over the intercom. "You know he handles mostly divorce cases."

"He handle yours?"

She hooked a finger to beckon him closer. "You ever need one, baby—trust me on this. Get the nastiest shyster in town. If you don't, your prospective ex will. Believe me, Reuben, Freddy Cape is the one you want."

Reuben laughed.

Heidi pressed the bar on the intercom. "Reuben Styles, Mr. Cape."

"What's that overgrown shitkicker want?" Freddy's voice came back impatiently from the speaker.

Reuben leaned over Heidi's desk to press the speaker bar for himself. "A divorce, you blood-sucking social parasite."

Freddy crowed delightedly. "Now you're talking. Second door on the left, have your wallet out."

Heidi's mouth became a glistening bright red O. Her eyes brightened with the speculative malice only scandal involving a formerly dear friend could kindle.

"No kidding?" she breathed. "I thought maybe you needed a defense on a drunk-and-disorderly, the way your ear looks."

Reuben shrugged. As he headed down the hall toward Freddy's office, Heidi jumped up and leaned over her desk.

"Hey," she called, the silk of her blouse liquid with jiggle, "you want some company some night, I'm in the book."

Freddy had his feet on his desk. Glancing up from a *Playboy* centerfold, he grinned at Reuben and then tossed Miss October aside.

"Hey, cowboy. Let's hear your tale of woe," he said.

Reuben found the room far too warm. Yanking his shirt collar, he sank into the chair Freddy indicated. He was suddenly grateful to be sitting down. All at once he was sweating heavily, all nerved up as if he were back in high school, facing a surprise quiz. The flippant announcement over the intercom now felt like childish bravado. He wiped his damp palms on the thighs of his work pants.

Back when they were both students at Greenspark Academy he could never have imagined that one day he would be sitting in Freddy Cape's law office with his guts roiling and his head swimming, about to reveal the mess he had made of his life to Freddy— Freddy who had once topped a bottle of beer with pee and gotten an already foozled Sonny Lunt to drink it on a bet that Lunt would drink anything.

They'd have to update the yearbook at the next reunion. He

could see a page of cock-eyed *What are they doing now?* snap-shots: Top left: Freddy Cape in his lawyer suit with the power tie snapping Heidi's bra while she strutted her tit job; center: once sweet-sixteen Laura, the Last Virgin in the Senior Class, in those bits of randy underwear; bottom right: himself, Greenspark's pitching ace, in greasy overalls and hangover, with his ear cauli-flowered by an angry, thieving bitch of a cheating wife. And not to be forgotten—bottom left: Sanford Harold Lunt Jr, a.k.a. Sonny, leaning against the fender of his truck by the side of the road, dick draped over the stub of his right index finger, his open, booze-raddled face raised to grin while he fails to notice he is pissing all over his work shoes. No matter—Sonny's shoes proba-bly thought piss was shoe polish by now.

"You okay?" Freddy asked.

Reuben blinked. He was still sitting in Freddy Cape's office, his life still a frigging train wreck. No wonder he had thought of Sonny. "Laura left me last night. This morning she cleaned out all our bank accounts."

Freddy's eyebrows popped up with the violence of toast from the slots of an oversprung toaster, and he whistled his amazement.

"I got eleven dollars in my pocket," Reuben said, "and what's in the till."

Freddy shook his head. "Who fucked up your ear for you?"

Reuben hesitated.

"Spit it out, man," Freddy prodded.

"Laura clocked me with a coffee mug this morning. At her folks' house."

The lawyer winced. "Please tell me you didn't clock her."

"I didn't."

He met Reuben's gaze with un-Freddyish solemnity. "Before we talk about money, let me get one thing straight. If you've ever set-tled a domestic dispute with your fists, find yourself another law-yer. If I take your case and you subsequently engage in abusive, threatening behavior against your wife, I'll quit. I've had too many of you backwoods cowboys get shitfaced and go around to teach the bitch a lesson. I don't care what she did to you or what she does to you in future—we do this by the rules or not at all. You clear about this, cowboy?"

Reuben nodded.

Freddy reached for a legal pad and a pen. "Any possibility of a reconciliation?"

"She was pretty definite this morning, she wants out."

"And while you were still reeling from getting your ear bashed, she made a trip to the bank." He flipped another legal pad across the desk to Reuben. "I need all the numbers. Net worth, before and after this morning, your income and hers and where it comes from. All your assets, liquid and real. The quicker you can provide me with your income tax returns for the entire span of the marriage, the better. I need her current address. Who's got the kids?"

"I do."

"How'd that happen?"

"She left in the middle of the night—went to her folks down the road."

"She indicate whether she wants them or not?"

Disconcerted, Reuben shook his head. They were with him; she was the one who had left. Surely they would stay with him.

"I need their full names, ages, and Social Security numbers. Your mother still with us? Is she your dependent too?"

He began to make hasty notes of Freddy's requirements.

"Tell me about last night."

"She came home just after one, from a prayer meeting that started at seven-thirty and usually breaks at nine. She goes to church every day, just about—four, five days a week and most of Sunday. She does the church books too, and that usually takes up a lot of Saturday. Been a lot of nights lately she's cruised in in the wee hours."

"I heard she was born again. The Reverend Smart's flock, right? So you think she's fooling around when she's supposed to be at church?"

"I know she is," Reuben said. "With the Reverend Dick himself."

Freddy sat up straight. "You're shitting me."

Reuben sat in silence, his throat constricted, his eyes suddenly watering.

"You're really sure about it?" the lawyer asked.

Reuben made no response.

Freddy tapped his pen against his legal pad. "I've heard rumors about that guy . . ." He chewed his lower lip and then changed the subject. "How are you going to operate while we chase your funds?"

"Line of credit."

The lawyer grimaced. "Jesus. Can you do it—hold on, I mean?"

"You mean," Reuben said with a slow grin, "are you ever going to get paid?"

Freddy laughed. "Of course I'm going to get paid. I asked you if you could hold on."

"One way or another I will. How much of a piece are you going to tear off?"

Freddy told him.

"Is this legal?" Reuben demanded, genuinely shocked. "Do you buy the K-Y?"

"Buy cheap, you get cheap. This isn't something that can be repaired with a wad of chewing gum and some baling wire, cowboy. Just because we go back I'm doing you one hell of a favor. I'm going to let you walk out of here without leaving me a retainer."

"I don't want any special treatment—"

Freddy groaned. "Oh, shit in a handbag, Reuben. You can't afford pride and principles. Gimme one of those eleven big ones you got in your pocket and shut up before I change my mind."

Reuben dug out his wallet.

"I'll get you whatever your regular retainer is," he said, "somehow."

"Nine hundred ninety-nine more of the same." Freddy stretched across the desk to pluck the single bill from Reuben's hand. He sank back into his chair, swung his feet to his desk and began to fold the bill into small triangles.

"Listen up, cowboy. Law says marital property gets split down the middle or as near as makes common sense. Your problem is Laura's disappeared your liquid assets. Possession counts. She's got it, you don't and I hope to Christ you can prove you ever had it. The best you can hope to recover is your half. In the meantime she's entitled to half your business and your real property. She's likely to get custody if she wants it. That means you'll have to pony up child support until each child is eighteen. She's gainfully employed, right?—so you shouldn't have to cough up alimony. Now tell me what you want out of the divorce."

"My kids," Reuben said without hesitation. "My business. The farm. I can buy her out, can't I?"

"With what?"

"The money she took. I'll mortgage the farm."

The dollar had become a silvery green paper crane in Freddy's

busy fingers. He offered it to Reuben. He held it in his palm, trying to make head or tail of it. It was a crane that kept wanting to
sort itself out into a dollar bill, like one of those shrink-trick pictures that could be either a pair of candlesticks or two opposing
profiles.

"One," Freddy said, "you have to prove she's got that money
and that it came from your business. You can't mortgage the farm.
Half of it's hers."

"Half of it's my mother's."

"So Laura can only claim a quarter ownership. All right. You'll
probably have to buy Laura out of her share or trade it against
something else."

Reuben nodded.

"All right," Freddy said. "You won't get your kids unless you
can prove Laura abuses or neglects them or that she's schizo-
phrenic, suicidal, alcoholic, drug addicted or a convicted felon. Or
unless she voluntarily gives them up to you. Cheating on you, lying, absconding with your assets—none of it costs her custody. If
you're lucky you'll get them a couple weekends a month and vacations. You'll also get the bills for the kids' educations, insurance,
medical care, orthodontic care and corrective lenses."

"They're with me now. She walked out on us."

Freddy shrugged. "If she doesn't change her mind, they're
yours. Just don't expect anything. The fact is, they just stopped being your kids. Now they belong to the court system, and the bias
in custody is with the mother."

Reuben raked a shaking hand through his hair. He wanted to
bolt from Freddy's office, but he didn't know where he would go
or even if once he was on his feet he could stay on them for long.

"With luck," Freddy said, "and if Laura gets a lawyer with any
sense we should be able to hold onto the homestead and your
business—the house because half of it belongs to your mother, and
the garage because you've got to have the means to earn a living.
Whatever else happens, you will never have sole custody of your
children. The best thing you can do for yourself and for them is to
resign yourself; Laura is their mother and even if the court departs
from the usual disposition and gives them to you, you will have to
allow her access to them as defined by the court."

Reuben blinked. Freddy was fading in and out.

The lawyer's hand darted to the intercom. "Mrs. Lasker, would
you bring us a couple of cold Cokes pronto?"

Freddy went to the window and stared out at Main Street, with his hands in his pockets. "Break time. You look like shit, old man. It's a bitch going through this."

"She walked out on us," Reuben repeated.

At Heidi's light knock Freddy opened the door and relieved her of the requested beverages.

Reuben appreciated Freddy protecting him from Heidi's avid eyes. The Coke tasted wonderful. He felt as if every cell was sponging up the cold sweet nectar in blissful gratitude.

Freddy sat on the edge of his desk. "It shouldn't matter if you have a girlfriend, but if you want custody you'd better keep it in your pants for the duration. It's not fair, but that's the way it is. And now I think about it, don't have sex with Laura either."

Reuben couldn't help barking a rueful laugh.

"It's a legal thing," Freddy explained. "It amounts to reconciliation if the court finds out and you have to go through filing all over again. It may not seem very likely to you at this point, but it's extremely common for estranged spouses to jump into the sack together, out of habit or convenience or because the prospect of losing sexual access to their old partner is a turn-on. Do yourself a favor and make up your mind you're done with the marriage, Reuben."

But I don't want this, I don't want a divorce, he thought. *I want Laura back. I want a working marriage. I want my family whole. I don't want to go through this shit.*

Staring at his sweating palms, he was suddenly aware of his hands as objects. His life was in them. They were enormous, hard and ridged with calluses and scars, the nails broken as the shoulders of a paved road after frost and washout in spring, and they never looked clean, even after the harshest soaps. His wrists were so thick they were hardly distinguishable as wrists at all. He had lived by his muscle and his sweat all his life and had taken pride and pleasure in the use of his body and his skill and integrity as a workman.

What he looked like was of little interest to him. It was only when he saw it mirrored in the faces of other people—in Laura's most often—that he was reminded how easy it was to take him for a brute. It was then that he felt this distance from himself, this dismay at his own powerful body—the loom of his own existence— made repulsive and alien to him in the mirrors of his wife's eyes—then that he felt helpless. It was as if he had had a terrible accident and now all his strength and skill could not free him. There was no relief, no escape from the impalement; indeed, his body was part of the trap, the medium of his suffering.

The hell with the money, he thought. *It's gone. It's going to Freddy and some other goddamn lawyer. I'd forget I ever had it if she'd just come back.*

Freddy went on. "I can't say it often enough—if you want a chance at custody you have to live like a monk. And whatever Laura does, don't lose your head. Do all the dealing that needs to be done through me—let me do what you're going to pay me so handsomely to do."

"Reminds me of the rules Sixtus Rideout laid on me when I was sixteen," Reuben said. *"No drinking on the job, no chicks, no buddies hanging around, no credit*—only I forgot the most important one: I left the register open."

Freddy laughed. "You may not be wealthier but you'll be healthier and you're already wising up. You know, it brings me a lot of satisfaction, promoting chastity, sobriety and moderation."

It was a relief to laugh, though Reuben still had an interior ache something like muscle strain deep in his gut. It felt the way it had just after tearing down the Eldorado.

"Speaking of someone who's no model of any of those virtues," Freddy asked, "have you seen Joyce lately?" He smacked his lips. "Remember when she and Heidi and Laura and Janice Shumway were cheerleaders? Joyce could still wear her uniform today. Aerobics, she tells me. I don't know about you, but I think what Jane Fonda's done to keep up the tits and asses in this country is more than adequate reparation for her sucking up to the North Vietnamese during the Big Muddy. What the hell—the world moves on. We're buying sneakers from the Red Chinese these days and Richard Nixon's pontificating on world affairs when he ought to be in a federal pen somewhere, trading cigarettes to get some punk to blow him."

This time Reuben's laugh was wholly painless. Everything felt looser again. "Where's your respect for our institutions, Freddy?"

"I'm a divorce lawyer. How could I have any respect for our institutions?"

"Do you talk like this in court?"

"Me?" Freddy mocked offense and then grew serious again. "This is going to take months to work out, cowboy, and it's going to be about as pleasant as a hemorrhoidectomy with a rusty chain saw." He flipped some business cards onto the desk in front of Reuben—his own and an assortment of therapists and counselors of one kind or another. "Talk to someone. It helps. Your kids need to talk to somebody too. Call me if you feel the urge to do anything stupid. You can reach me at home or by car phone anytime. On your way out of here, hold still long enough for Heidi to take a Polaroid of that ear. I'll start running paper, serve Laura as soon as we can and see if we can locate your cash. Cheer up, cowboy. Give it a couple of years and you'll be stupid enough to get married again."

XXX

The CB Crackled almost as soon as he was in the truck.

It was Jonesy. "Boss, your mother's looking for you. She says she's okay but she sounds anxious. You want me to scoot up the house and check on her?"

"I'll call her."

He thought of last night guiltily.

She knew how to operate the CB in the kitchen. Sometimes it took her awhile to answer it, but this time she was so prompt, he knew she had been waiting on him.

"What's wrong, Ma?"

"I'm not sick," she replied, "but you best come home."

She sounded upset, all right.

"Don't speed," she added.

So he jammed it.

Frank Haggerty's Subaru was in the yard and his father-in-law met him on the porch steps.

"Ede's all right," Frank said.

He brushed past him.

His mother was in her usual chair, a cup of tea at hand. Her color was nearly normal but she was fluttery with distress.

Lucille heaved herself to her feet to greet him. He bent to give her a reassuring scratch behind the ear.

"Laura left half an hour ago. She came to take her things," his mother said. "I've been trying to reach you since she got here."

"I was out of the truck."

"I never thought I'd see the day," his mother went on querulously. "Maureen and Laura came through the door without so much as a by-your-leave and never a decent word to me from either of them the whole time. Laura's lived under this roof like my own daughter."

"I apologize, Ede." Frank was so agonized he couldn't meet either hers or Reuben's eyes.

The old woman ignored him and addressed her complaint to Reuben. Her voice quavered. "She took the children's things."

Taking the stairs two at a time did nothing to calm Reuben. He had been chasing his money while Laura set about stealing his kids.

In each of the children's rooms the drawers stood emptied from the dressers, the closet doors ajar with only skeletal hangers dangling in them. The pillaging had been uneven. Desks and bookcases were untouched and many of their treasured if rarely used toys and mementos had been left.

His father-in-law huffed behind him.

"Now calm down, son," Frank said in a voice so thick with distress it belied his own advice. "You know the kids have to go with Laura. She and Maureen have gone to pick them up at school. They'll be just down the road at our house. You'll see'm any time you want—every day, so long as you're sober. I promise you."

Reuben shouldered past him to the front bedroom.

Laura's jewelry box was gone. So was everything else of hers. His shirts had been knocked to the floor and his good suit hung like a suicide in the otherwise emptied closet.

He groped his way down the front stairs to the small room off the dining room that served as his office at home. It was where he kept their income tax records and other family papers. The file cabinet was still locked, but it was newly dented and scarred from a tire iron that Laura had flung to the floor in frustration, among a litter of black shards he realized abruptly were the remains of all his old forty-fives and albums.

"Goddamn," Frank said mournfully as he trailed Reuben. "I'm awful sorry about this. The way this was done. We were supposed to be helping move her things and the kids, and the next thing I knew she's smashing up your records and beating on that cabinet. I put a stop to it soon as I heard the noise. She didn't get any sleep last night. Her emotions got ahead of her."

Reuben crouched to touch the relics of Chuck Berry, Little Richard, Jerry Lee Lewis, Eddie Cochran, Buddy Holly, Creedence—the joyful noise utterly silenced.

"She could have stayed home last night and slept in her own bed," he said.

Frank cleared his throat apologetically. "I asked her outright. What the hell were you getting home at that hour, I asked her. She says it's none of my beeswax. I said right back to her, My God, you can't blame Reuben for being suspicious, any man would be." He sighed. "She looks right through me. I expect you've got the right of it and she is carrying on with somebody. I'm sorry, son. She's my daughter and she'll be my daughter however bad she acts. I have to stand by her. And I warned you, I warned you over and over to get yourself straightened out, didn't I? There's always two people to blame when a marriage breaks down. You did your share."

Reuben toed the shards. "I wonder how she'll sleep tonight, the day she's put in. You know what she did with her morning?"

"She was going to Reverend Smart for counsel, she told me."

He snorted. "She stopped at the bank first and stripped my accounts of every last cent. Everything. How the hell am I going to support my kids if I lose my business?"

Frank's Adam's apple bounced wildly. "I didn't know. I never had the slightest idea she was going to get up to these shenanigans. Look, we'll go down to my house and sit her down at the table and get this straightened out. I'll give her the straight of it."

As Reuben looked around at the disorder in the room he realized his gun rack was unlocked and empty.

Frank's restraining hand closed upon his forearm. "I took'm, son. I know I had no right, but I couldn't leave them, not in good conscience. Took Frankie's twenty-two as well. I'll give'm back when you've steadied down."

He shook his head. "I know you mean well, but I can get another gun in under ten minutes and I won't even have to pay cash for it."

"I know, I know. It just ain't a good idea, you keeping that shotgun around. I wished to Christ you'd thrown it away after your dad used it. It's like a rotted chicken around your neck. It stinks of a bad death. I told Ede I was taking it and she told me where the key was."

"Never mind. I don't care where the shotgun is. I'm not going to use it, on myself or Laura or that holy joe con man she's screwing."

His father-in-law gasped.

"That's right," Reuben said. "That's who her boyfriend is. Her married minister."

Deep unhealthy color suffused his father-in-law's face and throat, past the open collar of his shirt. Frank's fists clenched and unclenched spasmodically.

"Mother of God," he muttered angrily. Then he turned stony. "I can't stand that oily son of a bitch but you're raving. You're paranoid. If she's got herself involved with another man, it's probably one of those fellas at Willis', somebody with an eye for a vulnerable woman. And you're the one who set her up for it."

"Suit yourself," Reuben said, "you'll have spit in your eye soon enough and then you'll see. Let's go to your house. We'll wait there for the kids and Laura."

Frank nodded tightly.

Reuben called Tiny Lunt and told her tersely they had a family problem. He asked if she would come and sit with his mother while he did some necessary errands. Tiny said she was on her way.

Listening to him make the call, his mother seemed visibly relieved at the thought of company. She bestirred herself to fill the kettle and began to fuss over cups and napkins.

"The house is all at sixes and sevens," she said.

"You know what Tiny's house is like," he reminded her. "She won't notice."

"That's the point," the old lady sniffed. "I know what her house looks like. Mine doesn't."

There was no one yet at the Haggertys'. The smell of coffee in the kitchen evoked a throb in his aching ear. He didn't drink coffee himself but Laura lived on it and so did her folks. His people had always been tea drinkers. Waiting in Frank and Maureen's kitchen for the kettle his father-in-law put on to boil was a distressingly familiar state. He couldn't sit; he paced, lurking at the windows that looked upon the yard.

"You must need some money to keep the business running," Frank said as he busied himself preparing Reuben's tea. "How bad a fix has Laura put you in?"

"The worst I've ever been in," he admitted. "Ma's got a little bit but a week in the hospital would wipe it out even with her insurance. Besides it's hers—I wouldn't touch it."

"You let me talk to Laura, now. You get hotheaded, you won't get anywhere. She'll just dig in her heels. Somebody must have filled her head with bad advice some silly woman had a husband pull that kind of trick on her. I'll make her understand you can't meet your obligations to her and the kids if she beggars you."

Reuben put little faith in his father-in-law's influence with Laura. The only silly woman behind Laura's financial marauding was Laura herself, acting on the advice of the Reverend Richard Smart, the Cadillac preacher.

"I saw a lawyer this afternoon."

Frank pinched the bridge of his nose wearily. "Damn, I hate this. Who?"

"Freddy Cape."

"Mother of God. He's a shark."

That's funny, Reuben thought. *I'm numb from the waist down, it's my blood in the water and Laura's bite just fits the marks.*

"The kids are old enough to be allowed some say about which one of us they live with. When Laura and Maureen come back with them, I'm going to ask them where they want to be. If they want to go home with me, what are you going to do?"

His father-in-law's shoulders sagged. "For pity's sake, they'll be right here within walking distance. Is that so bad? You want to put them through making a choice between you and Laura over less than a quarter of a mile through the fields?"

He stared at Frank a moment and then got up and left the kitchen to sit on the back steps in the gathering gloom. His head ached with remnant hangover, with the blow to his ear and the strain of one of the most hellish days of his life. He shivered with the cold.

Laura had walked out on him and the kids last night and today she was taking them away from him, and somehow he was a bastard for wanting them to stay with him in the only home they had ever known. And yet asking the kids to make a choice between the two of them was like cutting the baby in two. He knew how that would feel because giving them to Laura was already tearing him in two. Weekends and vacations, Freddy had said.

They would be just over the fields here at the Haggertys'. He'd be able to look out the windows of their bedrooms in the farmhouse and see the lights of the rooms they would sleep in in his in-laws' house. His father-in-law would make sure Laura let him see them every day. So Frank said. He didn't believe it. His father-in-law's authority over Laura had ceased the day she married; bolting it had been a motive in getting married. She had the bit in her teeth now. There was no way to make her stay at her parents'; she could move the kids away anytime. He washed his face with despairing hands.

Frank stood in the open door behind him. "Come in out of the cold."

"Where the hell are they?"

His father-in-law squinted into the twilight as if he thought he could just make out headlights down the road.

"Getting late," he admitted.

The phone rang inside and Frank went to answer it. Reuben followed him.

"It's Frankie. Wants to talk to you," his father-in-law said.

Reuben took the phone. "Where are you?"

"At the garage," Frankie said. "Got off the bus here. Nana said you'd gone to Nana Haggerty's."

"I'm waiting on your mother."

"Mom came to school. Got Coach to yank me out of practice. She said she and Nana Haggerty had Sam and Karen in the car outside and she wanted me to go with her, someplace she said was safe. I told her I was already someplace safe, what did she mean? She said get your stuff and come get in the car, and I said not without talking to you first, Dad. She was ripped at me. What's going on?"

"I don't know. She told me this morning she's quits with me. She took your things and picked up Sam and Karen at school. Your granddad was under the impression you'd all be staying with him and Nana Haggerty, but if that's so, she's late. What you say makes me think she's gone someplace else."

"This sucks," Frankie blurted.

"Yeah, it sucks. Frankie, I love you."

"I know," the boy said in a choked voice.

"Ask Jonesy to close up long enough to bring you home. Tell him I'll be in for at least a few minutes before it's time to lock up."

He told his father-in-law what Frankie had reported.

Frank's face crumpled. "Goddamn."

The sound of the wagon and its headlights flashing into the windows made both of them jump. They moved to the door in unison. Maureen was driving and there was no one else in the car.

Frank became apoplectic. "Where's Laura! Where's Karen and Sammy?"

Maureen straightened her skirt and thrust her chin at him pugnaciously.

"Safe," she said.

"Safe! They were never in any kind of danger! You told me they were coming here," he shouted. "You told me they were going to stay with us!"

"This is Laura's business," Maureen said. "She knows what's best for her children. She's got a right to keep them from the influence of a man who gets drunk when he's supposed to be taking care of them."

"Laura knows shit!" Frank bellowed at his wife. "She's screwing around on her husband and kidnapping their children away from him and robbing him of the means to make a living and you're helping her. Have you lost your senses? The man's entitled to see his children, he's entitled to be allowed to support them! You lied to me, you and Laura, bald-faced lied to me!"

"It's cold out here and I want my supper," Maureen said and marched up the steps.

Reuben followed her. "I need to talk to Laura, Maureen. Give me a phone number. I'll see her on her terms, where she wants to set it up. I just want to see the kids and talk to them. Please, Maureen, you don't have to tell me where they are. Just a phone number. Or she could call me. Get her to call me, please?"

Maureen shook his hand from her arm and slammed the door in his face.

Frank roared after her impotently. "Goddamn it, Maureen!"

Reuben grabbed his father-in-law's arm. "Get me a phone number, Frank. Or get Laura to call me. That's all I ask. Please."

"I'm sorry," Frank said. "I didn't know. I never thought it would come to this. I'll do everything I can.

"Reuben," he called from the steps, "stay off the booze."

Reuben gave him a nod and threw the truck into gear.

* * *

Face up and face down, the cards on the table did not yet even hint the outcome of the game of double solitaire his mother and Tiny Lunt had laid out. Frankie squatted on the floor, scratching Lucille's stomach. The old bitch's demonic red eyes rolled in ecstasy. Frankie jumped up and Reuben embraced him. Frankie hesitated and then hugged him back.

"What happened to your ear, Dad?"

"Nothing that won't heal."

"My goodness, that looks sore," Tiny clucked.

Reuben greeted her with a peck on the forehead and then did the same to his mother. Tiny cooed but his mother did not look up from her cards.

He scooched down to the old lady's level. "Ma, I want to apologize for the bad language last night."

Her eyes flicked toward Tiny, who nodded approvingly. His mother struggled between embarrassment and a certain pride that he was making what amounted to a public apology.

"Men swear in their cups," she said.

It was neither an acceptance nor an excuse but her way of underlining the offense for which he hadn't apologized.

"I made a meatloaf," Tiny said. "Supper'll be ready in half an hour. Ede and I have had a real nice visit, haven't we, Ede?"

His mother nodded and turned over a card.

He took Frankie into the office and shut the door. The broken records had been cleared away.

"I cleaned them up," Frankie said. "She shouldn't have done that. I wanna know about your ear."

The glint of excitement in his eyes made it clear he wanted to hear Reuben had found his mother's boyfriend and done him some damage. Reuben wished it were as easy as punching somebody out. The truth in all its petty ugliness was unavoidable.

"Laura busted a coffee mug on it this morning."

The cockiness of the fight fan went out of Frankie in a puff.

"Why?" he cried.

"Must have been my face."

The attempt at joking fell flat. Wariness shadowed the boy's features. Though familiar with his mother's instinct at the height of an argument to reach for the nearest object and pitch it, Frankie had never seen her draw blood. He had not been there when Reuben caught the knife with his bare hand. Nor had he ever been present when she punished Reuben's ears.

"You didn't do anything to her?"

It hurt being asked. "You saw her this afternoon—did she look like I'd done anything to her?"

Frankie shook his head. "You didn't call her a . . . some bad name?"

"No."

"She just smashed it into your ear?"

Reuben found himself excusing it. "She's wrought up—you said it yourself. You know how we've talked about teenagers acting up and mouthing off and so on, as part of growing up, getting ready to leave home? Maybe she's doing things that seem crazy to us to get herself worked up enough to get herself free of what's making her so unhappy."

Frankie's voice was tremulous. "Us?"

"Me," Reuben said quickly. "Just me. It's me she's unhappy with and me she wants her freedom from, not you and Sammy and Karen or she wouldn't have taken them off today and tried to persuade you to go."

As reassurance it only succeeded in reminding his son of the bad things that had happened.

Frankie looked away into something Reuben couldn't see. "A lot of my things are gone. Not my stereo or my records but my clock-radio, my bats and balls, my basketball, my baseball cards. The only clothes I've got are the ones in the laundry. It's like we were in the middle of moving somewhere else; there's stuff where it's supposed to be and then there's big holes. Sammy's room and Karen's—" he said and then he choked and wiped tears hurriedly from his face.

Reuben reached out to him but Frankie backed away. "She told us this morning she couldn't live with you anymore on account of you're not a Christian. Sammy asked her right away where we were going to live, and she said she was working it out, there had to be arrangements made. I asked her why she came in so late last night, and she said she was praying with the people at her church, what to do. I asked her if that's why she'd come in late the other nights and she said yes, it was."

"Do you believe her?"

Frankie looked at the floor. "No," he said. "Not about that. She was lying her head off."

Reuben put his hands on Frankie's shoulders. "I know you love your mother. Believe it or not, I still have feelings for her too. She must be very unhappy with me to have taken up with someone else. I don't understand why she's doing what she's doing, taking Karen and Sammy and cleaning out the bank accounts, she won't talk to me—"

"What did she do?" Frankie interrupted. "What did you say about the bank accounts?"

That was a slip. Reuben hadn't meant to dump that on the boy. His head ached fiercely. He was overdue for another slug of aspirin. He wanted several hundred beers too. Wearily he rubbed his forehead. "This morning she turned the bank upside down and shook out all our cash assets."

"Why? How can you do business, how are you going to work the cash flow?"

"I'll worry about that, Frankie."

"And so will I now I know about it."

It had seemed like a good thing, teaching Frankie how the business worked, that it wasn't just a matter of doing the repairs and pumping the juice. He guessed Frankie would have to know what Laura had done sooner or later anyway.

"Lawyers'll sort it out and we'll survive."

"Lawyers."

"I had to see a lawyer, Frankie."

"Jesus," the boy muttered. He wiped his nose with his sleeve.

Reuben passed him a tissue and Frankie blew his nose. "I have to call him now, in fact."

"What'd you do to her anyway?" Frankie asked. "You knew she was unhappy, why didn't you do something about it?"

"If I'd known what to do about it I would have."

Frankie just looked at him and then jerked the door open.

"I'm going to take care of Two," he said in a hoarse voice, and then he spun about and hurried away.

XXXI

"What's Up, Cowboy?" Freddy asked.

He told him.

"You speak to her?"

"No, never saw her. She led my father-in-law to believe she and the kids were going to stay with him down the road, but apparently that was never her intention."

"Any ideas where they are?"

"No. I expect she's turned to her church for help. I don't think she's got any friends outside of it anymore."

"Stay away from that church, cowboy. I know this really goes against the grain, but don't go looking for your kids or Laura. I'll locate them." Freddy paused. "How's that beer taste?"

For a long moment Reuben didn't reply.

"What beer?"

"The one you're sucking up—or is it bourbon? That was what you were sucking up at Joyce's wedding."

Reuben looked at the bottle he'd taken out of the fridge after Frankie went out to the barn. He rolled it thoughtfully across his forehead. It was cool and wet with condensation.

"Don't bullshit me, cowboy, you were so hungover this afternoon you could hardly stand up."

"I'm still hungover, Freddy. Do we have to deal with this now?" It sounded like a whine.

"Yes, my son, we do."

"Look, my wife's fucking somebody else and all I wanted to do was crawl in the bag and pull it over my head."

Freddy grunted. "That was last night. How often do you crawl in the bag and pull it over your head?"

"Jesus, I don't keep count. I don't do it that often. I couldn't work if I did, Freddy."

"You drink every day? Get shitfaced on the weekends?"

He didn't get it. Why was Freddy twisting his tit about drinking? Drinking wasn't a crime. He wasn't a drunk. This wasn't about him drinking. Laura left him because she wanted to leave. Because she didn't want to be married to him anymore. Because she had somebody else.

"Fuck you, Freddy."

A long, tired sigh came over the line. "Fuck you too, cowboy. You came to me with your life all fucked up and asked me to help you bail out. I don't have to do this, you know. I could tell you to go hire someone you can afford. Or I could shuffle paper for you and call that good enough. I'm trying to give you some genuine help, you asshole. Listen to me. When you're boozing you're not dealing with what's going on and you may be making it worse. Is this getting through to you, cowboy?"

Suddenly Reuben was near tears. His throat felt choked with sand.

Freddy plowed on. "Let me tell you something you don't seem to have figured out yet. It's not working. The problems haven't gone away, they've turned into a shitstorm. Booze is not a cure, it's not an out, it's not a fix. You need a clear head—you'll never need a clearer one. If you can't stay sober on your own, get help. I'm going to give you some numbers, people you can talk to about it."

Reuben wrote the numbers, first names and last initials, on a scrap of paper.

"I'll talk to you tomorrow," Freddy said.

Reuben hung up. He looked at the scrap of paper, then he crumpled it up and threw it on the floor with his busted records. He took the beer into the downstairs bathroom and tipped it into the basin. He ran the water after it to flush away the smell of it and then he took some aspirin, washed his face and hands. He had a long look in the mirror. No broken veins in his nose, no permanent flush to his face like Roscoe Needham or Alf Parks or one of the other old drunks. His hand was steady.

Frankie came in from the barn and washed up, and they sat down to eat Tiny's venison meatloaf. Either the aspirin or the food or both kicked in, and Reuben's headache lifted abruptly.

"I have to go back to work," he told his mother.

"I'll stay awhile longer," Tiny volunteered. "Ain't got a thing to go home to. Me and Ede, we'll throw together some coffee cake for your breakfast."

"Can I go with you, Dad?"

It lightened his heart just to be asked. It might not be his company the boy wanted so much as Jonesy's or the distraction of working on an automobile, or maybe he didn't want to be home if his mother showed up again. At least they would be together for a little while longer. Frankie grabbed his jacket and gave Lucille a hug, for which she washed his face with her tongue, making him laugh. It was good to hear it.

*　*　*

The boy parked his boots—big boots now, he was all gangly feet and hands these days with no idea where to put them—heavily on the dash.

"While I was taking care of Two, I thought about it." Frankie kept his gaze fixed on the passing countryside. "I've never been very good at figuring out how to make Mom happy either. I tried to remember times when she was happy—you know, maybe there was some common denominator. I could only think of a few times she seemed to be having a good time—other than when she's on Two. She's always happy then, isn't she?" He paused. "Have you been real unhappy with Mom?"

Reuben sighed. He looked into the dark woods on either side of the road for an honest answer. It saddened him, the boy trying so hard to be grown-up about it.

Frankie prodded him. "You said you still have feelings for her."

"Good ones and bad ones, all mixed up. I'm angry at her, I won't kid you about that. I'm very confused right now, Frankie. I guess if she wanted to come home I'd try to work it out with her."

"Why'd she have to take Sammy and Karen away like that? The business with the money's just nuts," Frankie blurted. "I thought Mom made her own money. Why does she need the savings and your cash-flow accounts? I mean," he took a deep breath and rushed it out, "if you get divorced, you have to divide up your money and stuff anyway, don't you?"

"Yes. She won't talk to me. I'm hoping your granddad will get through to her and maybe she'll talk to me on the phone soon."

"If she talks to me I'll tell her she *has* to talk to you, okay?"

"You don't have to, Frankie. You don't have to be any kind of messenger."

"I'm not a little kid. This is my life too, so stop being so protective of me."

Reuben smiled at him and he smiled back.

"Guess you told me."

"Guess I did."

At the garage they caught up on the pending work orders to the beat of oldies from the radio. Reuben found himself glancing at Frankie frequently, checking his mood. His older son had grown so much in the last year, the last week—he changed every day.

As a toddler Frankie had dangled his sneakered feet in the toilet here, had dragged crayons in crooked lines over the painted walls, had slept in a playpen next to the desk. He had taken naps on the mattress in the back room. He had learned to ride his first two-wheeler on the apron around the pumps. And what Frankie had done, so had Karen and Sammy. The sign on the garage had read *Styles & Son* since Frankie's birth, *Styles & Sons* since Sammy's. Frankie would never choose to divorce himself from this place he loved, from Reuben—would he?

✳ ✳ ✳

Returned to his marriage bed again that night, he heard Frankie down the hall, clearing his throat and blowing his nose. What was worse—the silence from the empty bedrooms of two of his children or the sound of weeping from the one who remained? A confused fragment came into his mind—*Rachel weeping for her children*—was it the Bible or *Moby Dick?* Wherever it came from, it was where his soul was, with *Rachel*. The devious-cruising *Rachel*, he remembered suddenly, *after her missing children. Moby Dick.*

He felt himself thinning, stretched like skin being cured on pegs. The room around him was dark but he could see everything almost as well as by day. It was as if his eyes could feel as well as see, as if all his senses were on red-alert but for what he didn't know. He stayed that way for what seemed like hours, every cell making itself known to him, from his throbbing ear and his headful of zombie brain cells, to the thickened skin on the soles of his feet, the beard prickling his jaw, his broken fingernails and scarred and callused hands, to Thing flopping indifferently upon his thigh.

His mind kept circling back to the idea a few beers would wet his dry mouth and loosen his throat and relax him into sleep. But he made himself stay in the bed, pretending he had lost the use of his legs and couldn't get downstairs to the refrigerator. He stared at the ceiling, at the inside of his right forearm, then his left, at the inside of his eyelids, and then tried the ceiling again. He listened to the roaring of his ear. His hand found Thing, but Thing wasn't interested. Thing must be suffering from the same terrible accident that had ruined his legs.

Bleary and desperate for sleep, he finally rolled out of bed and went downstairs. To the couch. Lucille padded out of the kitchen and lay down next to it, within reach of his slack hand. She slobbered and grunted and stared up at him, apparently relieved to have him back where he belonged. She dozed off. He lay awake until there was enough light to give it up and go tend the nag.

* * *

The state cruiser in the driveway at his in-laws was so familiar he had a moment of déjà vu before it clicked in it was Terry's, not Frank's. Presumably Terry was at his folks' to mediate between the two of them.

In Greenspark, Heidi received the tax returns and other papers eagerly. Reuben didn't stop to say hello to Freddy. He'd talked to Freddy Cape more in the last twenty-four hours than he had in the previous twenty years. As far as he was concerned, another twenty years' pause in the conversation would be about right.

Terry Haggerty was filling his cruiser's tanks at the pumps when Reuben pulled in at the garage.

Reuben took the gas gun from his brother-in-law. "How's your folks?"

"Chewing on each other. I just stopped to ask you if you have to fuck up everybody else while you're fucking up yourself."

Reuben holstered the nozzle. "This one's on me, Terry, just so I can get you out of here faster."

"Wait a minute," Terry called after him. "Don't turn down the state's money, asshole."

Reuben realized wearily that he was tense with fury and he didn't know where it had come from. Terry'd been needling him for years and he had rarely ever let it get to him before. It was a brother-in-law thing, Terry younger and challenging, and himself resentful of Terry's quick judgment. But Laura's brother was one of Frankie's favorite people. There were days and moods when Reuben could see Terry in the face of his older son.

In silence he took the credit card and wrote up the slip.

Terry switched about like a nervous cat. "I don't suppose you'd talk to me about what's happened between you and Laura?"

Reuben handed him the form for his signature. "I'm already sick of talking about it. It's hard enough talking to Frankie."

"How is he?"

"Messed up—what do you think?"

Terry took his credit slip and folded it neatly into his wallet. "Trish and I would love to have him stay with us this weekend."

Reuben thought of the way the house was, those empty places Frankie'd talked about, what kind of weekend the boy was going to have staying home. Terry and Trish would take him to some mall to play video games. Terry would rent kung-fu movies to watch with Frankie while Trish teased them about it and stuffed them full of homemade tacos.

"Ask him. A little distraction would go a long way."

Terry nodded. "Great. I'll stop by the house this evening and pick up Frankie unless he calls Trish and says no go. Maybe you'll call too if you feel like you can talk to me. I'd like to help. I'm pissed at Laura for the way she's acting. Jerking the kids around— that's lousy. Anything I can do to make it easier on the kids, I want to do, okay?"

Reuben nodded. Terry was being careful not to extend any particular sympathy to him. Laura was his sister, after all, and while he knew her faults well, having suffered them exquisitely as a boy, he had also kept a careful account of Reuben's sins and omissions.

"My dad's worried about you," Terry said.

"I'm not drinking, Terry."

"Good. Don't start. I see it over and over again. Some joker consoling himself with a bottle starts brooding about his wife handing him his walking papers, and all of a sudden it seems like a good idea to go right back home and blow the bitch away, give her a shotgun divorce, she wants out so bad. Then the joker's put himself in a corner where there's twenty cop cars in his yard and his options are down to a long hard go caged up in a zoo like Shawshank or maybe Thomaston if he's lucky or toeing his own shotgun or letting the SWAT team take him out. I hate calls like that—I don't want to get one and find out my sister's the stiff and my brother-in-law's the joker."

Reuben closed the register. "Relax. Your dad's got my firearms and I'm not homicidal or suicidal. I just want my kids back."

He met Terry's cop's eyes long enough to satisfy him, and Terry nodded and left. His brother-in-law meant well and he was good to Frankie, who needed all the family he could get.

* * *

He worked alone Friday night while Jonesy took his girlfriend to the movies in North Conway. Frankie went to Terry and Trish's.

Sonny Lunt bopped in with a six-pack in one hand and tossed him a can. Reuben hefted it and flipped it back to him. Sonny's face was a comic study as he almost didn't catch it.

"Hey, take it easy on the suds," Sonny protested. "I thought you might like to tip a few with me. Close the place up and then go close up some bars, check out the pro-am circuit."

Reuben shook his head.

Sonny carefully set the shaken can aside to settle, unyoked another, popped it and offered it to him. He waved it away. Sonny shrugged and drank it himself. "Stopped to see Ma and bum a meal and she told me Laura fired you. I figured you'd be up for a blow out—do some serious brain damage."

"Thanks for thinking of me, Sonny. I'm working tonight."

"Not all night."

"No, but I'm can't go drinking with you. I'm paying Freddy Cape too much money I don't have to advise me, and he's told me to stay sober and out of trouble."

"I'd fire the little prick," Sonny said. "He's just trying to keep all the pussy to himself. Freddy, huh? He was Joyce's lawyer, you know. Took that asshole she married right to the cleaners."

"Which asshole was that, Sonny?"

Sonny guffawed. "The rich one, dear. I wasn't worth the trouble to hire Freddy. Anyway the little prick wasn't even through law school when me and Joyce went boom, it was that long ago. Back then he was hangin' around Hahvid Yahd or wheresomeever it was with the peaceniks, wearing his hair to his asshole. After a while he got sick of picking crabs out of his teeth and cut his hair and turned into a shyster. Good move on your part, ol' hoss. Ma says Laura's snatched Karen and Sammy and left you with the change in your pocket."

Reuben hadn't supposed it would be impossible to keep the details from Tiny. Anything she couldn't pump out of his mother she'd have gotten out of Frank.

"Where you working now, Sonny?"

"Over the mountain, in East Ap. You changing the subject?"

"Ayuh. How'd the good folks of East Ap slip up and let you into their corner of heaven?"

Sonny burped. "Funny thing. Just today I saw something in E.A. made me think of you. Then the first thing Ma says to me tonight is you and Laura split up. I was going by this farm, passed it a dozen times in the last couple of days and all of a sudden it hits me. Sitting in the yard's a '59 Eldorado ragtop. It was so fucked up, it took me all that time to realize that was what it was. I thought maybe you'd already had a go at it."

He had to laugh.

"Had a 4-Sale sign on it," Sonny continued. "You don't want to go buy it and tear it apart for the fun of it? I missed the last time you did it, be a kick to see you do it. We could get all messed up and tear it apart together."

"Love to but I can't afford it right now."

"Farmer owns it only wants a hundred and a half."

Reuben shook his head.

"Hey, the Lord will provide," Sonny said.

"I'm not too crazy about the provisions the Lord's made recently on my behalf. And I doubt the IRS, the Texaco Corporation or Freddy Cape take the Lord's scrip. Or junker Eldorados."

Sonny sighed. "You're gonna curl up around this like a porkypine, I can tell you are. Work eighteen hours a day and be mis'able."

"I'd like to get my kids back, Sonny."

Sonny crushed a can and high-handed it into the trash can. "Yeah. Well, good luck to you. Just tell me sometime what God gave us divorce for if he didn't intend we should go out and pull a few horror shows."

"I got enough of a horror show going on right now."

Sonny barked a laugh. Reuben glanced up in surprise. He hadn't meant it as a witticism.

XXXII

Jerking Him out of a Sweaty, angry dream the telephone shrilled at him like an alarm. When he rolled over to fumble for it, the clock was going on seven. The last time he'd looked, it had read four and he'd wondered if it could be wrong. He was in Laura's bed again. Or was that in his dream? No, he really was upstairs, in the bed that was supposed to be theirs.

"Reuben?" Terry Haggerty, sounding chagrined. "Laura just came by and took Frankie with her."

He closed his eyes but he knew he was awake and it wasn't part of the bad dream.

"This wasn't some kind of setup. I didn't expect her to turn up. She must have found out from my mother he was here. It was his choice to go with her. What could I do? She's his mother, you don't have any kind of legal custody arrangement. I'm really sorry, man."

"Not as sorry as I am." He tried to slam the receiver into the cradle but his hands were shaking and he missed it.

He had to lean against the bathroom wall while he voided his bladder. Frankie could have called him, he could have told him what he was doing. *Why hadn't he called?* He dressed and went downstairs. His mother looked up from her tea and toast.

"Frankie's with Laura," he said and took his jacket and went out.

It was a snow sky, white and low, and the air was very cold. Two tossed his head at the sight of Reuben and shifted from one hoof to another in his stall. The gelding seemed to welcome the saddle. How many days had it been since it had last been exercised? He swung into the saddle, Two dancing a little and Reuben allowing it to express its excitement, before giving it a nudge toward the barn door. The first flakes stung his face as he walked the gelding through the barnyard toward the bridle path that led to the woods. Slowly they picked their way over frozen grass and mud and through the woods and down the hill to the Haggertys'. Wood smoke flagged the chimney. From the kitchen window Maureen in her bathrobe looked out at him with her face as stiff as pond ice.

He tied Two to the paddock fence and stroked his nose. Two nickered softly.

"If I had a gun I'd shoot you," he told the beast. The gelding jerked its head away as if it understood. "Then I'd put it in my own mouth."

The gelding curled its upper lip and snorted with seeming derision, and he let go of its cheek strap and set off walking home.

Once home again he tried to eat, but three forkfuls into the pancakes his mother had made, his stomach turned over and he went into the bathroom and heaved.

"Hungover?" she asked, tight-lipped.

"Don't I wish," he said and left.

In the truck he had his usual attack of guilt and turned around and went back inside to kiss her cheek.

"I'm sorry," he said. "You going to church?"

She nodded. "Ruby's going to take me."

When he left her she was still stiff-necked with anger at him. The odd thought struck him that maybe he'd come home and discover Laura had come by and taken his mother away too.

From the garage he rang Freddy to tell him Frankie had gone to Laura.

The lawyer was sorry to hear it but more concerned to reiterate his previous advice. "Don't go looking for them. And stay sober."

"Hey, Freddy," he asked, "what *am* I supposed to do?"

"You still shoot hoops at the meeting house?"

"Going there now."

Freddy said he'd be right over.

He kept some spare clothes in the back room. From the battered old trunk beside the mattress what came to hand first were the sweatpants Frankie had given him for his birthday a few weeks earlier and then the cutoffs Frankie preferred for himself. Underneath them, a couple of pairs of Sammy's shorts, hand-me-downs from Frankie.

The phone rang in the oily emptiness of the garage. He wanted it to be Frankie calling. By the time he reached it he was in a cold sweat.

"Dad?" Frankie spoke in a voice so low it was almost a whisper.

"Where are you?" Reuben asked.

"I'm okay. So are Karen and Sammy. That's all I can say right now."

Then the line was dead in his hand. He dropped the receiver and put his fist through the wall.

* * *

He'd broken a good sweat and the high school kids were working him hard by the time the lawyer turned up. Freddy watched for a couple of minutes, joining the jeers and catcalls of the kids and bystanders. Reuben didn't mind the needling about his decrepitude as long as he was keeping up with the punks. Once Freddy ventured onto the floor, Reuben pressed him as hard as the kids had him. There was a certain satisfaction in establishing he could still block anything Freddy had.

Reuben bought him a Coke from the machine in the hallway to the men's room, and Freddy took it eagerly.

"What's that I hear?" Reuben asked. "Is that the sound of Freddy Cape with his mouth shut?"

"Fuck you, cowboy," Freddy said.

"By the time I get you paid off, Freddy, you will have."

The thought made Freddy laugh with satisfaction. "How you feeling?"

"Everybody came in here this morning asked me that. Do you folks know something I don't?"

Freddy lifted an eyebrow. "You work this hard every Sunday?"

He nodded.

"Between the sugar in this Coke and adrenaline," Freddy said, "I'm as pumped up as Joyce was on toot at her last wedding."

"Come again? Coke? Joyce?"

Freddy knuckled the end of his nose and sniffed. "Grass is a little quaint these days, and flake's better than a feather down the throat for helping a girl keep her figure. Besides, Joyce can afford the high-priced high. Weed is just too high school. She and old Chipper snorkled their way through most of the nose candy in the county at that reception."

"I wasn't in a noticing mood."

The lawyer grinned. "No, I guess you weren't. Had a big night yourself. I heard your brother-in-law caught you screwing her in the coatroom."

Reuben punched another Coke from the machine. "I was so wrecked the details are all a blur, but I didn't actually get into her. I'm embarrassed to have to remember any of it."

"Well, I did get into her—not at the wedding but way back when—and I remember every second of every time. Took some of her last divorce out in trade too. I don't do it as a rule—fucking and business don't mix—but with Joyce, one minute you're giving her a little encouraging hug and the next thing you know your dick's wet and she's smiling like the cat that got the cream."

It was all good fun, but Reuben couldn't shake the sense of a long doggy snout jammed into his crotch. And all his good neighbors inquiring after his health when he wasn't sick—they were minding his business for him with all the best intentions, but he couldn't helping wishing they wouldn't. He supposed he wasn't any more entitled to the privacy of his wounds than anyone else.

After that a long, empty Sunday stretched ahead of him. He filled it up. Did the maintenance on the wrecker, a meeting at the firehouse, a rescue shift in the evening. Came home to find his mother weeping inconsolably. The farmhouse groaned with the wind and cold. It came to him this could very well be the rest of his life.

* * *

He took his jacket off the peg at eight on Monday and told Jonesy he had errands to run. Jonesy nodded and went back to his work.

The grammar school in the village had been overcrowded even when he had attended it. In the early sixties a new school for the fourth- to eighth-graders had been built a mile south of it. The buses had been emptied and parked, and school was in session by the time he got there.

The principal's secretary jumped up when Reuben came through her door. Through the open door to his office her boss, Brian Buckley, glanced up. Buckley tensed and started to rise.

"Reuben!" the secretary exclaimed. Doris Wright had been secretary at the grammar school when he went there. She had gotten white-haired and smaller, but she could still name every kid in the school on sight and recite their genealogies back to whenever their people had settled on the Ridge.

"Doris. I want to see Karen and Sammy."

Buckley came out of his office, his hand outthrust in greeting. "Reuben, come on in."

Buckley was an outsider. He'd been hired when the new school was built and had dug in with a will, but nobody had ever forgotten it was his wife—Cheryl Priest from the Back Narrows Road— who was native. Anyone with a question or a problem always dealt with Doris first. Buckley thought it meant he was a good administrator and Cheryl never told him different. Doris smiled reassuringly. This was one time Buckley would have to be involved.

Reuben was in a cold sweat of nerves and he didn't want to palaver with Buckley, but he took the chair the principal indicated to reassure him he was in control of himself. "You know what's going on, don't you, Brian?"

Buckley nodded. "I heard."

"I'd like to see Karen and Sammy. Just talk to them so they understand it's not my choice to be apart from them. Laura has no legal right to keep them away from me, you know, but I didn't come here to try to take them off the grounds or away from Laura. I just want to see them."

The principal shifted uneasily in his chair. "I wish I could help you, but they aren't here. They never came to school this morning."

"Oh." Reuben felt like seven kinds of fool. It was getting to be a familiar sensation. "I never thought she'd keep them out of school."

Buckley assumed an expression of professional sympathy. "I'm sorry you're having problems. If there's anything the school can do for the kids or if I can do anything for you personally—"

Reuben came to his feet. "Sorry to bother you, Brian."

Buckley offered his hand again. "Good luck."

Behind her desk, Doris blinked at Reuben over her bifocals. "From me too. It's a shame."

* * *

The lake was restless on the Ridge side of the Narrows where he stopped and got out of the truck. The dark, hopeless water looked as deep as any sea, deep enough to house monsters. As always he thought of the little girl, like a broken tree branch, falling, floating through the opaque depths. Always, his first thought on sight of the lake was of her. And then, always, he wondered if her murderer had had the same first thought. If her murderer was still alive. It was as if India had never lived even her nine short years. Like a drop of blood instantly invisible and dispersed beyond recall in the depths of the lake, a child's murder was absorbed by his community. By himself too. It was part of them, at some cellular level. He couldn't say no one was ever punished for it, only that no one was ever charged or tried. A murder unsolved in the first twenty-fours, it was said, tended to remain that way. So there was nothing special about hers, except a conspiracy of silence and guilt and perhaps that was not unusual either. How could you balance a child's death? Justice was meaningless.

A few flakes of snow whirled out of the zinc sky and spat into his face.

He got back into the truck and crossed the Narrows and a few minutes later passed through Greenspark's downtown. On the nether side he pulled into Willis' Ford Isuzu and parked near the service bays. Laura's T-bird was in the employee lot.

As he approached the side entrance of the glass-walled showroom the barbered heads of the salesmen rose in unison and alarm widened their eyes and brought them tensely to their feet. Dale Willis, a wide, nervous grin on his doughy mug, came lurching out of his office as Reuben came through the door. Willis hustled toward him.

"Reuben," he said heartily, as if he thought he were there to buy a fleet of trucks.

Reuben kept on moving toward Laura's office. Willis pumped along next to him, trying to put himself in front.

"Laura's stepped out," Willis said.

"Her T-bird's in the lot. There's not going to be any trouble. I just want to talk to her a few minutes."

Willis shook his head and planted himself in front of Reuben. He jerked his head at one of the salesmen, and the man reached for the phone.

"Nobody needs to make any calls, Dale."

"She doesn't want to see you or talk to you. Be sensible and go away before the cops show up."

Reuben brushed him out of the way. Laura's office was empty, but she'd left in such a hurry she'd abandoned her handbag. A thread was caught in the zipper. She always liked that shade of blue—it matched her eyes. He pulled it out and began to twist it around a finger. Willis stopped the doorway, and when Reuben looked up, he had a forty-five in his hand.

"Oh, for shit's sake."

"Just behave yourself," Willis said. "Put your hands on the wall and spread your legs, be a good boy."

"Semper Fi, Dale," Reuben said, being a good boy. "Call out the Marines. Don't you want to stop and get your uniform out of the closet, get a trim maybe—you don't want to let the Corps down, do you?"

Willis' mouth sagged with disappointment when his frisk failed to produce so much as a slingshot. "I'm not the one in the shit. Look, I got nothing against you. We've done business for years, I hope to continue doing business, but Laura's been here for years too. I'm real sorry you're busting up, but I've got an obligation to protect a valued employee and I won't tolerate having my place of business disrupted. So you just sit down there and be quiet for a while. You want a cup of coffee or something?"

"I want Laura to let me see my kids."

"They're not here. You shake that out in court, friend, that's what court's for. I've been through a divorce, you know, I've got some sympathy for you. I lost my kids too. I've been a much better father since I have to make an effort to see 'em."

Reuben didn't think Willis would use the gun, ex-jarhead or not. He sat down in Laura's chair and put his boots on her desk, noticing he'd picked up some of Two's leavings in the treads—in the course of filling the woodbox for his mother that morning, no doubt.

Along with pictures of the kids on the wall Laura had one of the Reverend Smart, a studio shot that made him look like a TV evangelist. Reuben reached up and plucked it off the wall, looked at it for a minute and then put it on the desk and dropped a heel on it. The glass crunched gratifyingly and some of the horseshit on his sole smeared across the preacher's face.

Willis jumped at the crack of the glass. "Don't do any more damage or I'll have to file a charge against you."

Reuben opened her top drawer and saw the usual Laura mess—paper clips clotted with lipstick from uncapped tubes, orphan earrings and stray backs, slips of pink paper with messages on them, a scatter of hard candies wrapped in cellophane twists, a fan of religious tracts and a litter of business cards.

"Stay out of her desk."

He ignored him. Willis had developed a squeak in his voice. Pretty soon the car dealer would be piddling down his leg. In the bottom drawer Reuben found a Bible and a couple of prayer books. Ah, well, perhaps a few minutes with the Good Book was just the ticket. The book opened naturally to "The Song of Solomon," where another picture of the Reverend Richard Smart acted as a bookmark. This one was a snapshot, taken at some informal church function—an outdoor setting, picnic tables, the Reverend Dick in a short-sleeved, open-collared shirt and Laura in a sundress, at his side, his arm around her waist. If you didn't know who they were, it would be easy to take them for man and wife. Her head was tipped to look at him. She looked happy. Shit, she looked deliriously in love. He tried to remember if she'd ever looked at him like that and knew she never had. Smart, he supposed, was the kind of man women thought good-looking. Maybe that was all there was to it—two people getting the hots for each other and everything else, marriages and kids and their own beliefs, falling by the wayside with their pants.

He slipped the snapshot into his jacket.

"What's that?" Willis said. "You oughtn't to be going through her desk."

"So shoot me. Where were you and your sidearm when she was going through our bank accounts?"

"I don't know anything about that—"

Terry Haggerty stuck his head in at the door and looked relieved not to find any blood on the walls. He glanced at Willis' gun and grimaced.

"Jesus, Dale. Was there any call for that?"

Willis puffed up. "In my judgment, yes."

Terry jerked his head toward the door. "Come on, Reuben. Thanks for calling me, Dale."

"Have a nice day," Reuben told Willis in passing.

The dealer looked pissed.

Outside, Terry gave him a good shove against his cruiser and kicked his feet apart. Willis and all his employees watched avidly from behind the glass walls of the showroom.

"Dale already played cop with me," Reuben said.

"You stupid fuck." Terry frisked him anyway. "What did you think you were doing?"

"Trying to talk to Laura, that's all."

"You let your lawyer talk to her lawyer and stay away from

her. You were lucky I'd already told Dale to call me, you got stupid like this. Next time you pull a stunt like this, it'll be on someone else's shift or the sheriff'll take the beef and you'll end up in court, catch yourself a weekend in jail and a protection order. If you never want to see your kids again, keep it up, jerk. You're making all the right moves."

"Thanks, Terry," Reuben said, "you're a sweetheart the way you look out for me."

Terry went all red in the face. "I couldn't do anything. The kid was crying, Laura was crying—what was I supposed to do?"

"Call me and let me talk to him. Let me talk to her."

He shook his head. "Maybe I should have put him on the phone to you, but I can't make her talk to you. What the hell do you think you could say at this stage to make any difference?"

"You talk to her," Reuben said. "You've got a number, don't you?"

Terry nodded.

"Tell her to meet me for dinner at Jean-Claude's next Sunday night. Tell her she can come home anytime she wants. If she doesn't want to come home, she really wants out, tell her to let the kids come, at least for now. We'll work out a fair arrangement. Tell her I surrender. The war's over. She can have whatever she wants."

Terry looked at Reuben in disbelief. "You don't get it, do you?"

"What do you mean?"

"She's got what she wants. You got nothing to negotiate with, man." Terry lowered his eyes. "Go on home, please."

✳ ✳ ✳

The wind was up as he crossed the Narrows and it churned the gunmetal lake water, tearing the last dead and ice-encrusted leaf from the trees that had held them stubbornly past the bleeding of their colors and the first snowfall. Behind the rising cloud cover the sun was a blurred and feeble blotch.

Within a half hour Freddy was tearing him up over the phone as Reuben leaned against the wall of the garage and picked horseshit out of his treads with the flat blade of a screwdriver. He muttered, *Right, Freddy.*

"You pull this shit again, you can find a new lawyer," Freddy said. He paused. "You didn't happen to find out anything?"

"Saw a bank deposit bag she must use for Dale's business because it wasn't our bank."

"You're thinking she might have shifted your funds to Dale's bank? Which one is it?"

Reuben told him. "What happens now, Freddy?"

"Sit tight, cowboy. Don't let it get to you."

Joe Nevers stopped in to warm his hands at the fire. The years were wearing him down, exposing the bony structure of his face and skull, of his knobby old fingers going through their husbanding of the cheroot. Bar the hectic red cold burn on his cheekbones, his skin had become almost translucent, from the lids hooding the arctic blue of his eyes, stretched taut over the blue lightning in his temples. It furrowed around his thin lips, gone a grayish purple, as if stained with blueberries. The caretaker took a look at the hole in the wall and grinned.

"Took it all a mite too seriously," Reuben admitted.

The old man winked. "Ah well, if things don't work out, you can always get work in the demolition business."

XXXIII

The Spin of the Cap Was Loud in the quiet of
the closed garage. The bourbon tingled his lip and nose, and Reuben paused to savor that sensation before he let it flow into his
mouth. He held it there and breathed deeply before he let it slide
on past his tonsils. He closed his eyes and remembered the widow.
The weight of the glass like buffed stone in his hands. She had
called it a jar. Brought a jar with me, she'd say. Let's have a jar.

"Let the good times roll," he muttered.

Rocking back on the office chair on its wheels, he fished the
snapshot he had taken from Laura's Bible out of his pocket. He took
it to the stove, opened the fire door and consigned it to the fire.

" 'Burn, baby, burn,' " he advised it and raised the bourbon in
salute.

Then he parked his ass in the chair again, hung his reading
glasses on the end of his nose and opened his books. An hour later,
he pushed the chair back with his heels, checked the lowered level
in the bottle and had another knock. When he tried to get out of
the chair he staggered.

> *Young man*
> *I was once in your shoes*
> *I said*
> *I was down and out with the blues*
> *I felt young man more dead than alive*
> *I thought the whole world was jive*
> *that's when someone came up to me*
> *and said young man*
> *take a walk up the street*
> *there's a place there called the YMCA*
> *they can start you back on your way*
> *it's fun to stay at the YMCA—*

he sang with more lung than tunefulness as he lumbered around the stove.

A sudden rattle at the door broke through the noise he was making, and he spun around to see who it was and nearly fell down, catching himself on the chair by the stove.

Joyce made a face at him through the window and rattled the door again.

"Shit," he muttered and went to let her in.

"I wouldn't have expected you to be a Village People fan," she grinned.

"Heard me, huh?"

She whipped a gauzy scarf off her head and waited for him to help her with her black mink coat. He hesitated. He had an idea the beastly expensive things weren't supposed to be handled like ordinary coats. But actually touching it freaked him out—the lush silkiness was like a woman's pubic hair. He fumbled to get it by the satin lining and then poked around to find a hanger for it. It looked very out of place among the greasy coveralls and jackets on the pegs.

Joyce picked up the bourbon bottle and sniffed it.

"You should have called me," she said, "you were gonna have a party."

She looked great, he thought. Jesus, she looked great. It was as if he smelled something good to eat; suddenly he was salivating. He swallowed and his tongue felt huge in his mouth.

"You want some?" he asked.

"Some what?"

Face reddening, he gestured toward the jar.

"Sure," she said and laughed.

He found a tea mug and slopped some of the bourbon into it.

"Cheers," she said.

They drank and then she dropped into the desk chair.

"You know, you're going to find this hard to believe, but someday you're going to look back on this and realize it was the best thing."

It wasn't actually the first time someone had offered him this particular bit of condolence. They were invariably divorced themselves.

"I don't know how it lasted as long as it did," Joyce continued breezily, then abruptly changed tack. "Actually, that's bullshit. I do. I know exactly how it lasted so long. It took me five years to write off Sonny, didn't it?"

"Let's not talk about it," he said. He didn't want to stand up anymore. He sat down on the floor with his back against the wall. Joyce's legs twitched sleekly in front of him as she crossed her ankles.

She stared at the bottle. "We haven't seen much of each other in a long time. I haven't forgotten how you took care of . . . the baby . . . and me when Sonny was away." Her face was taut with strain, her eyes dark and mournful. "Don't tell me it doesn't hurt. I've been through two divorces. I lost my kid too. There isn't anybody who knows better than I do what you're going through."

He didn't know what to say. He nodded.

She sat up and smiled ironically. "I heard a rumor Laura's having a fling with her minister—"

"Oh?" Reuben knew there was talk, but it wasn't coming from him. He'd told Frankie and his mother and Freddy Cape and no one else.

Joyce was disappointed in his lack of reaction. But after a moment's thought she smiled, satisfied by some mental process of her own that it was true.

"I'm not surprised. It solves a lot of problems for her—"

"That's good to know," he said with heavy sarcasm.

"Really," Joyce laughed. "Haven't you ever wondered why these hellfire and brimstone types are always getting into trouble over sex? It's the compulsion and fear they have about it that makes them religious in the first place. They try to get control of their sexuality by scaring themselves shitless. It's a self-fulfilling prophecy after a while—a cycle of temptation, sin, repentance and forgiveness and here-we-go-again. And the great thing is they still get laid."

He laughed raggedly.

"I wonder sometimes if I had more guilt about it," Joyce continued, "if I'd have even more fun."

They both laughed and she held out her tea mug and he spilled the last of the bourbon into it.

"Poor Laura," Joyce said. "She married you to get away from Daddy and Mommy and surprise! you turn into Daddy and she turns into Mommy. She didn't want to be Daddy's little girl anymore, but that was all she knew. And you didn't want Daddy's little girl, did you? You wanted a grown-up woman to fuck and have babies with. How'd we miss each other anyway?" Joyce grinned. "I saw her after she had the last one . . ."

"Sammy," he filled in automatically, wishing he could think of a way to tell her politely the last thing he wanted to listen to was her facile analysis of his failed marriage.

"—Sammy. She told me she didn't want him, you forced him on her." Joyce shrugged. "Funny, isn't it? It's the women who don't want babies get pregnant and the women who do, don't. Whatever. By then she knew she wasn't making it as a wife and mother. She told me if she didn't have a job, she'd go nuts from staying home with the kids."

"I know," he said. "I tried to help."

Joyce looked at him pityingly. "She said you were a shit about money. You wanted her to have her own so you wouldn't have to give her any."

Rocked, he wanted her now to just stop but he couldn't get his mouth in gear. He was numb and starting to feel sick.

"She called you Mr. Toothpaste," Joyce went on. "She said you had a thing about putting the cap back on the toothpaste and how it had to be squeezed out from the bottom. But you let the kids use it like squirt guns."

"Christ," he muttered. "I never thought it was that important." But he didn't know. Maybe he had been a shit about it. About money too. Did people start hating each other over the goddamn toothpaste? She hated him. It wasn't just she'd stopped loving him, if she ever had. She just out-and-out hated him.

"I don't want to talk about it anymore, please."

She looked him over speculatively and uncrossed her ankles. "Okay. Let's talk about you and me."

His insides lurched. He didn't move. He couldn't.

Her smile flickered off. "Oh, for Christ's sake, I thought you might like a roll in the hay for old time's sake. Cheer you up, baby. I've always had a thing for you. We both know it's not going anywhere, so what's the harm in having a little fun together?"

"I can't," he said.

Her eyebrows knitted delicately. "Just because Freddy Cape told you to keep it in your pants. He tells everybody that. He's quick enough to unzip himself."

"I can't," Reuben repeated angrily and hauled himself to his feet. "I can't."

Shock blanked her face a moment, and then she smiled and reached out to take his hand.

"Oh, baby, I'm sorry." She squeezed his hand. "It's not uncommon, you know, especially when you're going through a break-up—"

He freed his hand from hers. "I got half a load on anyway. Even if I thought I could manage it, the booze would probably sink me."

She stood up and moved closer. "Let me help. I'm good at this."

He laughed wearily and her lips pressed against his, she pressed her body against his. He hadn't shaved and his beard was prickly and she said ouch and laughed and kissed him again. She drew his hand to her breast, to her thigh, she was good at this, she felt as good as she looked, and desire kindled in him but it was very far-away, like the dead light of the moon.

"Shit," Joyce whispered in exasperation after a few moments of dead-end groping. "My lousy timing again."

He got her coat for her. "I'm sorry."

"Me too," she said, grabbing her scarf. "Goddamn it."

She gave him a hug that he thought could best be described as a no-hard-feelings one and then he was alone again. It was a relief to watch her taillights slew away into the night. He couldn't help sniffing around her, he thought, just the old monkey at work, but he didn't really want her. She knew what she was doing, telling him all that shit about Laura said this and Laura called him that, to make him feel shitty and hate Laura for it. Joyce was good at it, all right. The biggest turn-off came from the certainty if he did fuck her, she'd make sure to bump into Laura tomorrow and let her know. While there was a certain nasty appeal in trying to hurt Laura back, he found he was sick of ugly feelings.

He glanced at the clock and guessed he could go home now. Or not. It hardly mattered. Hardly.

" 'Young man,' " he muttered, sweeping the books back into the drawer. " 'I say, young man, there's a place you can go.' "

The mattress in the back room was cold and lumpy. He stretched out on it and closed his eyes and waited for sleep to come or not come, with or without dreams, good bad or indifferent. For time to pass and take him with it, drifting through the hole in the world.

* * *

In East Ap he found the farmer with the junked Eldorado and bartered it off him. A tune-up on his four-wheel drive and a pair of snow tires was as good as cash, the farmer said, in which his creditors might express an unhealthy interest. Reuben sympathized with him. He couldn't afford the parts even in barter to rebuild it any more than he could afford the work he would do for the farmer. He couldn't afford to work for anything less than cash, but it didn't matter because there was no way he could generate enough of *that* to meet his quarterly taxes or pay his distributor enough to keep his pumps open.

In a state of gleeful light-headedness he hauled the Cadillac ragtop all the way from East Ap. It was an extravagance much like taking his mother out to a restaurant and buying her the most expensive meal on the menu. When his financial house of cards finally collapsed, the cost of a prime rib and a bottle of imported burgundy, never mind the cash value of the work he had agreed to do in exchange for the Eldorado, would amount to a fraction of the bottom line.

When a luxury imports dealer from Lewiston, who occasionally farmed out work to him on the classic American makes some of his customers collected, stopped to gas his sedan, he pitched Reuben, not for the first time, to come work for him. To the dealer's surprise Reuben took his card and told him he'd give him a call in January, if he could wait that long.

"No shit," the dealer said. "What is it, your distributor finally succeed in starving you to death, or are you just tired of working for yourself?"

"Getting divorced."

His grin faded. "Oh. Sorry to hear it. I've been through it myself. Never again; next time I'll just shoot the bitch and take my seven years at Shawshank. Well, don't forget to call me. This might turn out to be the best thing ever happened to you."

Reuben doubted it, but he was getting used to people offering him inane comfort.

* * *

Freddy got a temporary custody arrangement approved that would return the kids to Reuben two weekends a month and for Christmas Day. When a permanent arrangement was made, he assured Reuben, the kids would come and go between Laura and Reuben as they pleased so long as the two of them lived in close enough proximity. Freddy thought it worthwhile to seek an agreement that neither parent would move out of the county.

On the first weekend Laura did not bring the children to her parents' house to be picked up, as agreed. Reuben's mother cried on Tiny Lunt's comfortably upholstered shoulder. Reuben worked and played long hours of basketball with anyone who was willing and tried not to think too much about it or the fifteenth of the month when push was going to come to shove.

On the seventh he arrived by appointment at Freddy's office to talk about the fact he was for all intents and purposes bankrupt. Freddy closed the door behind him and handed him an envelope.

"Merry Christmas," he said, "and Happy New Year."

Inside were cashier's checks covering the quarterly taxes and payments to the distributor and a deposit slip on a new bank account for twenty thousand dollars. Reuben almost dropped them.

"Mother of God, Freddy, where did this come from?"

Freddy plopped into his chair and parked his Italian shoes on his desk. "Only the Shadow knows."

Reuben shoved the envelope across the desk. "I can't take this."

The lawyer rolled his eyes. He flicked the envelope back. Then he passed Reuben a sheaf of papers. "You can't afford to be proud, cowboy. Sign where indicated and be thankful for large mercies."

He buzzed Heidi.

Reuben looked at the papers. They were standard personal loan forms, due in eighteen months and at a rate of interest that hadn't been available in fifteen years. The lender was a Delaware corporation called Podners.

Heidi popped in and Reuben shook his head.

"No," he said.

Impatient, Freddy gestured Heidi out. She shrugged and closed the door again.

"I can't service a debt of this magnitude, Freddy. What happens if I can't pay it?"

"They'll turn it over. None of the parties involved is risking anything they can't afford to lose—might even benefit them in terms of their tax liability. The worst case is you wind up with some silent partners."

"I'm sorry, I appreciate the gesture, but I can't take on potential partners when I don't even know who they are."

Freddy sighed. "I worked my ass off putting this deal together. You got friends, whether you know it or not. There's plenty of people remember you had your own business at eighteen and plenty know you pay your bills. Sign the papers, cowboy."

Reuben knew his mother's financial status as well as he knew his own, and she couldn't have done it. He would also be surprised if Frank Haggerty had enough extra and besides, his father-in-law wouldn't be shy about it. There wasn't anybody else in his little corner of the world he could imagine who could afford the kind of money that had been put up.

He supposed there were professionals in Greenspark, businessmen, men like Piers Larsen and Freddy's partner, Norman Bosque, who might have the extra to invest. It still made no sense to him. Freddy himself could easily be one of the investors. For all Reuben knew, Freddy had mob connections and when the note came due, he'd find himself running a chop shop for the mugs-and-thugs.

It came down to a choice between losing the last fifteen years of his life outright or accepting the bail-out. So what if the costs included running another set of books for a wide boy named Rocco? In the end he did what he had to do, and the former Heidi Robichaud notarized it, while pressing her left breast against his forearm. It felt less like a tit than a bald tire, he thought.

* * *

Snow filled the driveway of the old caretaker's house on the Monday morning after a hellacious late storm fell upon the Ridge, Easter weekend. The old man's wagon was there under a shroud of snow, but his four-wheel drive was not. On his way to work when the pristine fall in the driveway disturbed his eye, Reuben turned around and went back to check Joe Nevers' house. He found the caretaker's cat yowling on the stoop.

The morose fellow running the mom-and-pop store near the grammar school told Reuben Joe had been in the night the storm hit, asking about the widow. The proprietor was aggrieved; it seemed she'd stopped at the store to buy liquor and sideswiped his parked truck on her way out.

Reuben found the caretaker's four-wheel drive parked off the road above the widow's house and her current Cadillac lodged against a dead oak at the bottom of the drive. The steep road had made the old man cautious enough to leave his truck at the top of the hill and walk down. It wasn't the first time the oak had stopped one of the widow's boats. The snow around it was considerably disturbed, as if someone had tried to dig it out. He found the shovel.

Inside the summer house the old caretaker was as dead as the tree. Next to him on her bed the widow herself was nearly so. Her pulse was faint and irregular and her breathing pained and shallow. It was difficult to believe it was her at all. She was so old—he struggled to remember when he had last seen her. Surely she had not looked so very . . . old. And sick. Her hair—what there was of it—had gone completely white. It seemed obvious something had her in its claws—cancer, cirrhosis—something mean.

As he bundled her in blankets to keep her warm until Rescue arrived, she stirred. Weakly she rolled her head against the pillow. Drawing the blankets up to her chin, he realized her breasts were gone. She was more skeleton than flesh, as if she'd already died and been buried in some hot, dry place. He was shaken to numbness.

A shallow cough expanded and wracked her wholly. He brought her water and held her head while she sipped it.

"Shit," she grimaced.

Her mouth was loose and the water dribbled from one corner and there was a rumble in her flat, scarred chest that might have been a laugh. He wiped the dribble gently away.

Her eyes focused on him.

"You," she said breathily. It was a huge effort and she closed her eyes. He waited a moment and then, thinking she had slipped again into unconsciousness, started to rise to go out to the truck to call for Rescue. But the coughing seized her again and he hovered anxiously.

It let go of her and she was slack and gasping for a moment, her eyes rolling in her head. And then they found him again and she struggled to speak. He bent his ear.

She mouthed the word and it came out in two slow gasps. "David."

"As soon as I can find him," he promised.

And she closed her eyes.

* * *

Letting himself into the caretaker's empty house later that day, he found Gussie's current address and number in the old man's address book. He gave her the news. Gussie was as composed as he had expected her to be; that was the way she and her brother had been raised. He told her as much as anyone had been able to figure out: Joe had gone to one of his houses in the face of the unseasonable storm out of concern for his client, a woman known to have a drinking problem, and terminally ill. Attempting to free her vehicle from the snow, he had suffered an apparent coronary. The woman had attempted to care for him, but the phones were out, the roads impassable, and she was in a fragile condition herself.

"Old men and snow shovels," Gussie said. "Damned old fools. And the poor woman? I remember her. She never had any luck, that woman. Her boy, then her little girl."

"She'll be out of it soon, the doctor says."

"I'm glad he wasn't alone." Gussie told him she would call back later to make arrangements when she had a little while to let it sink in.

Under numbers for the widow's other residences in Falmouth and Boston was the name and number of a woman identified in Joe Nevers' Palmer script as the business manager. The house numbers were on recorders referring him back to the same woman's number. Presently he was connected with a brisk Brahmin accent.

"Is it the caretaker?" Ruth Gale asked. "He said if anything ever happened to him it would probably be you that called."

"That's part of it," Reuben told her. "He died over the weekend."

"I'm sorry," she said with polite formality. "I'll track down Mrs. Christopher and let her know."

"She knows. Joe died at the summer house. She was there."

"How unfortunate. How's she taking it?"

He detailed the widow's condition—touch and go and terminal in a matter of months anyway, according to the admitting physician.

"Oh, Lord. Do you know what's killing her? Cirrhosis?"

"Dr. Hennessey says metastasized cancer, but he doesn't know the original site, only that she's had a bilateral mastectomy, a hysterectomy and a large part of her intestines removed in the last year."

"Oh, my God," she said. "I had no idea. I go months just speaking to her on the phone. I haven't seen her in over a year."

"I thought you might know where David was."

"I'll find him," she said.

She asked him to fill in for Joe, at least temporarily, and that's how he became the caretaker of the summer house, for two days, until David fired him and hired Walter McKenzie.

XXXIV

Next Day He Met a power company crew at the widow's. After the Cadillac was moved out of the way they took down the oak, and the utility guys repaired the lines and restored the electricity. Ruby Parks cleaned the house while Reuben replaced broken window glass. With the heat back on, the place would be comfortable by the time David arrived. He towed the Caddie to the garage but left it untouched. David could see to its disposition.

It was a melting day under a harsh blue sky. Everything was wet, from the softening unseasonable snow to the road surfaces, the fields, the stoops where melt water fell from the gutters. At noon it was nearly spring, but after that the wind came up and by four a winter cold stung his face and hands when he had to go outside to pump gas. It made his ears ache. He stoked the fire in the stove and brewed himself strong tea.

Work kept him from closing up until past suppertime. He didn't know if David had gotten into Greenspark. Since he hadn't stopped at the garage Reuben assumed he was either still en route or at his mother's bedside at the hospital. Swinging by the summer house to check the heat, he was surprised to see the place lit and a new red four-wheel drive with rental company's plates on it parked there.

David opened the door before he could knock. In the months since Reuben had last seen him—five, seven? it seemed a long time past, when dinosaurs shook the earth, before Laura left and took his children with her—David's skin had darkened with exposure to a stronger sun. His resemblance to his mother in her younger years was uncanny. For a moment Reuben thought he had cut his hair, but when David turned away, he saw it was tied in a loose braid. It was longer than ever.

David shivered, stepping back into the long shadows of the hall. "Come in out of the cold."

Silently he took Reuben's jacket from him and led him to the big room, where he had a fire going. The place seemed hollow and empty. The few times Reuben had been in it, it always had.

David offered tea and he said no. David hesitated, then went to the kitchen and came back with a bottle of Wild Turkey; Reuben held up his palms to fend it off. David smiled and took it away with an undisguised relief that evoked in Reuben all the old feelings of shame and guilt and pity and admiration. He knew what it must cost David to go through the ordinary social act of offering a guest a drink. He slumped onto the couch. The heat was seductive; he realized he was tired.

David hauled a rocking chair closer to the fire, took off his glasses and rubbed the bridge of his nose wearily. "I heard you and Laura busted up."

Reuben stared into the fire, astounded at how much it hurt to even think about. "How's your mother?"

Resting his head against the chair back, David dropped his glasses back onto his nose and stared at the ceiling. "I didn't know who she was. I thought I'd gotten the wrong room."

"I'm sorry," Reuben said.

He shrugged. "I don't know about you, but it'll be a relief to me. And to her. It must have been absolute hell for you, seeing that diseased old woman and realizing you used to screw it."

Reuben stood up. "I'll be going now."

David came to his feet hastily. "I shouldn't have said that, I apologize."

"Never mind, David. It's all water under the bridge."

"Yes, I know. It was still a terrible thing to say," he said softly and abruptly changed the subject. "When is Joe going into the ground?"

"Not until it thaws a little more. Two weeks maybe. The arrangements are still in the air. Gussie's not in the best of health, it's an effort for her."

"I'd like to be there."

"I'll let you know." Looking at him, Reuben saw the nervous exhaustion in the strained muscle of his jaw, the shadows under his eyes. "Are you all right?"

David smiled in reassurance and walked with him to the door. As he gave Reuben his jacket, though, David touched him, a casual brush of his fingertips over the front of his pants. Reuben started. David was no longer smiling. He moved closer and his mouth brushed Reuben's. Reuben flinched. David laughed. It was an exhausted, embarrassed sound.

"You're fired," he said. "I'll take the house keys now."

Wordlessly Reuben handed them over. David spun the ring of keys casually around one finger.

"Send me a bill for what you've done. I saw the Caddie at the garage when I passed. I want you to have it."

"I don't want it."

"I know that. Use it for a paperweight, burn it, sink it in the fucking lake, I don't give a shit. Tear it apart for me. I'd like that. Good night, old man. Take care of yourself."

There was genuine affection in David's voice. He closed the door gently between them.

* * *

Joe's cat was all on her lonesome and Reuben went again to the caretaker's house the next morning to feed her. He changed her box and checked the heat. Walking through the empty rooms with his eye turned for roof leaks and broken windows and the little things that can go wrong in an empty house, he was conscious of the unnatural emptiness and the reminders of the old man still in the air. The place smelled of Joe's cheroots and his clean old man soap-and-aftershave, the aged wool of his work pants and shirts, the polish he used on his work boots, the cat box in the shed, a dry, ashy flavor of mourning and loss, even a very faint undertone of freshly baked bread. The only alterations that had been made in this house for decades had been the conversion of a ground-floor bedroom into a bathroom, complete with cripple bars, during Joe's second wife's last illness. Bar the wear and tear of time itself Joe's house was just as it had been when he had brought his first bride to it back in the twenties.

Reuben couldn't imagine Gussie, failing steadily to the depradations of a crippling arthritis, would ever come back to live in this house. It would pass into other hands, some young family's, most likely, and be renovated. The greatest change would not be new wallpaper and appliances but the shattering of the library quiet by the high-pitched voices of small children, the shrieks of childlike abandon as they slid down the banisters, the intrusion of the television's incessant chatter, the eighteen-wheel thunder of some kid's rock on a boombox, the music of other pleasures, some woman's laughter and the rhythmic creaking of the bed in the room under the eaves, with its views of both the mountains and the fields and orchards of Joe's property.

Old but not too old to feel the old man's absence, the cat twitched through Reuben's legs. Maggie. He remembered her name. Maggie the cat. He picked her up and gave her a good rubbing behind the ears before he left.

At work he moved the Caddie out back, next to the hulk of the Eldorado. A vision of sinking the widow's Cadillac into the lake kept recurring, but it was just a fantasy; the lake didn't deserve to be so sullied. In the end it took three minutes and one phone call to take care of the damned thing.

In the late afternoon David brought the red four-wheel drive to the pumps and filled the tank himself, waving Jonesy back to his work. Reuben went on with his own. Behind him he heard David accept Jonesy's condolences on his mother's condition as he paid for the gas, and then David crossed the bay toward him.

Reuben didn't look up.

"Mother's stable," David said. "I'm moving her to Falmouth tomorrow. Walter McKenzie will look after the property here." David looked around. "Where's the Caddie?"

"Just arriving in Falmouth," Reuben said. "I had it towed. You missed it by an hour and a half."

David laughed softly. "You win that one." He paused. He spun abruptly on his heel and strode out.

Reuben saw him again late that month when they lowered the caretaker's old bones into ground just this side of frozen in the graveyard not a hundred yards from Joe's own back door. The thickening tops of the old elms rattled mockingly. Gussie was too fragile to be there, but most of the town was. David's expensively tailored overcoat only made him look more thin and frail.

He was still more boy than man, Reuben thought. Peter Pan. The Lost Boys. Tick Tock, the alligator with the clock in his tummy. Tinker Bell. Even as a kid that story had given him the creeps. Years later he'd read William Golding's *Lord of the Flies* and thought there it was again. The Lost Boys. Pan was a pagan god; if you were a Christian, all those old Greco-Roman deities were in fact other names of the selfsame Lord of the Flies, whose name was Legion. Grand reading and terrific poetry but there was no need to name the devil. The raw meat and bones was nothing more or less than human nature. Boys were cruel. People were cruel. Time was cruel; it had teeth like an alligator.

But it was kind too; it relieved the sick and the old of grief and pain and loneliness. Old Joe was out of it, more or less gracefully and with minimal pain; he was beyond the tick tock of the clock forever, consigned to the embrace of the earth he had tended like a garden. His bones would sweeten the thin acid soil of the Ridge.

David left with everyone else while Reuben remained to repair the breach in the earth. After replacing the sods he stood in the silence amid the markers. Overhead the trees clawed and raked at each other with a noise like chains dragging, and a branch cracked and crashed to the ground. Always the change of seasons raised troublesome winds. There'd be power lines down this evening, and the trees would give up their dead wood to the reap of the wind. It would be something to listen to as he lay awake tonight.

* * *

Autumn stained the Ridge before David called again. He didn't say his mother was dead or use any of the conventional euphemisms.

"It's over," he said tersely.

Two days later he lingered, loosening his tie, in the cemetery and watched the box sinking into the hole. He had cut his hair; it was shorter than Reuben's. The undertaker departed and still David stood there by the stone wall, his eyes hidden by the dark lenses of his sunglasses, riveted on the process as Reuben backfilled the grave. When Reuben stepped down from the backhoe and began to replace the sod, David took off his jacket and tie, rolled up his sleeves and helped, staining his white linen trousers with the clay soil and the grass. That done, they piled up a variety of wreaths upon the grave. David picked up his jacket and stood staring at the newly sodded, slightly faded green patch that marked the grave.

"Think she'll stay down?" he asked.

"Never had one that didn't."

He laughed harshly and clasped Reuben's hand. "I thought when she was gone I'd be able to breathe again, but I still feel like she's sitting on my chest, only she's turned to stone."

"Give it some time."

An hour or so later, David wandered into the garage and put the kettle on. He still wore the suit, but his shirt was sweated through and his shoes ruined; clearly he had been on a traipse. Reuben wiped his hands and drew up a chair next to the cold stove. David made them both tea and they sat there together in a companionable silence that was like the old days.

"Tell me about the war between you and Laura," David said out of nowhere.

"Don't you read the papers?" Reuben asked. "Watch the tube?"

"Yeah, but they lie. And they get things wrong."

He shrugged. "Very human of them. I don't want to talk about it."

David leaned forward. "Remember the day after the baby died you were so hungover and I gave you the beer. Hair of the dog, right? Spill. Think of it as hair of the dog."

Reuben rattled the kettle and refilled it and put out the crackers and peanut butter, and then he joined David in putting his feet on the fender of the stove.

"First we worked out a temporary custody deal," Reuben said.

* * *

He remembered waiting in the Haggertys' kitchen, his father-in-law sitting opposite him at the table, waiting for Laura to bring the children that first time.

Good born-again Christian that she had become, Maureen couldn't abide being in the same room with him. She had taken herself to her sewing room, and they could hear the angry mechanical sting of her machine above them. Reuben's mother was at home, baking for the kids. When Reuben had left the house she had been talking aloud to Lucille. She had been doing that awhile now—went on for half an hour at a time sometimes. She didn't seem to know she was doing it either. He thought she had had some kind of little stroke, the kind that releases eccentricities and insignificant craziness.

The appointed time came and went while he twitched and wondered whether he had gotten the time wrong or the clock was broken. He waited an hour past it. He called Freddy and Freddy called Laura's lawyer and then called him back and said so far as her lawyer knew she had been going to comply. He waited another hour and called Freddy again. Then he went home and listened to his mother talk to the dog.

On Monday they went back to court. The lawyers worked everything out again and the kids were supposed to be home for Christmas. His sister, Ilene, made the trip from Oregon to be there. His mother talked to the dog all day Christmas Eve with increasing excitement. Laura didn't bring the kids and his mother wept again.

Ilene went back to Oregon and he went back to court.

The hearing was the first time he had seen Laura since the morning after she had left. He had a moment's confusion; she didn't look like Laura anymore. She was a stranger, smaller than he remembered and nowhere near as pretty. Oddly cold eyes, wary as a snake. He wouldn't have looked twice at her on the street. He wondered if it was the same with her—if she barely recognized him and was shaken by the thought this man was once her husband who had seen her naked and possessed her and seen her, bleeding and writhing, expel his children from between her legs.

It was hard to concentrate on the legal arguments. Laura's lawyer explained that Laura was a devout Christian who regarded the safeguarding of her children's souls as a paramount duty. Her failure to turn over the kids at Christmas was really an exercise of freedom of religion—a mother seeing to the religious devotions of her children through the Christmas holy days.

The judge reprimanded her anyway, but that was the limit of it. Freddy protested. Reuben hadn't seen his kids in months. What right did Laura have to impose her religion on her kids or to take the kids out of public school and put them in church schools without Reuben's consent? Weren't the children his as much as hers? The judge hemmed and hawed and said she was the custodial parent for the moment and she could take them to church and put them in any state-accredited school she wanted. Freddy said Reuben had never consented to Laura's custody of the children.

The judge left the kids with Laura while Freddy kept hammering at another agreement that would take them through the divorce. Laura didn't comply with that one either. She fired her lawyer and hired a new one, who consequently needed time to acquaint himself with the details. This tactic worked so well she proceeded to fire and hire lawyers until it was a joke at the courthouse about how soon every lawyer in the county would have had a turn in her employ. The judge began to be seriously irritated.

Freddy asked for custody and the judge ordered the kids removed from Laura—and into state care.

* * *

"Freddy went bugshit," Reuben told David. "The judge threatened him with a contempt charge."

"Sonny got into it too, didn't he?"

"I don't know what Freddy did exactly, but he called in some favors or something and the state placed the kids with Sonny's mom. She's been taking in foster kids on an emergency basis ever since her own kids grew up."

But when the social workers turned up to take them, Laura went out the back door with the kids. Freddy had had the foresight to have a private investigator watching that back door. With his information the state cops located Laura and tried to serve a contempt of court order as well as the DHS order. She went out another back door and took sanctuary in her church.

While the concept of sanctuary has a strong romantic appeal, in the U.S. of A. it has no legal weight whatsoever. The state proceeded to serve the legal orders. Terry Haggerty somehow wangled permission from his commanding officer to be there, so there'd be somebody the kids knew. Consequently the Sunday front pages all had it: a four-color shot of Karen clutching Terry's hand and Sammy with his face hidden in Terry's armpit. It was a cherry on the whipped cream, Terry being Laura's brother and a state cop too. There was another photograph of Laura, looking like Joan of Arc on the way to the stake, handcuffed between a couple of state bulls the size of pro wrestlers. And the most important one, the wide-angle of the brawl between the cops and the preacher and his brownshirts.

"*Highlights at Eleven.*" Reuben grimaced. "It was like watching one of those clips from the middle of some civil war in the back of beyond, except the faces—" He stopped. "I couldn't bear watching it but I had to. I felt like a man on a desert island, eating bits and pieces of himself to stay alive."

"Indeed," David murmured.

When Terry's cruiser arrived with the kids Reuben was waiting for them on Tiny's back stoop. It was the first time he'd seen them since Laura took them. They looked different too. They'd done a little growing, of course; they couldn't help it. But they were changed. The boys' hair had been shorn nearly to boot camp baldness. All of them wore unfamiliar clothes—a dowdy dress on Karen that fell past her knees, Mormon missionary suits and ties on

Frankie and Sammy. And they were pale and shaking, as if they had just crawled out of a train wreck.

"Sammy thought he'd been arrested and was being taken to jail. Frankie and Karen were furious," he told David. "I saw what Laura and I were doing to them. It made me sick. I apologized to them. I told them if they wanted to go back to her, I'd take them and there wouldn't be any more fighting about who they were going to live with. I was trying to make it stop and all I did was scare them some more. They didn't want to go back. They thought I was going to make them go live with her. I thought I'd screwed up before—"

He got up and went into the bathroom and threw the dregs of his tea into the toilet. He splashed water on his face and took some aspirin. David was huddled around his own cup of tea when he emerged. They sat in silence for a little while and then Reuben realized he needed to tell the rest of it.

Within hours the reverend and his cohorts were bailed out. They convoyed straight to Tiny Lunt's. It was still the Sabbath but just barely. The kids were in bed and Reuben back home and on the phone with his sister, telling her how it had gone. The preacher and his posse pounded on Tiny's door like night riders, bringing Tiny downstairs in her flannel nightgown and runover slippers. The kids crept from their beds and watched from the upper windows.

"What do you people think you're doing, getting decent folks out the bed the middle of the night?" she demanded.

"The Lord's work, Mrs. Lunt," the preacher replied. "A mother is waiting for her children. We've come to fetch them to her."

"Judge placed'm here, Reverend, and seeing as how I haven't heard from the Lord myself, I'll just be keeping'm. Now you and your gang beat it 'fore I call the cops."

The Reverend Smart was not to be deterred. In the ensuing struggle to enter her house he knocked Tiny down. She broke her hip in the fall. Once the fracas started Frankie came hurtling downstairs to defend her, but by then it was too late. All three children were forced into waiting vehicles.

Tiny got herself to a phone.

Freddy met Reuben at the hospital and took him back to the Ridge and spent the morning there with him, shooting hoops at the meeting house. He wasn't letting Reuben get into trouble.

Sonny took charge of the getting into trouble. He and Charlie and some other male relations—Lunts and Partridges and Priests—collected up tire chains and baseball bats and went to the church in Grant to set things right.

Freddy was disgusted. "Cowboys," he said as he and Reuben watched the live broadcast of the second brawl at the church.

Sonny and Charlie earned themselves three weekends in stir, where they amused themselves rattling their bars at the reverend, who got six months on a plea-bargain. Laura was fined and got a weekend in stir herself. Reuben was astounded at the leniency of the court—the preacher had committed a felony, a kidnapping, and they *plea-bargained* it? And allowed him to declaim in court on the separation of church and state and freedom of religion.

So far as he could see, what Laura and her co-religionists meant by separation of church and state was that their membership in their church exempted them from having to observe civil law. Freedom of religion for them meant freedom to force their religion on everybody else. He thought the judge was scared shitless—and why not? The judge—like Reuben and Freddy Cape and Tiny Lunt and Terry Haggerty—had received written and telephoned death threats and suffered some form of midnight vandalism—tires slashed, home or office windows broken. Be that as it may, the judge did give Reuben full custody, and the state cops, with riot guns, went into the hostile community of Grant and took the kids away from Laura and brought them home.

"Don't tell me us white folks don't know how to have a good time," Reuben said.

David grinned.

"At least you've got them back." He went into the lavatory and rinsed out his mug. "Time for me to go."

Reuben reached for his hand and David clasped it and threw his other arm around Reuben's shoulder and hugged him. He tensed. David, sensing it, released him.

"Take care," David murmured and left with an abruptness that made Reuben feel like dogshit. David had only wanted to comfort him.

XXXV

There Was More He Hadn't Told. Frankie
came back with his front teeth broken from a stray fist during the
melee at Tiny's. Sullen and withdrawn, he displayed a newly angry
and dictatorial hand with the two younger children.

Karen—when Reuben sought to embrace her, she turned into a
rigid, thorny little tree. Often she seemed to be two people, the
hard bark of the one on the outside protecting the one living on
the inside. She was deaf to both love and authority, and her laughter had a bitter edge to it. She looked at the world with eyes too
old and knowing for her age. In her presence Reuben felt as he so
often had in Laura's—as if he were the fly-blown corpse of a gutted deer, something so unbearable that his existence could not
safely be acknowledged.

Sammy ceased speaking altogether. For the first few weeks at
home he had gotten up in the night to smash light fixtures with his
baseball bat, piss his name all over the walls and tear the stuffed
animals of his babyhood limb from limb. It took almost infinite
patience to cope with it, but gradually he was becoming calmer.
Ilene had sent him a short-wave radio and Frankie had helped him
raise an antenna on the roof. Reuben was becoming used to finding his younger son asleep with a pair of headphones askew on his
head, in the green and red light of the radio's readouts.

Once the children had been returned to his custody, he arranged through Freddy to allow Laura to see them regularly, on
her oath on the Bible she would comply by the agreement. She
swore the oath. He didn't know what brought her around—her
brief experience of the county jail, the whole godawful hooraw
and its effect on the kids. Maybe she was just tired of the power
struggle—and he didn't care so long as she stuck to the agreement.

Then Sammy wouldn't get into her car when she came to pick
him up for the first scheduled weekend with her. Frankie tried to

talk Sammy into it and, when that didn't work, tried manhandling him into Laura's car. Sammy fought back and the two of them went sprawling onto the ground, pummeling each other. Laura demanded the kids stop it and get into the car. Karen applauded ironically while Reuben separated the two boys.

Red-faced, tear-stained and snot-nosed, Sammy picked up his duffel and headed for the back door. When Laura grabbed him he shoved her aside.

"I'm not going," he said. "I hate you."

Laura started blubbering but the kid ignored her and went back into the house.

"Let me talk to him," Reuben said.

"Leave him alone," Karen blurted.

Laura turned on her. "Nobody asked your opinion."

"Shit," Frankie muttered.

Karen picked up her knapsack. "I'm giving it anyway. I guess if Sammy can stand up on his hind legs and refuse to spend his weekend being prayed over, then I can too."

"Guys," Reuben said, "let's go in the house and have some cocoa and talk it over."

"Talk it over," Karen sneered. "She makes Sammy sleep in diapers, Daddy. Tell him, Frankie."

"It's true," Frankie said. "They're going to exorcise him if he doesn't quit pissing the bed."

Reuben looked at Laura, but she wouldn't look at him.

"I see. All right. This isn't going to work this weekend, Laura. Go on home. Some time next week we'll get together, you and I, in Freddy Cape's office and we'll talk about this. We need some ground rules."

"Give in to them," Laura said. "It's so typical. They walk all over you. You're ruining them."

"Humiliation doesn't cure incontinence," Reuben countered. "And neither does exorcism. And while we're on the subject, I'm not getting into any more pissing contests with you. Call Freddy, please."

Watching her drive away, all he could think was, she's crazy. She's stark raving nuts. They all are. Not misguided, not well meaning. Just fucking out of their gourds. Exorcism. They'd be burning witches if they could get away with it. They'd had his kids for months. Jesus. He took a deep, shaky breath and went inside to see what he could do for Sammy.

* * *

A message from Freddy summoned him to Greenspark some weeks after he'd seen David. The reception desk was empty, Heidi nowhere in sight. He leaned over the desk and groped along the intercom for the button marked FREDDY, above which Heidi had taped a newsprint image from a movie ad of sad, bad Freddie Krueger, and pressed it.

"*Hey Hey, Lord Lord, Yeah Yeah, Ah Huh,*" Reuben sang in falsetto, "*Freddie's daid, that's what I said.*"

Freddy stuck his head out of his office. "Hey, cowboy."

The lawyer grabbed him by the elbow and hustled him into the office with a positively furtive air. He shut the door firmly behind them.

"Gotta show you something."

He turned on a portable television set on the credenza opposite his desk—something new. With a videotape player next to it. Freddy punched up the tape.

It was somebody's homemade porn. Shaky camera, bad angles, jerky action, wretched lighting and worse focus—no sound, thanks for small favors.

"Oh, come on, Freddy," Reuben said. Then it hit him. Laura. That shithead preacher.

Struggling between disbelief and the undeniable fact of what he was looking at, he watched a moment longer and then lunged for the off button.

"Sweet Jesus," he said. "I'm trying to see how funny this is, but my sense of humor seems to have cramped up on me. I think she's done her worst, she's screwed up as bad as she can, and then you come up with this. Is she crazy, Freddy? I didn't see it when we were living together, but I swear to God, the shit she's done, she's out of her mind."

Freddy handed him a Coke. "I don't know. I'll grant you she's screwed up."

Reuben slumped into Freddy's chair and put his feet on Freddy's desk and knocked back the Coke while the lawyer played an audiotape of a conversation—a confrontation—between a woman named Judy and the Reverend Smart. It seemed Laura had displaced this Judy in the reverend's affections. Once the reverend had somebody else, Judy had repented of her adultery with him. Now she wanted a public repentance from him. And of course a break with Laura. He blustered a lot but basically it came down to no way, sister. But Judy had been secretly recording him. She knew his predilections and she still had a key to the cottage he used for his assignations. She had hidden in a shuttered closet there and videotaped the reverend dallying with Laura. Then she had brought the tapes to Freddy, knowing he was Reuben's lawyer. Not to help him out in any way, just to get back at Laura.

"I told her you'd never use this stuff; it would hurt your kids too much, never mind the personal humiliation," Freddy said. "In any case, it would be a conflict of interest for me to represent her in a separate actions against the reverend and his church. I sent her to another lawyer."

"I can't believe people actually do this shit to each other," Reuben said. "I didn't have a thing to do with it unless you want to blame me for Laura, but here I am in the middle of a stiff-dick preacher scandal anyway. I feel like somebody pitched a truckload of horseshit into a jet turbine just as I walked into range."

"I'm sorry," Freddy said. "There's no way to suppress this stuff. Judy Crouse has got her own agenda. A lot of people are going to see that videotape before this is all over. There's one advantage for you in it. With a suit involving a sex scandal I think the church board is going to be a lot more amenable to rolling over your money rather than deal with another suit prolonging the stink."

"Forget it, Freddy. I quit. I don't want the money anymore. If I go under without it, I go under. I'm out of this mess right now."

Freddy leaned over the desk to hiss into his face. "The hell you say. Look, cowboy, you can't go pull a rock over your head. This shit's coming down whatever you do."

Reuben thought about it for several long moments while Freddy paced. "How long before this goes public?"

"Judy's lawyer's taking it to the church board tomorrow night. I'd guess the story, if not the tape, will make the eleven o'clock news."

"I think my kids need a trip to Disney World."

"I do too," Freddy said. "Think they need a trip, I mean. I don't want to go with you. You need money?"

"That's an amazing question, coming from you. My credit card's clean and I'll run out the credit line. I might as well be bankrupt for eighty thousand as seventy-five."

Twenty-four hours later, Reuben was suffering shell shock at the price of the tickets to the Magic Kingdom. He let the kids enjoy it a few days before he told them why they had taken such an abrupt vacation—it wasn't something he could keep from them forever. All he'd hoped to be able to do was keep them out of the sight of television cameras when the scandal broke. Finding the words to explain they were at Disney World because Mommy had gotten herself videotaped in embarrassing circumstances with her boyfriend was a lot trickier. It took them a little while to get back into the spirit of the vacation but they did, Frankie a little grimly, Karen and Sammy a little shrilly.

The tamer outtakes made the papers as grainy stills—the video was fortunately of very poor quality, which didn't stop even more horrible copies playing the crummier bars and VFWs across the state for a couple of years. Mouse-trapped, the preacher repented movingly and resigned, with full media coverage. So did Laura. The reverend's wife stood by her man and forgave Laura, and everybody got right with Jesus. And in short order the reverend decamped to another community and founded a new church, and Laura followed. The distance made it almost impossible for the children to have any time with her, even if she had been willing to work out the problems they had with it.

✳ ✳ ✳

There wasn't a lot of choice. They went on with their lives.

The transfer back to Greenspark Academy from Laura's church's high school had been difficult enough for Frankie. Once the further scandal broke it was unbearable. One day he came home and announced he wasn't going back. Reuben figured a mental health break wouldn't hurt him and let him work at the garage for a couple of weeks. That didn't work any miracle cures, and all of a sudden he and Frankie couldn't talk to each other about anything without an argument. Frankie quit the garage, which Reuben thought was exactly what the kid wanted to do— the opportunity to tick off his old man—and Frankie found himself a job with the town crew.

At about the same time Reuben's mother took a bad turn and kept on turning, until one evening she died on the way to the hospital. Between what his mother left him and the legal settlement with Laura's church, Reuben cleared the bulk of his debt but didn't quite get out of the hole.

One night Frankie came in from a dance at the academy with

booze on his breath. He wasn't drunk, so Reuben didn't say anything about it. The next weekend Frankie was very late coming in and threw up on the back porch. Reuben didn't say anything until the next day, when he asked Frankie how he liked his hangover and then took his keys and grounded him for a month for driving drunk.

Barney the tomcat disappeared for three weeks and then staggered in one day, emaciated and half dead, and expired on the mattress in the back room of the garage.

Joyce got married a third time. On a flawless June day she gave birth to a girl she named Antonia. In the wee hours of the next day Reuben bailed Sonny out of the drunk tank in Greenspark and took him to Tiny's to sleep it off.

A wave of break-ins of summer places on the lakes culminated in the beating and rape of a woman visiting her summer home between Christmas and New Year. When she escaped and sought shelter in Miss Alden's cottage, it turned out to be fatally booby-trapped and the rapist was killed, with his brother and step-brother, who were along for the ride. Miss Alden shot herself.

Frankie went back to school. Nearly every weekend night he came home at least lightly toasted, though he was supposed to be in training for one sport or another. He spent a lot of time hitching while Reuben held the keys to his truck. Then one wet night five Greenspark Academy students wrapped a souped-up Mustang around an ancient obdurate white pine. Reuben heard about it on the scanner and volunteered Frankie and himself to go help clean it up with Maxie Sweetser. After that Frankie steadied down for a while.

Frank Haggerty choked to death on a chunk of TV dinner turkey while watching a football game. Maureen had become very arthritic and Terry moved her into his home to take care of her. Within the year he had to move her into a nursing home, but by then Trish had left him, taking their twins with her.

One night Reuben caught Frankie lighting up a butt behind the barn—confirming suspicions of several months—and Frankie ratted on Karen, who did indeed have a pack of Marlboros in the leather sack she carried as a handbag. He made them both smoke every cigarette they had, one right after the other, until they were green in the face. He grounded them and fined them their allowances and was smelling tobacco smoke on Karen within the week. By then he was sicker than hell with an ear infection and was too miserable to be able to think what to do about the two of them smoking.

Laura abruptly filed for a change to shared custody, a physical impossibility without a matter transporter. The kids went into court and told the judge they didn't want to see her, period. Reuben said whatever they wanted was fine with him. The judge hemmed and hawed and frowned and allowed the kids were old enough to be consulted. But not old enough to just write off one parent. He decided Laura should see the kids once a week under the auspices of a family therapist for a period of six months. She and Reuben would share the cost. Laura never showed for the appointments. Karen and Frankie dropped out of the sessions after the first couple of times, but Sammy took a shine to the woman counselor and went for a while on his own. Reuben paid for it.

Karen grew beautiful and wild as blue flag by the water's edge. One afternoon Reuben caught her smoking marijuana in her room, and she ratted on Frankie, who had been toking up out in the tack room. Frankie had a good three ounces stashed in the battery pocket of a flashlight. Karen had less than half an ounce of weed in her handbag, along with half a dozen condoms she claimed were a joke a girl at school had planted on her.

Reuben thought he had made his stand on marijuana clear. And it wasn't enough, obviously. Probably silly of him to hope it would be. He sat the miscreants both down to point out—again—that weed, despite the easing of laws on possession for personal use, was still illegal—as indeed, the purchase of tobacco products was for them as minors. He didn't want it in the house, he didn't want them using it, and if either one of them or both got busted for it, he would let them enjoy the experience of the county jail, and they would have to pay for the services of a lawyer and whatever fines they were assessed. Oh, and they were both grounded for the next six months. And fined Karen her allowance and docked Frankie half his wages for the same period, since obviously if they could afford pot, they had too much disposable income. Groans and outrage.

He had been concerned at the influence of Laura's prudery on the kids and didn't want them growing up as abysmally ignorant of sexual matters as he had. Providing them with what he could find for books and pamphlets that seemed appropriate to their ages, he had tried to impress upon them the need for protection from disease and unplanned pregnancy. From the way they received the information, he suspected he was behindhand with both Frankie and Karen—they were embarrassed and dismissive.

"You don't have any business with these things even as a joke," Reuben finally told Karen when he went in to say good night to her. "You're too young to have sex. Your girlfriends are too. Sex is a lot more powerful than weed, sweetheart, and you can get seriously messed up with it. The miserable, unfair truth is it costs girls more than it does guys. A condom can't protect you from all the crap that comes down on a girl with a reputation—"

"Reputation?" Karen said. "Did you actually say reputation? Talk about out of it."

"Right," Reuben said. "As I was saying, a condom won't protect you if it breaks or slips off, and it's not just a matter of not getting knocked up anymore—"

"Do you have to be so gross?"

"You're the one with the rubbers in your handbag," he pointed out, "—so I'm saying you're too young and don't do it because I don't want you to get hurt."

Karen pulled her quilt up to her nose. "Yeah, yeah. Turn out the light, will ya?"

Gussie Madden died while Joe's estate was still in probate, and hers got all tangled up with his. Joe's house stood empty while Walter McKenzie took care of it. When Walter realized he couldn't take on all of Joe's old caretaking properties, Reuben picked up the slack. It was easy work that took him all over the Ridge and brought in some extra winter income and somebody had to do it, so why not?

One hot day in June, Frankie graduated Greenspark Academy and a week later was gone, off to see the world on a Navy ticket.

Sammy grew straight and tall and carried a basketball under one arm with him everywhere until he seemed naked without it. He told Reuben irritably to quit calling him Sammy. It was a baby name and he was shaving, for crissake. He was Sam.

Sam-I-Am, Reuben teased. *I do not like green eggs and ham.*

Sam smiled a smile that still looked like a Sammy smile to him. One day Reuben was forty.

✳ ✳ ✳

Rain-sweet air and the newly thawed damp earth mingled with the burgeoning green of a cold day in spring, thrilling him with its sensory reawakening as he opened the earth for Gussie. In order to dig her a hole he had to shake up Joe's bones under the wild rose that had taken over the Nevers' plot. The roots fought the back-hoe's shovel something fierce and the rose shook with the plunge of the shovel. A fanciful thought came to him: what if he yanked up a root and brought up every stiff, skeleton and spare bone buried there?

With his mind on the job it was a moment before the motion in the corner of his eye distracted him and he caught a glimpse of a woman climbing over the stone wall between the graveyard and Joe's house. Elizabeth Madden's daughter—Ilene's friend Elizabeth who had run away from home over thirty years ago.

Why, she's a Nee-gro, old Walter had sputtered in his excitement the day before at the garage, after meeting her. *That ain't all. Oooh la la. I'm telling you. Oooh la la.*

Amused, he had disbelieved. Walter was getting soft.

But she was the very rumor Walter had imparted so gleefully, a dark lady indeed. Walter had said she meant to stay, to live in Joe's house in this out-of-the-way corner of the world where no others of her kind, whatever the current correct label was—woman of color, Negro, black—had ever lived in living memory.

Standing down from the backhoe to make his manners, he took off his sou'wester and let the rain dew his head.

Like him she was dressed for the weather, galoshes and a slicker, a bright red one, her head of black hair sequined with the drizzle. In the gloom and damp the diffuse light found a velvety warmth in her skin tone and enlarged the pupils of her eyes so they eclipsed the color and made it a silvery annular ring around their dark core.

Thirty, he guessed, or thereabouts—her hand in his was confident and strong. With his olfactories already stimulated by the rainy green earthy out of doors, she smelled good to him, of a light spicy perfume and herself, woman, woo-man. A blind man would have been intrigued.

African features were not an everyday sight for him, nor had the images available in the media ever drawn his eye very strongly. He was arrested—*we aren't in Kansas anymore,* he thought. The topography was a new world, warmer, much warmer, and lusher. He thought her nose, broad at the nares, high-bridged and arched like the nickel Indian chief's, was the most beautiful one he'd ever seen. Regal, sculptured, leonine, something in all those adjectives but there was a sensuality too and a sense of humor in her face—

that glittered through, like specks of quartz in polished granite—he shuffled through words and nothing really fit. Herself.

Before he had released her hand he thought he had the first in-
kling of what the old rose felt when the backhoe gnawed its roots.

Not since the divorce had he felt a serious tug toward a
woman, one strong enough to be worth the risk, and it was so unexpected and so strange—he felt like he had a leak somewhere inside; there was a trickle down the back of wherever it was and it
felt so damn funny—it took him a little while to be sure that was
what it was and not some discombobulation caused by seeing that
flaw in her eye that Gussie and India had shared. He told himself
there'd be a fellow turn up, husband or lover, but she settled in
and bought Needham's diner from Roscoe and nobody turned up
to lay claim to her.

He could almost hear Freddy Cape laughing like a hyena.

XXXVI

Summer Came on, and David turned up. He had become a man of such treacherously easy handsomeness that it was difficult to get past it. Like a beautiful woman, people took him at face value and dismissed him—pretty and rich and neurotic with privilege. Wealth makes a madman merely eccentric, and so David was just another one of those, a fool with more money than sense. He resumed his old habits, wandering the Ridge, making his rounds with the concentration of a man looking for a lost valuable. Or a hound tracking some quarry.

The first Sunday he was back he dropped in on the pickup basketball behind the library. Sammy was on a tear, making everyone else feel incompetent or over the hill. David finally threw himself down on the grass, gasping for breath. When Reuben passed him a Coke he popped the cap eagerly.

"Gawjus, your kid," he said in a mocking Yankee drawl.

"Karen?" Reuben grinned ruefully.

David squinted at the court. "Sam." He shook his wrist. "Hot."

Reuben froze. It was the first it really sank in—David's approach to him had not been a unique event for him. David really was AC-DC; he had sex with men as well as women. It had something of the shock of Laura's adultery. Suddenly it was obvious—he should have seen it, seen both the outline of the candlesticks and the profiled faces opposing each other.

David made a kissy face at him. "Relax, big daddy. Don't worry about your baby boy's virtue. I was just making an esthetic comment. As I might indeed make of Karen. He's a little young yet for my tastes, and by the time he gets there, he won't be any more susceptible than, say, you are."

Campy, limp-wristed—he was throwing it at him. Reuben didn't know how he was supposed to respond. So he didn't. David loped back onto the court. A few minutes later Sam drove around him and lifted off and stuffed the basket, and when he came down, David patted him on the ass, a rigorously correct athletic gesture, and then he looked over at Reuben with a little smile.

And after that it seemed like every day he had some excuse to stop by the garage, making sure Reuben saw him spend a few minutes with Sammy, kidding around. Sammy obviously liked the attention—he missed his older brother, and David drove a hot little sports car and was fluent in sports and the hard rock the boy was passionate about. It was a relief to have Sam's friend Josh hanging out at the garage for long hours, distracting and buffering Sammy from David's attentions.

There wasn't anything to it, Reuben told himself, just David yanking his chain for the twisted fun of it. Or maybe he just couldn't help himself.

Seeing Sam's face light up when David said one of these days he wanted to make a hop to Boston by Learjet to take in a Sox home stand and maybe Sam and Josh would like to come along to share his box behind home plate, he couldn't help a cramp of jealousy. Once or twice a summer he made the long drive to Boston with Sammy to sit in the bleachers. It had always been a big deal. And he remembered how Sam had loved flying to Florida and back; a ride in a Learjet would be such a thrill to him. He couldn't do that for Sam but David could; David could take Sammy to the top of the mountain and offer him the world.

For an instant he was scared and pissed off. He thought it likely that with a little effort David could seduce the pope out of his petticoats. It ran in his family—the thought snagged him. No, there wasn't anything to it but David reminding him of his own long-ago fall. He remembered David as a boy, sulking in the backseat of his mother's Cadillac. David had gotten his mother's attention with his acting out, and what he was doing with Sammy was getting Reuben's.

All right, he had it. Reuben decided the next time he saw David he'd ask him if he didn't want to go down to Fenway with Sammy and him and catch a game.

Only David stopped hanging around. Bored, probably. Sammy hardly seemed to notice. Reuben felt like an idiot. The widow had always been good at pulling the football away, and David had that in spades from her too. He couldn't be angry. He would do it, ask

David to go along—ought to have made the gesture long ago. For himself as much as the widow. He relaxed.

* * *

Watching the Sox blow a perfectly good lead to the A's, he tipped the beer with the drunk in it. Sam groaned and stumbled off to bed—kid couldn't negotiate his own feet once off the basketball court or a base path. Reuben stumbled himself over Lucille, recumbent next to the couch and doing her usual flawless imitation of a smelly, farting rug, but he didn't have Sam's excuse. The only growth he was experiencing was the weight in his bladder. He took Lucille out to take care of *her* bladder and they watered a lilac together. She'd probably piddle in the kitchen before morning and give him a look so downhearted when he found it he wouldn't have the heart to scold. He didn't think she could help it anyway.

As always, as he turned off lights and checked to make sure the oven and all the burners were off and then that the doors were locked—waste of time, locking the doors, with the windows all wide open and nothing but screens in them that an intruder could just pop right through—he wondered where Karen was, who she was with, what she was doing—useless fretting even before she rented that sorry-ass trailer but he always did it, locking up. High school dropout, working as a waitress, running around with a druggie shithead. His little girl, such a winning little girl. He'd done something wrong. Forgotten to invite some fairy godmother to her christening. He didn't know. He didn't know what to do about her, never had. She didn't listen.

Even with the windows open, the upstairs was close. Kicking off his shoes, he sat down on the edge of the bed and started to unbutton his shirt. Suddenly a little light-headed with the beer, he flopped back onto the pillows and let himself drift. He touched himself idly. He was thinking about her a lot—Pearl—and dreaming about her too. He didn't have any doubt about it, he wanted her—had wanted her from first sight and was afflicted with an adolescent fever of horniness—but he was afraid. Sensible of him, he thought, to be afraid. He didn't believe just because he could get hard to jack off again that he could count on it when push came to shove.

Close study hadn't changed his first impression of her. There was no sign she had any hang-ups about skin color, though the sanest-appearing folks were sometimes inconsistent and illogical and stark raving nuts on three subjects he could name, race being the first, religion and sex close behind. But she didn't appear to be much interested in racial identity, whatever that was for someone six of one, half a dozen of the other. Nor was she religious either, a huge relief. More trouble in this world over the color of people's skin and the skinny on Jesus or Buddha or Allah or Rin Tin Tin. Do unto others and put no false gods before. Be a lot saner world if people ever listened to what came out of their own mouths. Himself included.

She hadn't shown the slightest interest in horseback riding.

She was a prodigiously hardworking woman. Roscoe had let the diner go to wrack and ruin, and she was putting it to rights in aptly short order. Scrupulous but tough in her business dealings—he'd bought her old sedan and then Joe's Eagle from her, both of them quick turnovers, and enjoyed a little mental arm wrestle with her in the barter. And she was good-humored, absolutely necessary to survival since she had kept on that old goat Roscoe as a part-time employee, and Karen too, who'd been waiting counter for Roscoe since quitting school. Dealing with either one of them would drive Mother Teresa to cuss words. Mother-starved Karen had basically concluded Pearl was God.

Because Karen was working for her, he didn't loiter at the diner, so as not to look as if he were checking up on her. Or losing his cool over her boss. The most casual contact, though, was reassuring, for Pearl was easy to talk to, easy to be around.

All at once the world was sexier. He was suddenly more aware of what was going on between people—a man speaking in a low voice to his wife, the woman bursting out in laughter and squeezing his hand and leaning closer to him, a flushed young couple playing grab-ass near the tennis courts, the glitter of a woman's downcast eyes as a man flirted with her, two teenage girls watching Sammy on the basketball court, nudging each other, blushing.

He was bemused at the way it suddenly seemed everywhere he looked, on TV, in magazines, in movies, there were so many beautiful, sexy women of color. Not just black but Hispanic, Asian, Native American—there weren't enough terms for the variety. The way when your wife is pregnant you see pregnant women everywhere, or you buy a new truck and suddenly you see that make and model everywhere. He had become aware of skin in all its aspects—texture as well as color—and even the range of hue among his neighbors, blued-milk white to booze-purpled red to weathered olive leaped to his eye.

And he saw himself anew: *paddy, bogcutter, generic Danny-boy howling-in-his-cups misty-eyed Mick*. His wash baby blues, his fine-grained, transparent complexion creasing now with age and disregard for the harshness of sun and weather, his colorless hair, still with a thick, tight curl to it. All his own teeth too, he mocked himself, a poor man's pride. Cap-wringing shuffling semiliterate, the closest living relative of the great apes—some experts asserting, controversially, that the distinction is moot, and others that the Celt is the missing link between meat and vegetable, the nearest mammalian relation of the potato, *Gorilla Solanum Tuberosa*. Thus explaining the cannibalistic obsession with meat and potatoes. Science aside, he was the stuff of white trash.

How did she see him? The likes of him overseeing the likes of her. Not owning but doing the dirty work, bullying and intimidating and starving and raping and flaying the living, beautiful skin off fellow human beings for the owners and then the ex-owners, keeping the not-quite-freed down. Little comfort in the thought Africans and Arabs had sold Africans to the slavers or that the Irish have had their own millennium-long turn in the colonial barrel. How do you get past the dead, clanking weight of the chains your ancestors spun in life to where you're just a man and a woman? What's it got to do with a middle-aged mechanic with a hard-on, unreliable or not, for a good-looking woman?

He gleaned and deduced and absorbed everything he could about her. From Karen he learned she was thirty-five, a little older than his first guess. A good thing as far as he was concerned. Of age to know her own mind. He couldn't ask his daughter outright if Pearl had a fellow somewhere or had ever been married, but he didn't think Karen could have kept it to herself if she knew. Doubtless Pearl realized the same thing and perhaps had just elected to keep her business to herself. She was educated— overeducated for slinging hash—but she clearly knew what she was doing with the diner and he guessed she had her own reasons. Her last address Gussie's Georgetown home but with some years in Denver reflected in her accent that didn't quite cover up Florida.

Her presence made him examine the rut he had churned for himself. Rut. What a grand hoo-ha. His children were mostly grown, for good or ill, and in a few short years he would be alone. Oh hell, he *was* alone. And just what a woman like Pearl must be looking for, an aging, divorced grease monkey with a chronically limp dick.

Since divorcing he had had his share of offers from local women—single girls, widows, divorcees and some married women too—and had carefully overlooked them. It was easy turning down the married ones; he didn't want anybody else's wife—not only was mistaking another man's wife for your own still a killing offense in this neck of the woods, it was what his own wife had done to him. He didn't want a wife just to have a wife. He didn't even want a woman just to have a woman, he told himself—at least until he had fended off another one. Then he could admit to himself it was just an excuse, a way to avoid admitting he couldn't get it up anyway. There had been and were a lot of times when he most assuredly did want a wife again, and more when he wanted a woman. The tease of desire was in perfect balance with his fear of failure and was almost indistinguishable from it.

She hadn't gone out with anyone else—he would have known about it pretty much instantly. Trying not to play the fool but always feeling like one anyway, he made cautious moves that could be taken as neighborly acts if she wanted. Despite his attempts to be discreet his interest in her hadn't gone unremarked. Place too small, himself too transparent. Even Sammy in his adolescent daze knew, if from nothing else, the several weeks of hearing Reuben humming, whistling and occasionally singing, *"There's only one thing left that we can do. We gotta get you a woman."* Of course, the boy himself had a crush on Pearl.

Pearl knew. Hesitant as he was, cautious as he was, he had met her eye and she had met his and there had been that simple acknowledgment of awareness. *You. Me. Uh-huh. That's interesting.* And she had seemed to be content to let him set the pace.

* * *

Too hot to sleep he went downstairs in his socks and took another beer out of the fridge and sat on the back stoop, where it was a little cooler. Lucille heaved herself up, padded after him and collapsed next to him with a huge ooof of effort. She rolled a curious eye at him.

One day while mowing Pearl's lawn, Walter had had a fainting spell and afterward stopped at the garage and asked Sammy to finish for him. The boy had jumped at the chance and hurried over there and come back just as quick, mumbling she had been dozing under a tree and he had been afraid the noise would disturb her. And Reuben had gone to do the job.

It had been late afternoon, after she had closed up the diner for the day, and she had been something to see, sprawled in the shade of that tree in the casual vulnerability of sleep. Lashes soft on her cheeks and her breasts slowly rising and falling with the long breath of dreams. Skin-tight jeans. Soft bulge and furrow of sex. White-against-her-skin T-shirt straining over her breasts. A bra beneath the shirt but semitransparent, for the shape and shadow of her areolae were still visible. Buds. Tight-petaled flowers.

It had been a hot day too and there had been dampness darkening the roots of her hair at her temples, along her brow, and perspiration on her lip as she dozed under the tree. Her body had been turned, one hand flung hard right, the other trailing to the left, left leg cocked hard left, the other straight. Sandals kicked off bare feet—a little bit square, high arch, dark on the top, light on the bottom, with unpolished, neatly trimmed nails. There was something delicate and fragile about the bump of her ankle bone, the way the skin lightened at the top. He had wanted to touch that little island of bone so close to the surface. Ankle bone. Connected to the shin bone. Shin bone connected to the thigh bone, thigh bone connected to the hip bone—another place the bone was close to the surface, denim tight over skin tight over bone. She had a fine haunch in her jeans, a woman's haunch, woo-man, oh, he was wooed, all right.

He had cleared his throat—*Poor Sammy,* he had thought, *poor me too*—and gone to the mower both Walter and Sam had abandoned and cut the grass. When he had glanced back from the seat of the mower she was gone, the clatter and roar indeed having woken her. Later she had come back and given him a glass of iced tea, and he had let another opportunity to ask her out go by because he was afraid, so deeply afraid of failure.

He pressed down on his crotch and emptied the beer and held the dead soldier in his hand. Long-neck bottle, hard and smooth as he rolled it in his palms. Shee-it. Forty-one, forty-two too soon. He set the bottle down next to him and studied his nails. Cleaned'm during the game; never got it all but they weren't too bad. Still a little red strawberry juice stain that went well with the flaked edges and the ground-in dirt and grease. He'd spent part of the afternoon filling a pint box with wild strawberries from a patch on Joe's property—her land now—but he thought about Joe, missed him, the smell of his cheroots, his ironic blue eye, the kindness of the old man. Left the berries at her door, as he had fiddleheads when they were in season. Like a cat leaves a mouse, or parts thereof. Mighty hunter. Hadn't hunted in decades but he was hell on strawberries, they cringed when they heard the forest floor shake under his footstep.

He took the empty into the house and slotted it into the case in the shed and went upstairs. His keys were with his pocket change, emptied onto the nightstand. He sniffed his armpits—okay, he thought, for a hot night. He had showered after work, as was his habit. Shaved in the morning, and so he was halfway there again, and he stroked his jaw and decided it was a little rough. He wandered into the bathroom, muttering to himself he was nuts, and lathered his beard and went back to the bedroom and found his shoes and put them on and then went back to the bathroom and used the razor, very carefully considering he was tight, and didn't even cut himself once. He sniffed three different aftershaves and decided on the expensive one Ilene had sent him at Christmas time—Tuscany—he'd looked it up and it was part of Italy, not the aftershave but Tuscany, Tuscany was part of Italy. Supposed to be beautiful place, Italy, where the pope lived like the hole in the donut, but the money was inflated and Venice was drowning in the sea, a dirty, nasty sea full of sewage, Venice's own waste. He'd read all about it in the *National Geographic*. Venice wasn't in Tuscany, though. Venice was north, Tuscany south, he thought. Fancy stinkum was always alleged to be Italian, if not French. Places of romance where the men all ate pussy from an early age and the women were all satisfied, maybe, or was it just the rest of the world bathed regularly and didn't need to cover up sweat with perfume? Probably the stuff in the bottle actually came from New Jersey or Idaho or somewhere equally unlikely. Idaho, toilet-water maker to the world. Idaho Aftershave. Ida-ho, ho.

He picked up another beer—nothing but cans left, why had he bought cans at all? on sale or something but the beer always tasted tinny—on the way through the kitchen to the back door and popped it behind the wheel. Took Frankie's keys away from him for drinking and driving, he thought, and here I am with a nice cold beer in my crotch, tooling down Route 5. Nice and cool and smooth. His balls contracted pleasantly with the sensation. Better not spill it, look like he pissed himself. Too cool for school, Dad. They made the cans out of aluminum foil these days, at least that's what it felt like, and if he squeezed it between his thighs it would probably explode. Just thinking about it, he tightened his inner thighs and felt the cold can give a little and it made him hornier. It was only a couple of miles as the crow follows the center line.

If there weren't any lights on he'd go down to the Narrows and go skinny-dipping and then go home. Cold-water cure, colder than the beer, and less hangover. If the lights were on, they won't be on, she's an early riser, opens the diner while God's still drooling on the pillow, but if the lights *are* on, he could ask her if she liked the berries. Jesus, what a stupid idea, going around at nigh on to midnight to ask if she *liked the berries*. Never mind the berries. He should ask her if she'd like to go down to the Narrows, go skinny-dipping to cool off. He laughed and then it struck him it actually wasn't a bad idea, he didn't have to say *skinny-dipping,* he could say go for a swim and when they got there say, this late there's nobody around and I usually go skinny, d'you mind? Sure, she'd probably bat her eyelashes and say never mind swimming, let's just fuck, sure, Reuben, you drunk asshole. Sure. Be even funnier when he came up soft as Play Doh.

And he pulled off at the turnout to turn around, and there was a wink of light from the house on the hill. He swallowed the last mouthful of the beer. Maybe it was a night light of some kind. At the bottom of the driveway he could see the light was on the sun porch on the west side of Joe's house, and he caught a glimpse of her profile on the daybed and the light winked out. Sensible of her, sleeping on the sun porch in this heat. But she wasn't asleep, not just yet, and even as he hesitated, she must have heard the truck because she turned the light right back on.

He turned off the ignition to kill the noise that suddenly seemed obtrusive, like honking your nose in church during one of the solemn bits. It was too late to back out, he realized. He had at least to go speak to her and make some kind of explanation for being there. God, he was a fool. She was going to notice he was lit up—why hadn't he thought of that? He forgot about the empty can at his feet until it rattled on the gravel as he was getting out. He could see her, she could see him. He was glad of the dark that at least hid his blush. Forty-one and blushing, and why not? Man is the only animal, Twain wrote that.

But she didn't seem pissed off at his arriving so late—just a little curious. She sat with her legs tucked under her on the daybed, a sheet drawn up to her collarbone, and when he knocked politely, she asked him in. He could smell strawberries and then he saw the box of berries on the daybed next to her.

Embarrassed, apologetic, he grinned. "You're up late, Pearl."

"You too," she said, and apologized for her dishabille, by which she meant being in her nightshirt, though it was him who owed her an apology, but before he could tender it and get the hell out of there, she thanked him for the berries.

"It's too hot to sleep," he found himself trying to explain, and then his apology turned into a confession. "Actually, they're yours, I picked them on your land."

Seeming amused, she asked him to sit down. He looked about and there was a wooden chair handy, and he turned it around and put the back between them.

She picked up the box and offered it to him. He took a berry, confessing he had had quite a few while gleaning them that afternoon. She said she remembered doing that when she was a kid. He was looking at her and she was looking at him, and he thought it's all right, she doesn't mind me making a fool of myself, it's okay to be a human being with her. And he relaxed and grinned at her, and it seemed obvious now all he had to do was ask her if she didn't want to go out to dinner at Jean-Claude's some night and then whatever she said he could take his leave politely and go home. Or down to the Narrows. It was still too hot to sleep.

And she moved and the box rose on her lap and the berries inside rose too, right up over the edge like riding a jump in the road, and the box tipped and he reached to catch it and so did she and they both missed and came up with each other's hands. The berries as they spilled bruised and the air was full of their sweet tartness. Her fingers locked with his and he felt the tremor in them and saw her eyes darken as her pupils widened. He rose from the chair and went to her.

Her mouth tasted of wild strawberries and distantly, he thought he imagined, of wine, a fine, polished chablis that was right for strawberries. Slow kissing, murmurous bubbles of laughter, delighted discovering rapturous. He would have been content with languorous kisses for a long time if she wanted, but once they were touching each other, swapping spit and tasting each other's faces and throats and nowhere on the narrow daybed for him but on top of her full body, he was hard and hot and aching. She in her nightshirt, nothing on underneath. Pretty quick she wasn't even in the nightshirt anymore, and he had his shoes off and his pants open and then off and they were skin to skin. Naked, naked with each other, no shame or shyness or modesty, just the two of them like pieces of a jigsaw puzzle, made to fit together to make something more complete than themselves. Her skin fit her just right, he wouldn't change a thing. His own skin was hot and alive, the fabric of desire. He didn't want to stop and she didn't stop him. She said yes. Yes. Yes. Murmured it, said it aloud. Her fingers closed around his cock and she jacked him with a firm, sweet hand, she knew what she was about, and he almost wanted her to finish him that way. But for the tender heat of her cunt anticipating him as he worked his fingers in and out. She didn't ask to stop to take care of anything, and he thought she must be on the Pill or have an IUD or she would, a woman her age he didn't need to ask about it, did he? and he didn't have a rubber on him of course and he didn't care anyway, she had his cock in her fist and he was fingering her and she was hot and creamy as a stroke-book heroine and if he knocked her up, all right, it was worth the risk he didn't care and abruptly and simultaneously they shifted and she took him inside her, into the slick plunge clench tug.

After the first euphoric sensation he knew he had a problem, a flashback to his wedding night with Laura. He was so aroused he could not come. Even as she jerked under him violently, coming, he could feel her spasms around his cock and he wanted to feel that again and he did, she did it and did it again and did it again and he was amazed into incredulous laughter. And so was she, meeting his eyes with a question in hers, and he thought she understood the problem. And then she was trembling in her laughter, worked pliant in his arms as clay and her smoky eyes were merry and tearful and surrendering to him and he was taken by surprise. It went on for a long, intense moment, a tearing loose and unknotting, as if she were drawing it out of him in an oriflamme, like a pennant being drawn from a magician's sleeve. And when it was done he was light and floating and wanted to live forever. He kissed her all over her face. Licked sweat trickling from her hairline. She closed her eyes and shuddered wearily.

He shifted them around, wedging them on the bed together. The sheets were damp, they had sweated so much, and they were both running with it. He held her head against his chest and closed his eyes. His head was spinning.

XXXVII

She Had Him by the Ridge of the Nose,
waggling his head, demanding he wake up. It was getting light
out. Her hair was a mess, a wild tangle, and she had circles under
her eyes and her mouth was swollen. She looked like she'd spent
the night balling. Right away he was interested in doing some
more, but she wasn't having any, and she was right—Karen sometimes dropped by her house on the way to the diner. If she found
her father, still about a quarter-cut, in bed with her boss, it was
likely to mean a rough start to the day for all three of them.

Once behind the wheel again he felt a little unreal. He was on
the line between tight and hungover, and his head was beginning
to ache and his stomach was queasy. He didn't want to think
about not asking her about contraception. Or about jumping her
with so little preliminary. He felt like he knew this woman better
on the strength of a few weeks' acquaintance and even before this
precipitous roll in the hay than he had ever known the woman
who had been for fourteen years his wife. Knew her, he mused. He
knew her, she knew him. Odd the resonance of that archaic Old
Testament euphemism. Knowing. It had been more like recognition—oh, it's you?—or was it merely waiting so long, everything
was imagined before it happened and that's why it felt so familiar.

It was as if she had been waiting for him with her motor running. It crossed his mind maybe she'd been masturbating—what if
she had been? She was a grown woman—no virgin, bless the fellow who had seen to it for her, himself he never wanted anything
to do with another virgin again—she had her needs, thanks be,
and no lover until he had volunteered. His good luck. So maybe
he'd caught her halfway to flashover, and if so, needn't award
himself any medals but all right. He was alive again and if she
wanted to walk on his face for kicks, he'd buy her the spikes.

* * *

The clock-radio alarm went off—otherwise he'd have slept right through—and he flicked it off and stared at the ceiling for a long moment. He wouldn't go back to sleep; he was immediately awake and his head was bad, though he'd taken aspirin before he went back to bed. Then the shower went on as Sammy got there first.

The boy glanced up from the sports page and flung it aside. He watched Reuben pour orange juice and drop bread into the toaster.

"Got a head," Sammy said. It was a diagnosis, not a question, and there was no sympathy in it.

Reuben rinsed the juice glass and upended it into the dishwasher.

"Little one."

"You want some eggs or something? I'll cook."

Reuben nodded and Sam got up and went to the fridge.

"Lucille took a leak on the floor again," Sammy said. He used the same neutral tone of voice as before. "I cleaned it up already."

"Thanks."

Sammy looked up at him.

"You did it often enough for me."

The boy stood there with four eggs cupped casually in one big hand and suddenly he smiled. It was crooked and shy and incandescent with love and Reuben wanted to hug him but Sammy might think it was the hangover making him maudlin and guilty so he picked up the paper and stared at the sports page.

* * *

In Greenspark to run an errand, he went into the pharmacy on impulse. Even if she was on the Pill, there was still so much to sweat these days, herpes and AIDS along with the old familiar poxes—they said you went to bed with everyone your partner had been with for ten years back. She'd been living in big cities. New Sodom and Gomorrah, D.C. and East Babylon. Even if she was careful—but she hadn't offered or asked for protection.

He was making assumptions. Assuming she'd want to go to bed with him again to start. Still, he didn't intend to be empty-handed again. And she might appreciate the gesture—after all, it was protection for her against anything he might have as well as for him.

He knew he was as innocent of infection as a virgin, but she didn't. If she didn't want to use them he'd throw them in the back of the desk drawer and make a present of them to Sonny or some other bachelor when the occasion presented itself.

He met her in the parking lot outside.

Instantly he was acutely self-conscious. He had safes in his pocket, having refused to have them bagged like penny candy, and this was the woman he had had in mind in buying them. She was wearing a tight top and loose, gauzy trousers and sunglasses, and he was immediately aware of the body inside. He felt like a horny teenager with fevered designs on the girl he had gotten the bra off the previous Saturday night. Except he'd had her, though that made it sound like he was some kind of stud when it had been all her doing. She'd gotten him hard and he'd been able to fuck again and it had been the best job he'd ever done. Never mind it wasn't supposed to be the measure of a man anymore, the fact was he had been unmanned and she had made a man of him again. Screw the quacks and shrinks and therapists saying it didn't matter. Let them spend a decade flogging a limp dick and see how it felt.

Her hand flew to her hair and she acted as if she felt a little awkward too. Her coordination was a little loopy, hand a little shaky. Skating on the edge of exhaustion.

He had had time to think about what he wanted to say. She listened gravely to his apology for his uncouth behavior of the previous night, and he noticed her throat working as if she were really moved by it. And then she responded quietly that he owed her no apology.

Relieved, he tried to make a joke, asking if she wanted to go berrying with him, but it fell flat as she smiled tiredly and said she couldn't. He asked if he could take her out and again she said no. He began to feel it was going badly and his headache started to tighten. But she assured him quickly it was only she needed a night's rest. She didn't have an idea, he realized, what she had done for him, and he was overwhelmed and all he could do was ask if she wouldn't go berrying with him the following afternoon instead. No joke. Just to spend an hour or two together and maybe some berries would get picked and maybe not. And she said yes.

"My kids," he said.

Right away she picked up on it. No telling how they'd take his seeing her. She understood how things were with him and Karen, his not able to do a right thing or say a right word and Karen putting it up his nose with a vengeance.

They parted and he was lustfully fixed on the sway of her hips as she headed toward the pharmacy when she nearly walked into Roscoe Needham's niece, Belinda Conroy. Belinda had dumped a rat-brained retriever bitch on Roscoe after his collie died and Roscoe hadn't been able to cope with it and the cussed thing was running wild all over the Ridge. Belinda was a famous bitch in her own right, with three husbands hung out to dry and shopping for another one, as he knew from his own experience evading her. Handsome woman if you liked them with sharp tits and never a hair out of place. Be just the ticket if you didn't have any use for your balls. He'd already had one ballbuster for a wife, thanks anyway. Belinda and Pearl sort of bounced off each other like a couple of magnets with opposite polarities, but Pearl recovered and disappeared into the pharmacy.

Belinda saw him and waved and started to twitch his way. He dived into his truck and fled back to the Ridge, checking his rearview for Belinda's broom.

* * *

Just as his hangover was about as thin as ice on the edge of a puddle, at nearly closing time, Laura turned up to bitch at him about Karen moving out of the farmhouse into the trailer. There wasn't anything he could have done to stop her, and it wouldn't have changed anything anyway. Karen would still be running around with Bri Spearin. He couldn't stop her screwing the creep, or smoking dope or any other damn thing she wanted to do. Any more, he stopped himself saying, than he had been able to stop Laura fucking him over but good. Oh, Laura knew it. But she'd made a long drive to kick his ass. It was a way to say after all the shit they'd been through, he'd done a lousy job with the kids. As if she'd had nothing to do with it. Thinking back to the kind of shape Sammy had been in when he and Laura broke up, he couldn't believe he'd been so dim about it. How had he failed to see the signals that at least one of their kids was seriously bitched up? It was a miracle Sammy was as okay as he was now.

Laura had a further purpose: to announce personally she was going to take him to court again. Because Karen was out of control.

It felt like her heels were stomping the edge of ice in his nervous system, crunching and snapping it like thin bone. He snarled at her. He told her to get the fuck out. He'd never said anything like that to her before, ever, not in the heat of the worst battles they'd ever had. On a day when he'd been so happy, even ruefully savoring the butt end of his hangover as a kind of souvenir, she'd come out of her way to make him feel like homemade shit. He wanted to follow her out to her car and tell her she hadn't succeeded in castrating him after all, he had gotten laid by a real woman the previous night, and how did that frost her cake?

As he was locking up the register, it occurred to him if Pearl Dickenson had come to town while he and Laura had still been married, he'd have cheated on Laura without a twinge of conscience. If he'd had the choice back then, he'd have left her for Pearl. And taken Sam, of course. Ifs. If Pearl had been the mother of his children—or even their stepmother—they'd have all been so much better off. He found himself using his thumbs to squeegee a surprise onslaught of wetness from his eyes down his cheeks. It was like he had a bundle of fireworks inside him someone had lit and they were all going off at the same time, sparklers, whistlers, cherry bombs. Incandescent.

* * *

Sammy dropped an envelope casually in front of him at the breakfast table.

"Happy Father's Day," he said with a grin and nary a trace of a stammer.

Reuben picked up the envelope. A smooth rectangle of blue stiffened by the card inside, it bore Sammy's arduously drawn printing.

Sammy punched a brace of frozen waffles into the toaster.

"I took some chicken out of the freezer and put it in a marinade to grill for supper," he said. "Karen said she'd be here. She's bringing some potato salad and a dessert. Probably kifed it from the diner, so at least it'll be edible."

Reuben slid a clean knife under the flap and eased the card from the envelope. Crudely drawn cavemen—a Far Side cartoon. A slip of paper escaped from inside the card and Reuben caught it. A gift announcement: a subscription to *Sports Illustrated*.

"There's some freebies with it, supposed to come in the mail later," Sammy said with a shy grin. "Can I have the video of the swimsuit babes?"

Reuben laughed and rose to his feet to grab Sammy by the back of the neck and give him an affectionate cuffing.

"Maybe I'll just keep it."

"Gross," Sammy teased, "you're too old to be looking at the young stuff."

"You don't understand. I gotta make sure it's okay for you to see," he said.

"Hey, I'm doing research, Dad. I been thinking about sportswear design as a career," Sammy laughed.

"Oh, all right," Reuben said. "My son the fashion designer."

Sammy twirled around the kitchen, singing in falsetto:

> *The basketball coach kicked me off the team*
> *for wearing high heel sneakers*
> *and acting like a quee-een.*

Sammy tripped over his own feet and Reuben caught him.

"Sam-I-Am," he said. "You make me proud."

Flushed, Sam righted himself and grinned.

"Let's not get carried away," he said. "You know how easily I start to blubber."

The waffles bounced up with a clunk.

"The hell with those things," Reuben said. "Let's go shoot some hoops and eat breakfast at the diner."

"Now you're talking," Sam said.

He plucked the waffles from the toaster and frisbeed them to Lucille. The old bitch struggled joyfully to snap at them.

It was time, Reuben thought, time to get on with his life.